A POSSIBLE

Sebastian Faulks's books include the number one bestseller *A Week in December*, *Human Traces*, *On Green Dolphin Street*, *Charlotte Gray* and *Birdsong*, which has sold more than three million copies. In 2011 he wrote and presented the four-part television series *Faulks on Fiction* for BBC Two.

www.sebastianfaulks.com

ALSO BY SEBASTIAN FAULKS

Fiction

The Girl at the Lion d'Or
A Fool's Alphabet
Birdsong
Charlotte Gray
On Green Dolphin Street
Human Traces
Engleby
A Week in December

Non-fiction

The Fatal Englishman: Three Short Lives
Pistache
Faulks on Fiction

SEBASTIAN FAULKS

A Possible Life

A Novel in Five Parts

Please Return by the Date Shown

Reference Number: F168   Loan Period 4 wks

Club Internacional de Nerja

VINTAGE BOOKS
London

Published by Vintage 2013

2 4 6 8 10 9 7 5 3 1

Copyright © Sebastian Faulks 2012

Sebastian Faulks has asserted his right under the Copyright, Designs
and Patents Act 1988 to be identified as the author of this work

This is a work of fiction. Names and characters are the product of the
author's imagination and any resemblance to actual persons, living or
dead is entirely coincidental

This book is sold subject to the condition that it shall not,
by way of trade or otherwise, be lent, resold, hired out,
or otherwise circulated without the publisher's prior
consent in any form of binding or cover other than that
in which it is published and without a similar condition,
including this condition, being imposed on the subsequent purchaser

First published in Great Britain in 2012 by
Hutchinson

Vintage
Random House, 20 Vauxhall Bridge Road,
London SW1V 2SA

www.vintage-books.co.uk

Addresses for companies within The Random House Group Limited can
be found at: www.randomhouse.co.uk/offices.htm

The Random House Group Limited Reg. No. 954009

A CIP catalogue record for this book
is available from the British Library

ISBN 9780099549222

The Random House Group Limited supports the Forest Stewardship
Council® (FSC®), the leading international forest-certification organisation.
Our books carrying the FSC label are printed on FSC®-certified paper. FSC
is the only forest-certification scheme supported by the leading environmental
organisations, including Greenpeace. Our paper procurement policy can be
found at www.randomhouse.co.uk

Typeset by Palimpsest Book Production Limited, Falkirk, Stirlingshire
Printed and bound by CPI Group (UK) Ltd, Croydon, CR0 4YY

For Lawrence Youlten
As we lie . . .

'Si chaque homme ne pouvait pas
vivre une quantité d'autres vies
que la sienne, il ne pourrait pas
vivre la sienne.'
Paul Valéry from *Poésie et Pensée Abstraite*

If a man couldn't live a number of other lives,
he wouldn't be able to live his own.

PART I — A DIFFERENT MAN

Geoffrey Talbot was supposed to be a linguist, but spent most of his time at university playing games. He appeared twice for the First XI at cricket, but was not selected for the match at Lord's where his place was taken by 'Tiny' Trembath, a slab of a man already on Lancashire's books. At rugby, Geoffrey's headlong tackling in college games had earned him a game for the university itself against Rosslyn Park, but at Twickenham the man chosen at open-side wing forward was a graduate Rhodesian.

It was no surprise to Geoffrey that he fell twice at the last. His Hampshire day-school had told the pupils that their place in life would be the middle rank. Geoffrey's father worked as a jobber on the London Stock Exchange and hoped that Geoffrey, with his knowledge of languages, might one day go into the Diplomatic Service. Geoffrey's mother, who came from Limoges, had no ambition for Geoffrey; her main interest was in dog breeding, and the family house near Twyford Down was home to generations of yapping dachshunds.

After graduation, Geoffrey went to see the university appointments board, where a man with a pipe gave him some brochures from Shell and Imperial Tobacco. 'You're a personable fellow,' he said. 'I should think you'd do well in industry.'

'What about the Diplomatic Service?'

'They won't mind your sportsman's two-two — won't even ask — but their own exam can be tricky.'

In September 1938, after a series of rebuffs, Geoffrey found himself at a boys' preparatory school in Nottinghamshire, where he was to teach French, Latin and elementary maths. He had been interviewed by the headmaster in London at the offices of an educational agency and hired on the spot.

The taxi from the station drove through the outskirts of a mining town before the road opened up on some hills of oak and beech as they neared the village of Crampton. The school was set on high ground that overlooked a fast-flowing tributary of the Trent; it was a building whose elevated position and solitary brick tower gave it a commanding aspect; the grey stones were covered in creepers and the stone-mullioned windows held leaded lights. The headmaster's wife, Mrs Little, showed him upstairs to his quarters. She was a woman in her sixties who smelled of lavender water and peppermints.

'It's not a large room,' Mrs Little said, 'but bachelors can't be choosers. The boys come back tomorrow, but there'll be tea in the dining hall today at six. You can meet your colleagues. After tea, you have to forage for yourself. We don't allow drink on the premises, though the Head won't mind if you occasionally go down to the Whitby Arms.'

The room had a small sash window, with a view towards a wooded park. There was a chest, a shallow built-in cupboard with a hanging rail, a standing bookcase of four shelves and a single bed. When the house had belonged to a wealthy family, Geoffrey thought, this would have been a maid's bedroom. The shape of it seemed somehow to dictate the sort of life he would lead. The bookcase would need filling and the evening sun would help him read in the armchair with its loose floral cover; he would send for his old books from university and might even get round to the plays of Schiller and Racine; presumably there would also be a lending library in the town. He had never imagined he would be a schoolmaster, but felt the role settle on to his shoulders as easily as the black gown he hung up on the door.

His interview with the headmaster of Crampton Abbey had been brief. Captain Little, a tall, grey-haired man whose horn-rimmed glasses had one blacked-out lens, had made it clear that Geoffrey's principal job was to improve the performance of the sports teams. 'The parents do expect us to win a few matches, you know,' he said. 'It's more than twenty years since we beat Bearwood Hall at anything.'

After Geoffrey had unpacked his single suit and spare tweed jacket, he decided to go for a walk in the grounds. Beneath an oak tree next to the cricket pitch, he came across a wooden bench with the inscription 'J. D. Farmington 1895–1915'. The Battle of Loos, he thought. He wondered if Captain Little's sad demeanour and sightless eye had had anything to do with the war. Geoffrey's father had been in the infantry in France, but never spoke about it except if he had a coughing fit, when he muttered about the gas and made disparaging remarks about his wife's German dogs.

Geoffrey looked to his right, where the ground rose to a wooden pavilion. He pictured the nervous opening batsmen making their way to the middle to be met by a barrage from the opening bowlers of Bearwood Hall. Only a few weeks earlier he had himself gone in on a damp morning at Guildford to face Alf Gover and his brother-in-law Eddie Watts of Surrey; he had made only twelve and had been hit painfully on the forearm. He had no idea whether his knowledge of rugby and cricket would make him a good coach, but it could scarcely be difficult to motivate a group of energetic small boys.

There were wood pigeons and some noisy blackbirds in the trees that fringed a small football pitch behind him. Generations came and went in places like this, Geoffrey thought; they flickered through the huge front door with its iron bolts and bars, each new boy gripped by the conviction that he was alone in such straits — deprived of mother and home, beset by rules he

didn't understand, hoping the next hour might bring relief from
new sensations. It must be hard for a child to believe that his
experience, far from being unique, would in time dwindle
into something no longer even individual, as his tears were
taken up into the clouds. Geoffrey liked poetry and had a secret
ambition to write verses in the style of Rupert Brooke, but he
had never shown his undergraduate efforts to anyone, not
even the fellow members of the Marvell, a weekly reading
society.

A light wind blew as he set off back to the school to have tea;
walking along the crazy-paved path towards the terrace, he felt
apprehensive at the thought of meeting experienced members of
his new profession. He pushed open the tall double oak doors of
the dining hall and saw one of the two long trestles partly laid up
with a red gingham cloth. There was no one else there; Geoffrey
went in and sat down on an inconspicuous chair. Through swing
doors from a kitchen came a woman in blue overalls with wild
hair. She carried a plate that she set down in front of him without
speaking; it had two warm sardines on a half-slice of toast. She
reached over and lifted the teapot to pour him a cupful of deep
chestnut brown. Geoffrey, who was hungry after his journey up
from Hampshire, disposed of the sardines quickly, wondering if
he might need something else to eat later in the evening. As he
was preparing to leave, the double doors swung open and a bald
man in tweeds and brown brogues with thick rubber welts rolled
into the room.

He held out his hand and introduced himself. 'Gerald Baxter.
Classics and Under Eleven cricket.'

The maid brought his sardines. 'Thank you, Elsie,' Baxter
said. When she had gone back into the kitchen, he lowered his
voice. 'They get them from the bin. You probably saw it when
you came from the station. The old county asylum. They're all
quite harmless. Apart from one who fell in love with the maths

master and tried to stab him with the ceremonial sword above
the fireplace. Before my time, though. Do you want to come to
the pub?'

'Is that allowed?'

Baxter smiled. He had yellowing teeth and one gruesome
canine, coloured almost black. 'Old Ma Little warn you off, did
she? No, it's perfectly all right. Just not meant to go to the Hare
and Hounds in case we bump into Long John. Doesn't booze
with other ranks.'

'Long John?'

'The Head. After Long John Silver.' Baxter covered one eye
piratically.

The Whitby Arms was a fifteen-minute walk downhill. The
saloon bar was a large featureless room with a few coloured
photographs of vintage cars and a small coke fire; through the
servery Geoffrey could glimpse a dim public bar where men in
caps were drinking flat, dark beer. He could see why Mr Little
might have preferred the Hare and Hounds with its bottle-bottom
windows and coloured lights.

'Done any teaching before?'

'No, it's my first job.'

'It's not a bad life. Especially if you have a private income.'

'I'm afraid I haven't.'

'Nor have I,' said Baxter. 'A word of advice. Don't try and
become head of department or any of that nonsense. Then your
life is all timetables and meetings. Stay a foot soldier. Teach the
little buggers and knock off promptly when the bell goes. I'll have
the other half if you twist my arm.'

Although Baxter insisted on drinking only half-pints, he
managed to dispose of a dozen in two hours, most of which
Geoffrey bought for him. 'Still your round, I think, Talbot. Just
a freshener.'

Baxter puffed loudly as they made their way back up the

hill. 'I'd get a car if I could afford it. I don't mind coming down, it's the climb back I can't manage. I was wounded, you know.'

'Where?'

'I was with the Sandpipers.'

'The Sandpipers?'

'The 13th/25th. Won't be called on to fight again, that's for sure. Too bloody old.'

They were walking into the school grounds and the clock was striking nine. 'Are you up by the sick room?' said Baxter.

'Yes.'

'I thought so. My room's at the end, down the half-flight. Breakfast's at seven-thirty. Why not look in afterwards? I generally have a dry martini before Prayers.'

Geoffrey had been a schoolmaster for only a year when war broke out and he went to ask Long John Little's permission to volunteer.

'You could do well at this job, you know,' said Little. 'You're a natural. The boys listen to you.'

'I hope I'll be back soon,' said Geoffrey. He had really no idea how long the war would last. So long as the Russians and Americans were not involved, there would be, he imagined, an intense but brief struggle in Europe. The Scandinavians would offer little resistance, but the French could be relied on to hold out until British reinforcements came to help. Then he could return to coaching the First XI, who had scraped a draw against Bearwood Hall in his first summer in charge, and see if he could get some games for the Nottinghamshire Second XI himself.

'It's going to be a devil of a job getting any young staff at all,' said Little. 'During the last war my father had to dig a lot of old men out of retirement. They were making it up as they went along, keeping one step ahead of the boys in Hillard and Botting. But I shall still have Baxter.'

'Yes. He did his bit, I suppose.'

'Oh God, he didn't give you all the "Sandpipers" stuff, did he?' said Mr Little. 'I do wish he wouldn't do that. He had a game leg and never got nearer to the fighting than Étaples. He was a quartermaster in charge of handing out kit. Not his fault.'

'What about you, sir?' If ever there was a time to ask, Geoffrey thought, this was it.

'Messpot.'

'I'm sorry?'

'Mesopotamia. I was happy to miss the Western Front. This was a small price to pay.' He pointed at his eye. 'You'll be all right, Talbot. No trenches this time. It'll be all tanks and movement and high-level bombing. Write to us if you like. I know Mrs Little would like to hear. She's got quite a soft spot for you.'

'Thank you, sir. I will.'

As a graduate from an ancient university, Geoffrey was expected to become an officer. Out of loyalty to the county of his birth, he offered his services to the Duke of Hampshire's Regiment, whose honours included the Battle of Dettingen in 1743 during the War of the Austrian Succession (what on earth had that to do with Micheldever, Geoffrey wondered) and the Siege of Havana in 1762, where it had suffered heavy losses owing to dysentery. Ejected and reabsorbed in countless infantry shake-ups since Waterloo, its members were by 1939 known simply as the Musketeers.

After four months at officer cadet school in Colchester, during which he learned the rudiments of leadership ('Always let the men smoke during a briefing'; 'The first thing that happens in action is that the radio breaks down'), Geoffrey was sent to join the 1st Battalion in Norfolk. Looking through the window as the train left Swaffham, he noticed how the sandy pine forests started to give way to a different landscape, unchanged for centuries, dark, self-absorbed, as though its inhabitants had not often stirred themselves to make the journey to King's Lynn, still less the odyssey to London. He took a notebook from his case and began one of his secret verses – in pencil so an eraser would leave no trace of the clumsy first draft.

> The hedgerow cannot hide where last the may
> Like spring snow daubed it reckless white.
> Now, flowers gone, the thorns assert their day
> And this fair land is entering the night.

He wondered whether 'may' – by which he meant hawthorn – should have a capital 'M' or if that might make people think it referred to the month. 'Fair land' sounded archaic, but it echoed what he felt – such true affection for a part of England he had never seen before, heightened by the fact that it might soon be under attack from the skies. There was also an irksome echo in 'reckless white' – something second-hand, owing its existence perhaps to Shelley's 'hectic red'.

The 650 men of the battalion were assembled at a shabby Queen Anne house that had been offered to them by its impoverished owner. The bedrooms were designated 'officers for the use of'; the outhouses, barns and stables were filled with bunks and makeshift beds for other ranks, while the medical officer set up his surgery in the old butler's pantry. Geoffrey was instructed to present himself for dinner at the officers' mess in what had been the library, a pleasant room with a large fireplace and marble surround, above which hung the Musketeer colours in magenta and gold. There were oak-fronted cupboards and double doors leading into a comfortable sitting area – the last room, it appeared, the owner had been able to afford to heat and keep habitable.

Geoffrey had just taken a cocktail from the mess servant and was trying to conceal his sense of being all at sea when he saw someone he recognised. Standing with his back to the fireplace, smoking a cigarette in a bluff, aggressive way, was the monumental figure of 'Tiny' Trembath.

'What on earth are you doing here, Talbot?' he said.

'The same as you, I presume.'

'It's all a mistake,' said Trembath. 'I meant to go into the navy. Too late. Then the Gunners, but I failed the trigonometry. Now I'm in the bloody infantry. They look an absolute shambles, don't you think?'

Geoffrey found himself bristling a little, as though he had already developed a loyalty to the Musketeers. 'I expect we'll be billeted together,' he said, in a neutral sort of way.

Trembath looked Geoffrey up and down, as though imagining the prospect without relish.

'I suppose so,' he said eventually. 'I can't wait to get the hell out of here.'

On the fifth day there was a 'night op', the first time the junior officers were allowed out to take charge of some men without an NCO to keep an eye on them. They were meant to find their way, using compasses and a map reference but no torches, to a secret enemy position at Location X, where they would take possession of a Nazi flag to an accompaniment of blank rifle fire. This first part of the exercise was supposed to take only four hours, and from Point X they would receive their orders for the rest of the night, culminating in the safe transfer of the Nazi flag to secret position Y. Trembath and Geoffrey were in charge of A Section, but there was a second group, B Section, who would of course try to get there before them.

At five o'clock, when it was already almost dark, they started to black up their faces with burnt corks from wine bottles they had emptied the night before in the mess.

'Rather a fitting end for such a disappointing hock,' said Geoffrey, smearing his forehead.

'Don't be an arse, Talbot,' said Trembath.

The section walked for three and a half hours through the Norfolk countryside towards the sea, the men toiling under the weight of their packs and complaining that they were not allowed to smoke.

'You know damn well you can't show a light after blackout,' Trembath told them. 'Get a bloody move on or the other chaps'll beat us to it.'

Geoffrey had been put in charge of map-reading, not something that was easy to do by the light of a winter moon. Eventually they found themselves by a village green.

'For God's sake, Talbot,' said Trembath as the men sat on the grass. 'We're supposed to be going across country not on the bloody trunk roads.'

'It's hardly a trunk road, it's a village lane.'

'Here. Give me the map.'

While Trembath was wrestling with the outsize piece of paper, Geoffrey looked about him. On the other side of the road he thought he could make out the shape of an inn sign swinging gently in the breeze; and while Trembath struggled to get the map laid out to his satisfaction on the grass, he walked quietly over to it. Through the blacked-out windows came the sound of glasses chinking and low, contented conversation. Geoffrey checked the luminous hands of his watch: 20.45 hours. He eased up the latch of the front door and went down a short flagged corridor into a room with wooden settles and a small serving hatch. Silence fell in the room as Geoffrey asked for a pint of best bitter and the barman bent over the tap on a wooden barrel.

As he put down the glass on the counter, he said, 'Do you want a Lord Nelson with that?'

'Yes, please,' said Geoffrey. He hoped it might be a sandwich, or a pie, but it turned out to be a small tot of something that smelled of cloves. The beer, though still, was fresh; the Lord Nelson was sweetly aromatic. Two minutes later, Geoffrey was back with Trembath on the grass, ready for the battle ahead.

'Sorry. Call of nature. What do you think?'

'I think we should follow this path here.' Trembath prodded his forefinger against the map. 'Then we go across country.'

'Jolly good,' said Geoffrey. 'You take over the map-reading, I'll push along the stragglers from behind.'

'I say, Talbot, I—'

'No, I don't mind. It's your turn. Off we go. Fall in, please, men. Come along.'

Trembath's route took them through a field behind the pub, then into a copse, where he consulted his compass by the light of a match.

He sucked in his breath. 'I think the enemy will be well dug in. They'll have a bunker in some deeply wooded area, a natural fortification. That's my guess. I think if we follow this bearing, north by north-west, and just about here . . .'

There followed an hour of walking over fields, climbing fences, regrouping, head-counting and grumbling. The ground was becoming marshy and hard to walk through. Geoffrey, who was now beside Trembath at the head of the section, wondered what it must be like for the men who hadn't had the chance to play as much sport as he had; some of them were clearly city types on whom a ten-mile hike must be starting to take its toll. By now they were all knee-deep in water. Geoffrey trailed his fingers through it for a moment and licked them: salt.

Then the going underfoot seemed suddenly to change again; it was becoming drier, then sandy. Ahead of him Geoffrey could make out undulations – not hills exactly, but mounds or rises that stood out in the dark winter countryside.

And now there was something odd – yet familiar – about the soil beneath his boots, and in a moment, it came to him. He was walking on a seaside golf course. There were no flags to confirm his suspicion, the ground staff having doubtless taken them down for the night, but he could see where the cropped grass on which they were walking gave way to rough on either side of a fairway. Geoffrey had no doubt that 200 yards or so ahead, among the dunes, they would come to an even more close-cut area: the green.

'Trembath?'

'Yes?'

'Do you know where we are?'

'Yes, we're heading north-north-west on a bearing of—'

'No. More exactly. More colloquially.'

'What the hell are you talking about, Talbot?'

'We're on the eighth hole at Burnham.'

'The Royal North Norfolk?'

'Yes.'

Trembath said nothing, though he grunted a good deal.

'Can you make out that shape in the distance?' said Geoffrey. 'The one that looks as though it's built up with railway sleepers and filled with sand?'

'Just about,' said Trembath, non-committally.

'I was just wondering. Do you think that might be the enemy bunker?' said Geoffrey. 'A natural fortific—'

'Pipe down, Talbot. If we don't get a move on, B Section's going to beat us to it.'

At that moment, there came the sound of rifle fire about half a mile east of where they were standing.

'Too late, I think,' said Geoffrey.

'Quick,' said Trembath, 'let's get our men over there and ambush them.'

'We can't go forward on to the beach,' said Geoffrey. 'They'll have patrols there.'

'You sure?'

'Yes. Sergeant Turnbull said, "Stay off the beach, Mr Talbot."'

'Did he really call you "Mister"?'

'Yes. Look, we'll have to go back the way we came, then pick up the coast road towards Wells. The guns weren't far away.'

'Come on then,' said Trembath. 'Let's get a bloody move on.'

'We're on the eighth fairway now, so if we cut back through—'

'I don't want a lesson in course management. I played here in the varsity match.'

'Don't tell me you got a golf blue as well,' said Geoffrey.

'Halved my match at the eighteenth. The race is to the swift, Talbot. Come on.'

The men fell in and began to walk back the way they had come, but before they reached the seventh tee, they came to a halt. Ground that had earlier been marshy, then knee-deep in water, was now submerged by the sea.

'We're cut off, sir,' said Hill, one of the other ranks; known as 'Puffer', he was a tobacconist in civilian life. 'Tide comes in here at a hell of a lick. It'll be six feet deep in places.'

'How do you know?' said Trembath.

'Used to come here on holidays, sir.'

'Well, we'll just have to wade through it.'

'Can't wade, sir. It'll be too deep. And some of us can't swim.'

'Don't be so bloody ridiculous, man. It's only a few yards across. Come on. Get going. All of you.'

Reluctantly, holding their rifles above their heads, the Musketeers entered the icy tidal waters that cut off the eighth hole from the mainland.

Geoffrey felt his feet slip from beneath him. He was swimming – a clumsy breaststroke towards the higher ground he could make out just in front of them. He had never been much of a sea-bather and was finding the water almost unbearably cold. He was not alone in feeling the chill; a good deal of shouting and groaning came from the section as it half swam, half splashed its way towards the out-of-bounds beside the seventh.

To warm his drenched and freezing troops, Trembath told them to proceed at the double back to the coast road between Brancaster and Wells. As soon as they got there, they would be allowed to smoke; he had seen them stick their cigarette packets beneath their forage caps as they went into the water, like householders saving their most valued item from a natural disaster.

This order seemed to Geoffrey an idea of near-genius. He had thought the extent of Trembath's cunning might be to make sure his batting partner faced the fast bowler while he enjoyed the youthful leg-break lobber at the other end; he had never thought old 'Tiny' might be capable of such insight into the mind of the soldier. A few minutes later, smoking and steaming by the side of the road, the section caught its breath.

Geoffrey resumed map-reading duties, and shortly afterwards A Section, chilly but in good spirits, arrived at Location X – a telephone box set back between the road and the 'staithe', as the locals called the area of jetties and moorings by the sea. Here they were rewarded with hot chocolate, pork pies and more cigarettes before pressing on towards Location Y.

The bracing tidal water and the nicotine had left the men exhilarated, eager to outflank B Section, and attentive to all commands. They went at the double through the grounds of a stately house that looked, in the darkness, like a lunatic asylum, lacking only a water tower to set off its grim west facade. At one o'clock they found Location Y in a cherry orchard in the grounds of the shrine of Our Lady of Walsingham and an hour later they ambushed a complacent B Section on a country lane with thunder flashes and vigorous hand-to-hand fighting, resulting in the capture of the Nazi flag. It was not until they were back at battalion headquarters just after dawn that they saw that one of their number was missing at roll call. A. J. 'Puffer' Hill did not answer his name.

After breakfast, a search party was assembled to leave by lorry and retrace their steps, but was told to stand down when a telephone call reached battalion headquarters. An early-morning golfer, searching for his ball in the rough beside the par-five seventh, had come across the drowned body of a soldier, evidently beached some hours earlier by the retreating tide. Geoffrey was despatched with the medical officer to fetch him back as discreetly as possible; the course prided itself on rapid play (four-balls were banned) and the secretary was anxious not to disrupt the progress of the monthly medal.

'I suppose there'll be a dreadful stink about this,' said Geoffrey.

'I rather think there will,' said the MO, a man inured to disaster. 'You can say goodbye to any hopes of getting a company. You and Trembath will probably be put on a charge.'

'Oh God. Someone'll have to write to his wife.'

'They certainly will. He was probably the last Hill in Norfolk.'

Owing to their inexperience and to a plea in mitigation entered to brigade staff by their commanding officer, the guilty pair escaped court martial, though it was made clear to them that their lapse had put them into the slowest of slow lanes as far as advancement in the Musketeers was concerned. If there were distant lands to be invaded or glamorous staff colleges to attend, others would be chosen; if there was a gasworks to be guarded, theirs would be the first names put forward.

In the meantime, the battalion, like all the infantry who had not been out to the Low Countries and back through Dunkirk, bided their time. They trained and trained; they became good at what they did, but still they waited; in Lincolnshire, Norfolk, the Scottish Highlands, they sat frustrated, like athletes ready for a race that was endlessly postponed. They watched with envy when a small group of commandos was despatched to create havoc in Vichy French possessions in West Africa; but the mass of soldiery twiddled its well-trained thumbs, drilled, exercised and fed; and for Geoffrey the wait was made worse by the fact that he knew that when the 'balloon went up' he would be given only a secondary job. Europe was entirely under Nazi occupation; France had not put up the resistance that Geoffrey, raised on stories of heroic resistance on the Marne, had expected. The glorious nation of Pétain's Verdun – even with old Pétain himself back in charge – had fallen in a few days. Britain was under a 'total blockade' by German shipping and its main cities were being bombed every night.

So when in September he heard of a new irregular force being formed in London with a view to harassing the German occupier in Europe, he used a forty-eight-hour pass to offer his services in a flat in Marylebone to a toothy man who went by the name of Mr Green. This was the first time Geoffrey had been in London since the bombing had started and he was surprised by the damage already inflicted by the Luftwaffe. Much of the West End looked closed for business – boarded up, clenched, shocked. A different kind of person seemed to be at large on the streets of Piccadilly and St James's: self-important types of a certain age in ARP and Auxiliary Fire Service uniforms; young women in smart suits and nylons bustling to offices in Whitehall; men in soft shirts and chalk-stripe suits with time on their hands.

'What's the rest of your unit doing?' asked Mr Green, showing Geoffrey a chair. Despite calling himself 'Mr', he wore the uniform of an infantry major.

'Awaiting the order to move, sir.'

'Like the rest of the army.' Mr Green smiled. 'Restless, I expect, are you?'

'Yes. Rather.'

'Tell me about yourself.'

Geoffrey had been interviewed often; it was part of being young; but there was something about Mr Green that he liked – a liveliness, an indifference to convention shown by his loosely knotted tie and scuffed shoes. He told him about the Musketeers and poor 'Puffer' Hill.

Mr Green nodded encouragingly when he heard the story. 'Are you good with secrets?' he said.

'Yes. I think so.'

'Good. I had a girl in here the other day who was constitution-ally incapable of lying.'

'A girl?'

'Yes, it's not all cutting throats, you know. It's undercover work. Communications. Liaison. We've recruited half a dozen women already. But don't worry, your athletic prowess won't be wasted. Plenty of strong-arm stuff as well. Can you lie?'

'I don't think of myself as—'

'But in the interests of national security?'

'Of course I could.'

'Good. I see you're a linguist. What languages do you speak?'

'French fluently. Some German.'

'All right. I'll get our French bods to run the rule over you. Then you'll see a headshrinker.'

'Why?'

'Psychological fitness. It gets lonely in the field. Very lonely. Does that worry you?'

'No. I don't think so.' Geoffrey had never been lonely; he could barely imagine what it might feel like.

'We're taking on mostly civilians,' said Mr Green, 'but I can swing it with your brigade staff. I can fix a transfer. It's the PM's pigeon, the whole thing, so we can take short cuts through the army red tape. Are you keen?'

'I'm very keen indeed, sir.'

'Good man.'

'What happened to the girl who couldn't tell a lie?'

'I took her on. I had to. She was bilingual. She's in Portsmouth now, learning how to be deceitful.'

'I suppose there's not much else to do in Portsmouth,' said Geoffrey. 'Apart from dodge the bombs, of course.'

Geoffrey stayed the night with an aunt in a service flat near Marble Arch. He had dinner in a club in Pall Mall and walked back through the darkened streets of Mayfair. The large hotels were like ghost ships steaming quietly in the night, though occasionally from below ground he could hear the sound of tinkling gaiety. One of the most famous had moved its ballroom into the basement boiler area, laid a parquet floor among the lagged plumbing and set up a bar in front of the laundry. Guests in black tie and jewels danced to the sound of a jazz band as the German bombers droned overhead on their way towards the docks; while there was gin, the manager was convinced, they would continue to dance. The top-floor bedrooms were let out at a quarter of the normal price to those prepared to take a chance on a pilot jettisoning spare bombs on his way back to the Fatherland.

In the morning, Geoffrey went back to the flat near Wimpole Street to meet the 'French bods'. They consisted of a woman from Brittany who taught in a school in Brook Green and her husband, an engineer who had heard General de Gaulle's call to arms broadcast by the BBC on 18 June. On putting himself in touch with the general, as invited, he had decided he could see action sooner by joining the new British force.

The married couple sat side by side and asked Geoffrey about his life. He was not quite sure if, when he came to an English word, he should pronounce it with a French accent or say it with a stubbornly English one to show how Gallic the rest of the sentence had been. '*Je suis né près d'Andover,*' he said, but it made it sound as though his birthplace was called 'Dandover'. It was best not to mention 'Puffer' Hill. What was the French for 'Puffer', anyway? '*Souffleur*'? He had a vague idea the word also meant something indecent. He would avoid Hill ('*Colline*') completely, he thought, though he did venture a small joke about his regiment, ending '*qui s'appellent les "Mousquetaires", bien que nous soyons – heureusement – plus que trois!*'

Neither of the French couple smiled. He wondered if his use of the subjunctive had given him away as a foreigner. Would a village Frenchman really bother? The conversation moved into calmer waters: his mother, Limoges, the pottery industry, the Fall of France, the greatness of its people . . . Geoffrey had never considered his ability to speak French as much of a gift – any more, say, than the ability to ride a bicycle or play a square cut; he had just absorbed it at home. None of his tutors had ever questioned his fluency even when lamenting the infrequency of his essays, yet the woman seemed unhappy with his performance. Was there something about his accent, he wondered? Had he inherited from his mother, without knowing it, the equivalent of a Cornish brogue?

Her husband, however, nodded vigorously as he listened and seemed to sense – and share – something of Geoffrey's impatient desire for action. They shook hands firmly and Geoffrey was sent back down the passageway, where Mr Green showed him through to a small office that opened off his own. In it was a man in civilian clothes with a bald head and a pipe; he remained sitting and pointed at the chair.

'Dr Samuels,' said Mr Green. 'This is Talbot.'

Samuels looked at a list on his desk and nodded. Mr Green left them to it.

'What makes you think you're suited to this kind of work?' said Samuels. His manner was abrupt.

'I haven't been told a great deal about what it entails yet. But I speak French. I'm fit. I'm keen to help.'

'Think you could kill someone?'

'What?'

'Unprovoked? With your bare hands?'

'Well . . . If I was trained for it. If it was necessary.'

'What would constitute a necessity?'

'Self-defence. The defence of another.'

'The national interest?'

'I . . . suppose so.'

Samuels, who had been looking out of the window, swivelled his chair to look Geoffrey in the eye.

'We're going to do some word association now. I say a word and I want you to say the first thing that comes into your mind. No hesitation. The very first thing.'

'All right.' Geoffrey licked his lips. It was like taking guard against Alf Gover.

'Father.'

'Confessor.'

'Mother.'

'Superior.'

'Girl.'

'Guide.'

'Boy.'

'Scout.'

'Could you just pause a moment before—'

'I thought you told me not to.'

'I did, but you're just completing set phrases. I want you to tell me what picture or feeling the word evokes for you.'

'Right-ho.'

'Jew.'

'Israel. Bible.'

'One word only. France.'

'I see the shape of the map.'

'Let's try again. One word. France.'

'Loire.'

'Loss.'

'Death.'

'Victory.'

'Cricket.'

'Sex.'

'Lust.'

'I think that's enough of that. Do you have a girlfriend?'

'No. I'm in the army. We don't really meet women.'

'Before the war?'

'There were no women at the school where I taught. Apart from the maids, but they were from a mental institution. At university I might ask a girl from home to go to a college ball.'

'Did you sleep with any of them?'

'No . . . No, they weren't that sort of girl.'

'Would you say you had a strong libido?'

'I don't know. I don't know what average is. I do like girls.'

'Have you ever had homosexual feelings? In the army for instance?'

Geoffrey suppressed a laugh at the thought of the sweating Musketeers. 'They're not that sort either.'

Dr Samuels leaned back in his chair. 'If you go abroad you may see things you've never seen before. You may see things that none of us has ever seen. We don't know. Would you describe yourself as robust?'

'Yes, I think so.'

'When did you last cry?'

Geoffrey thought for a long time and shook his head. 'I can't remember. Perhaps when I was nine or ten.'

'Are you good at being on your own? Do you have resources? In your head?'

'I hope so.'

'Were you an only child?'

'Yes.'

Samuels stood up. 'This interview is over. I have no further questions.'

'My God, Talbot, you've got to get me in on this French lark,' said Trembath when Geoffrey reported back that evening.

'I'll see what I can do. Though I don't recall your French being up to much.'

'How the hell do you know? We weren't even in the same year.'

'We did a couple of conversation classes with old Madame Whatsit – when the man in your college was off sick. Don't you remember?'

'Vaguely,' said Trembath. He stroked the moustache he had grown since receiving his commission. 'I don't suppose you could give me a few lessons, could you? Just to brush up? I'm desperate to see some action. If I sit round here cooped up much longer I'm going to lose my mind.'

They had time only for an evening of Charles Trenet records before Geoffrey's transfer came through. 'The best way to sound French is to imitate someone,' said Geoffrey. 'As though you're acting. I always mimic my grandfather, who was a *garagiste* in Clermont. Marvellous old codger.'

'That's exactly it,' said Trembath. 'The way you swallowed the "r" in "*garagiste*" and "Clermont". Your Adam's apple disappeared below your top button. And don't forget, Talbot, I've never had the pleasure of meeting your grandfather.'

'Well, imagine you're Charles Trenet then.'

When the paperwork was done, Geoffrey returned to London. He felt wistful about saying goodbye to the Musketeers, though the fact was, he admitted to himself on the train, his sentimental affection for the regiment had not been reciprocated. They might one day sail to North Africa, he presumed, if they were lucky; and what sort of baptism of fire might that be – in the sands of Tunisia? Doubtless he would have been left in reserve with the baggage in some Algerian port.

At his final interview, Mr Green was joined by a man called Dawlish, whom Geoffrey liked a good deal less. Green might have been an enlightened manager in a family-run company; Dawlish had an air of deceit and cruelty about him. Geoffrey wondered if he had been transferred from another secret organisation of longer standing; he seemed to carry a history of calculation in his eyes, and Geoffrey could picture him disowning a stranded agent without a second thought: 'Talbot? Never heard of him.'

'You got a splendid report from the headshrinker,' Green was saying. 'Top rating. Your little trouble in Norfolk is of no consequence to us. I'd go so far as to say it was a recommendation. We're not in the business of hiring straight-up-and-down foot soldiers. Many of our recruits are foreign nationals. Most are civilians. We're after mavericks, people who may not fit in to normal life. Are you with me?'

Geoffrey had always felt that his best quality was exactly the opposite: the ability to fit in anywhere without a fuss. As he felt Dawlish's eyes bore into him through a pair of horn-rimmed glasses, however, he thought it best to say nothing.

'You start training at once,' said Green. 'We have a residential course near Brockenhurst in the New Forest. Here's a travel warrant.'

On his way to Southampton, Geoffrey called in to see his parents

and surprised his mother outside clipping at a runaway jasmine.
She disliked gardening, thinking it an English affectation and
watching with disdain as her husband struggled with the lawn-
mower. In France, grass simply grew.

Geoffrey's father came home from his office at lunchtime and
they were able to eat at a table in the garden. Mrs Talbot cooked
some young courgettes from the vegetable patch and served them
with a rice dish made from leftovers. It was surprisingly palatable,
though Geoffrey's father grumbled about eating the 'marrows'
before they were fully grown.

'What's the food like in the mess?' he said.

'Not bad at all. The regiment prides itself on feeding well.'
Geoffrey put down his beer glass. 'I have to tell you something.
I'm switching to a different outfit.'

'Not the RAF, I hope,' said his father, glancing up at the sky.
'I mean, bloody brave chaps and all that, but—'

'They live only a few weeks,' said his mother.

'No, don't worry. It's a sort of irregular outfit.'

'Commandos?' said his father.

'Not exactly. I can't tell you much about it. I shall be going to
France in due course.'

'Ah, sabotage, I suppose.'

'Which part of France?' said Geoffrey's mother.

'I don't know yet.'

'I wish I could come too. *Je voudrais bien voir.*'

Mrs Talbot sighed and sat back in her chair. Very faintly in the
background there was the sound of a single-engine plane, perhaps
a Spitfire, Geoffrey thought, on a training exercise from one of
the grass airfields in Sussex. Considering the war for civilisation
they were daily waging with the Luftwaffe, the noise was oddly
peaceful, not much more than the buzz of a distant bee in the hot
afternoon.

For a moment the three of them, the small family unit, looked at one another and Geoffrey had the sensation of time stopping, as though all his childhood summers were rolled into that moment: the slow days when sun glowed on the brick of the village almshouses with their fiery beds of dahlias and wallflowers tended by old men in cardigans; the bubbling white of the water that ran beneath the bridge by the church in which, flat on the grass, he would dip his hands to cool them, then splash his face; the road when he bicycled past the cottage hospital on his way home from school and saw the patients wheeled on to the grass to lie in the drowsy afternoon with a wireless faintly playing through an open door.

Then the Lysander was touching down on French soil on a night as dark as any secret-service planner could have wished. The little plane had come in beneath the German coastal radar and flown low for another thirty minutes before Geoffrey felt the bounce of its wheels on the grass field. It came to a halt, leaving him tilted back in his seat by the steep nose-to-tail slope.

'Thank you, ladies and gents,' said the pilot to the sound of unclipping seat harnesses. 'We have reached our destination. Please be sure to take all your belongings with you.'

Geoffrey and a female agent threw out their cases and clambered down a fixed port-side ladder. Of the half-dozen torches that had lit the landing strip, a single one remained alight in the woods beside the field, where Geoffrey and his partner were greeted with silent handshakes and went their separate ways. The refuelled Lysander was already turning into the wind for take-off.

Waking the next day in a village house at the end of a lane that led from the square, Geoffrey washed and shaved briskly before going downstairs. He was wearing clothes suitable for a commercial traveller; all of them were of French manufacture except the trousers, which had had their English label removed and a French one sewn in. He carried a packet of cigarettes made from '*caporal*' tobacco – the word 'corporal' supposedly showing they were superior to the tobacco of the simple '*soldat*', though still appallingly rough to his taste. On the other hand, the showy tie-pin, made in Lyons, was rather a good touch, he had to admit. 'Pierre Lambert' was his name; roofing was his business.

The lady of the house offered him some breakfast – stewed coffee, yesterday's bread and a scrape of jam with no butter. He was in the so-called 'Free Zone', where the French were allowed to police themselves without German supervision, but it was clear that their 'freedom' did not extend to the table. Geoffrey wondered if life might be better in the coastal Occupied Zone where at least the locals would have illegal access to what the Germans were piling on to their own plates. He ate beneath the grudging eye of his hostess, finishing what he was given and careful not to ask for more. The woman was not as welcoming as he had expected; she showed little gratitude for the fact that he was risking his life for her countrymen; there were no fine words or toasts to the freedom of the Patrie. Geoffrey felt she viewed him rather as just another player in the baffling number of organisations that beset her previously quiet rural life.

He walked for an hour or so to a nearby village where there was a railway halt, then took a train to the local town where he was to meet the head of the so-called 'Dentist' circuit, an Englishman who would be known to Geoffrey only by his code name 'Alain'. The journey was a pleasant one through fields of dwarf oak and walnut trees and the occasional grey-shuttered station, where the train took on water and Geoffrey could hear the birds singing as gleefully as though the Nazis were still bottled up behind the Rhine. He read his French novel and rehearsed imaginary conversations in which he explained to French or German security officers the vagaries of his life as a salesman. 'Yes, of course I travel a good deal. I miss my wife Hélène and our small child, whose name is Laurent. Would you care to see a photograph?'

Alain turned out to speak French with what sounded to Geoffrey like a Wolverhampton accent. He seemed worried and downcast. Dentist's wireless operator, a close personal friend of his, he explained, had been captured by the Vichy secret police a few days earlier.

'I had no idea,' said Geoffrey.

'Well, of course you had no idea,' said Alain. 'There was no one to transmit the news. And they took his set.'

They needed to make contact with another circuit, called 'Barrister', in the Occupied Zone not far from Bordeaux, Alain said; they had to ask Barrister's man to transmit a message asking London for a replacement wireless operator and set. 'So I'd like you to go and tell Barrister. As a matter of urgency.'

'Isn't that a job for a courier?' said Geoffrey, who had expected to be put in charge of blowing up power stations, laying the explosive, as he had been taught, flush against the machine. 'I mean, couldn't we get a friendly Frenchman to relay a message or post a letter?'

They were sitting in a tidy front room of a 'safe house' on the outskirts of the town. Through the window they could see the life of the citizens carrying on as it must have done for centuries, the postman on his bicycle, the women talking outside shops, the red-nosed man in the *bar-tabac* with his newspaper, a horse and cart on its way to a field. The absence of motor vehicles made it seem not merely quiet but timeless.

'The "friendly" Frenchmen are the worst,' said Alain. 'Do you know how many French and German security organisations we're dealing with? Fourteen. Do everything yourself. Never write anything down.'

'How do I get across the demarcation line?'

'By train.'

'But surely they—'

'Not in the train. Under the tender. The driver will explain.'

'So there are some friendly French.'

'The railwaymen are mostly Communists. They hate the Nazis. Go to the café in the marshalling yard at six. Ask for Benoît. Take a toothbrush.'

Geoffrey did as he was told and found himself led to the wheels of a locomotive tender. Benoît was a stout, red-faced man with a spotted neckerchief under his overalls who seemed to regard the evening's work as a joke of subtle if colossal proportions. Geoffrey was not sure who the butt of it was meant to be: himself or the enemy. Beneath the water tank was a space just large enough to take a man lying down, concealed from the outside by the vertical sides of the tender. When Benoît passed him in some wooden planks, Geoffrey was able to make a floor by resting them on the struts of the chassis and so convert the area, for which there was no other obvious use, into a coffin-shaped, one-man compartment.

'*Dormez bien!*' chuckled Benoît as he strolled off.

Geoffrey wondered, not for the first time, whether the French were taking the calamity of their defeat and occupation as seriously as they might. Through the spaces between the planks, he could see the rails and points go slowly by as the locomotive backed on to the train; they moved out of the siding on to the main line where he heard the sounds of the public address system, reminding him of visits to his mother's family in Limoges; then the stationmaster's whistle and the sound of steam escaping as the driver hauled on his levers and the train jolted forward, cracking Geoffrey's head against the chassis; then another, slightly less pronounced, shudder, for which he was better prepared; then another and another till the train picked up speed and the wooden sleepers began to move smoothly past beneath him.

This was more like it, Geoffrey told himself; this was an adventure. Why then, did it not feel like that? For some of the time he felt horribly enclosed, gazing at the floor of the water tank a few inches above his face; then he noticed the beginnings of cramp in his right hip and turned on to his side; but for most of the journey, for an hour or more, he felt only a sense of unreality, as though all of this was happening to someone else.

The train stopped at four stations and then again a fifth time in open country. Geoffrey was aware of a voice calling out to him. With Benoît's help, he extracted himself from his shallow grave and stood by the side of the track in the darkness. They were in the Occupied Zone, but far from any German or French police; he was free now to ride in the locomotive, alongside the amused Benoît and his fireman. As the train picked up speed, Geoffrey watched the dials and pressure gauges and found it hard to suppress an absurd schoolboy pleasure, while the pine-heavy scent of the countryside drove into his face.

After drinking some wine with his new friends at the station, Geoffrey found a barn in which to sleep before completing his journey by bus the following day. He met the leader of the Barrister circuit and delivered his message; he was told that Dentist would in due course receive coded instructions from a BBC broadcast advising them of a replacement.

He made his farewells and saw that he was for the moment a free man in an occupied country. How best might he impede the enemy?

For two years Geoffrey 'commuted', as Mr Green put it, between grass landing strips in England and France. Most of his work seemed to consist of putting people 'in touch' with other people. He met plenty of French patriots along the way, people who thought Pétain had been wrong to enter into official co-operation with the German occupier, but few of them seemed interested in doing much beyond making further introductions. In Paris he encountered a baker who had helped blow up an electricity sub-station near Rennes; but the Germans had shot twenty-five local citizens in reprisal while the baker and his fellow saboteurs had been driven out of town by angry residents. The Germans in the Occupied Zone were bad enough, but the French authorities in the 'Free' Zone were even more vigilant; and here civilian vendettas made any covert action dangerous: it was bad enough, Geoffrey quickly saw, having to deal with the Milice or the Abwehr without also having Mlle Durand falsely informing on a woman she thought might be stealing her boyfriend.

Geoffrey helped sabotage a factory near Clermont-Ferrand and arranged drops of guns and stores to small resistance groups that his own organisation had recruited, but it was what Trembath would have called 'farting against thunder'. Then, in the spring of 1943, the demarcation line was abolished overnight when the Germans, in a rush to protect the southern coast from the Allies based in Africa, occupied the whole country. At the same time they introduced a Statutory Work Order by which all young Frenchmen were required to go and work in German factories, and for the first time Geoffrey began to recruit French resisters in large numbers: better a hand-to-mouth life in the shadows, these young men told him, than the drudgery of a production line in Dortmund.

All of them, even the youths now living outside the law, were content to wait for some unspecified moment, some glorious day of action, and Geoffrey was frustrated by the delay. At one point he was tempted to rejoin the Musketeers, who had at least seen action in North Africa. In France, nothing happened. The British Secret Intelligence Service, covertly competitive with Geoffrey's organisation, was keen to build ever-larger networks of people who, so far as Geoffrey could see, then sat around and drank coffee with one another in risky public places.

So when in May he met a dark-haired twenty-five-year-old called Giselle (not her real name any more than his was Pierre

Lambert) he was enchanted by the fire of her impatience. She had worked as a courier for the Barrister circuit where she had encountered a fellow agent she described to Geoffrey. He had made an impression on her, this *rosbif*. He was very large — she gestured with her hands — and insisted on doing everything according to the 'book' (though could not say which book, or who had written it); he exercised vigorously each morning, was baffled by the lack of golf courses in the Landes and spoke French with a deplorable accent.

'*Mon dieu*,' said Geoffrey. '*Je le connais. C'est "Tiny".*'

'*Comment?*'

'"*Minuscule*". *Il s'appelle "Minuscule". Tiny.*'

Giselle looked doubtful, but Geoffrey explained that in English the alliteration with his surname gave it a certain lilt. They moved on quickly to discuss a plan Giselle was developing. A goods train left from the yards of Montauban early on a Wednesday morning to carry supplies up to the Massif Central. Its terminus was no less a place than Vichy itself, where the French puppet government strutted among the parks and boulevards of the old spa town.

With humour lighting up her dark eyes, Giselle outlined the plan for Geoffrey, herself and two good men she had recruited to their circuit, to dynamite the track and send a symbolic message to the people of France that the Resistance would no longer tolerate the flower of French agricultural produce being transported to the Hôtel du Parc and other troughs of official collaboration. Giselle was the woman Geoffrey had longed to meet — in almost every way. As over the succeeding weeks they sat long into the night, poring over railway maps, he grew light-headed on the spirit of her ingenuity and her sense of the absurd. In a moment of exhilaration, when she briefly drew breath from plotting, he kissed her full and silent lips and found himself enthusiastically kissed back. They regained their seriousness, agreed what they had done was '*pas professionel*', but did not rule out doing it again, perhaps after they had derailed the train.

They chose a section of track that was far from any town or village, in the hope that this would make it harder for the Germans to organise reprisals, and travelled there by bicycle two days before the planned attack. A resourceful schoolboy called Hugues found a way through the hedgerows and ditches, then led them through a damp culvert to an embankment. They slithered down to the track, where Geoffrey quietly insisted that his training, still remembered from his week at the country house near Brockenhurst, meant that he alone must supervise the laying of the charges, though at Giselle's insistence he allowed her also to clamp some of the plastic explosive against the rails. He told her that a lonely courier with the Dentist circuit had once been so hungry that he had eaten some of the explosive and had pronounced it quite satisfying, like a mild Swiss cheese. Giselle, her eyes alight with competitive fire, told him her father had drunk half a litre of engine oil and vowed that even after the war he would never go back to the thin olive variety.

They climbed back up the embankment, trailing fuse wire, and settled down to wait. The train went up with a satisfying explosion, though they were distressed that it seemed to contain some live animals as well as their products in the form of ham and cheese. If there were any armed guards or German soldiers, they seemed to have died in the blast, and the saboteurs were able to help themselves to some edible souvenirs; the driver of the train, who was unharmed, was a resistance sympathiser who congratulated them on their work and pointed them to the wagons with the best food. They were long clear of the area before the lights of armoured vehicles and motorcycles came across the fields.

When he next returned to France after a spell in London, Geoffrey was put in charge of a circuit in the Lot called 'Haberdasher', living in a deserted barn with a view of the river

Dordogne in the valley. With a supply of walnuts and fruit in the orchards and with cheese from the sheep on the hill it was sometimes difficult to remind himself that he had work to do. When the weather began to turn cold, however, he told his wireless operator and courier that he had important business near Mont-de-Marsan and set off to find what he could of the Barrister circuit. It did not take many enquiries to unearth a large man passing himself off as a Belgian handyman.

'Why on earth are you Belgian?' he said.

'To account for my accent, I think,' said Trembath. 'It means everyone looks down their nose at me. It's quite convenient.'

Trembath had a room over a café in a small town; he took a bottle of thin wine from a cupboard and filled two glasses.

'I'm bored,' said Trembath. 'Nothing ever happens. We just wait and wait. It's lonely. I sometimes see the wireless chap, but he lives miles away in a deserted manor house. He spends all day playing the piano in an empty drawing room.'

'Come and spend some time with Haberdasher,' said Geoffrey. 'We're planning great things. We expect the Allies to invade France from the south in the spring and we're looking at how we can stop German reinforcements getting down to the coast.'

Trembath pushed his big hand back through his hair; a smile spread across his placid features. 'All right, Talbot. I'm game.'

'We'll have to travel separately. I can't afford to be seen with a Belgian handyman. You know the name of the village? I'll see you at the crossroads at midnight the day after tomorrow. Have you got money? I've got plenty from London.'

Two nights later at the barn, they lit a small fire and sat either side of it eating bread with ewe's cheese and drinking red wine Geoffrey had bought from a man in Gramat. There was a message from Hugues, the keen schoolboy, telling him that Giselle wanted to see him urgently at a location between Brive and Ussel.

'Giselle!' said Geoffrey. 'What a firebrand.'

'I know.'

'Better than your solitary pianist. This is the war you wanted. This is resistance with a capital "R".'

The next day they set off by bicycle, Trembath following an hour behind. Their rendezvous was a remote farmhouse chosen by Giselle as the headquarters for her next operation, at the end of a long narrow track with a commanding view of the countryside.

It was evening as Geoffrey approached, standing on the pedals as the bicycle juddered over the potholes. He was invigorated.

He felt that his life was about to take a decisive turn. Why should it be here of all places, he wondered – this old farm that had seen the generations come and go and would see him in the grave as well? But then again, why not? What are places for – but to keep watch silently?

Dismounting, he wheeled his bicycle across the farmyard with its stinking midden. A chained dog barked as he approached the door. No one answered his knock, so he let himself in and walked down a gloomy passageway; he heard what sounded like a horse, or perhaps a cow, shifting on its hooves in a side room. Eventually the passage opened into a parlour where a log fire was burning. There were lit candles in wrought-iron sconces on the walls.

'Giselle?'

There was a scuffling sound from an old couch in front of the fire, and Giselle was suddenly standing in front of him. He had only ever seen her in her trousers or overalls, but she was wearing a dress with stockings and there was a ribbon in her hair.

She crossed the room and embraced Geoffrey, squeezing him to her. '*Ah bonsoir, mon brave, mon anglais. Que je suis heureuse de te revoir!*'

'*Moi aussi.*'

'*J'ai préparé un dîner un petit peu spécial.*'

'Il y a un autre qui arrive dans quelques instants. Un ami. "Minuscule".'

A commotion in the yard told them Trembath had found his way, and shortly afterwards he was sitting with them at the rough table drinking a local spirit made from apples while Giselle sliced a dry saucisson. She had prepared a slow-cooked dish of beef in wine and there were fried potatoes to go with it. After dinner, she began to describe her next plan. Pushing the plates to one side, she laid out a map on the table and pointed to where the German tank divisions were likely to be sent. She then outlined the best places on the main roads to attack them, though this would involve more than booby traps, she said; this would entail the full manpower of all the young Frenchmen who had fled to the hills to avoid working in Germany. They needed more weapons. She looked enquiringly at Geoffrey, who nodded his agreement and told her he would see what he could do.

While he was quietly thrilled by Giselle's plan, he was a little worried by her manner. She was as fiery as ever, as contemptuous of the Germans and careless of her own safety, but there was something detached about the way she spoke — as though in her heart she did not expect to see the events she was describing.

He looked across at Trembath in the candlelight. He was studying the map while clearly struggling to understand all that Giselle was saying. It was strange, but Trembath seemed not to respond to her as a woman, Geoffrey thought; his attention was fixed only on the briefing.

For a moment, his own attention wandered as he took in the details of the parlour, the row of copper pans above the range, the stone sink, the home-made wooden shelves with pots and jars. What must it be like in peacetime, and who really lived here? How strange was the dislocation of war, like a ghost universe. Then he looked at Giselle's slim, earnest figure as she leaned across the map, the light catching the red ribbon in her hair.

She smiled and said in English: 'So you are prepared to fight?'

'We are,' said Trembath.

A door that led further into the house swung open quietly. Two German soldiers stood with rifles raised, pointing them at the Englishmen, one at each.

Giselle sat down heavily and lowered her face into her hands.

'*Je suis désolée*,' she said. '*J'étais prise. Le mois de juillet. Ils m'ont torturée.*'

Geoffrey could not speak. He wanted to translate for Trembath in case he hadn't understood, but the outcome of it all was clear enough.

The two of them stood with their hands above their heads and were pushed at gunpoint down a passageway towards the middle of the house. Though he could hear Giselle sobbing, Geoffrey did not look back.

For a day they were held in a police cell in the local town; then, with other undesirables, they were put on a transport to Bavaria, where they spent a week in a makeshift prisoner-of-war camp. The conditions were tolerable, they agreed, and Geoffrey persuaded Trembath to do nothing rash in his desire to escape. Then one night the pair of them were taken out of the camp in a lorry and driven to the local railway station, where they were put into a cattle truck. There were about thirty others in the wagon, most of them Russians. The train moved slowly eastwards, though no one knew where they were going. There was no water or food, though every few hours the doors were drawn back and they were allowed out to relieve themselves while armed guards looked on.

It was about three in the morning when they were finally told to disembark. They were at a railhead with a long platform and what looked like a normal waiting room with flowers in wooden tubs outside. A German soldier pulled along by a dog on a chain told them to strip naked; he was not the lazy infantryman one might have expected to volunteer for prison guard, but, Geoffrey recognised from his enemy identification course in Brockenhurst, an SS officer. Other guards emerged from the darkness and shouted at them to hurry. Some of the men, exhausted and bewildered by the journey, were slow to remove their clothes, and Geoffrey saw one beaten with a rifle butt and another with a whip. The SS men drove them into a building at the end of the platform where they had their heads shaved by unspeaking men in striped uniforms. Still naked, they were told to dip their heads in a bucket of green liquid. Only the guards spoke, keeping up a continual hectoring: '*Schnell! Schnell!*' Hurry, faster, quicker. It was not the usual fear of rank that made the Germans so frantic, Geoffrey thought; there was no hidden superior they were trying to impress. It was something else. He caught Trembath's eye, but neither spoke.

They gave their names and nationality to a clerk who sat by the door. Geoffrey hesitated for a moment before deciding on his own name rather than that of Pierre Lambert; it would help the Red Cross to trace him. In the next building they were given striped uniforms and wooden clogs of their own, then herded at gunpoint down a path and into a brick block with the letter D chiselled into the stone lintel. Inside were rows of wooden bunks from floor to ceiling, designed perhaps for one person but holding two, three or even four men. There was a drainage channel down the centre and an ablutions room at the far end. A prisoner who appeared to be in charge pushed them to the end of the block, shouting orders at them in Polish. They climbed into a wooden bunk near the door, Trembath's bulk causing the man already in it to lie tight against the side. It was too dark to see this man's face, though they were aware of him scratching himself through the cold, uncomfortable night. None of the others showed any interest in the new arrivals; they had clearly seen many people come and go.

Geoffrey closed his eyes, his body against Trembath's. They would find the British officer in charge the next day, no doubt, and make contact through him with the Red Cross; he would want to get word to his parents in Hampshire and arrange for some parcels.

They awoke to shouted orders in Polish from a man who appeared to be a kind of dormitory prefect. Another Polish prisoner, this one more of a head boy, then inspected the block before ushering in two SS officers; it was a little like occupied France in the way the Germans had persuaded the vanquished to do the dirty work for them. Hundreds of shaven-headed men stood shivering beside their bunks; one or two appeared too ill to move and, on the orders of the SS, were pulled out by the others. Two were already dead and were dragged from the block by their hands. An older man who could no longer stand unaided fell to the ground by the drainage channel, where a German shot him through the head. Trembath leapt forward to remonstrate, but Geoffrey grabbed his arm.

A cauldron of soup was brought in on a wheeled wagon to the end of the room and the men went forward in silence to receive their ration. With no plate or bowl, Geoffrey could take only the bread, though to judge by the emaciated state of the prisoners he was not missing much in the soup. There followed a roll call that took almost two hours, the men standing in rows while SS men counted them off in an alley between two of the brick blocks. Then they were marched towards the camp gate, and Geoffrey for the first time could see what kind of place he had come to.

They were in marshy land with pine forests all round them; in the distance he could make out mountains, or their foothills. The camp itself had obviously been built for some other purpose before the war. The watchtowers were set into the perimeter fence at intervals of about a hundred yards and did not look particularly tall or robust; there was a second barrier of rolled barbed wire, while the main fence, to judge from the regularly spaced junction boxes, was electrified. Geoffrey walked next to Trembath through the gate of the camp and down a metalled road for about twenty minutes before the SS guards ordered them to stop at a building site. They were given shovels and told to start working; their job was to dig a drainage channel along the edge of the field.

Geoffrey could understand nothing of what the other prisoners, who were either Russian or Polish, were saying to one another. He felt as though he had become lost in someone else's war — some Transylvanian or Slavic nightmare that had nothing to do with Mr Green or the Musketeers. Who were all these East Europeans with their terrible histories, pine forests and slaughters? What had they to do with democracy and the RAF?

'These men look broken,' Trembath said from the corner of his mouth, working next to Geoffrey, glancing at his starved fellow prisoners. 'I think we need to set an example.'

'Not yet,' said Geoffrey. 'We need to know more before we start planning an escape, if that's what you're thinking.'

'It's our duty,' said Trembath.

Geoffrey stood up to stretch his back from an hour of digging and felt a sudden, excruciating pain in his side. An SS man with a whip stood behind him. The Pole to Geoffrey's right made a downward gesture with his arm: stay bent over, don't stand up. Along the line, Geoffrey saw an old Slav do what he had done — stand and stretch. An SS man drove a rifle butt into his face; when the man next to him went to help, they shot him through the knee. Another German officer, drawn by the sound, walked over to see what had happened. He took out his pistol and, to the amusement of his fellow guards, shot the man through the other knee as well. The prisoners bent down to the ditch and did not raise their heads.

They worked for twelve hours digging with a half-hour break

in the middle of the day, when a motor lorry brought water, a piece of bread and more soup. The site itself, perhaps twenty acres in extent, had many completed buildings, paths and roadways; it was surrounded by further wire through which Geoffrey could see what looked like bonfires in clearings among the trees, attended by further prisoners in striped uniform and overseen by SS men with guns and dogs. Columns of smoke with an unfamiliar smell emanated from the pyres.

Time spent in reconnaissance is seldom wasted, Geoffrey remembered from his course at Colchester. He would lie low and observe; and in planning his escape, there was no immediate hurry: the only sense of urgency seemed to come from the chance of malnutrition. It seemed that most of the prisoners in the camp were starving; they were being worked to death. He and Trembath needed to be on a train to the West to rejoin the war effort before they were reduced to the skeletal condition of the others.

There was a further roll call at the end of the day, followed by a watery soup of swede or turnip in the bunkhouse. For the hours of darkness they were left alone by the Germans with only the Polish dormitory prefect, or 'DP' as Trembath called him, telling them what to do. The ablutions room had a stone floor, a row of basins and yards of overhead pipework for showers. What it lacked was water. The lavatories were overflowing; a kind of pit had been excavated behind them, though many prisoners were too enfeebled to make the journey.

In the middle of the third night, there was a commotion as a group of six SS men came into the room for what they called a 'fitness test'. The prisoners were lined up naked and shivering while the Germans walked between the ranks. Those incapable of standing were hauled out by the DP and two other trusted prisoners. From outside, a few moments later, came the sound of gunshots; but it seemed a further cull was needed.

Geoffrey puffed out his chest and stood tall, though he was confident that even after the meagre food of occupied France he was in better condition than most. The concrete floor was cold on his bare feet. A further twenty men were taken out; others were pointed back to the bunks; but a line of fifty naked, shivering men remained. There was a laughing confabulation among the SS men, after which one with a long whip flicked it at the first naked prisoner. It grazed his side, leaving a weal below the ribs. The plaited leather was about six feet long with a metal-weighted tip; it took considerable judgement and wrist action to land the snap exactly — and this was their sport. When they had tired of legs and torso, their gaze turned to the men's genitals, a difficult target, but one that would cause the most pain. There was no gambling or sense of competition; the inflicting of agony was amusement enough. The guards were allowed three turns each before passing the whip on. Geoffrey turned his eyes to the ceiling where a row of dim electric bulbs was strung, wondering whether it was better to be prepared for the bite of the whip or to be taken by surprise. A man three along from him fell howling and shrieking to the ground while the guards laughed. Geoffrey, when his turn came, escaped with no more than a flick across the upper thigh, shortly after which the guards tired of the game and went to their own beds.

That night, lying close between Trembath and the Pole, Geoffrey thought how he might take his mind off where he was — off the pain in his thigh, the hunger in his belly — and open the gateway to sleep. He pushed his mind as far as he could from his surroundings. There was a particular cricket ground that had meant a great deal to him when he was growing up. It had a cedar tree in one corner, near the pavilion, a hedge that ran along the road and could be cleared with a mighty heave over midwicket, a bowling green at one end and cow pastures at the other. It was, for a club ground, remarkably flat and true; it was a place to score hundreds, though it never played quite as easily as might be expected, and you had to work for your runs. Now he imagined himself going out to bat on a bright Saturday morning in July, with perhaps a hundred people watching from deckchairs and benches at the side of the ground. There would be picnics on rugs laid out on the grass; boys practising their own games with smaller bats and balls; women in floral cotton print dresses; but above all there would be the concentration of the players in the middle – the intensity of struggle that was never sensed from the boundary.

He liked games with a morning start so he could make his mark at the crease with a stud from his boot in the brightest possible light. He talked to himself all the time he was facing, his lips moving, as he urged himself to watch the ball. That was all his self-instruction: watch it, fasten it to your eye like a fish on a hook. Once, against a slow left-armer, he had gone down the wicket, and as he swung through the ball, dispatching it high over long on for six, he swore he had seen at the moment of impact the slight mark made by the risen seam as its tough stitching met the soft face of the willow.

And to go into lunch undefeated on 48 or 55, to the congratulations of his teammates and the shy smiles of sisters and mothers and girlfriends; to sit at the long trestle and attack his plate of ham and tongue salad, biscuits and cheese, but not eating too much and drinking only a half-pint of beer from the barrel knowing that in the afternoon heat much more endeavour would be required of him because he so passionately wanted his side to win. Outside the pavilion he sucked on a cigarette and gazed up at the sky to re-accustom his eyes to the light as the umpires walked out again to the middle. He would turn to his partner. 'All right? Shall we?'

After they had been there a week, the Pole who shared their bunk died from typhus, and this gave them more space. They slept head to toe, and Geoffrey began, in a way he found ridiculous, to see the few square inches of space about his head as his own territory, and to resent any intrusion from Trembath's large feet. Once he concealed a rare piece of sausage that had come with breakfast in a small crack in the wood to give himself something to look forward to when the day was through. All afternoon he thought about it. Saving the 'unexpired portion' of the day's ration was the military term by which he dignified his action; in fact, his hoarding reminded him of his mother's dachshunds, who would take any prized bit of leftover from the human lunch that had been thrown in their dog bowl and carry it off to their baskets.

Before adopting their sleeping positions, he and Trembath would whisper plans to one another. There were tens of thousands of prisoners and only a few hundred guards. Among the prisoners there were many women, living in separate blocks, who might not contribute to a fight, though some looked desperate enough; many of the men were too enfeebled by sickness and starvation to be of use. However, there were still able-bodied men – many of the Russian prisoners of war, for instance – and there were skilled tradesmen: electricians who could help neutralise the fence, carpenters, blacksmiths and others who might help to arm them. It would be possible to overwhelm their tormentors by weight of numbers. They would at first take casualties from machine-gun and rifle fire, but were easily numerous enough to push on, capture the SS firearms, turn them on their owners, tear down the watch-towers, cut the wire and go free.

Trembath was becoming impatient. 'Listen, Talbot,' he said, 'it's important that we don't let ourselves descend to the level of some of these people. They've lost their dignity.'

'They're refugees,' said Geoffrey. 'They've lost their family, their homes, their money – their children in some cases, I think. But for us . . . It was certainly a bit rough in occupied France, but nothing like—'

'That's exactly it. They're civilians. We're soldiers.'

'Irregulars. That's why we're here and not in a proper PoW camp. Back in London once I heard that the girl who landed with me on my first drop by Lysander – she got captured and taken to some women's camp called Ravensbrück. They heard nothing more. The Red Cross doesn't function there.'

'Are you saying they killed her?'

'I think so.'

That night at roll call, the SS officer asked if anyone spoke French, and, without thinking, Geoffrey raised his arm. No sooner had he stepped forward and been pushed at rifle point towards the administrative buildings near the camp entrance than he saw that he had made a mistake. What had he been thinking? A better job, some interpreter's office work, an end to ditch-digging and beating . . . The collaborator's comfort? There was no such thing as 'better' in this place; there were only faster or slower roads to the same end. The smile on the face of the SS guard who accompanied him to the office was that of a man who knows but will not tell.

Geoffrey was given a new 'Special Unit' uniform with thicker stripes and told to wait. It was past midnight when they heard the distant sound of a train approaching through the pine forest. All trains sound the same in the night, thought Geoffrey: forlorn – and for a moment, a line from a Charles Trenet song sounded in his head. The rails rattled as the clanking wagons came closer; there was the outline of smoke and steam against the moonlit clouds, then the shape of the locomotive nosing through the night, slowing as it neared the terminal point, until the train of twenty wagons came juddering to a halt beside the platform and the engine let out a final gasp of steam. For a moment in the night all was silent.

Then the sides of the cattle trucks were unlocked and wrenched to one side, squealing on their metal runners, by willing striped prisoners of the Special Unit of which Geoffrey was now part. Inside there were no cattle or horses, but hundreds of people — children, women, men, old, young, jumping or falling down on to the platform, eager to leave behind the excrement and the dead bodies in the trucks. With an Alsatian dog snarling at his heels, Geoffrey urged and encouraged the people to dismount. They were French. '*Descendez. Vite. Messieursdames! Vite, s'il vous plaît.*' How pathetic it was, he thought, that he could only dignify his part in what was happening by saying 'please'. The French so loved their please and thank you and monsieur, madame; his mother and her Limoges family would be proud of him.

The members of the Special Unit pushed the people into lines while the SS officers screamed at them to hurry. '*Les hommes à droite. Les femmes et les enfants à gauche,*' Geoffrey called out, translating the German order. The prisoners' suitcases, bags and in some cases mere bundles of belongings were ripped from their hands and taken to large piles at the end of the platform, where other prisoners, many of them women, emerged from the darkness and took them swiftly back inside a building, like mice taking cheese through a hole in the wainscot. The new arrivals were haggard and startled, yet many still looked hopeful; there were men in good coats with yellow stars stitched to the lapels, women with neat dresses and hair they had managed to keep tidy through the journey from the west. Some of them held the hands of children purposefully to them; others were already like beggars, vagrants, living on the last scraps of energy; they looked to Geoffrey as though they would welcome any development that would let them rest. The majority, though, were stoical; they seemed hopeful, despite the dogs, the whips and the screaming, that some natural justice would prevail; Geoffrey saw them looking towards their future home, its strong brick buildings, its orderly air, with something like optimism.

The mothers and children came forward first. They were

pushed and piled on to the backs of lorries and driven off to one side of the main gate. The other women were divided, so far as Geoffrey could make out, by age and physical attributes. Those who seemed fittest for work were herded along the same route as he and Trembath had been, presumably to shaving and disinfecting; the older and frailer were loaded on to more motor transports. Some of the Special Unit were now pulling corpses from the train, while others began to hose out the reeking wagons. Geoffrey ground his teeth and tried not to breathe too hard.

He was told to join a motor lorry and to expect orders at the other end. He stood on a metal plate above the rear bumper, holding on to the tailgate as the truck trundled over an unmade road towards a white house beyond an orchard. Here there was a makeshift holding area, a sort of stockade, in which Special Unit prisoners, screamed at by SS guards, were struggling to deal with the multitude of people.

'*Schnell, schnell!*' the guards kept shouting.

In German, an officer who seemed calmer than the others told Geoffrey what to say. 'Tell them they must remove their clothes and leave them in piles here. Then they must go through that door. They will then be allowed to take a shower in this building. After that they will be given clean clothes and something to eat.'

But the words would not come to Geoffrey. He seemed dumb. He had lost all recollection of the French language. He cast his mind back to school, to home, Limoges, his mother . . . French, French. God, he was bilingual, but where were the words? *Ôtez les vêtements . . . Déshabillez vous . . . Demain, tout sera bien . . .* He cleared his throat and called, '*Attention!*'

There was the sound of a pistol being fired. A Special Unit prisoner lay dead beside him, shot by a guard impatient at his slowness. Women were beginning to cry, children to howl. No one knew what was going on or what to do. The guards began to scream louder, sensing the uprise of hysteria. Geoffrey felt a rifle stuck into his back. '*Schnell! Heraus mit der Sprache! Schnell!*' Speak up! Geoffrey's throat was swollen. He ground his clogged foot into the ground. It was speak or die.

'*Messieurs dames, attention, s'il vous plaît!*'

None of the Germans could understand French; that was why he was here. He could say anything. '*Je ne sais pas ce qui vous attend.*' I don't know what awaits you. He felt a hundred eyes on him. At last the French had in him what they had wanted: an insider who could explain.

'I don't know, I don't know, I've heard rumours . . . Why are you here and not in the camp? Are you old? Are you young? Are you dying? This place is not like any other. I have heard screaming . . .' Geoffrey found the words were coming in English. He didn't know if they passed his lips or whether they formed only in his mind.

But somewhere in the dark a French voice was speaking. It was telling them that there were clean clothes and, on the other side, hot food for them. Don't let that voice be mine, Geoffrey thought; dear God, don't let me lead them on.

They were starting to undress; some were going into the building. The tide of hysteria was beginning to ebb. The SS officer nodded at him and told him to keep talking. Through a gate in the perimeter wire he saw a flatbed lorry piled with pine trees driving towards a sawmill. He thought he heard the screech of metal teeth on sappy wood, too young to burn well, and saw another lorry leaving from the back of the mill with its load of pine logs cut to length, heading towards a building with a tall chimney that was pouring black smoke into the night.

The prisoners of the Special Unit were told to turn their backs on the white cottage, to avert their gaze, and, as dawn was seeping through the forests, Geoffrey was ordered back to D block. He clambered into his bunk alongside Trembath, too tired and ashamed to speak. He had lost his bearings, didn't know in any case what he might say.

'Listen,' said Trembath. 'Listen.'

There were wails and screeches coming from a building nearby.

'What the hell . . .'

'Oh God. It's the Frenchwomen.'

'Did you see?'

'No, once they were inside, we were sent away. The SS took over.'

'What happens?'

'They lock them in a shower room. An SS man puts in pellets through the roof. I saw a guard in a gas mask. We're not meant to see what they do. For fear that one day, when the war's over . . .'

Headlights of the trucks swept over the walls of the bunkhouse; they could hear the individual cries of children, men and women. Normally a lorry would have revved its engine loudly to drown the noises. All through the night was the sound of screaming and, closer to home, of men in the bunkhouse who had lost control. In the morning it was impossible to get into the ablutions room for the number of them hanging from the pipes in the ceiling.

It was a relief to march to the work site the following day, to dig with head lowered. Geoffrey wore the uniform of the Special Unit and feared that it made him conspicuous and liable for further 'special' duties. He did his best to keep his eyes on the frozen ground.

That night, he tried to understand what he had seen. He tried to place it, without feeling crushed by it. He had no idea what reserves he had, how great his desire to live at any price. The French people, he heard, were all Jews, some refugees from Eastern Europe, but most of them French nationals from Poitiers, Paris or Limoges.

Geoffrey was not sure he had met anyone Jewish in England. There had been a mathematician called Isaacs in the college next to his and, when he came to think of it, a physicist in his own college called Levi. Perhaps old Samuels, the psychologist who had given such a good report on him to Mr Green in London, was Jewish. These were names he recognised from the Bible, which furnished almost his entire idea of Jews, their history and beliefs. 'Heroic' was the word he would have used to describe them — frequently enslaved or exiled, yet able to draw on a limitless supply of soldiers, prophets and commanders: Saul, David, Solomon, Elijah, Moses, Daniel, Joshua, Gideon . . . Their stories had been repeated to him in Scripture lessons at his Hampshire school a hundred times; he had thrilled to the lions' den, the fiery furnace, the fall of Jericho and the parting of the Red Sea. What on earth was the point of taking a French seamstress from a backstreet in Lyons and transporting her across Europe to be murdered, on the grounds that some distant ancestor might once have plied his trade from Dan to Beersheba?

He turned on his side. The bunk now had a paper mattress that Trembath had bartered from an old Slovak. Geoffrey fixed his thoughts on England, certainties, and the life he had led as a child. He remembered his excitement on the September day he went to the village school and first encountered other children. His time at home was pleasant enough, but his parents didn't understand what a boy's world was like. Yet as soon as he met the children of the surrounding villages he found they all had the same enthusiasm for anarchy. There was no need to explain; once the bell rang and they roared into the yard, they all knew what to do. He was a pack animal who had found his place. Some of them won form prizes, some were good at football, others at art or adding up, but among themselves they made so few distinctions that they were surprised when life later seemed to push them into different channels. Geoffrey did not notice his own distinction in lessons or on the playing fields until his last year, when on seven occasions he went past fifty for the First XI and found himself steered once more toward the exam room, this time for university entrance.

Trembath was a bit of an ass in many ways, Geoffrey admitted to himself, but while he was still there, with his attachment to the proper way of doing things, it was possible to believe that the life he had known while growing up was not a mirage but a substantial and continuing thing; that it was the camp that was the chimera.

Working his way to the edge of the wooden bunk, his face away from Trembath's feet, Geoffrey began to hope that some divine intervention might come to their assistance. A Pole called Tomasz, who spoke a little English, told him that most of the prisoners candidly prayed for a miracle and that many of them had come to believe that one day the pine forests would part and that a shining chariot would sweep through, pluck them up and bear them all to safety in a place above the clouds.

The God of the Church of England was a vague and biddable person in Geoffrey's mind, not one that he had ever been encouraged to imagine closely. If Jesus was his son and Jesus was a Jew did that mean that God was also Jewish? He knew this speculation was childish, but his idea of religion was based entirely on the exemplary lives of Jews, including Christ, and it was difficult to think of God and religion in the framework of any other people. The questions of divinity and incarnation or of a life beyond this one were all posed in Hebrew; the odd meeting of universal and particular had found a pure expression in the black smoke from the chimney.

'For God's sake, Talbot. Are you afraid of something?' said Trembath. 'I'm not going to put up with much more of this. It's my duty as a British—'

'I know. But this is not a prisoner-of-war camp. The guidelines for officers don't apply here. I want to escape, too, but we need help. We need organisation.'

'You're like that bloody Roman general we had to read about at school. The Delayer. Cunctator. The chap who was always putting off the action. What was his name?'

'Can't remember. I think he was victorious in the end, though,' said Geoffrey.

'I don't want to stay any longer in this place.' Trembath had raised his voice and Geoffrey placed a restraining hand on his arm. 'I tell you, Talbot, I'd rather be killed outright than murdered on the quiet. Stuffed into a gas room with the Jews and the "nancy boys".'

Trembath's face was so close to Geoffrey's that he could feel his breath on his cheek.

'Even though I am one,' said Trembath.

Geoffrey was not sure that, despite their proximity, he had heard properly. 'What did you say?'

'I said, "Even though I am one." A nancy boy, I mean. Not a Jew. A queer.'

There was a silence while Geoffrey tried to digest what he had heard. He thought at first that Trembath must be joking, but soon saw there could be no reason for such an odd jest. Eventually he said, 'I didn't know.'

'I didn't tell. It's not something you go round shouting about. I wasn't always sure myself. Then something happened. There was a young corporal at Colchester. He seemed to have got my number. He was a very knowing young man. I used to sneak out and meet him every night. He made me see I'd always been like that, really.'

'God.'

'I won't tell you any more. I can tell you're embarrassed. But I couldn't see much point in keeping it to myself.'

'None at all. I'm . . . glad you told me.'

They were sitting in their bunk while many of the other prisoners had gathered round to hear Tomasz tell them a story. He could keep a hundred of them entertained with folk stories, legends or the entire plots of books his memory had stored. Geoffrey began to wonder if he ought to contribute something from his own education; he could pass it on to Tomasz to translate. His night-time discipline of forcing his mind into a better world now took the shape of trying to remember the various novels he had read. It was shocking how little had stayed with him. *Moby-Dick*, for instance: a sailor bent on killing a white whale that had bitten off his leg. Little else came back to him. Or *Jane Eyre*. A poor and ill-treated governess who eventually marries the man she wants, Mr Rochester; there was also someone called St John Rivers. The Poles with their taste for woodland spirits, angels and magical transformations were hardly going to be uplifted by that. So it would be *Great Expectations*, and he would do it serially, as Dickens had published it. He was pretty sure he had the plot by heart, until the end at least, when some of the revelations that ought to have been unforgettable had proved the opposite. Had he dreamt it, or did Estella actually turn out to be the daughter of Magwitch? He went over the story again and again in his mind, dividing it up into chunks that might take an hour to tell.

Somehow he fell asleep.

The next day at roll call, a senior guard told Geoffrey to step forward and asked why, if he was in Special Unit uniform, he was not on a special detail. Geoffrey replied that he was a French interpreter, on special duties only when required. The guard pointed him towards the administrative building and told him to go at once.

'*Nein*,' said Geoffrey. '*Ich bin Dolmetscher französisch. Interprète français.*'

There was the sound of a safety catch coming off a revolver. The process of trial and justice had reached its usual rapid conclusion and Geoffrey did as he was told.

For a day he helped sort belongings taken from those who had arrived by train from the west. There were baskets for currency or jewellery and great piles of clothes that were sent on to clothe German citizens at home. Some of the men's woollen items were destined, he was told, for infantry at the Eastern Front, and he wondered what the men would think if they knew they were wearing Jewish socks. Better that, perhaps, than the Jewish blood that was transported to Stalingrad for transfusions, taken by syringe from prisoners kept in cages for the purpose, so the superior soldiers of the Reich survived on the borrowed vigour of the Underpeople. Many of the other workers were women who had volunteered for a task that was at least indoors, away from the freezing ground and the Alsatian dogs. Glances were exchanged between some of the women and the SS guards; they were looks that made Geoffrey think there was a black market in sex, as in so much else inside the camp. What might go through the mind of a man who made love to a woman he viewed as less than human, of a lower species, Geoffrey wondered. Did it alter his opinion of himself, did it make him in his own eyes a bestialist?

The work lasted only a couple of days until a senior guard, noticing his still robust physical condition, sent him to join the Special Unit in the crematorium. A row of eight furnaces at knee height had to be kept roaring day and night with logs cut from the pine forests. Men shuttled to and from the doors where the trucks from the sawmill delivered the wood, unloading them on to wheeled wagons that were then pushed up to the ovens.

The corpses came in on trucks with chutes at the back that could be tipped on to slides that joined the mouth of the oven. Some of the stokers were given metal poles and detailed to prod the corpses down into the fire in groups of six or eight at a time, urged on by the screaming SS officers. Then the slide would be switched to the next oven. Geoffrey imagined the life of a crematorium worker at home, in Winchester or Andover; it might not be so very different, though of course there would be no more than a dozen corpses a day.

There were too many bodies. The lorries were backed up outside and he could sometimes smell their exhaust over the stench of the ovens. The delays drove the SS men to fury. Two guards took hold of a slow prisoner, held his hands behind his back and thrust his head into the oven. After a few seconds, they pulled him out again, demented and screaming, his head on fire. Geoffrey wondered if they did these things in order to keep their nerve up. It was as though the guards dare not risk lapsing back into the kind of life they must once have known. They needed to set an example to one another. '*Schnell!*' they still shouted. '*Schnell!*' No fire burned hot enough for them.

Geoffrey had a water bottle tied to his waist with string, though feared to drink from it. The intensity of labour was so great that when they stopped for half an hour at midday their places were immediately taken by others on rotation. There were no ablutions, and the men, many of whom had typhus, used the tin dinner plate for two purposes, chucking the waste into the flames as best they could. Those who collapsed or rebelled at what they did were thrown straight into the furnace.

At night, Geoffrey slept in the Special Unit block, outside the main camp, where his apparent composure meant that he was put on suicide prevention duty. The room was smaller than D block, and here the men were tortured not only by thirst and by the guards, but by the memory of what they had seen and done. Few were able to lie down in their wooden bunks to sleep. They had surprised a hunger in themselves for living, had found a will to survive so deep that it had taken them to madness.

Some sat against the wall holding their heads in their hands, scratching themselves raw. Some rocked back and forth, wearing away the skin on their backs against the cold wall. Some jabbered and screamed, or ran up and down the freezing barrack room; the most agitated were tied up to the ends of the bunks by their friends.

Geoffrey did what he could to calm them, though he lacked the languages needed, and most were in any case beyond words. He stuffed pieces of straw and paper into his ears to cut out the noises of Bedlam and turned to his memories of living. That night, nothing of England would come to him: no river, almshouse or cricket ground. It was these places that had now taken on the vague outlines of something he had dreamed.

Trembath had been right, Geoffrey thought. Better to die as a fighter, whatever reprisals the Germans took. If a hundred innocent men were shot to punish his revolt, it would only hasten what was inevitably coming to them. He wondered if 'Tiny' had made any progress with his plans, if he had connected with his doubtful French and schoolboy German to some other prisoners or whether he would make his stand alone. The thought of Trembath grabbing an SS gun and creating havoc even for a few moments was life-sustaining.

In the crematorium, Geoffrey met a Russian called Sergei who could speak a little English. He was a prisoner of war, not Jewish, and assured Geoffrey that all the Russians were determined to escape in order to get back to Moscow and help the Motherland repel the Fascist invader. As a result of two failed escapes, the SS had appointed Search Units from among the prisoners; these enthusiastic men were allowed to range over both camps to look for signs of planned escape. As well as personally searching their comrades and the barracks, they overturned stockpiled building materials, crawled into attic spaces, pipes and ducts — ostensibly to search, in fact to reconnoitre. A group of Russians had volunteered for search duty because it gave them so much freedom of movement; they had identified a weakness in the perimeter fencing where the Special Unit went in and out to tend the pyres in the forests.

The signs were discouraging. At intervals along the wire lay what Geoffrey had at first thought were bundles of rags that no one had picked up, but which were in fact the bodies of would-be escapers, shot from the watchtowers and left as a warning. Sergei believed that an escape was nevertheless being planned by a group of Search Unit Russians on the anniversary of the Great October revolution which, for reasons Geoffrey did not probe, fell on 7 November. He had less than a week in which to have himself transferred from the crematorium, though the chances of his being accepted into a Search Unit were remote.

Later that day the lorries from the gas chambers brought a consignment of dead women and children. After a week, Geoffrey had taught himself not to look at any aspect of the people who came in, especially their faces. He was not in any case on duty at the chute when the women came, but was carrying the cut logs in rapid relays to the furnace mouth. It seemed from shouts he heard from fellow-workers that some of the corpses were still living. When the number of people being killed was more than the gas chambers could process, the gassing time was cut to a barely sufficient ten minutes; then some last protective gesture had caused the women to hold the faces of their children tight against them and this perhaps had spared them the full effects of the gas.

Geoffrey latched his eyes on to the wooden logs and redoubled his efforts, beneath the, for once, silent stare of the guards. He had lids of skin that he could bring down over his eyes. He closed them when he could; at other times he fastened his gaze to the backs of his hands – to the veins, the pores – to keep the eyes from straying.

He heard the rumble of the chute and wished he had had lids with which to seal his ears.

He decided he would rather die now than go on. There was an SS man in the crematorium whom he had noticed eyeing him as he worked. He was a slight, feral creature with small black eyes. His name was Muller. An instinct told Geoffrey that the way this man stared at him was personal. At the end of his twelve-hour shift, as he was leaving the crematorium to return to the asylum of the Special Unit barracks, he asked Muller if he might transfer from the crematorium to the detail that worked in the woods outside the fence.

Muller looked him up and down. He seemed almost amused. 'Are you English?' he said.

'Yes. You speak my language?'

'Yes. I study before the war. Why do you wish to move?'

'I'm fit. I'm strong, I can do more work outside.'

'Those prisoners there live a few days only. It is the worst.'

Geoffrey felt Muller's gaze on him, sliding over his torso.

He said: 'If it would please you, Lieutenant. I would like to please you.'

The man's face froze over suddenly. 'Go, then. You disgust me.'

'Will you arrange my transfer?'

The fear left Muller's eyes. Contempt returned. He smiled a little. 'You want to die? You are a . . . coward?'

'You will authorise it?'

'Go and die.'

Geoffrey was dismissed. He went with a group of twenty prisoners through the wire to a clearing in the woods, where they exchanged their striped uniforms for rubber boots and waterproof overclothes. The job was to clear mass graves where the land had subsided, leaving ponds and pools of such fetor that even the Alsatian dogs would not go near.

They were near the section of the wire that the Russians had chosen for their escape, which was due in thirty-six hours' time. Knowing that his end was near, Geoffrey hurled himself into the work. He would have to complete only two shifts. He could do it.

'*Schnell!*'

The dogs for once cowered and whimpered. Geoffrey had an implement like a boat hook that he fished with in the swamp, hauling viscera and limbs out and carrying them to the pyres.

The quantity of ash cleared from the crematoria and dumped among the trees meant that nothing would grow; it looked like the surface of another planet. All the SS wore gas masks. One thrust a bottle at Geoffrey. It was vodka. He drank. The guards lifted their masks for a moment to drink. They passed the vodka round from guard to prisoner, from prisoner to guard.

There was continual screeching from the Germans. More. Faster. Harder. The prisoners were screaming, too, in Polish, Russian, Yiddish. Geoffrey's throat was raw with retching, raw with screaming. He shouted all the words he knew. Parts of human were dropping on him.

A prisoner turned on his guard, and was shot. Two men threw themselves on the pyre to die. One was hauled off and made to work again. Geoffrey pressed on with his eyes shut. His belly was empty, there was nothing left to retch. He took more vodka, more and more, then set back to work in blindness.

A day, a night in the asylum, a day again, bright sun over the pine forest, meaning thick ground mist tonight, back into the rubber boots, the clothes from the last crew dripping and he is in the woods again. This must be the last he knows of it, so he works in fury. Chloride of lime, meant to quell the stench, runs powerless from spleen and womb. An hour, another hour, a day. Inside the wire there is evening roll call and amid the clamour a column, fifty, sixty men, a Search Unit going out from the camp into the building site, their guards shouting. They are searching under planks and peering into pipes, secretly their pockets jammed with rocks and bits of masonry. From the watchtower a complacent guard looks down on them. The Pyre Crew is returning now as the sun sinks behind the woods and the men can barely pull their bodies home.

And the Search Unit is at the gap in the fence. There is a shot, there is always a shot. A body. More commands, a moment of confusion. Search Unit and Pyre Crew are crossing at the fence. The sentry is suddenly nervous in the watchtower and there comes a roar of Russian, fifty men hurling iron and rocks and rushing the wooden tower, which tips over, snapping on its legs, and Geoffrey is turning on his heel, with them now, with the Search Unit, running into the woods, scattering among the pine needles, through the lunar ash, running as though fresh from two weeks' rest, limbs free; steady, Talbot, pace yourself, leave something for the later stages; at least a minute gone before they hear the siren and the gunfire and the dogs.

In 1946, the autumn term at Crampton Abbey began on 17 September. The day before, Mrs Little knocked on her husband's study door before entering.

Mr Little's closest companion, a clumber spaniel called Heep, was asleep in front of the unlit fire, his aroma mingling with that of his master's Sir Philip Sidney pipe tobacco.

'We're at least three boys short,' said Long John, looking up from where he was making some calculations on a piece of graph paper.

'Doddington's not coming back. His mother can't afford it now his father's dead. And the price of coal, food, electricity . . . I shall have to cut the salaries. I wondered if I could sack Garrard as well.'

'But who'll look after the games pitches?'

'We've got this new chap starting. Franklin. I could ask him to do some mowing and maintenance as well as taking junior games.'

'How much do we pay Garrard?'

'The equivalent of one boy's fees for a year.'

'Oh dear,' said Mrs Little, sitting down and absently stroking Heep's head. 'Are we in a pickle, dear?'

'I think so. There seems to be no end of rationing in sight. The ministry says it'll last for at least five years. And now the parents are worried about what the boys are eating.'

'Matron wrote off to the ministry and they suggested Radio Malt to build them up a bit.'

'Could we get rid of some of the maids?' said Long John.

'We're down to five. And we only pay them pin money.'

Mr Little drew in a mouthful of Sir Philip Sidney. 'I must remember to invite the new superintendent of the asylum over one evening.' He puffed thoughtfully. 'I suppose what we really need is some sort of recruitment drive.'

'You don't mean advertising?'

'Good heavens, no. But we need to put the word about. That Crampton Abbey is a first-rate school. Has Baxter come back yet?'

'Yes, I saw him this afternoon.'

'I had to cut his salary.'

'Again, dear?'

'As a warning. After the maids found all those gin bottles in his room.'

'He'll hardly have enough for beer and cigarettes.'

'Good thing too. Anyway, I'm going out for my evening walk now. Come on, Heep. Come on.'

The spaniel rose stiffly from the hearth rug and followed his master out into the corridor, through the green baize door

and down the broad oak staircase, past the stone fireplace with
the ceremonial sword above, out into the still-warm air of the
Nottinghamshire evening. Habit had taught the dog that this
unwanted exertion, which might involve a walk downhill to
the village, would bring a scrap or treat of some kind in due
course.

Long John Little ignored the rose garden with its ornamental
arch and the wooded park that lay behind it, turning instead
towards the kitchen gardens with their sun-beaten brick walls on
which espaliered trees were heavy with fruit. He glanced into the
greenhouses, whose open doors gave a gust of tomatoes, while
the gravel paths between the cold frames crunched beneath his
feet. He calculated that he need serve only five more years before
passing on the headmastership to his son, at that time a junior
housemaster at a Midlands public school. His pension was not
adequate to provide for himself and Mrs Little in retirement, but
he hoped the governors might make special provision from one
of their contingency funds. Otherwise he would be condemned
to an old age in one of the unused wings of the house, whose
heating bills he could conceivably repay with a few Latin verse
lessons to the scholarship form.

The back gate from the kitchen gardens led into the village
churchyard, where Long John walked slowly among the grave-
stones and the heedless yews. On an impulse, he pushed open the
side door of the church and went into the damp-smelling interior.
The brass eagle on the lectern loomed wide-eyed and predatory
over the pews with their dusty kneelers. The organ needed over-
hauling, but there was little chance of the village being able to
raise the funds over the next few years; the steps up to the pulpit
were also a hazard, though anything that might cut short the
sermons of the local vicar, Mr Woolridge, was a blessing.

It had always struck Long John Little as curious that empty
churches seemed emptier than empty houses. A kitchen or a

sitting room was still the same with no one in it; but the silent organ, the bright stained-glass windows above the altar with its rather showy little cross, the board by the pulpit announcing the numbers of the unsung hymns, seemed heavy with absence. His footsteps loud on the cracked tiles of the nave, he went and sat down at the end of one of the pews – roughly where an eleven-year-old would sit on Sunday morning, the boys being ranged from back to front in school order, determined by their performance in Latin.

Little looked through his remaining eye at the memorial tablets on the damp walls. Most were for former vicars or village worthies, but two were for his own parents, his predecessors at Crampton Abbey. One was for R. M. Caird, 1885–1916, his school and university contemporary.

Long John did not particularly like small boys, but he felt a moment of sympathy for what they were put through on a Sunday – the creaking organ, the collects and the canticles, then Woolridge in the pulpit, each windy commonplace stealing moments they might have spent with visiting parents afterwards.

He sighed and looked over at his dog, who waited by the main door. Better to have died in Mesopotamia, Little thought, better a soldier's death with Bobby Caird, the only human being he had ever cared about, than the half-life he had led, with Advent, Septuagesima, Trinity, ticked off in this empty building.

Gerald Baxter had returned two days earlier from a holiday in South Wales with his sister. The boarding house they stayed in overlooked an esplanade and the landlady's cooking – blancmange and bony fish – was dismal, but there was a sailing club that took in temporary members in the summer and whose bar, by a vagary of local licensing, was exempt from the hours imposed on the pubs. There was also a nine-hole golf course that took him fifty-odd strokes to go round – more than enough to build up a thirst.

He arrived back at Crampton Abbey in a good state of mind. His mood dipped when he found out that the Head had trimmed his salary yet again, but he knew that after the debacle of the gin bottles he was fortunate still to have a position. Once he had unpacked and put his laundry out for the maids, he looked over his timetable for the new term. He seemed to have acquired a junior French class, which – unlike geography – would be more than just a matter of staying one chapter ahead in the textbook.

After a solitary tea in the dining hall, Baxter climbed the back stairs up past the new boys' dormitory, past a floor with a passageway that led he knew not where, and arrived at last at the top floor where the sick bay, idle for eight weeks, met him with its perennial whiff of liniment and iodine.

He walked a few paces down the corridor and knocked on a door.

A voice answered from inside. 'Who is it?'

'Baxter here. I wondered if you fancied a bracer at the Whitby?'

The door opened. 'Thank you,' said Geoffrey Talbot. 'Good idea.'

In the rear saloon of the Whitby, Baxter stretched out his game leg on an empty chair as Geoffrey brought another half-pint back from the bar.

'So,' he said, 'after you'd escaped from this wretched PoW place, what happened then?'

'It took me a long time to get back,' said Geoffrey. 'I was fortunate. Most of the escapers were caught in the vicinity and shot. A dozen of us made it to a railway and hid by a bridge. The first train was going east, towards Russia.'

'How the hell did you get your bearings?'

'The stars. Some men jumped on it just to get away from the dogs. Four of us waited for a westbound train. We jumped off at different times in Poland and Czechoslovakia. Eventually I got across the border into Germany beneath the tender of a locomotive.'

'Sounds uncomfortable.'

'It was a trick I'd learned in France. I ended up walking into Switzerland somewhere near Lake Constance.'

'What happened to the others?'

'I don't know.'

'And your pal?'

'Trembath? He died of bullet wounds in the camp. I found out later from the regiment. When we escaped, there was a riot. They managed to blow up a crematorium. Some of them rushed the guards. But not enough of them joined in.'

'Poor chap,' said Baxter.

'No, he wanted to do something. It was a good way to go.'

'Well, you didn't miss much here. I could manage another half if you're still in the chair.'

Geoffrey stood at the bar, tapping a half-crown on the wooden surface. Nothing seemed to have changed at the Whitby Arms, or at Crampton. Mrs Little was a fraction frailer, the stout calves not quite what they had been; the fabric of the building seemed tattier and, outside, the grounds were a little overgrown. Otherwise, it was as Geoffrey had remembered, with a more or less full school and a complete football fixture list, home and away, against the old enemies.

His way of managing what had happened to him was not to think about it. When he had returned to London from Geneva and filled in a number of forms, he was granted four weeks' leave. Mr Green required him to see Dr Samuels for further assessment, but after an hour he was passed 'fit for any disposition'.

France was liberated and the possibility arose that Geoffrey might do useful work in Burma, though Mr Green eventually offered him a position on the staff in London. When the service was wound up, Geoffrey returned to the Musketeers, though they had little of interest to offer a lieutenant who still had a bad mark against his name. Heavy losses in the Italian campaign meant that Geoffrey was grudgingly promoted captain and sent to Syria to help quell a mutiny among French troops. For the rest of 1945 he was on 'peacekeeping' duties in the Middle East before being officially demobilised from Musketeer headquarters in Hampshire.

He had spent a quiet summer with his parents and thought it better not to give them details of the 'prisoner of war' camp. Alone in his childhood bedroom, he tried to write some poems, but the things he now wanted to say seemed to be at odds with the words he knew for poetry. He played a few games of cricket for the local club, including one at the ground he had pictured at night in the wooden bunkhouse as the touchstone of a better life.

The weather was grey and overcast; there were only a handful of spectators, restless in the chilly afternoon. The captain was unaware of Geoffrey's ability and when asked where he would like to bat Geoffrey had replied, 'Anywhere you need me.' He found himself at number eight – he who had faced the Kent and Yorkshire opening bowlers. By the time he reached the wicket his side had already made a large score and the opposition, exhausted by its efforts, had put a small boy on to bowl. In an effort not to demoralise the youngster, Geoffrey checked an off-drive halfway through the shot and saw the ball caught by a surprised mid-off as it cannoned into his belly. He had made two. In the field, he wandered from third man to mid-on and back, feeling the grass through the studs of his boots, glancing towards the low hedge at midwicket and the Friesians at pasture. They were, in a way, as he remembered, but some force or light seemed to have gone from them.

He tried to feel that this world was his to share and know; that it was more enduring than flash-memories of pine logs and opportunely revving lorries. But when the opposition captain, going for a big hit over the pavilion, caught a leading edge and caused the ball to sky, then fall exactly where Geoffrey was standing at long on, he dropped it.

'You look miles away, Talbot,' said Baxter, offering him a cigarette.

'Sorry, I was just thinking about . . . Cricket.'

'Cricket?'

'Well, perhaps not just cricket. What it means. Or what it meant. To me.'

'Sorry, old chap. You're not making much sense. Shall I get some more beer? My turn, I think. Or if you wouldn't mind. Here's a bob. I'll just rest the old leg.'

When Geoffrey brought the glasses back to the table, Baxter said, 'Of course, I was never much of a player myself. But the Sandpipers put out a decent team. The 2nd Battalion won the divisional cup in 1921.'

'Yes, I heard they were pretty good.'

Geoffrey could feel his hand shaking and was reluctant to pick up his drink in case Baxter should see. There was a strange tightness in his jaw and in his larynx. There was a pressure behind his eyes and he felt as though he might faint.

'There was not much left of the Fusiliers, I can tell you,' Baxter was saying. 'Not by the time the Sandpipers had done with them.'

It had become a matter of urgency to Geoffrey that he should pass this first test of his resumed life. If he could not endure a friendly hour of beer and cigarettes with Baxter, what chance did he have of teaching a class or reading the New Testament lesson in church?

'So then our chaps set them an improbable total,' Baxter was saying. 'And we had this ferocious fast bowler who . . . I say, are you all right, Talbot?' Baxter was suddenly sitting forward in his chair.

Geoffrey looked at a coloured photograph of a vintage car above the horse brasses by the mantelpiece, then bent his mind to the job of answering Baxter. He summoned as much determination as he had used to get through any task in Poland; but however hard he tried, no word seemed to come. He merely nodded his head and gave what he could manage of a smile.

'Are you quite sure you're all right?'

There was silence for a few moments. Then the battle within Geoffrey began to resolve itself. He found a word. 'Yes,' he said; then after another pause: 'I'm fine.'

'Good,' said Baxter, sitting back in his chair. 'So. Do you think we'll beat Bearwood Hall this year?'

'Yes,' said Geoffrey, slowly at first, then growing in confidence. 'I see no reason why not.'

So he managed his return, a little at a time. The slow weeks of the endless autumn term consumed him: the seventeenth Sunday after Trinity, the eighteenth Sunday after Trinity, the Sunday next before Advent . . . It was a month of Sundays, a season, then a year of Sundays, with Geoffrey counting each week a small victory in his re-inhabitation of his old life. In the evenings he sat in his armchair and read detective stories before going down to the small masters' common room for a bowl of corn flakes at ten.

At the beginning of the next year he was made master in charge of dormitories, in place of Baxter, whose gin breath had been the subject of complaint. The breaking point had come when he signalled lights-out by shooting through a 40-watt bulb with an air pistol. The new duty brought no increase in pay, but it gave Geoffrey something to do, as he strolled the upper corridor, where half a dozen rooms held nine or ten iron beds in rows. He would occasionally sit on the end of one of them and talk to its small occupant, though he could see that the child did not feel entertained, but merely singled out. When he left the dormitory he could hear giggling, as the boy in question was teased about the special attention that had been paid him.

There was a similar layout of dormitories on the first floor, though the windows were taller. When the clocks went back again, the grey dusk seemed to hang in the corners of these sleeping rooms; the rough red blankets on the beds brought a touch of colour, though it seemed to Geoffrey it was that of the field hospital.

After the evening lesson in Scripture or Latin verses, the boys went on alternate nights across a chilly yard in their dressing gowns to the bathhouse. They were allowed nine inches of hot water in the bath and one such filling was supposed to be enough to wash three boys. Back in bed, they were allowed to talk until Geoffrey went round, one room after another, opening tall windows a few inches on to the night with the help of a boat hook, despite the pleas of the boys for warmth, then turning off the lights with what he hoped was a paternal 'goodnight'. The penalty for talking after this time was a beating; Geoffrey was licensed to use the slipper, though managed not to find it necessary.

In the summer term of 1949, Crampton Abbey chased the total of 128 set by Bearwood Hall, and thanks to some dropped catches and an innings of 54 not out by the Crampton wicketkeeper, a twelve-year-old called Cheeseman who played horribly across the line, they made it with three minutes to spare. Long John granted the school a half-holiday on the following Tuesday and presented Geoffrey with a three-guinea book token. Cheeseman, known to the boys as 'Cheddar' or 'Ched' for short, became a hero to his teammates but received corrective coaching from Geoffrey in keeping his left elbow up.

In 1951, Long John and Mrs Little retired to a remote wing of the abbey, and their son, a lanky and narrow-eyed man of about forty, known to the boys as 'Big' Little, took over the running of the school. He persuaded the governors to raise the fees to seventy-five pounds a year and sacked Gerald Baxter.

He told Geoffrey he was on probation, as there were some keen young masters at Repton who would like his position if he didn't care for it.

The years of rationing eventually ended, though their spirit was retained at Crampton Abbey, where the restriction on hot water remained, along with the daily dose of Radio Malt. Geoffrey's mother died of a stroke, leaving his father to dispose of a number of dachshunds. The decade was like a tundra, to be crossed with collar turned up, eyes averted, pushing on and adding up the days till it was over. Twenty-fourth Sunday after Trinity: Geoffrey's footsteps on the tiled floor of the nave as he went to read the Gospel, now his weekly task; twenty-fifth Sunday after Trinity: blowing his nose on his handkerchief as he approached the eagle lectern, his college gown billowing behind him . . .

There came news of change from the big cities: music, loud and raucous, imported from America then refashioned with jangling guitars and crazy haircuts, re-exported, booming. It was too late for Geoffrey Talbot, now aged forty-six, to whom the sounds he could pick up on the staffroom radio sounded simply barbarous. 'Yeah, yeah, yeah,' sang the boys, as they ran down the corridors. He put his hands over his ears.

The nursing sister, a woman called Miss Callander, asked him to go to tea with her in town on their afternoon off. They had poached eggs with anchovy essence under, then chocolate cake and strong Indian tea. They split the bill and enjoyed it well enough to make the afternoon a regular date. On one occasion they went to the pictures, though this involved a lengthy bus journey and the possibility of being late back for dormitory duty; the prospect so distressed Geoffrey that Miss Callander, despite loving Cary Grant and Deborah Kerr, whom she slightly resembled, did not press for a repeat.

One day in the tea room, she said, 'Geoffrey, I've been thinking.

I'm thirty-seven years old and I know how old you are. I don't want to seem forward or anything, but we do get on pretty well. You're a handsome chap and I'm a pretty well-organised girl. Do you think that together we might make more than the sum of our parts?'

'Mary, are you proposing to me?'

'Isn't it a leap year?'

Geoffrey looked down at his tea. 'I don't think I can.'

'Why not?'

'There are things about me you don't know.'

'What things? Don't be such a stick-in-the-mud.'

'You're very kind.'

'I have no money. Just an ancient mother who lives in Rye. But it's nice there, by the sea. For our holidays. There's a wonderful golf course nearby. I could look after you pretty well, Geoffrey.'

Geoffrey sighed. 'I can't explain. You're far too nice. Too good for me. I'm better as I am. As a lone wolf.'

'If you change your mind . . .'

'I won't. But thank you.'

'Can I ask you one more time? In a year's time?'

'All right.'

One year later, almost to the day, she re-proposed and Geoffrey, who had been expecting it, declined. Miss Callander flushed for a moment in frustration; then her eyes filled with tears. The next day she handed in her notice, and at the end of term left for a new job in Dorset.

That spring, Geoffrey was filled with a strange yet irresistible desire. Giselle. He must see her again. He must find her. It seemed to him extraordinary that it had taken him so long – more than twenty years! – to understand that this was what he must do. The intervening period seemed like a dream – no, more like a slumber, from which he had finally awoken.

His father had died the previous autumn, and by the time the lawyers had finished with the estate there was a cheque for Geoffrey of some £300. The cost of hotels would be covered by his savings, though it was comforting to know that there was a reserve; he would have wine at dinner. He thought it would be a help to know Giselle's real name and made some enquiries in London, but was told that the records of his old organisation had been classified secret; some access might one day be given to the official historian, but the papers would be closed to the public for fifty years. In any event, the series of cut-outs used to protect the identity of foreign nationals meant they might very well have no record of the actual names of French agents.

Undeterred, Geoffrey set off on the cross-Channel ferry in the last week of July. His spirits were high. He laughed as he stood at the taffrail, watching the bubbling white water of the wash. What a magnificent expedition this was going to be.

In Calais, he asked a taxi to take him to a garage that would rent him a car. He had planned to take the train to Brive, but now that he was in France he fancied a motoring holiday and, with his schoolmaster's eight-week break, there was no hurry to be back. The *garagiste* tried to give him an ancient Renault, but a look of respect came into the man's eye when he heard Geoffrey tell him his grandfather had run a similar business in Clermont. By noon, he was on the road in a two-year-old Citroën DS, black with biscuit-coloured seats, and a *Guide Michelin* that the *garagiste* had thrown in for nothing. The gear change was on the steering column, but Geoffrey was familiar with the arrangement from an old Singer; the only awkwardness was waiting for the hydraulic suspension to pump the car up when it first started – that, and the fierceness of the foot brake. Before long, though, he had grown used to it, merely grazing the round button with the sole of his shoe, and was purring through the plane-flanked avenues of northern France. There was no need for maps: Paris, Orléans,

Limoges would be clearly flagged, and after that he would trust his memory.

Sometimes, he wandered off the *routes nationales* on to the Michelin yellow roads and allowed his instincts to direct him towards rivers, hills, and villages with dusty squares and a choice of cafés at lunchtime. He slept in auberges or small hotels where the patron would not let him sit down to dinner later than seven-thirty. One night he stayed in a converted windmill with no restaurant, so for dinner was despatched to an old woman's house down a dirt road ten minutes' drive away. Geoffrey had little appetite for food since the war but could appreciate there was care in the way his hostess had prepared the rustic dishes with herbs from the kitchen garden he could see through the back window. The bill, scribbled on a scrap of squared paper in old francs, was less than five shillings.

It took him ten days to reach Limoges, as he drifted down the byways. All the time he thought about Giselle. She would now be in her late forties, but that was no reason why she would still not be beautiful. Doubtless she would have married after the war; some local businessman would have snapped her up, Geoffrey thought. That didn't matter either. The fellow would understand old loyalties. Talking of which, it was her betrayal that he wanted to ask her about: after all this time she must be ready to explain what had happened. The Germans had caught her; they had tortured her and persuaded her to become a double agent – to lead them to people like him. Might there not have been another way? She could have left the area, moved north away from the Germans who were running her . . . Or perhaps there were other reasons, personal things. He saw her face very clearly when he thought about her: the wide-set, excited eyes, the thin straight nose and pale skin. The least she deserved was a chance to talk to him about it. She would be grateful for that.

It was evening when he set off for the farmhouse through the fields with their cylinders of rolled hay in the still-fierce sunshine. After half an hour, he admitted to himself that he was lost. He had remembered a village called Saint-Aubin or Auban, then a narrow road going north-west towards the hills, but there seemed to be no such place. He parked the car outside a small roadside café and went inside. Two men in blue overalls looked up from a table where they were playing cards. Geoffrey explained that he was lost and looking for a farmhouse on a hill; the two men looked at each other as though they thought him soft in the head. Eventually, the patron came through a bamboo curtain from the back. Geoffrey ordered a pastis and asked the same question. After some grumbling and eye-rolling, the man disappeared through the curtain, returning a few minutes later with a tattered map of the area. Geoffrey offered him a cigarette as they studied it together. By looking at the contours, he could work out where the high ground was. He remembered from the setting sun that the house looked west, so it was . . . He pointed at a hamlet on the map and asked the patron if there was an old farm nearby. The man shrugged; but Geoffrey left the bar with new certainty and turned the Citroën round.

Ten minutes later he was on the track up which he had bicycled all those years ago; the potholes were smoothed out by the car's airy suspension, but it was as though he could still feel them jarring through the seat of his bicycle.

The farmhouse had a van outside, and a motor tractor for which in wartime there would have been no petrol; there was still a dog barking. As Geoffrey slammed the car door and walked across the yard, an Alsatian came racing out of a stable, causing him to flinch and raise his arm to his face. The dog was on a chain and could not reach him, but snarled and bared its teeth.

Geoffrey hammered on the back door and waited. He heard footsteps from inside and remembered the corridor with the sound of a horse or cow in a side room. In truth, he was expecting the

door to be opened by a twenty-five-year-old Giselle and had to
hide his disappointment when a stout grey-haired woman appeared
in the opening.

It was difficult to know where to begin. Many years ago . . . A
young woman . . . Her real name . . . Did Madame have a daughter?
Did she know who owned the farm during the war?

The old woman stood with her arms folded across her chest.
Geoffrey asked if she had a husband and this question seemed to
vex her. It occurred to him that she must think he was from the
Inland Revenue, or the French equivalent; the farm probably did
all its trade in cash and kept few papers. He tried to reassure her
that he was genuinely looking for an old friend, but after a further
minute or so of fruitless questioning, she asked him to leave. When
Geoffrey persisted, she went across the yard towards the chained
dog and threatened to release it.

Back in his car, Geoffrey decided to make for a café in the
nearby village, a place in which he knew Giselle had sometimes
eaten. He ordered a glass of wine and sat outside. He could picture
her so clearly that he believed she must be close at hand. The few
freckles on her skin, the light in her dark eyes, the dress she had
worn that last night – why had she dressed so well? – the way
she tossed her head so her dark collar-length hair bounced . . .
He closed his eyes and squeezed her face into his presence. He
pushed with all the force of his mind to bring her bodily into
being, so that when he opened his eyes she would be sitting, young
Giselle, in the seat next to his . . .

Then he drove the short distance to the church and sat down
on a wooden seat outside. Giselle, Giselle, you silly girl . . . She
must be inside the building.

He wrestled the door open and ran up the nave. 'Giselle!' he
called out. Dear God, where was she hiding? Why was she playing
such a game with him?

He ran outside and back to the car. All the fields were empty

— all the sun-burned fields rolling away without the shadow of a girl as far as he could stretch his empty gaze. He drove into the village, fast, braking fiercely in the square, sending a cloud of summer dust over the outside tables of the café. He climbed out and sat down on a wicker-seated chair. He held his head in his hands. Giselle . . .

A waiter asked him what he wanted, but Geoffrey found he could neither move nor speak. His jaw rested on his thumbs, his temples were held by his fingers. No muscle would respond to his commands.

'Monsieur? Monsieur?'

Geoffrey said later that he had no recollection of his journey home: none. Back, somehow, at Crampton Abbey, he went to see 'Big' Little in the headmaster's study and told him he did not feel well. Little drove him to a doctor in town. After a brief examination, the doctor said he perhaps should see a psychiatrist, but there was no such person in town, nor in the next, larger town; people in Nottinghamshire, it appeared, did not go mad. The only place that a doctor of this kind might be found was in the old county lunatic asylum, the one which had supplied the maids for the school, and it was here, on a hot afternoon, after he had closed his surgery, that the doctor drove Geoffrey with his overnight bag.

There were some awkward days before he saw a doctor. He was in a dormitory with men who moaned and thrashed. Some sat against the wall holding their heads in their hands, scratching themselves raw; the most agitated, he believed, were tied up in straitjackets in a remote room.

Eventually, he was moved to a calmer place with a hot, stuffy day room, like a greenhouse, and a garden outside with wallflowers and Michaelmas daisies. He was given a white pill each morning and a blue one at night; the medicines gave him a thirst that tied his tongue.

He wrote to Little and asked for more of his clothes to be brought, as the doctors told him he would be with them for some time.

The hospital library had a few romances and adventure stories and some old copies of the *Illustrated London News*, but Geoffrey had soon read all he wanted. After three months, he received a letter from Mr Little saying his contract had been terminated and that his place in the spring term would be taken by Mr D. G. Farmer, MA (Strathallan, and Magdalen College, Oxford).

For many weeks, Geoffrey sat quite still, staring through the picture windows at the flower beds and the wall beyond. One of the other patients called him 'Statue' because he never seemed to move.

He had been in the asylum a year when a female nurse came up to him one morning and said, 'You have a visitor, Geoffrey.'

'Are you sure?'

He could not think of anyone he knew. His parents, Trembath . . . Gone. Baxter, he had heard, was also dead. Miss Callander would never want to see him. He could think of no one else alive. Unless, perhaps . . . Giselle.

'Yes, it's definitely for you,' said the nurse. 'I'll go and ask his name.'

When she returned a few minutes later she said it was a Mr Cheeseman.

'Cheddar?' said Geoffrey after a moment. 'Good God. What's he doing here?'

There was a small room where Geoffrey had sometimes seen other patients receive visitors; when he opened the door he saw a man of about thirty in a suit with his back to him.

He turned round. 'Mr Talbot?' he said.

Cheeseman was a handsome young man, with thick brown hair, a maroon tie neatly knotted and smooth-shaved skin with the taut lustre of youth. He smiled and held out his hand.

'Hello, sir.'

'Hello, Ched.'

'How are you, sir? I heard you'd had it a bit rough so I thought I'd drop in. I brought these. I don't know if you still like detective stories.'

'Thank you. Do you live near here?'

'No, I live in London. But I was going to see my grandmother in Nottingham, and it was on the way, so I just thought . . .'

A nurse came in with two cups of tea.

'Still keeping wicket?' said Geoffrey.

Cheeseman laughed. 'No! Believe it or not, at my next school I became a bowler.'

'But you could never—'

'I know! But one long summer I had nothing else to do and there was this old leg-spinner, the coach at the local grammar school, and I . . . Well, I just got the hang of it.'

'And your batting? Still playing across the line?'

'Ah.' Cheeseman smiled uneasily. 'I kept the left elbow up and all that. For a bit – just as you taught me. I got into the school eleven as an all-rounder. But I just play village stuff nowadays and . . . Well, I rather go after it, I'm afraid. From the word go.'

'Never mind. If you enjoy it.'

'Oh yes. I do. I hit quite a few sixes.'

'Whereabouts?'

'Long on, mostly.'

'I thought as much. Not very nice tea, I'm afraid.'

All the food and drink in the asylum tasted bad, Geoffrey found.

'It's fine,' said Cheeseman.

'Are you married?' said Geoffrey.

'No.' Cheeseman laughed. 'Too young. But I do have a girl-friend. Maybe one day.'

There was a silence.

'And you, sir. You didn't . . .'

'Marry? No.'

'Of course, I suppose the war and all that. That must have been exciting.' Cheeseman licked his lips.

'You could say that.'

Cheeseman frowned. 'My father was in a tank regiment. He was wounded in Sicily.'

'Wasn't he rather old?' said Geoffrey, who could not remember Cheeseman's father in particular.

'Just scraped in, I think,' said Cheddar. 'He was very keen. And quite short. They just dropped him in the gun turret. So he used to say.'

There was another pause and Geoffrey struggled to find anything to say. He didn't want to embarrass Cheeseman by talking about his own health, or about his war experiences.

Eventually, he had a thought. 'What work do you do? Do you have a good job?'

Cheeseman grimaced. 'Not really. I work for a law firm in the City. It's pretty dull, to be honest. Quite well paid, though.'

They heard a trolley clanking down the corridor towards the ward. It was Cheeseman's turn to be struck by an idea.

'Do you have a television here, sir? I mean, can you watch the Test match?'

'No,' said Geoffrey. 'There's a wireless in the day room, but the others don't like cricket. They like pop music.'

'Bad luck, sir. We're doing quite well. I was listening in the car. What do you think of Colin Cowdrey?'

'Plays very straight, they say. Very well coached. Wonderful slip fielder, I believe. I'm afraid I've never seen him play.'

'I'll take you to Lord's one day when you're better. There's a chap in my firm can usually get tickets. It's about the only consolation for working there! Who was the best bat you ever saw?'

'Frank Woolley,' said Geoffrey without hesitation. 'He was imperious. He once scored a double hundred in each innings. No one else has ever done that.'

'Left-hander, wasn't he?'

A nurse came in to take away the empty teacups. The air seemed heavy when she had gone and Geoffrey felt his inspiration had run dry. Cheeseman licked his lips again and cast his eyes round frantically, through the window and out to the garden where two or three patients were walking slowly over the grass.

The silence hung thickly in the corners of the room until at last the lunch bell rang and Cheeseman said, 'I suppose I'd better be going now, sir. It was very nice to see you. I do hope they'll let you out of here soon.'

Geoffrey took Cheeseman to the main door of the building and shook his proffered hand.

'Thank you for coming, Ched. Very decent of you.'

Then he watched him drive off in a blue Ford Zephyr, sounding the horn once as he left the car park but keeping his eyes fixed on the road ahead.

Geoffrey did not go into lunch that day. He sat in the day room and cried. All afternoon, his tears fell on to the linoleum floor, making such a pool that the nurse eventually had to clean it up. 'Come on, Geoffrey,' she said, banging the head of a mop against the leg of his chair, 'pull yourself together.'

A week later there was a parcel for Geoffrey from London. Buried deep in layers of protective packaging was a small portable television with a built-in aerial and a pair of earphones.

Three months later, Geoffrey was out, discharged; and three months after that, he found himself a job in Hampshire. He had persuaded 'Big' Little to write a reference for a post he had seen advertised, and Little did so, adding the postscript: 'If there is anything further at all you would like to know about this candidate, please do not hesitate to ask me.' He had underlined the words 'anything further at all', which was a code headmasters used as a warning signal – usually that the man in question was too fond of boys. It also meant that the new employer could offer a reduced salary.

Geoffrey still had £200 of his inheritance left, and used some of it to buy an old car. His new school was near the area where he had been brought up, though not so close as to provoke mawkish thoughts. It was a notch or two below Crampton Abbey and sent most of its pupils on to schools with strong discipline but poor academic records.

He was put into an old cottage on the edge of the estate, overlooking the main road. It was meant to be for a married couple, but there were none that year and it was really too dilapidated for a woman to tolerate, Geoffrey thought. He didn't mind it, though. There was a kitchen garden behind, away from the road, and more than enough room inside for him and his belongings. He even took some pieces of his parents' furniture out of storage.

It was that summer, at the end of his first year, that his life shifted and changed for good. It was after a country wedding where he knew almost no one; and in return few people noticed a tall, grey-haired man with a slightly startled expression and flecks of dandruff on the shoulders of his suit. He was fifty-five years old, though looked older, in his late sixties perhaps, and nothing in his manner – mild enough, but dry – would have made other guests linger or introduce themselves.

The bride was blinking, wearing too much make-up, not quite able to believe what she had done, but buoyed by the approval of her parents and old-timers like Geoffrey Talbot. The groom, Nigel or Michael, bespectacled, sweating in his hired suit, was feeling lucky to have even for a day won some approval from his father-in-law. At the same time he was dreading the speech that would be his to make in the marquee on the cropped lawn among the bought-in bedding plants, after which his accountancy exams and married life in Clapham would seem a sweet relief.

No one seemed to know what Geoffrey was doing there, but a young man was polite enough to speak to him and discovered he was a cousin of the bride's father . . . Some childhood holidays . . . Long ago, Great Yarmouth . . . He was surprised to have been invited, but, yes, what a lovely day. He'd noticed earlier in church how some old chap was listening to the Test match commentary via an earpiece attached to a radio in the pocket of his morning coat. He chuckled at the thought of John Arlott describing the action at Headingley. Better that, said the young man, than listening to the women in the row in front as they whispered about the bridesmaids and their tangerine taffeta dresses.

During the first speech, made by a long-standing friend of the bride's family (commonly known as the Old Bore's speech) Geoffrey Talbot stood a little apart. He smiled at the attempted witticisms, nodded at the marital advice and raised his glass at the appropriate moment — but all like a man who had studied a book on wedding behaviour. Apart from his brief exchange with the polite young man, he spoke to no one.

Yet that evening, listening to the wireless in his kitchen, with the window open on to the vegetable garden at the back, in his shirt-sleeves with stiff collar and tie abandoned, Geoffrey Talbot was not unhappy. He had found a German station to which he listened frequently in an attempt to make up for the missed lectures and unread books of his youth. He still sometimes dreamed he was resitting his Finals, with better results.

His salary was enough to live on, and he had invested what remained of his inheritance in wine, so that he had a cellar full of half-bottles of burgundy. He had also had the pleasure of seeing Cowdrey, May and Barrington at the crease. After the wedding he opened some wine to go with the lamb chop and fresh vegetables that it was easily within his power to organise. This is not bad, he thought, as he ate at the table on the small paved area at the back of his cottage, where he barely noticed the sound of traffic from the main road at the front.

Then, suddenly, at about ten o'clock, when he was clearing up in readiness for bed, a feeling of enormous fatigue came over him – so great that he could walk no further but had to lie down on the sofa in the main room. The strength seemed to drain through his calves and his hands and his back. The millions of instances of lifting, heaving, scraping and hauling he had made in his more than fifty years alive seemed all at once to exact their toll. The efforts of crawling as a baby, of running as a child; of driving, cutting, hooking on the cricket pitch; the pounding of military drill; the reaching, digging, straining and the dragging logs to the furnace, the back-strain of tipping the chute – to say nothing of the hours of running, running through the forests or the everyday lift of boxes or suitcases or books – seemed to have left him with no further power in his body as it was.

Let someone else live my life for me, Geoffrey thought, with the skin of his cheek against the rough material of the sofa cover. I have loved my life, I have been violently loyal to myself, but now I have lived it long enough.

His dandruffy jacket over the back of the chair, his battered black shoes on the rug next to him, Geoffrey inhaled the exhausted, dried-rose smell of the old upholstery and closed his eyes.

He awoke some hours later in the befuddled dark, groped his way upstairs, stripped and climbed into his bed, pulling up the eiderdown over him as the first chill of early morning came into the cottage.

The next day he felt changed. The ropy veins on the backs of his hands were the same; the ache in his arthritic hip was where it always was and the world came to him through the network of nerves he had relied on since infancy. Yet he sensed a difference — not a medical or morbid change, more the touch of an unsought grace.

No one at school seemed to notice anything, but Geoffrey, quite happy at the blackboard or on the slow walk to the cricket pitch, with the afternoon sun slanting through the elms and the boys chattering as they ran past him, knew that some subtle rearrangement of particles had taken place within him; he felt with joy and resignation that he was not the same man.

My father made us all sit round the table. 'Children,' he says, 'one of you is going to have to go into the Union house. They've offered me that — to take one of you off my hands.'

We all looked at each other. John was the oldest so he'd be all right, he could work. Meg was the only girl and she was the apple of Pa's eye. Tom was the baby, he was only two. I reckoned it was between me and Arthur, the third and fourth ones. It was a long evening. I didn't know whether to speak up for myself or not. Me and Arthur kept staring at each other.

We were living in two rooms on the first floor of a house in Mason Street. Once we had all four rooms but then we had to let off the bottom two for the rent. Ma and Meg and the baby Tom slept in one room. Me and Arthur shared a bed in the other one. I don't remember about Pa and John, where they slept. They were out a lot.

In the morning, Ma said, 'I'm sorry, Billy, it's you.' I knew it would be. The place was called St Joseph-in-the-West, but most people called it the Bastille. I was seven years old and small for my age because we never had enough to eat. I said goodbye to Tom, but he didn't know what was happening. Meg was crying and making a big to-do. John had gone out with Pa to look for work. Arthur shook me by the hand but he couldn't look at me.

My mother put on a bonnet and walked me quickly down Mason Street because she didn't want people to ask where we was going.

It was half an hour to walk there. I'd seen the place once before when we were on our way to see Aunt Annie in Hoxton. It was a big grey building with an iron railing in front of it. Ma pulled the bell and you could hear it ringing inside but half a mile away. We waited and my mother was shivering. After a long time we could hear footsteps inside and then the sound of bolts being drawn. The door opened and a big man in a black hat was standing there.

'My name is Mrs Webb,' said Ma.

The man nodded. 'Leave the child.'

He pulled me inside. I called after her but the man pulled the door closed. I never saw her again.

I was in an arched hallway with a brick floor. I turned back to look at the door and felt the man's hand on my shoulder. I wondered if my mother was still outside. The man pushed me forwards and we went into a wide corridor with no windows.

We came to a sort of lobby and I was told to sit on a bench outside an office. There was more light here and I could see we were at the junction of two long corridors. I wondered if I'd ever see the outside world again. A man in workhouse grey clothes came and took me down till we came to a wash house with no windows but two gas jets. Here they made me take all my clothes off and put me in some water in a kind of square trough and a man scrubbed me with a brush. Then they cut my hair off and shaved my head. They gave me clothes made from some stiff material that smelled bad and some boots with nails in them that didn't fit proper. One was bigger than the other. There were blue socks.

They took me to another room and told me to wait outside. When I got in there I was face to face with the Master. I thought he'd be a swell like the people I'd seen when I'd gone with my father to St James's Park one time. But he was a rough type with whiskers and small eyes. There was a hot coal fire raging in the grate and he mopped his forehead with a red rag. He said something about believing in God, but Hard Work came first. There was framed pictures with words in them on the wall but I couldn't read.

I was shown a bed in a room that was like a barn with wooden rafters. You laid down in a sort of hole in the floor in a row like you was being buried except there was nothing on top of you, just a blanket. There was a straw mattress to lie on. Above you was the beams and on the walls there was more writing but it wasn't in frames, it was printed in big letters. In my room it was all boys, from littl'uns not much more than Tom's age up to John's age which was fifteen. There was a trough at one end you could use as a privy but I didn't want the others to see me. They wanted me to sing a song or say a rhyme or something because that was what new boys did.

The Master came in and he had a cane so no one moved. His wife, the Matron, she came in too and she had a stick. Mostly the man in charge was a pauper in the workhouse uniform called McInnes and he was given a bit more food to keep order. It was dark when the bell rang in the morning and we all had to get up quick and put our boots on and go to the hall where there was prayers. Then you went to these benches and sat down at a long table for breakfast. And you'd see the girls then, they come in from their corridor, but they were down the other side of the room and you couldn't talk to them. Breakfast was something in a bowl, they called it 'skilly', it was a liquid with oats in it. You just wanted it, you wanted it bad, but there were no spoons or forks. You drank it, then used your hands.

Us boys went to the classroom to do lessons. The teacher was McInnes. He was the only man in the Union who wasn't thin. He had a red angry face and he beat you with a stick on the hands. We had no slates to write on. There was a blackboard and sometimes McInnes wrote something on it. 'What's that?' he said and you all looked down because you didn't want to catch his eye. 'It's a four. Say after me. Two and two is?' That was all we took away from the lesson because that was all he had to give. I never knew for sure if what he'd wrote on the board was a four or a two or anything else. Then he made us sit silent and if anyone said anything he'd get thrashed on the hand. Jimmy Wheeler got his bones broke like that.

In the afternoon we went to another room where there was piles of rope. You had to unthread the rope and some of it was tarred. It was called picking oakum. When it was in its strands you carried it to the end of the room and it was put in crates they took off each day to the dockyards where they used it to seal the gaps in the timbers of the ships. We did four hours every day and it made your eyes hurt because there wasn't enough light and your fingers had to be strong. Some of the little boys was crying because it hurt them so much.

I close my eyes and I'm back in that place. I wasn't alive, I was only breathing. At night in the bed in the floor I slept. I pulled the blanket right up over my head. I didn't have thoughts. I didn't know nothing to think about. And I didn't dream neither.

No one came to see me. There was no word from my parents. I began to stop thinking about them so I could get through it.

I didn't make friends because no one did much and I was one of the smallest so none of the other boys was interested in me. At dinner one day I saw a girl across the other side of the room, a yellow-haired girl in one of them funny caps they wore. She smiled at me and I didn't know what to do. I looked out for her after that but we could hardly ever speak. Over the weeks I discovered little things about her. She said she'd never known her father but her mother had took in washing and had lived in a bad way in Poplar. There was too many other children and

Alice had a half-sister called Nancy who was in the Union house too.

I'd been there about two years I think when I saw a strange thing one Sunday morning. We had different clothes on a Sunday. They gave us a black coat you put on over your uniform. I was walking with the other boys through what they called the airing court towards the chapel. I saw men paupers come out of their building which was on the other side. They was being pushed along two-by-two by the Master.

There was a pale-faced man who looked like he might fall down. I was turning away when I recognised him. It was my father. I called out to him and tried to run across but McInnes slapped me back into line.

My father saw me. I saw his white face against the grey brick of the airing court behind him. His eyes met mine across that yard but he looked down at his feet.

He didn't want to hold my eye. He must have been ashamed of the boots he was wearing. Once he was a shoemaker and he had a good business. He said it was the Crimean War that done for him. When I first heard that word I thought he meant the war was a crime, it was certainly a Crime for us. He was apprentice to his own father before him and went out as a journeyman till he had twelve shillings to start up on his own. The shoes fetched two shillings a pair so he made a profit and he took on other men to work for him. That's when he took the house in Mason Street, with five children and all. He bought leather on credit. He had twelve skilled men working out for him but they all got the war fever and sailed off to the Crimea to fight. Then the price of leather went up through the roof. I remember this when I was still at home. He was proper knocked over.

Sunday afternoon was different because the children could go into the women's room if they had a mother in the Union.

There was a reverend come to say grace before dinner which was bread and a slice of cheese and jugs of water. This was the best dinner. There wasn't much of it but the cheese tasted good and it put you in mind of better things. The reverend went on talking and they just wanted to eat the bread and cheese and get over to the women's room. One Sunday I persuaded Alice to smuggle me in with her when she went to see her ma. When dinner was over I asked the monitor to go to the privy, which was a cesspit out in the yard. But I hid behind a buttress and when the children went past for the women's room I slipped in between Alice and Nancy and because I was small no one noticed.

The door opened on to the women's room. The children went flying in. It was a madhouse. There were women crying, children cartwheeling, there was sobbing and laughing and jumping and kissing. I never seen Bedlam but it must have been like this. I lost Alice for a minute, then I saw her and ran over and she put her arm round me and whispered to her ma that she was my mother too if anyone asked. We gathered tight to her on the bench and Alice and Nancy rattled off their stories and told her all the things that had happened in the week. She had her arms round them and I held on to her sleeve.

It began to calm down a bit. The visit was half an hour and you could see the clock on the wall. With ten minutes to go it all changed. A lot of the children stopped talking and just stood with their heads on their mothers' shoulders. They held on to them without speaking.

The bell came like a blow. Some of the children started to snivel and cry. The bigger ones took it bravely. You couldn't hang about because the monitor was shouting at you. Alice and Nancy kissed their ma and turned to go. Their ma took me against her shoulder for a moment and kissed the top of my shaved head.

*   *   *

About once a month we were allowed to go for a walk outside the grounds of the Union house. They picked about twenty boys and twenty girls and you walked in what they called a crocodile. It sounded exciting but it just meant you walked in a line of twos and you weren't meant to talk.

One time I got myself with Alice and we managed to say a few words. We came to a sort of park and there was a big clean house with gas lamps outside. We was told to wait outside then ten of us was told we could go indoors.

I pushed my way to the front and dragged Alice by the hand. I was mighty curious to see inside and I thought I might take something, a gold ornament or the like. I knew how to do it. Once we was inside I lost all thoughts of stealing. It was . . . I don't know the word. It was light.

A lady in fine clothes was smiling at us. She was quite old and not pretty to look at, with grey hair piled up on her head, but she smiled and just kept on smiling. No one did that. She took us into a huge room with a wood floor so polished it was like a mirror and there was other children there, about ten of them in smart clothes. They looked suspicious. There was paper streamers on the walls and the mantel. We was sat down on the floor and the lady played on a piano. Then a maid with a white cap came in with trays of cake and drink.

She put the tray down next to me. I'd never seen cake like this, big pieces with chocolate, ginger and dried fruit. I passed the tray to Alice and she passed it on to Jimmy Wheeler and he passed it on to the children in the fine clothes and they took pieces of cake and they ate it and they edged away probably because we smelled of the Union.

The tray came back to me and I passed it on, so it did another circle. I was looking at the paintings up on the wall with a cow standing in a river and this thing hanging from the ceiling. It had candles stuck in bits of glass. Everything in the room was light.

Suddenly the lady stopped playing the piano and came over to where the children was sitting. She took a new tray from the maid with more cakes on it.

She knelt down and held it out to me. 'Take some cake,' she said.

I didn't know what to do.

Alice could see. She spoke up and said, 'We didn't know we was to have any, Miss.'

The lady laughed. 'Go on. Take some. And then take some ginger wine.' She handed me a glass. I had never held a glass before.

We were in that place for more than an hour and when we got outside the others wanted to hear about it. I looked at Alice and she looked back at me. It was too much to tell.

A little time after this we were given stumps and bats and a ball to play in the yard of the Union house. I think they were given to us by the lady with the piano. They didn't want us to play cricket too much in case it gave us an appetite but once a week we could have a game. I liked to do batting.

Some dinner times we had cheese and bread, sometimes meat and potatoes and sometimes what they called broth, which was the worst because it was not much more than warm water. But I grew big enough to go into the men's section and this was frightening because of the talk and the way they carried on. Forty men in a room, some of them simple-minded with no shame. Then they coughed all night.

I didn't do lessons now, I did work with the men. We did corn-grinding, which was four of us turning a capstan. It was attached to iron bars that went through the wall to a flour mill outside. Some men did their bit, some tried to get out of it. The young lads were made to do the most of course. It was better than stone-pounding. For this I was sent to a hut where a man called Bolton was in charge. We was all told to break a

hundredweight of stones into powder that would go through a
sieve. They give you an iron bar with square ends and you put
the stones in a wooden box with an iron bottom. I never knew
what we was doing it for. Perhaps it was to make spoil for
mending roads. After an hour or so you'd get an odd feeling in
your fingers from the bar. The stone was still there in the box
just like you'd never touched it. Bolton said he'd have you sent
to prison if you didn't do your hundredweight. Some of the
men was jabbering and looked all done in and some of them
just give him the evil eye. Then white blisters would come up
on your fingers, then they'd burst, so blood was running down
the iron bar. It was better to work through it.

An old man told me he'd once been in a place where they used
to grind bones for fertiliser. He liked it because bones wasn't so
hard as the stones, but some of them wasn't boiled and they still
had bits of gristle on them. There was a big fight one day in the
bone-grinding hut because the men wanted to eat the flesh that
was left on the bones.

I lived for each Sunday when I would see my father if I was
lucky and I dreamt that I would one day make him recognise me.
There came a Sunday when he wasn't there and I feared the worst.
He'd looked awful pale the week before.

The next day, when I was on my way to the corn-grinding
shed, the Matron grabbed my arm and said, 'Webb, come with
me.' I thought she'd found out I'd stolen some cheese, which I'd
done two days earlier but I'd give it to Alice when I passed her
in the yard the next day. You could easily get sent to the police
and then you'd go to prison. I knew plenty of men who'd been
there and come back to the workhouse and said you were better
off in prison because you got more to eat. Some men who were
starving in the streets got themselves arrested on purpose. But
once you were a criminal you were done for, you were marked
for life.

Matron took me to the Master's office. 'Webb,' he said, mopping his head with his red rag, 'your father has made an application for your removal. Being in employment he's able to provide for you, at least for the time being. You will no longer be a burden on the parish. You leave on Sunday.'

'I thought maybe my father was . . . dead. He didn't look—'

'No. An acquaintance has found him employment of some kind.'

After ten years in uniform I was given a jacket and trousers. They said they could lend me the workhouse boots but I had to sign a receipt for them.

The Master pushed the piece of paper over. 'Sign here,' he said.

I made a mark. Seven years in the schoolroom that was.

He looked down at the paper, but he didn't meet my eye. He pretended to be busy with the fire. One day, I thought.

It was more of an alley than a street, with big uneven paving stones. Bailey Rents it was called. It was one of those streets you don't go down if you don't live there. There were no numbers on the doors. Some had a flag or a splash of paint or a shoe in the upstairs window so if you came in drunk you knew which was your house. There were half-naked children making mud pies by the standpipe. I asked round and found out which was my pa's place and I waited for him.

As I stood there I thought about all the Master told us about a Sober and a Righteous life. All the stuff the preacher told us too. If you don't have money those choices is just a thing you can't afford.

My father came home when it was dark. There was a young lad with him who looked in a poor way. It was Arthur.

'You'd better come up,' said Pa.

We stepped over two men on the stairs. The banisters had gone for firewood but the room Pa and Arthur was in was not so bad. It had furniture from the landlord – a table and two chairs. The windowpane was broke and was covered over with paper but there was a fire and some coke for it. He was paying eightpence a night for the room, he said. There was a mattress in the corner that he slept on and Arthur and me would have to do the best we could.

'Where's Ma?' I said.

'She left me. She went with Meg and the baby. They went to her mother in Greenwich. Then a few years back I had a letter from Australia. Didn't she write to you?'

'No. I didn't know she could write. What about John?'

'He joined the merchant navy. You better get some work, Billy.'

My father was a wall worker, which meant taking an advertising board to a fence or part of a wall where it could be hung. The best places were next to busy roads. My father would get the boards in the morning from some place near the Jews' Cemetery and put them up early. He had to take them in again at night. It was a lot of walking for a man his age but he got paid a shilling a week for each board and when things were good he had more than twenty so he got Arthur to help him. Arthur earned the odd sixpence running errands for other people so when I found them they were making about twenty-five shillings a week. The only trouble was that there was a long gap between putting up the last board and going to take down the first one in the evening and Pa spent most of it in the Turk's Head in Green Street. Of his twenty-five bob a week he was spending more on beer than rent. But still that night we had potatoes, mutton, bread and butter and Pa sent Arthur out to the pub for a jug of beer. We also had hot tea with plenty of leaves in it.

I had no training, the Union had taught me nothing but how to steal food so I had to try casual work. I got up before dawn. I ate some bread and drank some tea before I set off for the docks. I thought I'd be the first to arrive but when I got to the riverside there were hundreds of men waiting in the darkness. Some of them were smoking pipes or talking to each other, most of them were just looking at the gates.

It was past dawn when the bell went off and there was a rush for the entrance. Men you'd thought was dead on their feet was suddenly fighting one another to get through. What we were all aiming at was the hirers but they'd got themselves into wooden stalls or sometimes behind railings like a cage inside the dock. We were running up and down looking for one who looked more like he'd take you on, trying to catch his eye. I got to one man who was behind a wooden bar and as I reached to grab his ticket I was pushed on to the ground by a big man behind me. I got up and punched him and then I ran off to another pitch because I thought they wouldn't want to hire a fighter. The last cage on the dock was run by a man with two chained dogs. Most of the hirers looked frightened of the mob but this man took his time. There were maybe two hundred men and he was taking twenty for the day. Men were climbing over one another's shoulders to get at him. When he'd got the ones he wanted he threw the last five tickets out and let us fight for them. It was a test. I got one of them, though I had to half throttle another man to get it off him. I was wrong. They did like fighters.

You got fivepence an hour and sometimes there was only two hours for you to do. I went back every day for a year but I never thought the game was worth the candle. I saw men broken in half for a few pennies. I saw one man collapse and die at the pay box at the end of the day for three shillings and sixpence.

The man with the dogs was called Mr Riley and after about six months of casual he took me to one side and told me I could have regular work.

'Can you read?' he said.

I thought I would be found out if I lied. 'No,' I said.

'Good,' he said. 'You're from out the gutter, in't you, Webb?

You understand them men out there. They're animals, ain't they?'

'Takes one to know one,' I said. I didn't care.

He laughed and clapped me on the shoulder. 'That's what I like about you, you little bastard.'

He used me as an errand boy and a spy. As well as being paid a penny extra, sixpence an hour, to labour, I had to bring reports on all the workers, just give them to him by word of mouth and he gave me a tanner a time. I never asked what he did with the information but I think it was so he could pay them less. He took the ones who were strong in body and weak in mind and worked them half to death.

I'd got a taste for beer and because I was bringing in money I could buy it in the pub. In the Turk's Head one day I met the man my father worked for putting up boards. He was talking about men he knew who did bill-pasting which was better paid because there was a skill to it and I said I'd like to try it.

He laughed. 'You need to be able to read, you mug. Else you put the wrong bill up.'

I thought about hitting him but I saw my father's eye just in time. I finished my beer and went out into the street. I badly wanted this job and I had to think of a way. So I went down to Leggett's cook-shop in Houndsditch and talked to the proprietor, Sam Leggett, who was a know-all and a villain.

Leggett had some story of being the son of a gentleman the wrong side of the blanket, he was certainly a bastard. His cook-shop served convicts and ticket-of-leave men who were desperate to pick up some labour so they didn't go back to thieving. He said he'd been a policeman for a time and got free lodging by going into houses that was unoccupied. He knew the ropes. Once he was put to lodge in this cook-shop while it was having repairs and then the owner died so he took over.

I had to buy a bowl of his leg-of-beef soup to get his ear. I gave it to one of the convicts he lodges while they're on their ticket of leave from prison.

'Sam,' I said.

'Mr Leggett to you,' he said.

'Mr Leggett,' I said, biting my lip, 'I need to learn how to read.'

When he'd had his laugh of me with all the men in his foul cook-shop he gave me the name of someone he thought could help.

'Shall I write it down on a piece of paper for you, Billy?' he said, wiping his fat greasy hands down the front of his apron. 'Oh, no, silly me.'

All the convicts laughed again and I had a mind to kick his shin and to hell with the reading.

He gave me directions. 'It's right next door to the House of Accommodation,' he said. 'So if you sees nice ladies make sure you can afford it, young man.'

The thing about Sam Leggett is that he did know everyone. Even the police used to come ask his advice, so I don't know why the convicts trusted him. Somehow he kept the two groups apart. He told me there was a teacher fallen on hard times who would help me read if I could catch him sober.

This teacher was a Mr Stevens who lived in a place called Eagle Court off Old Ford Road. It was low buildings round a yard where children were scrapping in the dirt. They had a cat tied up by its legs to a rail. I tracked him down to a front room on the first floor of one of the filthier houses. Knowing his taste from old Leggett, I'd took along a bottle of beer from the Turk's Head. He was wearing a smart coat that had come undone along the seams and a waistcoat under. From the smell of him you could tell he hadn't washed for a long time. He told me he was doing odd jobs at night and I asked him how much he made. He was getting twelve shillings a week and that was mostly going on drink. I'd saved up five pounds from my work at the docks and I said I'd pay him a shilling a night to stop in and teach me how to read. We shook hands on it but I had to bring a jug of beer every time too.

My father and Arthur had moved to a house in Crow Street. There was another room there that came free when the old lady died. I went to see the rent collector who was called Worthington and told him I'd take it. I gave him four weeks in advance and it saved him a lot of trouble. It was a top floor and you had to go down to a privy in the yard at the back by the wash house but it wasn't so bad. Where did I get all this money? Same as everyone else. I worked in the docks, took the extras that come along, and what I was short of I found ways of laying my hands on. I didn't like to take watches and the like because then you had to go to a fence like old Abe Brown in Shadwell. I didn't take money either, like a dip, it was more if there was something left lying around. Sometimes I took food instead. Those years in the Union taught me to watch and wait your time. When big numbers of people are being fed, that's your best chance. No one can keep a watch on that much stuff coming in and out. So I'd go to an hospital. Or once I took a whole truckle of cheese from a cart round the back of St Joseph-in-the-West. I enjoyed that and it meant I could save my wages.

Next time I went back there was to tell them I could provide for Alice Smith, and I fetched her back to my room in Crow Street.

Alice was nineteen years old now and she wanted to make a home. For the first time in all those years we talked to each other good and proper and I heard about her life before she went into the Union. It was worse than mine because she had never had a father and the mother could never make ends meet taking in washing and then doing out-work for tailors and cigarette-makers and that. But in the Union the girls had had a teacher who knew something more than McInnes, so Alice knew how to read at least and she could help me after my lessons with Stevens. Together we used to practise writing. We used chalk on the walls of our room in Crow Street so when my pa came up one day for some tea he said, 'It looks like you two's living inside the covers of a book.'

Alice and me had been living together for a year when I went back to the Turk's Head and told the man I'd met there that now I could read and I would like to get a job as a bill-sticker. I had to pay five shillings for the introduction, but I met the supervisor, who was called Sidney Mitchell and lived in a tidy house by the canal in New North Road. I was taken on straight off for twenty-four shillings a week, which was enough to live on. There was a knack to getting a bill nice and smooth on a bumpy board but it wasn't too hard and I was quick about it. The tricky thing was doing it up a ladder so's you had to balance your paste and brush and bills in a wind and not fall off and break your ruddy neck. Some of the old chaps didn't fancy it so I got to be a ladder man and by the end of the year I was making nearly two pounds a week, working twelve hours a day.

Me and Alice got the back room as well and we had a sink for washing in, and after another year we got Alice's ma out of the Union and put her in the back room. She was good as gold, brought in a bit with some sewing and that, kept the place tidy and you could say we were all sailing along pretty well.

Alice was a lovely girl with her yellow hair and her plump bosom. We curled up in bed at night for warmth as much as anything, but it soon led to other things. She was always soft on me saying I was her hero because I rescued her from a life of misery but I told her she could have walked out any time, she didn't have to wait for me. 'Don't be silly,' she said. 'I had no money and no home. What was I going to do – sleep under the arches of the Great Eastern?'

I felt a lot of love for Alice Smith. She'd known me when I was dead out on my luck, just living through a minute at a time. But she was a right funny thing. She worked hard and she kept the rooms looking nice and she didn't drink much, but she had a temper and when she lost it she was like another person. She could say rotten cruel things. She was like a cat in a corner and she just lashed out at whoever came near. It didn't matter if it was me she loved most in the world, I'd still get it full in the face. Instead of calling me 'Billybones' or one of her pet names she'd start to call me William which was not a name anyone ever called me.

Before long she was expecting and we were married in the church on Mare Street. She had a little girl called Liza and not long after that I got made supervisor even though I was only about twenty-three. So now I was making two pounds ten shillings a week and then we got Alice's sister Nancy out of the Union too.

I think we were happy. I never had the time to ask. Three years after Liza, Alice had another baby girl and we called her May. By the age of thirty I had all the rooms in the house in Crow Street, I could read and write properly and I let old Stevens have one of the rooms downstairs for a song. Arthur and me built an extension on to the yard at the back, so we had a kitchen for the whole building next to the wash house. It was backing into the same thing on Grove Street and the man who lived there said could we put a door through between the two extensions, so when the police came he could run straight through our house. I said I'd agree to it if he paid me the cost of all my bricks and he coughed up seven pounds.

Alice was looking after the girls and teaching Liza to read. My father had shown her how to make slippers and he could get off-cuts of leather cheap so Alice had a little business going and our Liza could soon give her a hand.

Then one day I came back about eight o'clock in the evening from Wanstead and Alice had been took very ill. She was sat in her favourite chair by the window but she couldn't speak and one side of her body seemed to have froze up. The girls had been waiting for me to come home. They'd been down to ask old Stevens but he was dead drunk.

To cut a long story short, we got her to the sick asylum which was really just another part of the old workhouse where they put them as was too worn out or ill to do anything more. When I took Nancy to see Alice there, she said, 'We're back where we started, aren't we, Billy? In the workhouse.'

Well, I wasn't having this. I'd heard of a place that had started at the workhouse in Carshalton but they'd made it into a proper hospital and moved it to Putney. It was called the Hospital for Incurables and me and Nancy went over to have a look at it. We had a good talk with the doctors there and they said they would go and have a look at Alice in the sick asylum and then they would write and tell me what they thought.

'Can you read, sir?' said the doctor.

'Of course I can read,' I said. 'What do you take me for?' I'd dressed up in my best clothes.

The doctor stammered a bit and said he was sure he could help.

I said, 'You'd better help, doctor, because she's the kind of poor patient you should be having.'

The long and the short of it was they come over and took one look at her and said, Yes, that's one for us — and me and Nancy packed up some clothes for her and we took her on the omnibus along the riverside. I don't know if my Alice knew what was going on at all. Her eyes were staring straight ahead and she hardly ever seemed to blink. She needed help being fed and dressed.

Nancy said we was happy to keep her at home and she thought Alice would prefer that, but the doctor said they might be able to do something for her in the hospital and anyway Alice didn't know what was going on. I wondered why they thought they could cure her in a hospital for Incurables, but I was glad she would be looked after and kept warm. They said to leave her for a month to settle in before we went again to visit.

We gave it five weeks, then the three of us – me and Nancy and her and Alice's ma, who was getting on a bit by now – set off again for Putney.

Well, the hospital still looked pretty new and the corridors had just been distempered. The gas jets were all working and the stone steps were clean. I wouldn't deny that it was gloomy – it was a big old place, like they expected a lot of people in London to have Incurable illness. But the fact of the matter was that this hospital was a better place than any of us Smiths or Webbs had ever lived in before. The patients were common people like us but the food was uncommon plentiful. The nurses had clean clothes and starched headdresses. The doctors wore dark suits and neckties. Nancy's mouth was hanging open as she looked it all up and down.

The doctor in charge was able to see us for a few minutes. This was a tall man with a beard, not the one we'd seen before. He said something like, 'The nervous system is still a mystery to us, Mr Webb, but we are making some progress. Gentlemen in Paris using the method of . . .'

I didn't take it in. Nancy told me afterwards that what it boiled down to was they wouldn't have a clue till she died. Then they'd look at her brain and they'd see a little spot or something that told them what illness she'd had.

'What sort of medicine is that?' I asked. 'That waits till you're a goner before it can find out what the matter is? She's only thirty-two.'

Ma Smith said at least she'd be fed properly and there was no denying that. Also Alice was not half as bad as some of the poor wretches in there, people dribbling and shaking and thrashing their heads up and down, moaning and soiling themselves. You could tell that some of them had once been something. The nurse said there was a gentleman downstairs who'd been a doctor himself and at least two were clergymen.

Nancy and I went to see Alice every week to start with but she seemed to get worse. After a year or so there didn't seem much point in going. She stared straight ahead of her and she dribbled. Her lovely yellow hair was going dry and grey. She couldn't even take herself to the privy any more, the nurse told me, and they put her into bed most of the time. I don't think she knew who me and Nancy were.

It was hard for us to go and see this person, who looked like Alice, who looked like the little girl I'd seen in the Union in her white cap, but wasn't Alice any more. She was someone else. So we stopped going to see her so much, it was more like once a month and then every two or three months and eventually just at Christmas and once in the summer.

Back in Crow Street things were going along pretty well, you could say. That man Worthington who was the rent collector had a small line going himself and he asked if I could put some money into a house he was going to buy and then repair to let out. He'd got most of the money he needed from the bank. It was a weaver's house in Bethnal Green which had one big room on each floor. Over the years they'd put up partitions and there was now six families in it, two on each floor and one of them still let out space to a weaver to put up his loom. It was horrible. It was infested with all sorts of vermin, not just flies and lice and that which everyone had, but rats too. Worthington had got a deal off the owner who was fed up with it because they could never collect the rent that was owing. The idea was to knock out the partitions, fumigate the thing and then repair it.

You need a bit of go, a bit of spark. There was nothing me and Worthington did that others couldn't have done just as well if they hadn't been all day in the Turk's Head. One of the ladder men who worked for me had a nasty little terrier. I give him an extra shilling in his pay to lend me the dog and that saw off the rats. I got Arthur in with a sledgehammer and that took down the partitions. Arthur was living rent-free in Crow Street so he owed me a favour. Him and a bill-sticker with a nice steady hand did the painting. We did have to pay a proper joiner to replace the banister and do a fair bit of work about the place, but that and the roof repair was the only big expense.

I don't know what happened to the families we kicked out but they all owed months in rent anyway. Worthington was good at finding decent families to go into the three floors and he got them all to pay ten weeks' rent in advance. With the income we were paying back the interest and some of the loan to the bank and keeping a small profit.

It was an awful slow process. I was running the bill-sticking business and that was making enough for all of us in Crow Street so long as everyone else did their little bits. But it was stuck where it was and it was very small money really. So when Worthington come up with another house I jumped right in with him.

In five years we had four houses up and running. I put Arthur to run the bill-sticking and I became a landlord. I was the man they all hated. The costermongers, the catsmeat men, the coffee-stall owners, the prostitutes and their bullies, the dossers, the drunk old teachers and all the others. I was the enemy to them. Not that many of them could afford the rents that me and Worthington could ask for these houses once we'd done them up. I'll own that we did put some of them people on the street. And the new houses that the charities were building, the tenements and that, they couldn't afford them neither. That was the funny thing about housing for the poor — the poor could never afford it.

In all of this Nancy was my helper and my companion. She and Alice was only half-sisters. Both the fathers had disappeared at the first sign of trouble which was what had led old Ma Smith into the Union. They were different creatures. Nancy was thin and dark. People who didn't like her said she was sly, but she wasn't. She was the daughter of a pauper with an older half-sister, no money and brought up in a workhouse. She had nothing except her wits to live on. She learned to be quiet, we all did in that place. But she could read and write and she was quick with things — like with the doctor at the Incurables she understood better than me what he was saying. She was good at being in the right place at the right time and she was good at not being there when you didn't want her. She had a big barking laugh on her too. You didn't hear it that often but when something tickled her or when she'd had a drink, you'd wait to hear her and it was like the donkey on Clapham Common. 'Penny a ride, boys,' her mother used to say.

She looked after my girls, Liza and May, like they was her own and they loved her like their own mother, though they called her Nance. When her mother was too run-down to shift for herself, Nancy looked after her too. In the evening Nancy cooked supper for everyone who was there which might be all of us and my father and Arthur too. She didn't have a temper like Alice. I wouldn't say she was all sweetness, Nancy, but she never complained and she had a smile in her big brown eyes that could set the room on fire.

The first time she came into my bed I had a feeling it was wrong. Alice had been gone four years and they said she was never coming back, but even so. I looked at Nancy standing naked in the firelight.

We knew what was going to happen. It was Saturday and I'd been drinking all evening in the Turk's Head. There was a lovely clean smell to her hair when she put her head on my chest. She told me she'd never been with a man before but she'd waited long enough. She took my hand and put it down there and it was lovely. She held on to me all night like a monkey on a branch. I couldn't get enough, it was awful, I felt like a savage.

A couple of years later – just when I got my fourth house with Worthington – Nancy had a baby boy and we called him Dick.

We still used to go and see Alice in the Incurables twice a year, but we never told her about Dick, not that she would have understood.

When Liza was nineteen she married a dairyman who had a cottage in Camden Town. May was sixteen and Dick was just four and they came to the wedding in the same church in Mare Street where me and Alice were married. Nancy bought a new dress and looked beautiful. Although she drank a bit on a Saturday, she had been a good and faithful wife or like a wife to me.

The days went by. It must have been five years after Liza was married I had a letter and I could see from the envelope that it was from the Incurables.

I said, 'Prepare yourself for bad news, Nance.'

I began to read and pretty soon I found my legs wouldn't take my weight so I sat down at the table. It was from a Dr Charwell. I got it still in front of me as I write these words.

Dear Mr Webb,

I am writing to inform of a change in the condition of your wife, Alice Webb (date of birth unknown, circa *1852*), who became a patient at this hospital almost fifteen years ago. About six months ago, as you know from your last visit, she began to attempt speech. Following exercises with the nursing staff, she has regained the powers of communication. She recently reported the return of sensation to her lower limbs. Despite atrophy of the femoral muscles, she has regained the ability to walk. A few weeks ago, her improved co-ordination and dexterity meant that she became able to feed, clean and clothe herself.

It has long been our belief that her particular symptoms were the result of a localised trauma rather than of a degenerative paralysis. Such recoveries are comparatively rare but by no means unprecedented. I have no doubt that the diligent nursing and medical treatment she has received while under our care have contributed significantly to this happy turn of events.

Following a final examination by Professor Elliot, the visiting neurological consultant, we expect to discharge <u>Alice Webb</u> from our care on September 12th. We trust you will be able to make arrangements for her journey home.

A week later, I had a letter from Alice herself.

Dear Billybones, I know the doctors have wrote you about me. It is a miracle. They have give me back my life. I can hardly wait to see you and our dear little girls again. Thank you and Nancy for coming to see me in the hospital. I have missed you all so dearly and am longing to be back in our house again. Ever your loving Alice.

'What the devil are we going to do?' I said.

Nancy was crying. 'I can't believe it,' she said. 'After all these years. What's she going to be like?'

I didn't know. I thought perhaps in her own mind she didn't know that nearly fifteen years had gone past. I thought perhaps she thought she was still a young woman and that Liza and May were little girls. She'd been as good as dead and you can't be that poorly and just come out the same as what you was before. There must be some change, some damage in her head. That's what I told Nancy.

'And what do we say about you and me?' she said. 'And about Dick? We can't hide the boy.'

I didn't know what to say. Dick was at the Board school and was going along well enough but I thought it wouldn't harm him to go away for a bit. So I got Worthington to give him a room in one of his houses. He was only nine but it wasn't like I was sending him to the workhouse. There was an old lady there who'd look after him and I'd pay his keep. Then I told May that when her mother come home she wasn't to say nothing about Dick.

What I was really thinking was that we'd wait and see what Alice was like and then we could decide.

Well, we got the house ready. We had the whole of the top floor at this time and May put flowers on the table and Nancy cleaned everything up nice while I was out at work. I didn't write and tell Liza anything yet. She was expecting a baby herself and I thought it was best to leave her alone.

The day came and I set off in the omnibus for Putney with a heavy heart. I had to go into the office on the ground floor and talk to the Matron who made me sign some papers for her discharge. This time I could sign my name well enough.

Then I stood in the hallway on the cold stone and waited for my wife to come back to me. I looked up and saw her walk round the turn of the stone steps. She was wearing a black dress they must have given her and her hair was pinned up on top of her head. She was holding the rail as she came down and although she moved slowly she seemed able to manage fine.

When she saw me, her face lit up and she hurried the last few steps and threw herself into my arms. She clung on to me crying for a long time. When she lifted up her face to me there were tears all down it and it was swollen red.

'Oh, Billy, I can't believe it. I'm so happy, I can't tell you.'

'Come on then,' I said. 'We'd best be getting back.'

Alice wanted to say goodbye to the nurses and there were lots more tears before I got her out of there and on to the omnibus going down West Hill towards Wandsworth. She sat holding my hand and staring out at the streets and all the people in them. Sometimes she turned back to look at me and her face was all shining like a child's, like she couldn't believe her good fortune.

'There's been some changes at home,' I said, as the omnibus was getting towards Battersea Bridge. 'Liza got married. A dairy-man called Roberts. They got a nice little cottage up in Camden Town. And she's expecting.'

This knocked her back but not in the way I expected. I thought she might think Liza was still only three or four years old but she was just surprised we hadn't told her.

'Well, you couldn't take it in, could you?' I said.

'I took in most things all right,' she said, and I wasn't sure what she meant by that. But I thought of the times Nancy and me had been to see her and talked to one another in front of her and it made me feel uneasy.

When we got back to Crow Street, Alice walked in as though she'd never been away. I mean, she said how much better the house looked and how well me and Arthur had painted it and that, she said nice things about it — but then she went up to the top floor and settled down in the chair she used to sit in before.

We had a big supper that night with a shoulder of mutton and boiled potatoes and a steamed pudding and there was beer and wine to drink. We put Alice at the top of the table with her mother and her half-sister on either side of her. My father sat down with us, but he didn't seem to know what was going on. Afterwards old Stevens came up from his ground-floor room to take a glass of wine.

I looked at all these people flushed and talking away in the light of the candles and the single gas jet and I wondered what I was going to do.

Alice was back like she'd never been gone. She looked much older, all grey-haired and quite frail, but she didn't seem to think that anything was changed at all. But to me she was dead. I was looking at a ghost.

That night I showed her a little bed in the back room we'd had made up special. She looked surprised.

'Can't I curl up with you, Billyboy? It's been a long time.'

'I know. I need a bit of time to . . . to get used to it.'

She kissed me on the cheek. 'Didn't you miss me?'

'Of course I did.'

Nancy was watching through the half-open door.

'You're a funny old thing,' said Alice. 'Go on then, I'll see you in the morning.'

Nancy started off sleeping in the front room but in the middle of the night she came through to my room and got in with me. She held on to me tightly and her face was just an inch from mine. 'I'm not letting you go, Billy,' she said. 'Even if she is my sister. Even if she got you first. You're mine now. I've made you the man you are.'

She wrapped herself tight round me and made me do things to her. She could be wild like that. I knew what she said was true. I was nothing till that night she first came to my bed when I'd been drinking and she stood there undressed. And since that day I'd never looked back. For more than ten years Nancy Smith had shared not just my bed but all my thoughts and all my hopes. She was right when she said she had made me the man I was. I couldn't go back to what I'd been before.

The days went along and I got to know Alice again. In some ways she was just the same old Alice, and this made me feel terrible.

But half my grown life had passed without her and in that time I'd changed. I'd grown like a plant towards the sun, and the sun was Nancy.

Perhaps that was the problem with Alice, that she hadn't changed at all. It was almost like she'd been asleep for fifteen years. Sometimes I felt like a murderer, like a traitor who'd betrayed her trust. Sometimes I felt like she was still a child and I had to treat her like one. Other times I felt angry that she didn't seem to understand — she didn't even try to understand. Surely no one could just imagine that everything stays the same for ever?

Alice kept asking if she could come back to my bed and one day I thought I'd just better tell her. It was a Saturday and I took her off to Victoria Park. It was a hard thing to do, but if my father was right then I was the man to do a hard thing.

We sat down on a bench under a tree and I said, 'Alice, we've known each other almost all our lives. We seen some rough things in that Union house. And in Crow Street it wasn't easy. That night Liza was born.'

'I know, Billy. You were lovely. I remember when you held my hand.'

'I won't let you down, Alice. While I can work and breathe I'll take care of you. You took me in that Sunday to the women's room and for that alone I'll never let you down.'

'My ma give you a kiss, didn't she?'

I swallowed. 'I'm happy that you're well again. They say you'll live a normal life. But you were away a long time. And I'm not the man you left behind.'

'I can see.'

'Me and Nancy had a child. A boy. He's called Dick. He's nine years old and he's coming home soon to live with us. I want you to meet him.'

Alice didn't say nothing. She sat there on the bench looking straight ahead of her over the grass towards the trees. There were tears running down her face on to her collar, just silent tears running down. She looked so far away I wondered if she'd gone away again into her illness.

She held my hand for more than an hour while the people came and went, the mothers and the couples arm in arm and the children running after hoops and balls. Still the silent tears were running down her face.

It was starting to grow dark and the park-keeper sounded a bell. Alice turned her face towards me and squeezed my hand.

'Can we go home now, Billybones?' she said.

'Yes, come on then.'

We stood up and started walking. 'Can I take your arm some days?' she said. 'When there's no one else?'

'Yes,' I said. 'Yes, you can.'

In the next few years we had a lot of deaths. First it was Ma Smith and then old Stevens downstairs. We did up Stevens's room so it looked as good as new and Alice moved in there. She took in some work for pin money, sewing and that, but she had her meals with us and cooked a fair bit too.

Then one summer my pa was taken ill. He took to his bed one day and said he was never getting up again. I did get a doctor to come and see him but he said there was nothing he could do, the cancer was all over him. This doctor told me where I could find some medicines that would help the pain and make him sleep.

I sat by his bed and I thought about him when he was a young man and he had his business and twelve men working for him. He'd had a bit of a twinkle about him then. He thought things would work out all right for him after all.

Now I saw his unshaved face and his sunken eyes. He was a man on his last legs.

'Did I ever tell you, Billy,' he says, 'about the ones we lost? Your ma and me? There was another little girl besides Meg. We lost her when she was four or five. And there was a stillborn, a boy, between Meg and you.'

'P'raps if that boy had lived I'd never have been born,' I said.

'P'raps.' He heaved up a big sigh. 'I sometimes think I wasn't a good father to you, Billy. When I had to send you to the Union. But you was the only one who'd survive it. And otherwise we was going to starve.'

'I understand.'

Then my father said, 'Being a father . . . When you're a lad you think your pa knows it all. He's like a god to you. But he doesn't. You just make it up as you go along.'

'I know,' I said.

'And then you know you got it wrong. But it's too late.'

'You didn't mean no harm,' I said.

I looked down at his bed and into his eyes, which had all red rings round them. He was finished. Once he thought he could win, but life had beaten him, like it beats everyone.

We carried on living in Crow Street till my younger girl May got married too, then I took all the money I could from the business I had with Worthington and I paid down a deposit on a cottage in Clapham which had belonged to a railwayman. I took a loan from a mutual society and me and Nancy and our boy Dick moved in.

Arthur went off to Australia where he hoped to meet his mother, my mother, though I don't know if he ever did because he couldn't write. For a time Alice was the landlady in Crow Street, but her health wasn't so good really and Nancy said she should come and live with us in Clapham. I was very pleased with this and I was glad it was Nancy who suggested it. So now it's the four of us. And this is where we are.

Alice has a room on the back of the house that looks out towards the railway. She sits by the window there quite a bit of the day, and sometimes she goes down into the little square of garden at the back. She's got quite a knack with flowers and she's planted some tomatoes under the window, where they get the sun.

Nancy's taken my name, she's Mrs Webb now, and Alice has gone back to being Smith. No one in this part of London knows any different. Nancy's very good to Alice, she's careful not to crow. She's generous with what we've got and what we've made together.

Once I came home early and I saw them playing cards in the front room. It was like all the years fell away and they was in the mothers' room in the Union house on a Sunday, waiting for the bell to go. It was like nothing in between had ever happened. They didn't hear me come in and I stood in the doorway looking at them. Alice's eyes were fixed on Nancy's face while she dealt the cards. She looked quite calm, but puzzled.

I don't think you ever understand your life – not till it's finished and probably not then either. The more I live the less I seem to understand.

Dick's a bright lad and he did well at the Board school. Now he's got a job as a clerk in the City. He goes off early in the morning in a collar and tie. He's a good, clean-living boy and he wants to make an impression.

And when I die all the memories of my own life will go to the grave with me, God willing, and Dick will never have to look back at them. And his children will never even know what my life was like. They'll know nothing of grinding stones and lying down to sleep in what felt like a coffin and being hungry and ashamed all day and night and being beaten by a teacher who couldn't write himself and being sure you kept your mind so empty that you had no thoughts at all. And that's what I've done for them, that's my gift to them and to all their children ever after, so don't talk to me about being hard.

PART III — EVERYTHING CAN BE EXPLAINED

Elena Duranti was a wild girl who spent most of her time alone in the woods near her parents' farm. Her mother said she was 'shy', but the truth was that she found other children irritating. She knew what they were trying to say even as they began to labour slowly towards it; and when they got there it hardly seemed worth the trouble. She wasn't proud of this impatience and felt uneasy about being friendless, but she had only to spend a lunch hour hearing Bella make conversation with Jacopo to know that she was better off on her own.

Elena's father, Roberto, was a boatbuilder and the only human being she was never bored by. Perhaps this was because he said so little as he stood at the bench in his workroom, planing yellow curls from the planks of wood or bending over them with his set square and spirit level. He had long, shaggy hair that hung over his eyes and a beard that even in his thirties was threaded with grey. Elena would stand in the sawdust, her skinny legs bare beneath a cotton dress, hoping that Roberto would occasionally remember she was there. She watched how he measured and sawed, how he made the joints firm with screws and glue, and tried to remember it all for when she would build her own private hideaway.

She pestered her parents for a bicycle. Her mother, Fulvia, worked as a cleaner at a school in the nearby city of Mantua, and one day Elena pointed out to her a showroom that made her sick with longing. The black tyres had a new rubber smell and the colours on the metal frames — purple, lime and gold — were entrancing. She spent a long time looking at the straps and buckles on the saddlebags. Above all, it was the handlebars she craved; she pictured herself with her backside stuck high in the air, crouching with her face over the front wheel and her hands on the racing grips; she would raise one arm to swipe a bottle from a drinks station and ease her aching back. But the machine that arrived as a present from her parents on her ninth birthday in June 2029 had neither fluorescent paint nor fragrant tyres; it was the cast-off of a neighbour's son who had outgrown it. It had no saddlebag or lights; and worse, it was — and there was no denying it — a boy's bike.

Determined not to let her parents see her disappointment, Elena rode off as fast as the machine would let her. Within a week she had stripped it down and oiled it up; she fixed the gear-change and with some savings bought an elementary tool kit. She longed for a puncture. Ignoring Fulvia's cries of alarm, she went out on to the main highways, then lanes and farm paths and eventually off-road into the woods and hills. One day, deep in a glade she was fairly sure no human being had ever visited, she found a clearing that she thought ideal for a hideout. With timber offcuts from Roberto's workshop and some old tools he'd passed on to her, she set to work. For a roof she used a piece of corrugated iron she'd seen abandoned by a path, and for guttering some scraps from a skip at a building site. What she was most proud of was the drain: a three-metre run that voided into a natural ditch.

Inside, she put up shelves; and on these she put a few action figures, dolls and other toys she thought robust enough for the outdoor life. The place of honour was taken by a French eighteenth-century plaster Madonna that her father had picked up in a junk shop on a visit to a client in France. It had been badly knocked about over the years, but Elena repainted it a virginal blue. Through the centuries the figure had retained a one-eyed, minatory stare that was both comic and alarming.

The Madonna was left on the shelf, but the others became actors in long-running stories concerned with natural disasters. There was never a question of mothering them, or putting them to bed or seeing them marry one another; the American doll with the yellow hair had no time to spare for the fashion catwalk when she was needed to mastermind an airlift from a flooded infant school. Elena had a number of plastic soldiers she deployed in battle formations, trying to give the Indian braves a fair chance against the Soviet artillery, but the killings and explosions bored her and she preferred to integrate the military into the lives of the town.

Here their stories became more personal. Where she had been happy to tell her parents at the dinner table about fire and avalanche, she was reluctant to reveal too much of her suspicions about the closeness between the head firefighter and his deputy.

'She has no friends,' said Fulvia to Roberto. 'It's not natural.'

'She's happy, isn't she?'

'Yes, but living all day in that make-believe . . .'

'The teachers told me she's doing well,' said Roberto. 'She reads a lot up there in her little hut. She studies animals. She knows about the planets. And solar navigation.'

Fulvia was not convinced. 'Maybe she studies too much. I see her bedroom light on till all hours. And she's so thin.'

Roberto laughed. 'Listen, if you're worried, take her to see the doctor.'

Fulvia smiled and shook her head. 'She's just your little pet, isn't she? For you she can do no wrong.'

'She is what she is. We'll never change her.'

The local doctors' surgery had been reduced by lack of funds to little more than emergency services, but eventually Fulvia was able to secure an appointment for her daughter. The afternoon was airless and hot; they sat in a dusty waiting room for almost two hours until at last the name 'Duranti' was called over the system.

The doctor was a bearded man in shirtsleeves. He looked exhausted. There were blooms of sweat in the armpits of his shirt and heavy bags beneath his eyes. He made Elena strip to her underwear, then bent her arms back and forth. She touched her toes. He shone a light in her eyes.

'Does she have periods yet?'

'Not yet.'

Elena was taken away and put in a tube that rumbled. A nurse took her back to the doctor's room with a batch of blurred photographs. She felt humiliated at having to walk along the stone corridor in her vest and pants. The doctor told her to sit down while he took her blood pressure. Then he rubbed the inside of her elbow with alcohol and slid a needle into her vein; as he leant over her she could smell the cigarette smoke on his clothes. He put a small test tube of her blood into an envelope in his out-tray as he sat back in his desk chair and riffled through the scans.

'Skinny little thing, isn't she?'

'Well, she eats enough for two,' said Fulvia. 'I promise you she—'

'I understand. You have a family history of heart problems, it says on her notes.'

'Yes,' said Elena's mother. 'My mother died when she was forty-nine and her mother at the same age.'

The doctor put down the scans. 'Well, despite all that Elena's heart is normal,' he said. 'Physically, she's perfectly well.'

'She has no friends.'

For the first time, the doctor smiled. 'A few years ago we might have sent her to a counsellor for that.'

'And now?' said Fulvia.

'For people like us, ordinary people, that profession has disappeared. Take your little girl home, Signora, and stop worrying. She's a funny little monkey, but if I were you I'd just enjoy her company when you can.'

Later, on the bus going home, Elena said, 'Why did he call me a monkey, Mama?'

'It's just a friendly word. It doesn't mean anything.'

Elena could see that her mother was disappointed that the doctor had found no cure for her. Fulvia's face looked strained and old as she rested it against the bus window. Will my mother also die at forty-nine? thought Elena. Will I?

'Shall I tell you why I'm not a monkey?'

'If you must,' said Fulvia.

'It's because a monkey doesn't know it's a monkey. A human being knows it's human. That's what sets us apart from every other animal on earth.'

'If you say so, Elenissima,' sighed her mother. 'What would you like for dinner?'

It was not at first the idea of the monkey's brain that interested Elena, but its looks. She inspected herself in the mirror and came to admit that she was, in the word of a book she had studied, simian in appearance. She had furry arms, large eyes and a flat chest. She didn't have the golden skin of Cinzia, or Laura's long and slender legs. So be it, she thought. The project of my life is to make the most of what I have.

Although she read electronically at home, the library at school had printed books they let her take away; Elena carried them up to her hut in her new saddlebag. The teachers at her school were startled by the range of what she knew and allowed her to attend some of the senior classes, sitting at the back, taking notes in her small, exact handwriting. But before she settled down each afternoon to read in the old car seat she had lugged up to her hideaway, there were sporting activities.

She divided Italy into its regions and represented each in turn over a cross-country course of her own devising. The gearing on the bicycle was primitive and some of the ground was boggy, so there were parts of the course where she had to dismount and push, at the run. The Tuscans were accident-prone, she discovered. Her local district of Veneto tended to place well, though it was always hard to beat Campania, especially if the dashing Emilio Rizzo was in the saddle. She tried hard not to have favourites, but it was surprising how certain riders came to dominate the timings.

She waited till it was almost dark before she closed the padlock on her hut, jumped on to the bicycle once more and sped back out of the woods, down the hill, bumping over the paths and then along the main road back to her parents' farmhouse, where the lights were coming on for dinner and Pedro, the sheepdog, was waiting anxiously for her to feed him.

One rainy evening she hurried home particularly fast because they were expecting Roberto back from a business trip to Trieste. When she had fed the dog, she helped Fulvia prepare a sauce for the pasta, then settled down to wait. The electric car made no sound, and the first thing they knew of its return was when the door swung open to reveal not just her father, with rain dripping from the brim of his hat, but a second person: a boy in a ragged cape with hair more tangled even than Roberto's. Elena could not make out in the dim light of the kitchen whether he was brown-skinned or just dirty.

'I've brought someone for you to play with, Elena,' said Roberto.

'Why, Papa?' said Elena, appalled.

The boy took a step into the room.

'What's his name?'

'Number Two Hundred and Thirty-Seven. I took him from an orphanage near Trieste.'

'But what's his real name?'

'He won't say. Maybe we'll call him . . . Trieste. Where I found him.'

'He's not a dog.'

'What do you suggest, then?'

'We should ask him. Does he speak Italian?'

'Yes,' said Elena's father. 'But he's quiet.'

The boy took a step back towards the door.

Elena stared at him and wrinkled her nose. 'Perhaps Bruno. Because he's brown with dirt all over.'

The boy took a step forward again, and became Bruno.

'Let me show you where the bathroom is, Bruno,' said Elena's mother.

'How long is he staying?' said Elena.

'For ever,' said Roberto. 'We're adopting him.'

Elena fumed. For a week she refused to speak to her mother or father, let alone the intruder. She ate dinner in silence, then cleared her plate, went upstairs to her room and locked the door. Bruno gazed at her with dark, puzzled eyes. He could speak Italian fluently, it turned out, though with an accent, and in a harsh, high voice. Scrubbed, dressed in clean clothes and shorn by the barber, he looked clean, but still, to Elena's eyes, barbaric.

When the registration paperwork was finally done, they put Bruno on the school bus with Elena. She sat at the back with Jacopo and Cinzia, leaving him to find a seat for himself; her fear was that since they were the same age they might put him in her class. At school, he was sent for assessment and, to Elena's relief, was placed in the B stream, which was taught in a different building; she could continue to pretend that he did not exist. By day, she redoubled her concentration on the work at school and in the evening she leapt on to her bicycle and disappeared to her hideout in the woods.

'It's not natural,' said Fulvia. 'Poor little boy.'

For want of other company, Bruno allied himself to Pedro, and spent the early evenings throwing stones over the field with the dog at his side. He tried to teach him to fetch sticks, but Pedro seemed to have no retrieving instinct. He regarded Elena's father, meanwhile, with a steady reverence and worried for his well-being; when a contract for a boat went to a different company, Bruno took some convincing that it was not the end of their livelihood. Like Elena before him, he watched Roberto at work with drills and planes, though, unlike her, he didn't want to copy him or take part. He liked to stand nearby at all times, slightly closer than was comfortable, as though he feared his protector might vanish as inexplicably as he had appeared.

Roberto occasionally looked down at the solemn boy and smiled. He seemed to enjoy Bruno's company almost as much as Elena's.

'My God, you look alike,' said Fulvia one day when she brought in some drinks and saw them standing side by side. Both of them looked pleased.

There was a commotion one day at school. A boy called Alfredo ran squealing from the B-stream building with blood pouring from his nose. Elena was watching from her side of the school and, with a mixture of amusement and horror, saw Bruno being marched out by the teacher. It seemed that a group of boys had been taunting him about being an orphan, and had called him, among other things, a pirate and a 'Slovene peasant'; they had suggested an improper relationship with his 'sister', Elena. It was this last idea, so comically far from reality, that had proved too much for him.

As the bus approached the school that winter afternoon, its

headlights bending down the industrial landscape, Elena saw the misery in Bruno's eyes and feared what might happen if he gave way again to anger. She pushed into the crowd.

'Come here,' she said, grabbing his arm. They were the first words she had spoken to him. She shoved him ahead of her on to the bus, into a seat against the window, and placed herself next to him on the aisle, a thin barricade.

It was dark as they left the commercial warehouse zone and found the country roads. When they were nearly back at their village, Bruno said, 'Can I come with you one day to the woods?'

Elena did not answer, looking at him with distaste; but one Sunday, in a rare moment of feeling sated by her own company, she said, 'You can come for half an hour. Now.'

'Do you have a cave?' he said, running to keep up in case she changed her mind. 'A hideout?'

It was the first time she had seen him smile, and she noticed that he had a twisted tooth on the left side of his mouth.

'Maybe,' she said.

She let him ride her bicycle. He was almost as fast as Emilio Rizzo, and, with a pang, Elena knew the long era of her secret games was over.

'It's unusual to find one of these in a wood,' Bruno said, picking up what looked to Elena like a common daffodil.

'How do you know about flowers?'

Bruno shook his head, unwilling to talk about his past. 'Do you believe in God?' he said.

'Don't be silly,' said Elena.

'I do,' said Bruno. 'I believe in several gods.'

'Like an ancient Roman? Like a pagan?'

'It's better than believing in just one.'

'And what do your little gods do?'

'There's one who's in charge of the dead. There's a god of

luck, the most important one. There are lots of others. Maybe there's a god of love.'

Elena stifled a laugh.

'Let me ride the bike again,' said Bruno. 'Time me round the course.'

'I have to get the stop-watch.'

'From your secret place? I won't look.'

Bruno broke the course record, though Elena didn't tell him so. He offered to time her in return, but she was reluctant to come second. She suggested they go into the forest where the wild boar were still hunted.

'If one of them charges you,' she said, 'you have to wait till the last second, then jump to one side like this. The boar run fast but they can't change direction.'

'I'll remember that,' said Bruno.

After a few minutes and no sign of a boar, he said, 'Did your parents want another child?'

'I've never asked. I was happy with things as they were.'

'Now I've spoiled your life.'

Elena stopped walking and looked back into Bruno's expressionless eyes. 'It can't be helped,' she said.

Bruno did not flinch. He said, 'When I used to lie down to sleep at night in the orphanage I felt as though I was the only living thing in the world. I felt I could howl in the darkness and no one would hear. Do you feel like that when you lie down and close your eyes? As though you're dying?'

'No,' said Elena. 'I have my thoughts. I have company in my head. Sometimes I can order my dreams.'

'You're a very strange girl.'

No one had ever spoken to Elena in this way before. 'Let's go back,' she said.

'No. Don't be frightened. We can stay out here. Talk to me. Talk to me, Elena.'

He hadn't used her name before and she thought it sounded outlandish on his foreign tongue.

Elena's decision was based on little more than curiosity, though even then she knew it might have long consequences.

'Go on, then,' she said.

Talking to Bruno confirmed Elena's belief that there had been no one worth talking to before. Her life changed. At school, she remained aloof from her classmates and worked hard. Jacopo, Bella and the rest of them stopped making any effort to include her in their circle; at break time, since she couldn't join Bruno in his playground, she stayed in the classroom and did that night's homework in advance while he stood at the wire fence staring out towards her building like a starved prisoner. When the bell rang at four, the first one of them on to the bus reserved a seat for the other. After a time the other children didn't bother to ask if it was free; eventually they stopped chanting 'incest' and 'pervert'.

Bruno was the first person of her own age whose company had not annoyed Elena; but she was cautious about sharing her privacy, and at first gave out her secrets meanly, one at a time. When she did so, Bruno didn't laugh or mock her; he seemed to think her universe quite logical. There was joy, she found eventually, in sharing her intimate thoughts; her fantasies were not diminished but enhanced by having someone else who could participate in them, and the breaching of her wall of solitude was less painful than she had imagined.

'It's extraordinary, isn't it?' said Fulvia to Roberto. 'I thought she'd never speak to the poor lad and now she can't bear to let him out of her sight.'

'It's as though the rest of us don't exist.' Roberto sighed. 'I miss my little girl.'

As a child, Bruno had somewhere learned to ride a horse and

he persuaded Roberto to ask a neighbour if they could have the
use of two ponies. Within a few days, Elena could ride well enough
to canter beside him. They left her hut behind, and rode out
beyond the boar forest, to a ridge where no tyre track or hoofprint
had broken the ground. They made a base beside the ruined stump
of an oak tree. It didn't seem necessary to construct a shelter or
bring up their belongings; it was enough to be on this hill with
its white stones, with the call of the crows above. They sat in
silence, looking back over the woods towards Mantua, which was
just visible across the plain.

They imagined all the people in their factories, at their work,
in shops and streets and flats with laundry hanging out and food
cooking for the evening, willing the office clock to run down and
release them. They thought how strange it was that they would
never know these people and wondered if their lives were as real
or as urgent as their own.

On the ridge, they were detached from the anonymity of the
world — embodied for them by the chimneys, towers and smoking
outlines of the view. Elena's heart might be pounding from the
ride and her mind might be beating with thoughts, but the solid
earth and purple wildflowers were part of a harder reality, and
their indifference to her puffing lungs was a consolation.

Back at the farm Elena allowed Bruno entrance to her room,
a privilege denied even to her mother. Here they talked about
people they knew, or had seen in films. Bruno seemed able to
invent stories and people at will. He gave Elena accounts of the
imagined home lives of the teachers that made her ache from
laughing. He constructed a life for the driver who delivered food
in one of the huge electric wagons despatched from the industrial
zone outside Mantua; it included a spell in the French Foreign
Legion and five years in prison. Bruno gave him a violent wife
and beautiful twin daughters with ideas above their station.

Elena didn't try to match Bruno's invention, preferring the

wonder of the real world. She explained to him some of the awe she had felt on discovering how humans had evolved; the puzzle of how and why they had developed a sense of self-awareness and had become burdened with the foreknowledge of their own death – a weight no other creature had to bear.

'But wasn't that original sin?' said Bruno. 'Wasn't that the curse that God put on Adam and Eve?'

'I don't know. I haven't read the Bible.'

'How can you not know the Bible?'

Elena laughed. 'It's just stories, isn't it? I'd rather deal with the real world. It's so intricate and beautiful.'

'We weren't given a choice in the orphanage. Hearing the Bible stories was the best part of the day.'

'There are more scientific explanations for things now,' said Elena. 'Scanners are very advanced.'

One day Bruno suddenly pulled off his shirt and said, 'Look.'

Elena climbed off her bed and crossed the room. Bruno turned round and showed her his back. There were scars – large, raised weals that ran across his back, from one side of his ribcage to the other.

Without thinking, Elena reached out and touched one with the tip of her finger. 'Does it hurt?'

'No. Not now.'

'Who did it?'

'Some people.'

'At the orphanage?'

'No. Before that. But I don't remember where. There was a long journey by train.'

He turned to face her, taking her hand away, but holding it between his own. 'Never tell your parents. Promise.'

'I promise,' said Elena.

Her eyes were full of tears, but Bruno was smiling faintly, as though showing her his scars was a repayment for the way Elena had shared her private world with him. He carefully tucked his shirt back beneath his belt.

Sometimes it seemed to Elena that her thoughts were not fully validated until she had shared them with Bruno. His sharp edges helped reshape her; the friends she'd never had shone out of his alarming eyes.

Roberto and Fulvia's village had once been prosperous from maize and tobacco, but it suffered more than most in the Great Slump. Local agriculture reverted to smallholdings and self-sufficiency; the village came to be no more than a dormitory for people who worked in the city. By the time Elena and Bruno were seventeen, Italy was almost as it had been in the early twentieth century. Money was concentrated in few places, mostly in the north; private enterprise continued to find funds for scientific research at postgraduate level and successive governments to provide elementary teaching for children, but there was not much in between.

Bruno had started to read a good deal of history at school, where he had been moved into the A stream. It frustrated him that Elena seemed so unaware of the twisted shape of the society they lived in. He explained to her how financial institutions had all but bankrupted the developed world; she understood, but couldn't see what she was meant to do about it. She had one life to live. And surely every human being in history had been born into a world that was in some way peculiar: blown out of shape by cataclysm. After all, she told Bruno, the planet Earth only existed because of a galactic explosion at the start of time. 'You're such a scientist,' he said in despair.

Then one summer evening, when Elena and Bruno were sitting by their oak stump, she had a message on her screen: 'Come home at once. Emergency.' They rode their horses back to the neighbour's farm and ran home to find Elena's father being carried out of the house by ambulance men with a blanket over his face. He had suffered a stroke; it need not have been fatal, and a few years earlier would not have been; but the district's solitary ambulance was on another call, and when they finally got there it was too late.

Elena sat down in the kitchen. My father is dead. He who only a few minutes ago was living. The rest of time, she thought, starts now.

She went out into the stony field, knelt and lowered her face between her knees. She picked up handfuls of soil and let them trickle from her fingers on to her bowed head. She had been snatched up violently and did not recognise the place where she had been put down. She lifted up her eyes to the hills, as though some help might be there; but all she sensed was how long it would take to realign herself to this new world.

Bruno was furious. His protector had been taken from him by the bastard god of luck who had once more shat on his life. He disappeared from the house to be alone with his anger.

The days that followed were so full of things to do that Elena had no time to grieve. It was more than a week before she and Bruno were able to escape the clotted atmosphere of the house. Up by the oak tree, while the horses cropped the grass, Elena felt again the hard indifference of the earth. This time it was no consolation.

For the first time, tears came, not squeezed drops, but full drenched sobbing, as Bruno held her in his arms.

'He was so . . . *kind*,' Elena said.

'He was a god,' said Bruno.

As they held on to one another, Bruno did what no one had managed for Elena. Drawing on the limits of what he knew, he cobbled together a patchwork of physics, history and wishful thinking – a hypothetical universe in which Roberto lived on, planning such a reunion with his daughter as would make them laugh at the pain of their brief separation. In this version of existence, even as she smiled a little at its improbabilities, Elena was able to hold her father tight.

Roberto was buried in the village churchyard after a Christian service. Bruno was familiar with the words and the hopes they expressed; Elena was puzzled by the way the priest merely stated a belief in everlasting life without trying to make a case for it. They went to please Fulvia, who, having nowhere else to look, had turned to religion in her time of loss.

Afterwards, there were the mourners to be comforted and fed in the farmhouse kitchen. Elena took round plates of cake and sweets; Bruno poured cheap fizzing wine. Both longed to be alone and were dismayed when cousins from Verona sat down and made themselves at home, engaging Fulvia in reminiscences of Roberto as a boy.

A few weeks later, Fulvia told them at dinner she had some news to give them, and something in her voice made Elena glance swiftly at Bruno.

'Children,' she said, 'I've heard from the bank how much money is left. Roberto put aside enough to pay for one year of tuition for Elena at the university. That money's in a separate account. For the rest, there's just a tiny bit we'd saved. We can no longer afford to live here. I've asked them to sell the house and the farm. I'm moving to a flat in town. I've found work as a cleaner, starting next month. Elena, there'll be room on the couch for you, but, Bruno, from the end of this term I can no longer be your mother.'

'But, Mama.' Elena leapt up with her arms outstretched. 'Bruno's doing so well. He's joined the A class. You know how much he reads.'

'I do, I do,' said Fulvia quickly. 'He's an absolute mine of information. I'm sorry, Elenissima. Dear Bruno.' She put her hand on his wrist.

'I . . . understand,' said Bruno, the emotion of the moment making his accent thick again.

As she watched him struggle with his thoughts, Elena felt a surge of love and panic.

'But what will you do?' she said.

'Try to find work,' he said. 'Like everyone else.'

In less dire times, Bruno would have been able to finish his studies; but there was no public money any more.

They rode together one last time to the oak tree on the ridge. The city of Mantua was invisible under heavy cloud.

'Where will you go?' said Elena.

Bruno's eyes were barely visible, his head lowered against the drizzling rain. 'Probably Trieste,' he said. 'I might find work in a boatyard.'

'Stay in Mantua,' said Elena. 'There must be something you could do there.'

'What? Rubbish collection?'

'But you'd be near us.'

'No.'

Elena put her hand on his arm. 'But you've been happy with us?'

Bruno breathed in heavily. 'It was better than the life I had before, but I never thought it would last. All the time I worked and read I didn't expect it would lead to anything. I read because I was interested. I learned to live in my imagination.'

Elena stiffened under his coldness. 'But what about me? I mean, you and me. We're . . . friends.' In a moment of horror she thought she might have imagined it all. Her eyes were fixed on his face.

Bruno didn't smile or soften. 'I didn't have a friend before, so

I didn't know what it might be like, Elena. And was that it? Was that friendship?'

'It's more than that.'

'How do you know?'

Elena flushed. 'The other girls at school, people who call them-selves friends, they gossip and laugh and . . . Well, they have fun, I'm not denying that. But you can see there's no real close-ness. They don't feel what we do — that they're almost the same person.'

'How do you know that Giulia doesn't have that feeling for Marco?'

'Because they only talk about clothes.'

'And what can you compare me with? You always said you never had a friend before.'

'I didn't need one. Now I never want to be without you.'

'Is it "love", then?' said Bruno. 'Is that what it is?'

'Of course it is.' Elena stood up in agitation. 'You are so perverse, Bruno. Try to be real for once. We're not in one of your stories. This love won't come to you again.'

'Is it what you felt for your father?'

'No. It's different. And it's more wonderful because it's with a stranger.'

Bruno ran his hands through his hair. He looked up at Elena and said, 'I've never felt what I think is meant by joy or happiness, except through you.'

'Thank you. You can stop there. That's what I wanted you to say.'

But he went on, 'Perhaps when I was young — in that camp and then the orphanage — my means of feeling these things was . . . burned away. Sometimes when I've seen the light in your eyes, when you're laughing, I've felt it then. But I don't know whether it's your happiness or mine. And I think perhaps that makes me sick.'

'No, no, that's what I feel,' said Elena with a cry, sitting down beside him, gripping his wrist in her hands. 'If that's sick, then we're both ill. That's what I love about you, Bruno. I can take joy in a creature . . . in a person who's not me!'

She threw herself into his arms and he held her against his chest. He stroked her hair. 'But how can that be?' he said.

'I don't know. It's just the way it is. And if you leave you'll take away my only chance.'

They sat on the ground for a long time, indifferent to the rain. Elena burrowed close under Bruno's coat, feeling his heart against her breast. Self-awareness told her time was passing; then she held him tighter and for a moment could forget.

For Elena, life without Bruno was much like life before Bruno: solitary. The difference was that by now she had made her anti-social oddity into a socially acceptable career. Her teachers had no doubt that she could make a life in research; she was the most advanced student they had ever had at the local school. She needed no urging and very little guidance from them; her knowledge already exceeded theirs in all areas of biology. The university tutors allowed her into the second year at college, since her written work, submitted with her application for finance, had already covered the first-year syllabus. This meant that with the money Roberto had left, there was only one year's worth of fees to find, and such was the promise of Elena's work that the regional board agreed to lend the sum in full.

It all seemed so unlikely to Fulvia, as she went off in the late afternoon to her office-cleaning job. Why on earth was her little girl so good at something – anything? But it was also a relief. She watched Elena carefully to see if she was strained or unhappy, but there was never any sign of it; this complicated work came naturally to her and she was perhaps, thought Fulvia, one of those rare people who just find a niche that fits their shape.

Their apartment in the city was on the third floor of a modern block where the bass notes of the neighbours' entertainments boomed through the wall. Elena slept on the living-room couch, which opened up to make a fairly comfortable bed. She stayed late at the university library in the evenings; she timed her return to coincide with Fulvia's at about ten, when they would share some pasta with beans and talk about the day.

After Fulvia had gone to bed, Elena used her screen to search for signs of Bruno. He might have changed his name, she thought; he had always been reluctant to accept that he was a Duranti, feeling it was arrogant to claim kinship with Roberto in this way. Elena sent messages to him, but he never replied; perhaps he had also changed his ID. She felt sure that he was angry, that a sense of his small gods always ready to ruin his life had prevented him from viewing the love he felt for her as real. It was as though he thought it better not to let the feeling near him.

She loved him, but he was not there. His absence was a wound that never ceased to seep and throb. It was absurd, she told herself. What mattered was the love they felt; whether or not they were in the same room was of no significance. It would not be long before, as physical mass, they were both decomposing underground; so what did it matter if meanwhile their bodies were in different places? How could that possibly be important?

So much did she rely on her rational brain to guide her life that she was angry when it failed her now, when no process of reason could stop her wound from aching.

When Elena graduated, she joined her university's last remaining research programme, but needed work to pay for dinner and rent. She managed to find a job at the warehouse that despatched food wagons to outlying areas; she had to reconcile the orders and the loads, make sure they added up. She wondered what fantasy

Bruno might invent about her private life: a short one, probably. When her doctorate was complete, she was offered a teaching post in the department of neuroscience; the pay was hardly better than in the food depot, but the work excited her. She thought of Bruno all the time, there was never a moment when he was not in her mind; but she was able to have other thoughts, to keep him at the edge of her awareness. If she felt him spreading out to occupy a larger or more painful space, she renewed her concentration on the work at hand. In an odd way, it helped.

What most excited everyone in the field was the idea that they might one day discover the physical basis (or 'neural substrates', as they put it) of human consciousness. No one was quite sure what they would do with the information when they found it, but like the unconquered moon before 1969, it was there for the taking.

The breakthrough came with the invention of a scanner that gave detailed images of brain activity. Early scanners had offered information in broad, coloured swirls; but the new SADS (synaptic activity dual spectroscopy) scanner showed what went on in the actual synapse. Chaos, apparently. There was far too much information to be helpful, until a German postdoctoral student called Alois Glockner enlisted the help of a commercial software company to help run the scans at super-slow speed. After many months of studying, he observed something striking: that there was a moment when all the data that a creature gathered from its five senses seemed to cohere with the input from its large internal organs. For a moment what was known as 'binding' took place, followed by 'ignition': so the creature – be it human, dolphin or crow – had the sensation of being a 'self'. The moment passed too quickly to be useful; but Glockner saw it, recorded it, and, like all good brain explorers before him, planted his flag on the relevant part. He called it 'Glockner's Isthmus'.

In the light of Glockner, Elena's university appealed for funds to buy a SADS scanner. Their plea was answered by a private individual – a woman whose grandfather had made many millions in the world of finance. His bank had been hired by the Italian government in 1998 to find a way of presenting the Italian economy as being ready for the European single currency and had, by sleight of hand, concealed billions of lire's worth of debt. Perhaps, given what followed, there was a sense of guilt behind the donation of the SADS scanner, but no one in Elena's department cared about the motive; they blessed the woman who had answered their plea and queued up to use the wondrous machine.

The main part of the mystery remained unanswered. Glockner had illuminated the moment of base-level consciousness; but where in the brain was the additional faculty of self-awareness that had enabled human beings to write, record, plan, compose, explore and become aware that they were human? This question was soon the focus of every university department and every hospital lucky enough to have a SADS scanner.

Elena's researches came to a halt when she returned one summer evening to find her mother dead on the bathroom floor. At the age of fifty-three Fulvia had succumbed to the heart weakness that had carried off her mother and her grandmother.

My God, thought Elena as she sat on the side of the bed waiting for the ambulance, to think that as a child I used to long for solitude . . . And now my father, Bruno and my mother . . . gone.

The undertakers arranged for a cremation in Mantua, but an impulse made Elena take the ashes back to the village where she had been brought up. She found Roberto's grave, borrowed a spade from her old classmate Jacopo and dug a hole large enough for the wooden container. She tried not to think about what was inside. She imagined the crematorium was not too fussy about which ashes went into which urn; the contents could equally be a makeweight of flour, other people, or sand.

As she knelt on the damp grass, Elena looked down at the small box. The atoms that had made her mother had existed since the start of time, and in the great economy of the universe would be recombined for further use, she told herself – wishing at the same time she might sometimes be spared the starkness of such knowledge. Her only hope was that for Fulvia this was a proper ending, a satisfactory termination and release. If science was correct and there was only everlasting matter in the brain, then proper death – eternal extinction of the individual – was hard to come by.

Perhaps, thought Elena, standing up, wiping her eyes on the backs of her hands, the difference between individuals was equally unclear. If not just the brain but the quirks that made the individual were composed of recycled matter only, it was hard to be sure where the edges of one such being ended and another person began.

She stood, straightened her spine and sniffed. She walked back along the road that led past the farm where she had grown up. A chained dog leapt up and barked as she passed the gate. There was a light on in the kitchen, but she did not let her eyes stray from the path that led from the farmhouse and up into the hills beyond it.

Elena had no clear plan in mind, though she was aware of a desire to have contact with her past. Her footsteps took her where they had led her so many times before, and soon she was at the site of a ruined hut, its corrugated-iron roof torn off and its drainage run smashed by large white stones.

In the mud she could make out the head of a blue-painted plaster Madonna, its broken gaze still threatening. It would have made more sense to her if there had been no trace left of what had surely been another life, different from the one she now inhabited. For all that she accepted with gratitude the shape of her childish self, she felt nothing in common with the little girl who had strained her lungs to bursting point to bring Emilio Rizzo across the finishing line.

On her return to Mantua, Elena found a letter from a woman called Beatrice Rossi, a Roman who specialised in the brains of dogs. Dr Rossi had read a paper of Elena's and wondered if she would like to meet.

Elena knew of Rossi by reputation, and it was not a good one. Beatrice Rossi was puzzled by the idea of dog memory. She noticed that when a mongrel puppy called Magda slept, she seemed to have dreams that agitated her. Since Magda had never left the laboratory, however, she must be having access to some genetic or race memory of events. Rossi reasoned that if she could trick the dog's brain into thinking it was asleep while it was actually awake, she might be able to observe a very superior dog in action — a super-dog with access to some sort of collective unconscious. Early indications were encouraging, and in her excitement Dr Rossi made exaggerated claims. Magda's enhanced awareness would be nothing like that of humans. It would be as elevated, yet canine; 'And this', she wrote, 'is what Wittgenstein meant when he said that if a lion could speak, we would not understand him.'

In the final experiment her team injected a carefully prepared solution, going into the dog's brain via the eye socket, like the old asylum lobotomisers. Five researchers held their breath, like astronomers waiting for a new planet to float into their view. Magda ran around a bit, barked twice then fell into a profound sleep from which she was only roused some hours later by the sound of her biscuit tin being shaken.

The problem was not that the experiments had failed, but they had cost the impoverished Roman taxpayer a large sum of money. Dr Rossi had thought it wise to disappear for some time to Grosseto on the Tuscan coast.

Grieving, lonely and desperate, Elena overcame her scruples and bought a ticket to Grosseto. She went to the given address and rang bell D on a house that overlooked the sea. Having read only learned articles by Beatrice Rossi, she expected a grey-haired, bespectacled academic. When the door of the apartment opened she was surprised to see a handsome woman of about forty with dark hair cut just above the shoulder, dressed in black boots, navy skirt and tobacco-coloured cashmere sweater. Elena also noticed red lipstick as Dr Rossi smiled her welcome and rebuked the dogs, introduced as Mario, Magda and Coco, who greeted the newcomer.

They went for a walk along the beach under the high grey cloud, with Magda, the dog who had failed to reveal the divine secrets, trotting through the shallows of the sea with the others in her wake. It was a cold spring day and Elena found her city coat was hardly warm enough to keep out the wind.

After the day of the burial, she had shed no more tears for her mother; but the loss had made her weary. Every dry-eyed step in the sand was an effort when her body cried out for rest. She felt loss like a weight across her shoulders, as though that high, indifferent sky were bearing down on her. She looked out to the grey sea, through the grey invisible winds, as though she might see in them the shadow of her parents or of the one living man who could bring her peace. She saw only empty air and the nerveless agitation of the waves; she felt absence not as a void but as a force.

'So I've read your papers,' Beatrice Rossi was saying, 'and I think we could work together. What I like is your impatience.'

'Not very scientific, I'm afraid.'

'Which of the old theories irritates you most?' said Beatrice Rossi.

Elena was glad to hear flippancy for once. 'The idea of the self as a "necessary fiction",' she said. 'That electrochemical activity in the brain has generated this clown, this self-delusion, which natural selection has then favoured.'

Beatrice Rossi laughed. 'Yes, that's annoying.'

'There are plenty more,' said Elena.

The wind whipped Dr Rossi's hair back from her face. 'Oh yes,' she said. 'What about the point-and-click theory? That we are like early home computers. That the self is like the icon of the trash can — a false cartoon representation of the real work done on the hard drive.'

Elena found herself warming to this woman, even while an academic part of her urged caution. They walked on till it began to grow dark, sharing their frustration that even the SADS scanner had not been able to provide the solutions it had promised.

'Stay for dinner,' said Dr Rossi. 'There's a good restaurant five minutes from my flat. Do you like fish? We'll drink wine and you can stay the night if you don't mind being woken by the dogs.'

In the end, Elena stayed three days with her new friend. Dr Rossi was affectionate; she called her 'darling'; she made her laugh.

When she returned to Mantua there was a handwritten message on paper waiting for her at the university.

'I was sorry to hear about your mother. I've been abroad. A lot has happened. I will be in touch with you again, if you allow me. My screen ID is below. Bruno.'

Elena was thirty-two years old before Bruno felt ready finally to meet again.

Bruno had use of a small house in the Sabine Hills, he said, about an hour and a half from Rome; they agreed a date, and in a sultry August, during the summer vacation from her university, Elena took the train south.

An hour after her arrival in Rome, the electric taxi turned off the main road to Rieti and began to take her up through hills that seemed untouched by the events of the last hundred years. Never having had much in the first place, they had had little to lose — these villages each with its dusty square, single food shop and narrow main street edged by tiny houses and tubs of dry geraniums.

The car was running along a ridge from which they could see nothing but green, wood-covered slopes and the foothills of the Apennines. Elena wondered if she would recognise Bruno after all this time. He might be bald or prematurely grey. He might have become a businessman, complacent, easy-going, bland; he could have become embittered — an outsider with a sense of grievance. Even if he was unaltered, was she herself the person who had loved him once? If we change, can love exist outside us? Is such continuing love the embodiment of our former selves?

One of his recent messages had told her in a factual way that he had married a woman called Lucia, that they lived in Zurich and had a daughter called Caterina. Elena felt no happiness for him in his married state, yet neither did she feel downcast. Whatever his feelings for this Lucia, they seemed irrelevant to what she and Bruno had known; his other family was beside the point.

As they came into the village, she felt her mouth go dry. She was scared he might be different. No: she wanted him to be changed — so it would be easier to live without him; she wanted him to have descended into the run of the middling people she saw each day, dealt with politely and cared nothing for.

Alas, that wasn't true either, she admitted to herself. She didn't care what pain the unaltered man would bring her: so long as he was all that she remembered, then her life was still a flame — not a chain of days, but a chance of glory.

The car turned between two buildings, up over ruts and potholes, the rubber tyres popping and grinding as they rose to a hilltop where there stood a modest rectangular house, tile-roofed, alone. Elena paid the taxi and made her way forward slowly, dragging her case over sharp white stones. The door of the house was locked and there was no bell or knocker; so, leaving her case, she walked round to the other side, where the valley was spread out beyond an olive grove. And there on the terrace she saw him, the intruder, standing, braced, waiting for her.

She stopped for a moment to compose herself. He was wearing a Panama hat and he had a beard, but she knew every contour of his body, the smallest inflection of his stance – his head to one side, the large hands hanging loose, then turned palm-out to welcome her.

He pushed back his hat a little so she could see him. Beneath the beard his face broke into a lopsided smile, pulling at his left eye, revealing the twisted incisor.

As she went towards him, she stumbled, so he had to step forward and catch her.

He lifted her and held her tightly to his chest. Upright again on her own feet, Elena pressed her face to his shoulder.

There was a maid called Silvia, a young woman from the village with a child who clung to her leg as she prepared dinner. The noise of clashing pans rose through the house.

Bruno showed Elena to a bedroom where she unpacked and tried to regain control of herself. She washed her face in the bathroom, applied some make-up to her eyes and managed an uncertain smile.

She left the room with automatic steps, went quickly down the stairs and out on to the terrace, where Bruno was waiting, now hatless, in clean clothes. He looked bedraggled from the shower, almost as he had looked the first day he stepped in with Roberto from the rain.

He handed Elena a glass of cold wine and poured one for himself.

'It's a beautiful place,' she said, raising her glass to him.

He smiled, raised his in return and sat down at the long table overlooking the olive grove.

Then at last he spoke. 'Thank you for coming. After all this time you'd have been quite within your rights to . . .'

'I know.'

His voice was deeper than she remembered. Had it acquired a different accent, too?

'Where have you been?' she said.

'I joined the army. It was the only work I could find. We had a detachment in the Middle East Peace Force.'

'Why didn't you contact me?'

'I had no money. I had to make a life.'

'But you could have kept in touch. A message once a month.'

'It was easier my way.'

'Not for me it wasn't.'

Bruno drained his glass. Elena twisted her hands. She wanted time to run much faster, so she could have enough evidence to see if he was still the same man.

Silvia brought tomatoes chopped with garlic and oil on toasted white bread.

'Tell me what you've done,' said Bruno.

When she had finished, he said, 'I always knew you'd be a scientist.'

Elena shrugged. 'And you. After the army?'

'I did what I told you I might. Boatbuilding. I went to Lucerne, in Switzerland, where they still had money and orders. And then I began to write in the evenings. I had a room in a house that overlooked the lake. The landlady gave us dinner at six and then I was free to work.'

'What did you write?'

'Books.'

Elena laughed. 'What sort of books?'

While he described them to her she wished she hadn't asked. She wanted to know each detail of the stories he told her about; she yearned to understand which part of his life or mind they had come from; she felt the need to take them – his imagined people and their fictional deeds – back inside herself, her own being, where she felt they must in some way have originated.

Silvia brought more food, Bruno poured wine; Elena felt contented, and, at the same time, alarmed. I don't need to live at this level of danger or openness, she thought. This intimacy is not necessary; no one is compelling me to open my inmost self and lay it naked, undefended, against that of another – merely for the joy of the communion.

The sun went down the sky; Silvia and her daughter left for her house in the village. They talked on and on, Elena explaining why her work was at a critical point, Bruno asking what kind of life she and Fulvia had had together. It was one o'clock before they felt able to reopen the events of childhood.

Elena looked at Bruno through the light of the gas lamp on the table. He was the same person. He was the boy who had wakened her ability to connect to others. Without him, what would she have been? He had acquired some confidence, but it had not changed him; there was still a natural tact that had kept him from referring to the childhood years till now. He had always had that sense of propriety, even when what he said was so direct. She watched him laughing as he reminded her of the accident that had befallen the Tuscans on the final leg of the regional cycling championship, when he had gone flying over the handlebars.

It was starting to grow light, the Apennine foothills becoming dimly visible again, when he finally pushed back his chair.

'You must be tired,' he said.

They went inside the house and upstairs to the landing. His room was one way, hers the other, but she went uninvited through his door with him. They took their clothes off in the faint light.

He held her in his arms and said, 'Elena, I don't know. I'm not sure if this . . .'

Through the thin cotton of his shirt she could feel the raised weals on the small of his back. She said, 'It's all right.'

He said, 'I think Roberto . . .'

Putting her finger to his lips, she said, 'Ssh.'

When Elena was awoken by the sun coming through a half-open shutter, she found that she was alone in the bedroom. There was a note from Bruno saying he had gone to the village for milk and bread. He had left his screen on the table by the window, as though he had been hard at work since dawn. Before she could stop herself Elena had settled down in Bruno's chair to read.

Another Life

At first I think it is one more settlement we are to capture and subdue. The clay houses and the ramparts of the citadel are familiar to me from my life as a soldier. How many such places have we passed through as we make our way east.

My horse Kasam seems to think so too. He rears up in expectation of the battle and begins to snort. I have to restrain him from galloping straight at the gate. He is a warlike creature, yet gentle when we are in camp at night.

I dismount and lead Kasam to a thicket of trees where green leaves suggest water. I tie his reins to a low branch and give him dried grass to eat from my saddle bag. He tosses his strong neck and whinnies with his own kind of pleasure.

I am told to ride ahead because I know some words of the languages we encounter. We know that a column of reinforcements leaves our homeland every month. In mountainous country I ride Kasam to a peak, look back across the plain and can see a tower of dust on the horizon. It makes me glad to think of the young men with their hearts full of hope as they journey across the sand.

Among the trees, I find a stream with clear water. I go back to Kasam and lead him to it. He lifts his hooves slowly, then walks in up to his belly. He lowers his head to the current and when he lifts it after drinking there are clear drops on the whiskers of his muzzle.

Elena came up for breath and looked across at the Sabine Hills, green and indubitably real. She was laughing with relief, though she was also disappointed. She was pleased that the story was so far from Bruno's life and hers, yet for the same reason found it hard to take seriously. She knew already, after only one page, that she would never be able to read anything Bruno wrote as a normal reader would — objectively, with critical enjoyment. This was a great loss. Or maybe not — she had read so few non-scientific books that she had no way of telling if this thing was any good.

After a deep breath, she began to read again. The story was about a man called Imraz, presumably a Muslim soldier, one of the first to push out east from the Arabian peninsula, subduing towns and villages in the rush towards the Indian subcontinent, bringing the good news of the Prophet but without the time or the manpower to settle the conquered territories according to their holy law. Imraz was married, it turned out, and had two soldier sons, though there was frustratingly little detail about his wife.

By this stage, Elena had understood that Imraz was dead. The citadel of the opening paragraph was a kind of limbo where the dead lingered until their name had been spoken for the last time on earth.

Then, as Imraz wandered inside the citadel, Elena's eye caught on a woman's name.

Then I see a young woman I knew before I was married. Her name is Malika and I am surprised that she is dead.

I give the reins of the horse to Akmal, the friend of my youth, and tell him to wait for me while I run after Malika.

She is going into a house when I catch her by the elbow. 'Malika? What has brought you to this place?'

She turns and looks into my face. 'I died for love,' she says. 'For love of you, Imraz. Now I am waiting.'

'And are you not yet forgotten?' I ask.

'No. A poet wrote a song with my name in it. Until the last time it is sung, I shall be here.'

I stand on the threshold of the house. 'I did not know you loved me so much,' I say.

Malika lowers her eyes and I see the tears fall. 'I was afraid of what you would say. And I was afraid for your wife.'

'A man can love more than one woman, Malika. A man is allowed more than one wife.' I reach out my hand and place it on her arm. 'What could I have said to harm you? I would have been happy to know that you loved me.'

Am I Malika? thought Elena. Does he see me as someone he discarded or who was too timid to speak the truth?

Or am I merely Akmal, the 'friend of my youth'? She craved more detail and she feared it. Imraz seemed in the next section most of all concerned for his horse, Kasam, described as a 'close-coupled gelding', bred from a long line by Imraz's father. Surely this reflected Bruno's ease with horses and his love of them from some secret part of his childhood.

It took her almost an hour to finish. It turned out in the end that

it was neither the wife, the mistress nor the horse that really mattered
to Imraz; it was the father who counted — the ghost whom he was
now at liberty to release. The story ended:

I kneel and remember my father, whom I loved. Seven years
I mourned him. Seven years he appeared in my dreams as
though still living. For seven years it fell to me to tell him
each night, so softly, fearing to appal him, that he was dead.

I remember my father in the days of my infancy when he
held me in his arms and pointed to the stars in the sky. I sing
to myself the songs he taught me as he sat beside my bed. I
hear his voice again, modest and low, as he tells me of the
battles he fought and of the wounds from which he bled. I
see his eyes, loving and kind towards my mother and my
sisters. I do not think of him in the last days of his sickness
but as the young man who turned his face to the sun.

When I raise my head, my father is standing before me.

'You have come just in time,' he says. 'You have done
well.'

These are the words I have wanted to hear. I had not
known until he speaks how much I had wanted to hear them.
I lift my shirt and see a spear wound under my ribs. There
are weals on my back, as though from a whip.

'My time has come to disperse,' says my father. 'We are
made of fragments and they must go back. They have finished
with this man.'

My father has started to grow faint before my eyes. I reach
out my arms to embrace him as I have longed to do each
day since his death. But when I bring my arms together he
has slipped through them. Once again I reach out to him and
once more I bring back my arms empty.

Immediately a strong light begins to shine through him
and through the body of Kasam. I take a step back. I see the

outline of the man and the horse become vague and trembling. The energy that escapes their unravelling mass is for a moment so great that I can see by its light to the end of the world.

I can see each particle of matter that made them. In the flash of the skin of a dolphin as it shoulders the wave and the tip of the feather of an owl as it falls in the night. In the end of a leaf of a plant by a road, in the fifth of the six legs of a fly. I see time going fast over mountains and rivers, over cities and plains and down into the cold oceans.

I fall to my knees, scrape up dust, let it fall on my head, because this world I have been shown is grander by far than any world a god could make. I see a swarm of these specks as they surge and re-form in the hand of a human child to be born where different stars hang beneath a southern sky.

Then, with a new god in my heart, I start to make my long way back to the place of my undoing.

So fierce was Elena's attention that at one point, when Imraz showed such affection for his horse, she had to stop reading. I cannot, she told herself, be jealous of a horse — of a fictional gelding.

Not having read the Bible, she did not hear the borrowed rhythms, nor was she aware of a reference to Virgil's Underworld when Imraz reached out to embrace his father. What intrigued her was that this man was a soldier, as Bruno had been, that he had the same weals on his back. And who would have thought that the missing father would overshadow all else?

She had not long finished it when she heard Bruno call her name downstairs.

Soon after her return to Mantua, Elena received a message from Beatrice Rossi. 'Darling, you must come at once to Athens. We are on the verge. BR xx'

Beatrice was waiting for her at the airport, and on the way into town she told Elena what had happened. A dock worker in Piraeus had fallen from a scaffold and impaled himself on an iron bar extruding from a piece of concrete. It had pierced the underside of his jaw and had been driven up into his brain. The surgeons had sawn off the bar below the jaw on site, but had not dared try to remove it.

The odd thing was that the man had not lost consciousness. On the contrary, said Beatrice Rossi, he was extremely alert. He was talkative, highly focussed, with a prodigious memory and detailed plans for the future — more so, it appeared, than before the accident.

Dr Rossi had reserved a room for Elena in her hotel near Syntagma Square. 'It sounds as though the iron bar's done the job for us,' said Elena.

'Exactly,' said Dr Rossi. 'I think it's pressing on the area where the faculty of raised human consciousness is located.'

'The famous "neural substrates",' said Elena.

'The very ones! He's fully self-aware at all times, he can't just lapse back. So if we can scan him, we can find the precise area and see how it works.'

The accident had taken place ten days earlier and an item in a popular London publication had awakened the world's interest. Under the caption 'Kebab Man Puzzles Greek Doctors', it stumbled close to what was important about the patient, without quite getting there.

There were two problems for Elena and Beatrice in Athens: Dr Rossi was still regarded with suspicion in the scientific world, and access to the 'Kebab Man' was limited. However, in his hyper-alert state, he had welcomed the attention of journalists, believing he had something important to tell them.

'I suppose,' said Elena, 'if you can't get to see him as a scientist, you could pretend to be a reporter.'

'That would be the first time in history,' said Beatrice, 'that a doctor has gained access to a hospital room by pretending to be a journalist.'

Using all her charm, Beatrice Rossi persuaded the clinic to grant her an interview as a writer for an Italian scientific journal. It was one to which she had contributed; it was only the use of her mother's surname that was deceitful. In her half-hour with the patient, she convinced him that he should be scanned again with Beatrice herself present.

'He's a bit of a monster,' she told Elena that night. 'How often in an hour are you really self-aware, do you suppose? I mean, you drive a car and play the piano while thinking about something else . . . But really self-aware as only humans can be?'

'Maybe three or four times an hour?' said Elena. 'For a few seconds each time. Then I relapse into a sort of half-asleep, screen-saver condition.'

'This man is "on" permanently,' said Beatrice. 'The pressure on his brain is making him the most *sapiens Homo* who ever lived.'

During the first scan, Beatrice Rossi not only observed, but directed. Under questioning from the Greek technicians, she was obliged to reveal her identity and then, at the delighted patient's insistence, to take control of the process.

They scanned him for three days. The two women, Beatrice and Elena, made quite a pair as they arrived each morning at the clinic. Down the corridor they would walk together towards the scanning room, while staff, journalists and patients parted before them: Beatrice Rossi with her white lab coat flying open to reveal caramel skirt and black boots and Elena Duranti, the mousy sidekick, in her woollen trousers and glasses, padding along beside her.

On the fourth day they discovered the truth. The defining quality of human consciousness, the thing that had given the world Leonardo, Mozart, Shakespeare and had made humans little lower than the angels, was not an entity, but a connection. It was an open loop that ran between Glockner's Isthmus and the site of episodic memory. It was a link between two pre-existent faculties. It was fragile; it was, in evolutionary terms, very young — aged in the low tens of thousands of years. Through its speed-of-light pathway, the isthmus sensation of selfhood was retuned, refined and enriched by memory. The impingement of the iron rod had set the Kebab Man's loop to permanently 'open'; it had compromised his ability to lapse into normal or 'screen-saver' consciousness, the state in which humans happily perform for most of their waking hours.

For millions of years, the phenomenon of Glockner's brief neural unity had existed side by side with the faculty of autobiographical memory — but in isolation, like France and England before the invention of the boat. Then a mistake — a mutation in a single cell division in a single individual some tens of thousands of years back — had established a link. It was genetically the most successful mutation of all time because the endowment of self-awareness — particularly a voluntary self-awareness — allowed its possessors to infer thought processes in others and to predict what they were going to do; it let them empathise, guess, anticipate, manipulate, out-think, out-fight — and, where necessary, co-operate.

Drs Rossi and Duranti left the clinic in Athens to prepare their findings for publication. The following week, surgeons successfully removed the iron bar from the Kebab Man's brain, and he regained the ability to lapse at will into a normal and less demanding state of consciousness.

Elena and Beatrice sat on the runway, ready to take off for Rome.

'It seems almost an anticlimax,' said Beatrice Rossi, fastening her seat belt.

'I know,' said Elena. 'I know. But the fun will come when everyone works out what it means for their own disciplines.'

Over the Adriatic they toasted their discovery of why humans
are as they are with Prosecco from plastic glasses.

'You're famous!' wrote Bruno to Elena. 'All those afternoons in
your little hut. All those nights in your room reading! I am very
proud.'

Elena was offered the post of deputy director at the Institute
for Human Research in Turin, with the promise that she would
accede to the top job in due course. She was pleased to have a
position that enabled her to carry on with the work that fascinated
her and to have enough money for a comfortable apartment in a
pleasant section of the city. She wished only that the good fortune
had come a little earlier in her life, when she might have shared
it with her parents.

After the storm that surrounded the publication of her and
Beatrice Rossi's paper had finally died down, Elena had time to
think a little more about her own life – her own short time as a
possessor of this mutant link – and how she ought to spend it.

This meant Bruno. For the next two years, they continued
to meet at the house in the Sabine Hills whenever they could.
As they sat one day looking down over the olive grove into the
valley below, Elena asked if she could read the new story he
had written.

'I don't think you'll like it,' he said.

'I might. I've liked other ones.'

'I got the idea from *Nineteen Eighty-Four* by George Orwell,'
said Bruno. 'At one point Julia, the main female character, mentions
that she lost her virginity at the age of sixteen to a Party member
who was later arrested. I liked the way this man was of no import-
ance in Orwell's story, but central to his own.'

'I see,' said Elena. 'So it's this man's story?'

'Yes. He's a rogue, he doesn't believe in the Party. He's a hero,
yet he's just a footnote in Winston Smith's life.'

Elena let his choice of words settle. 'And me? Am I a footnote in your life?'

'No. You're the heroine.'

'That's an old-fashioned word.'

'But the trouble with me,' said Bruno, 'is that I have more than one story. You're the main character in this one. In the hills here. And here.' He put his hand against his head.

'And in your childhood?' said Elena.

'No. I was the main character in that. And then Roberto. And then you.'

'And would you like to know where you stand with me?' said Elena.

'I'm afraid to hear,' said Bruno. 'In my experience women are absolutists. They're liable to blame you for things that happened before you met and for things you can't change. Even for their own mistakes.'

'I never imagined you were so defensive,' Elena said.

Bruno was ready. 'On the one hand I see this abstract force, this flame, this life-changing thing between us. And on the other I see the material circumstances of living – the arrangements, places, flats, people, jobs. And I just think how can we best accommodate the two: the flame and the facts. The flame always comes first. We can bend the facts to accommodate it. But you . . .'

He waved his arm.

'I what?' said Elena.

'If you can't have all you want rolled up into one place, one ideal existence, you'd be prepared to throw out the best part. Out of petulance.'

'I would never do that,' said Elena. 'Never.' At the same time she felt a kind of panic at the otherness of Bruno.

At the age of thirty-six, Elena was preoccupied with the thought of children. While she knew she had another decade of fertility there were good reasons for being a younger mother. She had never felt the urge described by many women – as though reproduction were their deepest need. Perhaps it was because she had been an only child, she thought, or because the prevailing state of childhood – powerless dependence – had not appealed to her.

What had become clear was that if she were ever to have a child, she would like Bruno to be its father. She loved him more than she could ever love another man, so the idea of fusing her cells with his was a logical intimacy. There was also an urge less scientific. The pain of her relationship with Bruno lay in separation – not just in times and distances but sometimes, she felt, in the very fact that they were different beings. Even together they were apart. Their child would never suffer from this sense of being sundered.

In her laboratory, she smiled at such a fancy; but at home at night, glancing now and then at her screen to see if he had thought about her, it did not seem fantastic, it seemed true.

It was autumn when they next met – autumn with a hazy sun whose warmth and light seemed at odds with the smell of the damp chestnut leaves underfoot. It was a half-season, one that Elena remembered well from the woods above her village.

After they had eaten on the terrace and Silvia the maid had gone home with her daughter, it became suddenly cold. They went inside and Bruno made a fire from olive wood in the stone-floored fireplace. They sat in chairs on either side with their feet resting on a low, padded table in between.

'I've been thinking about children,' Elena said. 'Do you like being a father?'

'Yes. I was never a brother or son, so I don't know about that. But I think father is the role I would anyway like best.'

'And do you think we should have a child, Bruno? You and I? I'm still a good age for it. And it would be something for us to share.'

'A souvenir of—'

'No, not a backward look. A future. Something indisputable and together after all the time apart.'

Bruno stood up and turned so he was facing out of the window. 'I doubt whether Lucia would like it,' he said.

'She would never know. She doesn't know about this, does she?' said Elena, gesturing round them.

'No. But Caterina, she wouldn't—'

'I'm not the kind of person to turn up on the doorstep of your house with a babe in arms. I have enough money to look after a child well. I have no desire to break up your other family.'

Bruno turned back to face Elena and sat down again opposite her. 'Let me tell you what I did when I left you,' he said.

Elena fell silent.

'After my time in the army, I went back to Slovenia to try to find out more about my childhood. I found the orphanage in Trieste and they showed me their records. I had been there only nine months when Roberto took me away. I was recorded under the number Two Hundred and Thirty-Seven, Male, and the name Duranti was added later. He had visited several times to fill in forms and be questioned about his suitability to foster me. I was twelve years old and I remembered coming from another place — near Maribor, a big city in the north. The orphanage in Trieste gave me the address and I went there too. It was this orphanage in Maribor that I remembered so well. A huge building in a park with long corridors. It was like time falling away beneath my feet. Nothing had changed, it was still full of children. I felt they might lock the door and keep me there. And in some strange way I felt it was my fate, that I deserved it.'

In his agitation, Bruno had stood up again. 'I spoke to people in the office and they let me see their records. It was all quite easy.

The only trouble was, I didn't know my name. I didn't have one – though I had a vague idea that people called me Joe. Luckily the Maribor institution kept photographs, and after ten minutes or so we found me. I had arrived at the age of six. But they had no record of where I'd come from.'

'Isn't that unusual?' Elena had not moved from her seat.

'No. It was a time when some records were still kept on paper and would get lost or purged.'

'So the first six years of your life are a mystery?'

'I tried to find out about that camp I told you about.' He touched his lower back. 'I really wanted to know more, but I didn't have time, I had to work, so I hired a data expert I'd met in the army to help me. To cut a long story short, he found a trail. He also found my mother. And do you know where she was from? Trieste.'

'We're going round in circles,' said Elena.

'Not any more. My mother was Italian. She was not married and she gave me up for adoption because she couldn't afford to look after me. I wasn't really an orphan. Very few of us were. We were just the rejects.'

'And this place where you were badly treated?'

'It was in Ljubljana. I left just before my fifth birthday.'

'You poor boy,' said Elena.

'I am not that boy any more. But I don't want to be the father of your child, Elena. It would be too much for me. I don't know how to love someone properly. I never learned. I had no normal connections till I came to your family, and even then they were not really "normal". And what I might feel for our child is too much to contemplate.'

'But Lucia, she—'

'I don't love Lucia.'

'And your daughter?'

'I struggle to feel what I should. But with you . . . It would be different. And it would be too much. And there's another reason, Elena. I tried once to tell you before. But I failed. It was my fault.'

'What is it?' said Elena with a tightening dread.

'Eventually my army friend found and sent me a copy of my registration from when my mother had first left me in Trieste. Under the father's details, it had: "Name: Unknown. Occupation: Boatbuilder."'

'Like Roberto.'

'Yes. Very like Roberto.'

There was a silence.

'My God,' said Elena. 'You don't think . . .'

'Yes. I think Roberto was my father and that when he heard some girl had become pregnant and then disposed of the unwanted child, he tried to track me down. It took years to find me in Maribor and he couldn't—'

'Oh, God.'

'But he must have kept trying, and eventually—'

'Oh, Bruno.'

'He had me brought back to Trieste while he was filling in the forms to adopt me. I don't know for sure. There are many boat-builders passing through Trieste. But . . .'

Elena stared at the floor for a long time. Not since the day of Roberto's death had she felt herself so displaced. And as on that day, she could sense how long it would take her to adjust.

She felt Bruno's eyes scorching her lowered head. Many things – some that she was not even conscious of having been puzzled by – seemed to have become clear.

'I think you're right,' she said at last, looking up.

'I know we could easily have found out by a DNA test.'

'But what on earth would have been the point?' said Elena.

Bruno took a step forward. 'I should have told you before, Elena. That first night, I began to, and you said, "Ssh." I told myself that perhaps you suspected, perhaps deep down you already knew.'

Elena stood. She put her hands on his shoulders as they faced one another in front of the fire.

She looked hard into his eyes for what she knew might be the last time. She sighed. 'No,' she said. 'You did the right thing. Without you I would have been nothing. Less than nothing.'

A year later, Elena became director of the Institute for Human Research, and in her inaugural address touched on areas where the implications of the Rossi–Duranti Loop were still being worked out. These were many and unexpected.

One of the more amusing was in literature, where a Paris literary critic called Jean Guichard pointed out that readers who had struggled with Proust's long novel *À la recherche du temps perdu* could now see that the book's underlying premise – that experience was not fully lived without the faculty of imaginative recollection, or memory, being present – was a description of the function of the Rossi–Duranti Loop 150 years *avant la lettre*.

In clinical psychology there were implications for autism; in art history there was new light thrown on primitive painting, where it seemed that the caves at Chauvet and Altamira, far from proving humans had been 'human' earlier than had previously been believed, proved by carbon dating the exact opposite: that they could paint impressively before the key mutation. Like Darwin's big idea two hundred years before, the Loop was in itself quite simple; the fun was to be had in its ramifications.

Elena and her team had been able to show that it was 'neuro-developmental'. In other words, it took time to get going: the circuitry was completed at the age of about five and continued to strengthen as the individual grew, up to the age of sixty or more.

That was why older people were happier and wiser and calmer. The puzzle of babies — so human to the loving parent's eye, yet obviously not quite 'all there' — was also solved: the entrance to the Loop was like a hymen and was not open until the chemical activity of memories accumulated sufficiently to break it; the critical mass of memory needed was acquired after 58 to 62 months of living. A new scanner was able to show the moment of rupture in a five-year-old's brain.

The last objection to the theory was to the on/off nature of the link. If the iron bar had deprived the Kebab Man of the ability to switch off, did the normal brain not need an agency to switch on? Elena showed that the objection was unscientific. It did not need a 'soul' to make the motor neurones in the brain instruct the hand to scratch the head. The entire transaction was between pieces of matter. Why were connections between brain cells any different? Merely to ask the question was the mark of a seventeenth-century, dualist turn of mind. The idea of the 'soul' was dead, killed by the Loop; likewise the idea of self. Educated humans knew that they were merely matter that coheres for a millisecond, falls apart and is infinitely reused. On this defiant note, Elena collected her notes and left the platform to resigned applause.

There was a party after the lecture, at which journalists mingled with people from the institute and guests from European universities. Relieved to have delivered her talk successfully, Elena drank more wine than usual. To clear her head, she decided to walk for a while before taking the tram.

She had received honours from many institutions and it embarrassed her that it was she, more than Beatrice Rossi, who was chosen to receive medals and doctorates, bouquets and grand conference hotel rooms. The world had decided that the mousy one was the brains and the glamorous one the free-riding opportunist. Nothing that Elena could say about her colleague's dominant role would change the popular need to see things in the bright light of received ideas. In Europe, during Elena's lifetime, governments and unions, currencies and treaties, had come and gone with disorientating speed, but certain popular super-stitions, she supposed, would never change.

It was not just in the province of harmless journalistic clichés, however, that the world seemed reluctant to take on new ideas. Elena knew that most educated people 'accepted' the implications of the Loop without quite – in a true and personal sense – believing them. The number of those who adhered to the established reli-gions had dwindled, but cults of the mystical and the irrational attracted new members. Even for the minority who were strong enough to take on all the philosophical implications, the daily questions persisted. Knowing one was comprised of recycled matter only and that selfhood was a delusion did not take away the aching of the heart.

And the odd thing was, Elena now admitted, slightly drunk as she walked through the darkness of a warm spring evening, her lecture notes clasped in her hand, that she herself was one of those who carried on as though the work she had published did not exist. She knew it to be truthful, valid and endlessly provable, but she didn't allow the implications to affect the way she lived.

Back in her flat, she kicked off her shoes, made the large screen rise from its housing and chose an old film to watch. Then with a final glass of wine, she washed down a tablet of Elysiax. Synthesised under government licence, Elysiax combined the effects of THC, the active ingredient of cannabis, with that of MDMA, the basis of the old dance drug Ecstasy. It was available in different proportions of the two ingredients; Elena's preference was for the green, THC-dominant, tablet. She liked the marijuana sense of wonder and found the euphoric boost of MDMA prevented her from shaking her awed head too long over the sound of a six-string guitar, like a Laurel Canyon groupie in 1968.

She stretched out on the couch and closed her eyes.

Before Bruno she had had one lover, a fellow teacher in Mantua called Andrea. Fifteen years older than Elena, he was a large man with tweed jackets, a disagreeable wife and three children. She enjoyed his company and looked forward to the evenings when he came to the flat where she lived alone after Fulvia's death. But when he was away at a conference or with his family she hardly thought of him at all.

After she stopped seeing Bruno, she had had one more lover. Carlo was a musician in an orchestra in Turin, and she had met him at the opening of a new concert hall. He was handsome — much more so than Andrea — but reluctant. Having sex with him was unpredictable; he sometimes seemed aggressive, sometimes ashamed, and Elena had to coax him into talking afterwards. One day as they were lying naked on her bed, she began to laugh at the indignity of what they had just done. Carlo was at first affronted, then relieved. He put on his clothes and they became friends. It was a relief to Elena not to have to show her body with all its intimate folds to this violinist any more. Later, he visited her from Rome with his boyfriend.

That left Bruno. Making love to him had not seemed a separate act, but an extension of intimacy. How oddly well they seemed to fit together, she sometimes thought. He must have been a head taller than she was, yet when they danced, as he liked to do, her body slotted into his as though designed: her head rested comfortably on his shoulder while something of him swelled against her hip. In bed they were like a jigsaw where every piece fitted first time: not much of a puzzle, but a reliable delight.

To live, as now she did, without the fearful joy of communion with another person was not a decision that Elena had taken; it was an imposed state of affairs to which she had adjusted. Every day she relived the first evening at the house in the Sabine Hills. She remembered that even in the instant of her rapture she had told herself that she was not required to go along with it; that no one was compelling her to lay her innermost being, naked, against another self.

She saw Bruno only once more after he had revealed his suspicions about Roberto. It was three years later and, at her invitation, he came to visit her in Turin, to get a sense of her life, her work and where she lived – her soundproofed modern apartment, large, well furnished, with its high windows that overlooked the river Po, swollen and olive-coloured in the evening light.

They had dinner in a restaurant, then returned to talk further in her flat. It became clear to Elena as the evening went on that Bruno was looking for her forgiveness. He was direct, as ever, in the way he went about it.

Standing in front of her large fireplace with its marble surround, he said, 'That first night in the hills. I should never have let you . . . I persuaded myself that you knew, or at least suspected, that we shared a father. It was wrong of me, Elena, and I'm sorry. It's brought only sorrow.'

'You could have told me then. You could have spelled it out.'

'I loved you so much. I was desperate for the old closeness, the old warmth.'

'But you chose a new version.'

Bruno frowned and shook his head. 'When the moment came, I was weak. I acknowledge that. Try to imagine what it's like every day to wake up knowing that you've been rejected in the first and simplest relationship of your life. Your mother has disowned you. Every morning you begin at a disadvantage. It's like having fingers missing. For a second after waking you're like everyone else. Then you remember.'

'My dear Bruno, it was only a matter of money. It was not that she knew you, then decided that she didn't want you. She would have loved you if she'd known you.'

'It was only money the first time and it was only money the second time — when your mother also rejected me. The underlying reason doesn't really matter. It's the action and the emotion it causes. It means that you're forever vulnerable. Fearing abandonment. More than that — knowing that you're already rejected.'

'I'm sorry for you, Bruno. I'm sorry in more ways than you can perhaps imagine. Most of all I'm sad that some pall seems to have been cast over that friendship we had as children. Which was so wonderful to me.'

'And me.'

'But when it came to it, you could have been more rational. You could have spared us both.'

'Ah, but that's always been your way, Elena. Rational. The scientific path. You've taken it to its logical — its rational — conclusion. You've proved that we don't really exist. That we're nothing more than a table or a chair. That human beings contain nothing of value. So in your world none of this matters, does it?'

Elena lowered her eyes to the floor. 'I don't think that's what Beatrice and I proved.'

Unable to bear the weight of his guilt, Bruno began to attack her. He told her she had brought despair to millions. He became voluble, inflamed.

Watching him gesticulate, she saw his full weakness for the first time. She understood that this Bruno was not the boy who had ignited her own ability to respond to other human beings and was no longer the man she had loved with such hopeless passion. He was changed; he had become a different man.

*   *   *

Elena Duranti — now aged forty-nine, so at a dangerous age for females in her family — awakes each day with the sun slanting through the blind into her comfortable bedroom at the end of the corridor that leads from the front door of her well-maintained apartment. By the bed is a photograph of her mother, Fulvia, as a young woman; one of Roberto at his workbench; and one of herself with Bruno on a bridge in Venice taken fifteen years ago. Next to the pictures are her glasses and two bottles of pills: one that helps rock her off to sleep and one that stimulates the growth of tissue in the joints and spares her the stabbing of arthritis. The bathroom tiles are warm, the shower water is already at the optimum temperature, and while she stands surrounded by its soothing jets, she sucks a pastille that is all she needs for oral hygiene.

Clothes, which as a girl she regarded as a way of keeping out the cold, have come to mean more to her; she picks out dark trousers, shoes and soft woollen sweaters with something like pleasure as the smell of coffee drifts in from the kitchen. Then comes the descent in the lift, the blast of air from the city as she steps out on the pavement and her body moves off in automatic motion to the solar-tram stop.

Usually she is able to avoid introspection, training her eyes on the dark river and the bridges over it, on the people surging out from the subway and the bent trees along the embankment. When she gives way to reflection, she thinks only this: what luck that I, a farm girl, should have had a brain that was adept at making connections and retaining fact. How lucky, too, that my personality was such that I shrank from others and had time to cultivate the advantages my synapses had given me.

At other times, she is less sanguine. This is the lonely fate I have deserved, she thinks. For my childhood pride. Being bored by the other children at school, mistakenly thinking I was in some way above them. Shyness, arrogance — what was the difference?

Once, after her final parting with Bruno, she went back to their oak tree to see if she could find what she had been as a child. The earth was still unmarked and there were still crows in the air above; the city had sprawled a little further across the plain. She sat for almost an hour, looking for relief or enlightenment, but saw only that the white stones and the coarse grass had always known that they would long outlive her passion; they were neither indifferent, nor a consolation: they were simply a rebuke to the shortness of her life.

She had known as a child that old buildings had been there for hundreds of years; that, after all, was why people went to look at them and wonder at the ancient Romans who had trod there. Yet an absurd part of her had imagined she would in some way outlast the landscape and the man-made buildings. She found it humiliating now to recognise that she was after all one of nameless millions whom even the cheap shops on the ring road would comfortably survive and at whose vanished anonymity future tourists would gawp.

There is a *caffè* near the Piazza Rivoli where she looks in every morning as she changes trams. In the fragrant, wood-panelled room there are always the same people: Matteo, the proprietor, grey-haired and florid; Giuseppe from the clothes shop; and Ornella, the sly, dark girl from the lawyers' office. Others come and go, standing at the bar to gulp down coffee, touching their wrists against the payment reader, then dashing out. Elena likes to sit for ten minutes in the smell of roasted coffee and fresh pastry that takes her back to her childhood — or to some other time when life seemed more possible. The *caffè* has newspapers, printed out in a back room on recycled pulp; they don't have the delicate feel that she remembers from long ago, but they are convenient to read.

Looking through the tram window each morning as it goes up

the Corso Francia towards the Human Research Centre, Elena thinks: this is what I am, and it's a reasonable thing to be. There is no cause for sadness here; this is simply what it feels like to be alive. Often, she finds herself remembering the last line of Bruno's story, 'Another Life': 'I start to make my long way back to the place of my undoing . . .'

Everything she does seems heavy with loss. Often, her voice seems to have an echo, as though she is speaking into emptiness. The lines of her desk and screen suggest, by their rectangular edges, the absence of the human, of the random. There is nothing fissile in the room, nothing unknowable. At lunchtime she avoids anything that might perturb her heart. She takes pumpkin-seed oil on her avocado salad and eats fresh orange and banana slices with a handful of grains. Dear me, she thinks, I'm like some witless hominid plodding over the Serengeti.

She asks herself if this denial means she really wants to live. Why should she wish to prolong the time allotted to her, to check the coil of death unwinding in her genes? Perhaps, she thinks, as she sits back at her desk, she does not mind being unhappy. The idea that humans can capture a mere mood – 'happiness' – and somehow preserve it seems absurd. As an aim for a life, it is not only doomed but infantile. Yet she would prefer to carry on – living what she thinks of as a death-in-life – than not to live at all.

When she returns to her apartment in the evening, lies down on the deep brown sofa with a glass of Tuscan wine and watches the telescreen slide up from the floor, Elena admits that after a lifetime of scientific research she understands nothing at all.

She will watch an old film from 2029 – a story of other people running round, falling in love, chasing one another, making jokes. She drinks more of the wine from Montalcino. Then she closes her eyes and sinks deeper into the cushions. She is filled with memories of places she has never been – of a monastery in France with cloisters and a tolling bell; of a cabin up in the hills of California where there is music; of a house in England with smooth green lawns where boys play a strange game with sticks and a red ball.

She wonders if, when she awakes, she will feel as mystified as she feels now; or whether the hard edges of fact, of history, of her own past — of every cell that makes her what she is — are in truth as flexible as time itself.

PART IV — A DOOR INTO HEAVEN

Jeanne was said to be the most ignorant person in the Limousin village where she had lived most of her life.

The house she lived in belonged to Monsieur and Madame Lagarde; she had been there since she was a young woman, though no one had known her exact age when she arrived. The place was built of local stone with a tile roof and grey shutters; it stood on a bend where the road began to go uphill. On one side there was a path that led down to a few remote houses and then to the river where the local youths went to fish; on the other side there was an orchard that fell to a deep ditch as the road curved and carried on downhill.

The village was spread out, having started life as no more than a farm with some outbuildings and cottages; it was only in the last fifty years that it had gained an inn for coaches, a baker's and then a weekly market. With them had come some newer houses further down the hill, and these had been built round a square with cobbles. The Lagardes' house was of the 'old' village and the rooms inside were panelled with dark oak; they were connected by dingy corridors and single steps of stone to allow for its different levels.

Jeanne's room was on the ground floor at the back, overlooking the fields. It had a grey stone chimneypiece and a wooden prie-dieu as well as the bed, washstand and cupboard. The cost of logs for burning in the fireplace was taken from her wages, though there was no shortage of wood in the oak-covered countryside. Her job in the house was to clean and cook and look after the place as well as an old woman could; for mending fences or heavier work Monsieur Lagarde reluctantly brought in Faucher, the local handyman.

Lagarde himself had been bedridden for ten years following a stroke. He spent most of his time looking at his accounts and working out ways of making his savings go further. His wife brought him books, papers and pens each morning with his bowl of coffee and some bread and butter. The Lagarde family came from Ussel and had once owned several farms, but had lost most of its money during the Revolution. While he was little more than a second-generation bourgeois, Lagarde had cultivated a dislike of the 'rabble' – a term that for him took in anyone from a tax collector to the new mayor, and always included the village youth.

Partly as a compensation for his family's loss of property, Monsieur Lagarde had as a newly married man turned himself into a philosopher. He had boxes full of books delivered from sales in Limoges and Brive with impressive titles such as *On the Understanding of Human Nature* or *Essays on the Principles of Reason*. The bookcase in the parlour held leather-bound editions of the works of Montaigne, Pascal and Descartes, while in his bedroom there were translations of Seneca and the Greeks. It was thought that he alternated his reading of the philosophers with his work on the family accounts.

Jeanne had never heard the word 'philosophy', but always feared that her employer's careful housekeeping would sooner or later lead to his concluding that he could not afford her. Through decades of thrift she had managed to save a small sum of money, which she kept in the cupboard, but she had no idea where she might live if the family asked her to leave. One day when the mutterings from Lagarde's room sounded ominous, Jeanne went to find Madame Lagarde and told her that she would be prepared to work for no more than lodging and food; she would become one of the family.

Jeanne's life had not always been lived on such a low flame. Once she had had the lives of two children in her hands – Clémence and Marcel, the girl and boy born two years apart to Madame Lagarde when she was still in her twenties. The births had both been difficult, and Madame Lagarde had suffered from a sort of madness after each one. She said she felt as though she was falling from a cliff or riding a horse at speed into a stone wall; but she felt this moment of terror all the time. A doctor from Ussel gave her some sedative powders and advised her to hire a nurse or housekeeper to do some of the heavy work.

Monsieur Lagarde looked over the land his family still owned and went to the dairy where six young women were employed as milkmaids. He asked the dairyman about the personal history of each girl and discovered that the small, thickset one called Jeanne was an orphan who had simply arrived one day in search of work. She said she had been walking for four days after leaving a monastery where she had worked as a laundress. She had been at the dairy for three years and it was possible to make her work for nothing more than a bed of straw in the barn, with bread, cheese, milk and apples to eat. Unlike the others, she seemed glad of the work and didn't make eyes at the men who came to visit. She was also, the dairyman said, astonishingly strong for one so small.

'Let me speak to her,' said Lagarde.

He took Jeanne to one side of the farmyard and asked her if she liked children.

Jeanne squinted in suspicion. 'I don't know, Monsieur.'

'Did you have a younger brother? Or a sister?'

'I don't know, Monsieur.'

'What do you mean, you don't know?'

'I remember nothing before the orphanage. That's the first thing I know about.'

'And did you look after any younger children in this orphanage?'

'Sometimes. When I was older. On a Sunday.'

This qualification was all that Lagarde seemed to require. 'I'm going to offer you a position as nursemaid and housekeeper. How much do you think you should be paid?'

'That's not for me to say, Monsieur.' Her accent was so strong that he could barely understand her.

'I'll send a horse and cart for your belongings.'

'That won't be necessary,' said the dairyman. 'All she owns can be put in a bag.'

Monsieur Lagarde gave the dairyman a few coins for his trouble, remounted his horse and told Jeanne to walk behind him. An hour later they arrived at the village house and Jeanne was shown to a room at the back. At this time it had only a bed and a small table with a wooden crucifix.

'Come down the corridor to the parlour when you've unpacked your things,' said Monsieur Lagarde. 'You can meet the children, then my wife will instruct you in your duties.'

Jeanne's bag had a rosary that had been given to her by a nun at the orphanage, a single change of clothes, some grey woollen stockings and a shawl for winter. Finally, there was a plaster Madonna that was so badly chipped that the nuns had been on the point of throwing it away; they disliked its one-eyed, minatory stare, finding it alarming and comic in equal amounts.

She arranged these things on the stone windowsill and knelt down on the floor to say a prayer. Her prayers were always the same. She humbled herself before the Almighty, confessed her sins, thanked Him for His mercy and asked that the next day might bring no more hardship than the last. Sometimes she remembered to add that her final request was to be granted only if it was His will, as well as hers.

* * *

Jeanne was a steady nurse to the children. She was careful of their small bodies and aware of their social standing, but when it came to giving them instructions she knew no way but firmness. They profited from her certainty more than from their parents' vague ambitions. By the time they reached the age of eight and six, Clémence and Marcel were frightened of Jeanne, but they also laughed at her coarse voice and her face with its watery, short-sighted eyes. They feared her stern sayings, such as 'Tell the truth and shame the Devil', but noticed that the way she pronounced certain words showed she did not know what they really meant.

Clémence was a diffident girl who cried easily and hated the darkness on the crooked stair when she took her candle up to bed. She seemed always to be cold and had an exaggerated fear of insects; she was in fact scared of all animals, including dogs and horses, though this was so inconvenient for a country girl that she tried to conceal it.

Jeanne knew that her own upbringing had been unusual but presumed that the lessons she had learned from it would apply to any child. So Clémence and Marcel were scrubbed in cold water morning and night and made to say their prayers; they never ate until everyone was seated and never spoke unless addressed. As for their lessons, Jeanne, who could not read, was happy to see them go off to school in the next village.

She had never met either of her own parents and was told by the nuns that they were dead. One lesson had burned itself into her mind: that a child's happiness depends on the goodwill of strangers – in her case, Sister Thérèse, who supervised the cold dormitory where she had slept; and in the case of Clémence and Marcel, it depended on her.

Marcel was a simpler case than Clémence. While his sister was always struggling to make her natural inclinations bend to what the world required of her, Marcel had a temperament that fitted him for living. Cold water made him laugh, prayers made him hopeful and food made him content. He liked to ride the pony his father had given him, and the long walk to school each day was a chance to play games with the other children who journeyed to the next village. He was no scholar, but learned the essentials with only the occasional rap over the knuckles from the schoolmaster.

When she brushed Clémence's hair at night, Jeanne was touched by an emotion she did not understand. 'There, there, Ninou,' she used to whisper as she brushed, 'there, there.' She recognised it as a virtuous feeling, however; it made her want to protect the child from whatever lay ahead. What she felt for Marcel was fiercer. She had an urge to squeeze his shoulders in her arms and kiss the brown curls of his head. But she never allowed herself such liberties, and when they were safely in bed she took a candle to light her way downstairs, pausing at the parlour door to tell Monsieur and Madame Lagarde that the children were asleep.

Jeanne lived her life from one minute to the next, with no plan for the future and no sense that she would one day grow old or weak. By rising an hour before anyone else in the house she felt she stayed ahead of the others and that her disadvantages would not bring her to grief for at least another day.

She continually talked to God, her lips moving silently as she cleared the ashes from the grate in the parlour or scrubbed the front step. This was not prayer so much as putting her thoughts into words, but she had a clear picture in her mind who the listener was. He was the wooden figure on the cross in the village church where the children of her orphanage had gone every Sunday — a half-naked, bearded man with a wound in his side and a rough coronet of thorns on his head. Her time at the orphanage had given her a fierce sense of the supernatural. God had not only created the world and all that was in it, He was preoccupied with Jeanne for each moment of her waking day. He watched and judged her every action and unvoiced thought; he knew if her intentions were pure and if she told the smallest lie. She had no difficulty in believing in an invisible being. She understood so little of the material world – how water boiled, why a walnut fell from the tree – that she had had to take almost everything on trust. For her to believe that the organising power of the universe had chosen to make Himself invisible required less than to accept that – as Marcel had once tried to persuade her – the tides of the sea were drawn by the power of the moon. Of course God watched her and loved her; she felt Him near. Of course she could not see Him – otherwise there would be no need for Faith! And of course there were saints whose lives were an example, and naturally there was damnation for sinners; that was fair and just. And what was there in all this that was hard to believe?

From time to time Madame Lagarde thought she should try to educate her servant, though she lacked the stamina to carry out her good intentions in person. She had recovered from the mania that followed the birth of her children, but still suffered periods of melancholy during which she could barely stir from her room. The priest told her that she should busy herself with good deeds among the poor; the local doctor bled her with leeches. Eventually her husband paid for a well-known physician to come from Limoges.

He examined Madame Lagarde and sat by her bed for an hour before he delivered his verdict. 'Madame, I believe that one day your illness will be curable, but you have been born too soon. There is a doctor in Paris, a man called Pinel, who is beginning a new branch of medicine he calls "moral therapy". Perhaps you have heard how he freed the madwomen from their chains. One day, I suppose, we will understand how the mind works. Until then you must bear your fate as best you can. I suggest you take the air as much as possible, walk in the fields, ride a horse. Take a glass of wine or brandy with dinner. Try not to despair.'

'Despair is a sin,' said Madame Lagarde mechanically, though she was not properly religious, being no more than what she called a 'deist'.

Monsieur Lagarde regarded this advice as a poor return for the doctor's bill, and told him so. To placate his client, the doctor had a case of medicine delivered from Ussel; it contained twelve corked red bottles of sugared water, for which he made no charge. Monsieur Lagarde was happy to administer two spoonfuls of the elixir each day, as instructed.

In one of her brief periods of vigour, Madame Lagarde arranged for Madame Mechenet, the young wife of the mayor, to teach Jeanne the rudiments of writing and reading. This Madame Mechenet had recently given birth to twins and was preoccupied by them, but thought her 'position' in the village made it important for her to continue with some charitable work. She was a young woman with hair dressed in a fashionable way and she had a simpering manner that set Jeanne's teeth on edge. She sat her pupil at a large table in the parlour and spread out the letters of the alphabet, printed on wooden blocks. It did not go well. Madame Mechenet tried, without losing her dignity, to imitate the sound made by each letter. Jeanne looked at her blankly. They had got as far as the letter 'k' when a maid brought in the twins, and to Jeanne's astonishment, Madame Mechenet unfastened her dress and fed them, one at each breast, as though Jeanne's presence was of no more account to her than that of the dogs sleeping on stone flags by the fire.

Jeanne never went back for the second lesson and from then on referred to Madame Mechenet as 'that whelping bitch', a phrase that delighted Marcel and Clémence so much that they mouthed it silently to one another at any half-appropriate moment.

Madame Mechenet did not discover why Jeanne refused to go back and put it down to peasant idleness. 'I understand your servant prefers to remain ignorant,' she said to Monsieur Lagarde at church one Sunday.

'If so, Madame,' he said, 'it's not through any weakness. On the contrary, it's the fire of her character that will keep her in the dark.'

Monsieur Lagarde could not help feeling pleased with this remark; it was the sort of thing that he imagined a philosopher might have said. He repeated it to his wife, and later to Jeanne herself, who muttered something inaudible in response as she went down the passageway to her cold bedroom.

When Clémence was fourteen, Monsieur Lagarde decided it was time she went to a proper school and found there was a convent near Saint-Junien, run by the Little Sisters of the Ascension, that was happy to take her. Although the staff were all nuns, the girls were encouraged to learn social as well as religious graces. Clémence would be taught how to read music and how to do tapestry work; by the time she came home she might be ready to think about marriage. Jeanne helped her to pack a trunk full of clothes and toys, stopping from time to time to comfort her as she wept.

'Stop it, you silly girl. Stop it now.'

'I don't want to go, Mole.' This was what she sometimes called Jeanne because of her peering eyes and small size. 'What if there are insects?'

'Put on your flannel nightgown with the long sleeves. Think of our Lord on the cross. Did he care about insects?'

'And will you pack me some books to read?'

'What use are books? They'll have books enough there. That's what nuns do all day. They pray and they read.'

Clémence cried harder.

'And they fast,' said Jeanne. 'They fast all the time.'

Monsieur Lagarde called in Faucher to load the trunk on to the cart and to drive it home after he and Clémence had taken the coach to Limoges, from where they would take a smaller one to Saint-Junien. Marcel stood at the end of the lane where it met the stony road and waved his handkerchief. Madame Lagarde stood beside him, weeping.

'We can't get the cart up the road in winter, Mama,' said Marcel. 'So we won't see her till next spring.'

In fact, it was two years before Clémence returned; and when the coach for Ussel deposited her at the inn in the village no one recognised her. She left her trunk with the ostler, telling him it would be called for later, then walked into the building, bought herself a cup of chocolate and sat down with it outside. She wore a long coat with a fur collar and hat.

The landlord fussed round the strange young woman. 'Will that be all, Mademoiselle?'

'Yes, thank you.'

Madame Mechenet happened to be going past the inn on her way to her husband's house, accompanied by her twins, who were now old enough to walk. She paused for a moment as she saw Clémence and let her eye run over her clothes.

'Good morning, Madame,' she said in a tone of voice she imagined to be 'cultured'. 'What pleasant weather we are having.'

'Yes, indeed,' said Clémence, adding under her breath when Madame Mechenet was out of earshot, 'whelping bitch.'

Monsieur Lagarde was pleased with the change in Clémence. 'Goodness me,' he said to his wife, 'that's money well spent. Give her another couple of years and we can aim pretty high.'

Marcel was not convinced that his sister was as different as she pretended to be. When she had been at home for a few days he left a white mouse in her bedroom and waited for her screams.

After an hour Clémence emerged, holding the mouse by its tail. 'I think this may be yours,' she said to Marcel, dropping the creature on his bed.

It was Jeanne who was most affected by the alteration in her former charge. When she went to her room to help her prepare for bed, Clémence at first seemed reluctant to let her in. She tossed back her long chestnut hair so it fell over her shoulders and stood with her hands on her hips. Ignoring the unfriendly stance, Jeanne brushed past and started to unpack her clothes.

'Where did you get all these nice things?' she said.

'We're allowed to go to the shops. Some of the girls are rich and I asked Papa to send me some more money.'

'Do the nuns let you wear fur?'

'They're not very strict,' said Clémence, sitting at the dressing table. 'On Saturday they allow us to do what we like. Some of the older girls go into Saint-Junien and walk in the park. Last year one of them, a girl of eighteen . . .'

'What?'

Clémence looked at Jeanne but could not quite find the courage to tell her that the girl had become pregnant as the result of an affair with a clerk in the town hall. There had been a scandal. 'Nothing,' she said.

There was an awkward pause while Jeanne tidied the room, knocking into things, as she did when she was nervous or unhappy. She took the hairbrush and stood behind the chair. Then, as she looked down at Clémence's head, the separation and the change in her seemed to be of no consequence; she felt herself to be standing over the same frightened child she had known on her first day at the Lagardes' house.

'Shall I do your hair now, Ninou?'

But Clémence stood up and turned round. 'No, thank you, I can do it myself. And please don't call me that any more. In return I promise not to use that silly name I gave you either.'

Jeanne backed out through the door without speaking and went to the kitchen to prepare supper.

That night she could hardly find the words with which to shape her prayers. Her understanding of life was so small that she had nothing with which to compare Clémence's behaviour; she did not know that it was typical of girls of her age to try to loosen the ties of home. For two years her last thought as she laid her head on the pillow each night had been for Clémence. She had pictured her in the dormitory in which she herself had slept so many years at the orphanage, in her very bed, surrounded by strangers and harsh rules and – knowing her, poor girl – shivering in the cold. She had longed for the day Clémence would be back home in her own room and she could resume her care. Now some imposter or cuckoo had taken the place of the girl she had looked after. Clémence was dead.

When her daughter returned to the convent for her final year, Madame Lagarde seemed to go into a decline. She would wake in the middle of the night, then find it impossible to go back to sleep. She would walk round the room or take a candle and go downstairs to the parlour where she sat staring into the embers of the fire. To spare her husband from her nocturnal ramblings and to give him leisure for his philosophical studies, she moved her clothes and personal belongings into Clémence's room. She said the view was better and the bed more comfortable.

Jeanne was appalled by the change. She thought it wrong for a woman to leave her husband's bed and resented having to take soup and tisane upstairs to Madame Lagarde when she felt 'too tired' to come down. And what she saw in her Ninou's room distressed her. For days on end Madame Lagarde stayed in her nightclothes and took little care of her appearance. Her hair hung down loose and unbrushed, her fingernails looked dirty. Although there were books in the room, she never seemed to read. She merely sat by the window, looking over the pale green fields towards the line of poplar trees along the river. She said that sleep had deserted her, yet for long hours of the day she lay on the bed with her eyes closed.

In Jeanne's life, there had never been a choice of whether or not to get dressed. If she had decided one day at the dairy, she told herself, to stay up in the barn and not to milk the cows, she would have been thrown out on her ear. She wondered why Monsieur Lagarde stood for it, but he hardly seemed to notice.

When Clémence was almost twenty years old she brought a young man home to meet her parents. His name was Étienne Desmarais; his father was a lawyer and he wore a fawn coat with leather riding boots and a white lace neckerchief under his waistcoat. He had a way of holding his head on one side as he looked round the room – or down his nose, it seemed to Jeanne.

Monsieur Lagarde invited Monsieur and Madame Mechenet to join them that evening; Mechenet was no longer the mayor, but they were still the most distinguished couple in the village and the only people Lagarde thought worthy of meeting the man he expected to become his son-in-law. Dinner was sent up from the inn and arrived with a commotion of china on the back of the cart at seven. Jeanne grumbled that the food was no better than she herself could have cooked, though there was certainly more than usual, with an apple tart and cheeses to follow the dish of venison with morels and potatoes.

Young Desmarais stood before the fire and talked of his family's wooded estates near Châteaudun, which meant little to the Lagardes because they had never been that far north. He had been educated in Paris, he told them, and would probably return there to practise law when he had a little more experience. While he talked, Clémence kept her eyes fixed on his handsome face, allowing her gaze to flicker across the room only for a moment to see the effect he was having on her parents. Madame Lagarde had been persuaded to smarten herself for the occasion and sat next to her daughter, trying to look attentive.

After dinner, at which they had drunk wine, the conversation became wide-ranging.

'And, Monsieur,' said Madame Mechenet to Desmarais, 'do you ever imagine that you will one day live on your family estates?' She was using the false voice with which she had greeted Clémence at the inn.

'Ah, no, dear Madame,' said Desmarais. 'The eternal silence of those infinite spaces terrifies me.'

There was a pause as the others looked at one another and Desmarais put his head on one side. 'Surely,' he said, 'you recognise the quotation from one of our greatest philosophers?'

'Monsieur Lagarde is sure to know it,' said Madame Mechenet. 'He's the philosopher in these parts.'

Lagarde coughed and adjusted his waistcoat. He did not know.

'Pascal,' said Desmarais. 'He was referring to the heavens, of course.'

'Of course,' said Lagarde.

'Was he the man famous for his bet?' said Clémence, who remembered a few things from school.

'Indeed,' said Desmarais, and bowed towards Clémence's father to give him the floor.

But Pascal's wager — that, since we can know nothing, we might as well be good in our short life as risk an eternity of damnation by being bad — appeared unknown to him. Madame Lagarde stirred herself enough to move the topic on, but over the next hour the polite Desmarais contrived to offer his host a number of opportunities to redeem himself. He dangled famous lines for his completion and feigned forgetfulness about which philosopher's maxim had been 'I abstain'. But there was no answering light, not a flicker, in Lagarde's eyes, and Madame Mechenet eventually let out a half-stifled laugh.

Marcel caught Clémence's eye and mouthed the words 'whelping bitch', which made Clémence herself begin to laugh so much that she had to leave the room and the evening came to an end.

When he was nineteen, Marcel decided to join the army. He was just too late for the Battle of Friedland, but after two years of training, of mild adventures interspersed with boredom, gambling and chasing women, he found himself one summer night on an island in the Danube called Lobau, where his corps was billeted alongside Italian and German allies. He smoked a pipe in his tent and gossiped with his fellow junior officers about what they would do in Vienna when the battle was won.

It was his first experience of all-out war and it did not go as well as the generals had predicted. The Austrians were gathered on the plain ahead of them – a place they often used, oddly enough, for practice manoeuvres – and to start with the Allied infantry made progress on a wide front. In the evening, Marcel was among those ordered to finish the battle in a single day with a decisive attack on the Austrian centre. Soon they had driven the enemy back behind the high ground at Wagram, but as dusk gathered, Marcel's unit was cut off. The Austrians regrouped and pushed the Allies so far back that all their gains were lost.

Running through the half-light, in the noise of clashing steel and gunfire, Marcel no longer felt under the command of the emperor or part of a Grande Armée; it was more like the games he had played with the village boys in the hedgerows on the way to school. In the chaos, he shot at anything that moved and killed a man in a white uniform he later thought was probably a Saxon ally.

He was still deeply asleep in his tent when the Austrians surprised them at dawn. It was a long and awful day, as the massed French cannon on the island of Lobau poured shells into defence-less Austrian infantry, who plodded on until they were too few to go further. It was impossible to watch for more than a minute, whichever side you were on. On the morning of the third day, Marcel's corps, after a day of inaction, was ordered to advance again and by mid-afternoon they were entering a village called Markgrafneusiedl.

Marcel was with a dozen French infantry running down a street, past a baker and an ironmonger. He thought how strange it was that these shops would close only for a day or so while something called history was made; then they would resume their sale of bread and nails. He was in fact starving from his own exertions and for a mad moment thought of breaking off his advance to loot the baker's. Then there was a shout of warning. He turned to see a group of Austrian soldiers emerging from a side street. The range was too close to fire, but – raging and made strong by fear – they closed on the enemy with bayonets.

As for the rest of the day and the outcome of the Battle of Wagram, Marcel knew nothing for two weeks, as an Austrian blade had removed the left side of his face and left him on his knees, clutching at his still-intact teeth and jaw with bloody hands.

That night the stretcher-bearers got him to a dressing station where he lay, weak with shock and loss of blood. It was several days before he was in a proper military hospital, where it was found that his wound, though serious, was not infected and a surgeon asked if he would like to have his face repaired so that it as nearly as possible resembled what it had been before. The alternative, he said, was for him simply to clean and stitch what was left so that Marcel would look like one of those noseless beggars by the Paris roadside. Marcel told him to do whatever he thought best.

Three months later he was honourably discharged from the army and returned to the Lagarde family home.

*   *   *

He had written ahead to warn them of his wounds and to give them time to prepare a feast for the return of the Prodigal.

That evening, the family gathered in the parlour and Marcel began to tell them what had happened since he left the village more than two years before. It was difficult for him to speak because a part of his tongue had been sliced off, but he wanted them to know what it was like to march all night and, when you arrived at some foreign field half dead with exhaustion, to be asked to fight – to be expected to be at your most vital and alert, as a matter of life and death, to run, kill and pick up your dead. He wanted them to understand what he felt for the men he had been with in the chaos of battle in Austria and in the tedium of barracks in the damp foothills of the Vosges.

However, his father interrupted him to talk about the new mayor, a builder by trade, and to tell him of the money he had himself made by selling a parcel of land to a man from Cahors. Madame Lagarde said nothing, but stared at her son with a baffled expression.

Marcel tried once more to interest them in what he had done. 'The emperor himself gave us our orders on the third day,' he said. 'I saw him up close. He's quite short, not much bigger than old Mole. But he has a terrible glitter in his eyes. The generals worship him, but they're afraid of him as well. Marshal Bernadotte was relieved of his command in the middle of the battle.'

'We should tell Clémence that you're back,' said Madame Lagarde. 'I'm too tired to stay up talking now.'

'I'll send a message with the coach to Uzerche tomorrow,' said Monsieur Lagarde. 'What are you going to do now you're back, Marcel?'

'I'm going to train as a pharmacist.'

'And who's going to pay for your training?'

'I have some pay from the army.'

'And when that's run out?'

Marcel lost patience. 'Then I'll become an actor at the Comédie-Française. Or if that doesn't make me enough then I'll exhibit myself in a travelling show.'

What in fact he did was to spend many hours with Jeanne. He was not recovered enough to find work, so after a morning walk would settle himself in the parlour to read. When Jeanne had finished cleaning the house, she came and sat with him to do her sewing in the light of the broad window that overlooked the road.

'What are you reading?' she said to him one day.

'The Bible,' said Marcel. 'I expect you studied it at your orphanage.'

'We didn't study anything. We worked and prayed, that's all there was time for.'

'There was a fellow I met in the army who told me some stories from it,' said Marcel, 'so I thought I'd read it.'

Even the most religious Catholic families in the Limousin were unfamiliar with the book, taking their guidance from the sermons of priests and the example of the saints. Marcel was reading it for the first time, and with an astonishment he felt compelled to share with the nearest person, who happened to be Jeanne.

He read it as an adventure, his wonder increasing with every page. The brother's murder in the field, the son sacrificed by the loving father's obedience to a disembodied voice, the child floating in a basket among bulrushes, the sea rolled up and divided into towering walls of salt water, the old man gazing over into the land he would not live to enter . . . Above all, the cruel, unforgiving god and the inexhaustibly valiant men who struggled for life in the barbaric world this deity had made.

He took to reading it out loud, while Jeanne listened with a puckered mouth and a suspicious eye. Who were these Israelites who thought themselves so chosen and so great? Since she believed in a supernatural spirit ever present and invisible, she was not much impressed by the burning bush and the manna from heaven;

Israelite miracles seemed to her garish and false. She had in any case no clear sense of other countries or peoples. Even France was vague to her beyond the borders of the Limousin, and she suspected that the idea of 'France' had been invented by Parisians so they could grow fat on the riches of real places – Brittany, for instance, or the Languedoc.

Marcel tried to explain the whereabouts of the Holy Land. He pointed to it on a globe in his father's room, but then saw that Jeanne had no idea what this turning tin sphere was meant to represent. As he read aloud the story of the fiery furnace where the flames left the three men untouched, he found his throat thicken with awe. But when he looked across to the window at which Jeanne was sewing he saw that these extraordinary events meant nothing to her – because they did not relate to anything she had herself experienced.

Yet as the days went on, there came a slow alteration in Jeanne's attitude: she started to look forward to the readings, even while they appalled her. The stories of the Judges were the first to open a crack in the shell of her resistance. Samson she regarded as a fool who deserved, for his vanity and lust, to die in the dust of the temple he pulled down on his head. But when Jephthah prayed to his cruel god for help before his battle against the Philistines, there was something in his anxiety that she understood – especially when he tried to make his request more acceptable to God by promising to sacrifice, in the event of victory, the first living thing he saw on his return to camp. Jeanne had almost forgotten the vow when they came to the point in the story where Jephthah, returning victorious after the long day, was greeted by – of all creatures – his only child, his daughter running out to embrace him.

'Is this God of Israel true?' she asked one day.

'What do you mean?'

'He's not the real God, is he? He's not our God.'

'I think he's meant to be a version of Him,' said Marcel. 'But before He had a son.'

'Our Saviour?'

'Yes.'

'I don't understand.'

'No one truly understands. We don't really know how our minds work or why we are alive. That's why people have faith.'

'I know how my mind works,' said Jeanne.

'Not really. Not even the philosophers know. I have seen a man's brain on the battlefield and it looked just like something in the butcher's shop in Treignac.'

Jeanne told him to stop talking nonsense.

Marcel smiled. 'One day there may be someone who understands everything, every little bit of how our minds work, not just like a philosopher but like a scientist.'

'What on earth would be the point of that?' said Jeanne. 'It wouldn't alter anything.'

They seldom had such exchanges. Usually when Jeanne looked up from her sewing to Marcel's face, she thought only: this is not Marcel, this is someone else. The left side of his face was covered with skin that the surgeon had taken from his back in an operation he had learned on a visit to India. It looked to Jeanne as though the surgeon had run out of human skin and grafted on a section of pig near the forehead, where the bristle grew unnaturally thick. The graft, however, had taken well on the cheek and neck; it was Marcel's back, where it came from, that was slow to heal and needed daily dressing. Jeanne was the only person willing to perform this task, which she did with Marcel lying face down in his bed. When she had cleaned the area, powdered it and covered it with a fresh dressing, she would rub her hand briefly in the curls at the back of his neck, as she had never dared do when he was a child. She would not look at his face when he rolled over, though, because to her he was not the same person.

Marcel began to grow stronger; his spirits lifted when he looked across at the old servant and saw how she was being changed, a little, by what she heard him read. The kings of Israel seemed hateful to her, and she longed for their downfall with a peasant spite that made him smile. She never liked David, and it was no surprise to her when he began to cast a lustful eye on Bathsheba, the wife of Uriah, as she bathed naked. She exulted when David arranged for Uriah to be killed by placing him in the front rank in battle, not for dislike of Uriah but because it confirmed her low opinion of David. She was not concentrating when Marcel read of the subsequent visit of Nathan the Prophet. Nathan told a story about a rich man who had everything he could desire, but then decided what he wanted most was a single ewe lamb that belonged to a poor man. He took it for himself. When King David heard the story he was appalled. Clearly not seeing that it was a parable, but believing it to be a true report, he commanded Nathan to tell him who this man was, so he could punish him most severely.

Looking up to find Jeanne's eyes on him, Marcel paused for a moment before he read out Nathan's terrible answer: 'Thou art the man.'

Jeanne's mouth fell open to show her brown teeth. Marcel watched the dawn of understanding start to break across her face, then cloud, then lighten again. 'He means . . . the lamb . . . the wife . . .' Marcel said nothing, but nodded as she pieced together the meaning of what she had heard. It was the first time he had ever seen Jeanne at a loss for words. No high-sounding proverb or low country saying could tidy her thoughts away for her.

It pleased Marcel to see that even someone as resistant as Jeanne could be touched by the words of a book; it was a relief to him, since he had begun to wonder if it was he alone who was susceptible. Only the day before, in the quiet of his own room, he had read of the deaths of Saul and Jonathan in the Mountains of

Gilboa, then David's lament for them. It had for the first time made real to him the battlefield and the men he had himself seen die. 'The beauty of Israel is slain upon your high places: how are the mighty fallen!' he read, and the large book began to shake in his hands. He saw in his memory – clearly for the first time – the escarpment of Wagram, covered with the bodies of men he knew. 'How are the mighty fallen in the midst of the battle! O Jonathan, you were slain in your high places. I am distressed for you, my brother Jonathan . . . How are the mighty fallen, and the weapons of war perished!'

Sitting at the desk in his cold bedroom, Marcel put down the book so he could hold his head in his hands. Beneath his palms he felt the borrowed skin of his face, though only his right eye could shed tears.

The passing years did nothing to diminish Jeanne's reputation for ignorance. If anything, her fame became more widespread. Schoolboys on their way home hoped to see her working in the front garden so they could call out, 'What's the capital of France, Jeanne?' A red-headed lout once shouted, 'What's the king's name?' The gang hooted when she stood up from her task and said, 'King Louis. I know that, you little guttersnipe.'

This was almost ten years after Monsieur Lagarde's stroke. He survived for a further five, the last three of them entirely in his room with his unread books of philosophy, nursed by Jeanne.

After her husband's death at the good age of seventy-seven, Madame Lagarde, who was ten years younger, seemed to wake and stir. With some money he had left her, she bought new dresses from the draper in Uzerche during a stay with Clémence and her two children. She returned home with a trunk full of purchases, moved back into the marital bedroom and set about redecorating the house with the help of young Faucher, old Faucher's son. Jeanne watched suspiciously as rusty shutters were mended and roof tiles replaced. Madame Lagarde took all her meals in the parlour, sold her husband's books and declared that her life would begin again. Only a few months later, however, she disappeared. Jeanne took the coach to Ussel, where Marcel was working as a pharmacist, to tell him the news. Marcel returned with her and organised a search party among the villagers. At the end of the second day, they found Madame Lagarde's drowned body in the river, one of her dresses — a complicated affair with lace petticoats — having become tangled in the roots of the poplar trees she had so often stared at from her upstairs window.

Although there were murmurings in the village about Madame Lagarde's strangeness and her melancholy moods, no one actually believed that she had drowned herself on purpose. There were no stones in her pockets, no sign that her death was anything other than a grim accident, such as occasionally might befall a grieving and distracted soul.

Jeanne brooded on the death of her mistress. Although she believed the words of the priest who exonerated Madame Lagarde from all sin as he buried her in the hallowed ground of the village cemetery, Jeanne felt in some small way tainted by association. This unease hung over all the last period of her life, which began when Marcel moved back into his parents' house, bringing his wife Hélène and their three small children. Jeanne, who had been living in Clémence's old bedroom upstairs, returned to her cold place on the ground floor. It pleased her well enough to have a new generation of children to look after, particularly the baby, whom she bounced up and down on her knee, chanting rhymes that had emerged from the deep countryside to lodge, somehow, in her brain.

She made no judgement on what she had seen in her life, but each experience affected her idea of what the world was. Clémence and Marcel had shown her that people change and are not the same all their lives. Madame Lagarde taught her that sometimes they cannot change. The orphanage, the dairy and Monsieur Lagarde made her think that all that really counted was good fortune.

Marcel was kind to her and gave her money for the work she did, though she was too old and worn out to do much. As her eyesight failed and she could no longer sew, she was left to sweep the floor and tend the children when the parents were not at home. She still prayed morning and night, and this communion with her god was the liveliest part of her slow day. At night she pulled the blanket over her head. She had no thoughts then, and she did not dream.

One day she was too tired to go outside, but stayed by the fire. She liked to watch the shape of the flame in the logs. All her life she had been fascinated by the sound of the fire as it spat and licked at the wood, carving new shapes with the sharp edge of its heat, no two ever the same. Then she fell asleep in the chair and died.

Between the orphanage and the dairy there were ten years in which Jeanne — a growing girl, then a young woman — laboured where she could find work. She gained her unusual strength by helping the men build dry stone walls in the fields and by harvesting the crops in August. In winter she went to religious houses and asked for shelter in return for scrubbing and sweeping. Sometimes the abbot or the Mother Superior would take pity; at other times the double doors were closed in her face, even when it was snowing on the road. She grew accustomed to sleeping in outhouses, in cellars, on sacks or on bales of straw. When the spring came at last she could again find work on the land.

She tried not to make friends because she feared to become reliant on another. One winter when she was about twenty-five years old she found work at a monastery — not in the main cloisters, where no woman was allowed, but in the laundry. The others working there were women like herself, and a few who were soft in the head. Their conversation was coarse and Jeanne learned from it that human beings could behave in the same way as the animals in the field. The thought repelled her, but the wash house was warm from the steam of the water in the large wooden vats where they pounded the linen.

Because of her strength, Jeanne was at first made to carry the heavy cauldrons, which she and another woman did by inserting a length of wood beneath the iron handle and hoisting it between them on their shoulders like a yoke. Then she would refill it with buckets they carried in from a well in the yard. A friendly monk, Brother Bernard, would sometimes keep an eye on their progress. One of the girls sang the song 'Frère Jacques' whenever he appeared in the yard and one day he obliged them by joining in the last line with his bass voice – 'Din, dan, don, din, dan, don' – till Jeanne and her companion were squealing with laughter.

It was a cold winter and the ground froze hard. It became slippery beneath the wooden clogs of the women as they crossed to the wash house in the morning. There was nothing to distinguish one day from another except the visits of Brother Bernard. Jeanne found herself looking up expectantly each time the laundry door opened. She felt she was competing for his attention with Mathilde, who had now changed the words of the song to 'Frère Bernard'. He was younger than most of the monks; he had black curly hair and a puzzled, wounded look in his eye, Jeanne thought – like a dog that had been chained up too long. He smiled at the women and encouraged them in their work, but then fixed his eyes on some indefinite point in the distance, as though there was something there that only he could see.

When they took their break in the middle of the day he came and sat by the well, bringing apples or walnuts from the shelves of the refectory. He told Jeanne and Mathilde stories from the lives of the saints, but he never asked them about their own past.

One day, on an impulse, fretting at this lack of true exchange between them, Jeanne said, 'Why did you become a monk, Brother?'

He did not walk away angrily or rebuke her, as she feared he might, but said mildly, 'It was my destiny from a young age.'

Bernard began to visit every day and to stay for a long time talking to the washerwomen. He told them about the raising of Lazarus, the feeding of the five thousand and the time Jesus felt some vital strength leave his body in a crowded street and demanded to know who had touched him. A weeping woman knelt down and confessed that she had touched the hem of his garment in order to stem her 'issue of blood'.

A strange look came into his eye at this moment and Jeanne became convinced that Bernard felt that he himself shared something of this power — a power to attract and heal and make whole.

The women slept outside the monastery walls in an old apple barn that had a dozen straw mattresses on the ground or up a ladder on a platform beneath the rafters. That night as she lay in her straw bed Jeanne became sure that Bernard did have something of the Saviour in him. She had heard him speak of the Apostles and how they were sent forth into the world to carry on Christ's good work. They were chosen men who became filled with the Holy Spirit, and the heir of one, St Peter, was the holy Pope in Rome. So, ordinary men, she reasoned, could also have Jesus's power in their blood.

The wonderful thing about Brother Bernard was that she, Jeanne, was the only person who had seen this power. The abbot treated him as an under-servant. The other monks laughed at him. Being in charge of the laundry — spending the day with the old crones, the bastards and the halfwits who worked there — was the lowest task in the monastery. But Jeanne had seen the look in his eyes, as though Bernard could see through the surface of things

– through the trees, through the walls and into some comforting
and more truthful world that lay beyond them.

One day when Brother Bernard came into the laundry and
went close by Mathilde, Jeanne and another laundress as they
worked, Jeanne did what the woman in the crowded street of
Jerusalem had done: she touched the edge of his garment as he
passed by. It was a less delicate movement than she had intended
and she felt his hip bone through the cloth of his vestment. He
paused for a moment, then, as he moved on, gave her an understanding smile.

Having lived now for more than a quarter of a century, Jeanne
felt for the first time that it might be possible to open a door into
her solitude. Death had made her an orphan; life had made her
poor; and she had made herself go through each day with no
regard or trust for others. It had worked in its own way; it was a
life and she knew no other. In the smile of Brother Bernard,
however, she glimpsed a sort of heaven. She saw what it might
be like to let another creature see inside herself – and she imagined
what views she might be granted in return. Perhaps most other
people's lives were like that, she thought. What might it be like
not to be alone?

When the spring came, Jeanne did not leave the monastery to
look for work on the farms, where she would be paid, but offered
to stay and work for food and shelter alone. She was content to
wait and see what might happen. The fact that Bernard was a
monk was a comfort to her; it meant he would have no feelings
of the kind the coarser women talked about. Jeanne had long since
disqualified herself from any idea of love or marriage. What was
left, what was real, was the holy power that she alone had seen
in Bernard.

One day in May, Brother Bernard asked Jeanne if she would
like to meet him that Sunday afternoon. The abbot allowed the

brothers to walk in the countryside before Vespers and since the women did no work on Sundays he thought it might be a chance for the two of them to talk and pray. His eyes beneath his dark brows were full of concern.

Jeanne stammered out an agreement and Bernard pointed to a small copse on a hill beyond the local village. On the day, Jeanne cleaned her clothes and dried them as best she could. She had barely slept and found her hands clumsy even at this habitual work. When she arrived at the place Brother Bernard had pointed out, she found him already there, sitting with his back to a tree. He patted the dry leaves on the ground next to him and Jeanne sat down. She had never in her life before met someone without a purpose and did not know what she was supposed to do.

Brother Bernard turned to her. 'How old are you, Jeanne?'

'I don't know exactly.'

'Perhaps you are a couple of years younger than I am. Do you know where you came from?'

She shook her head.

He smiled. 'I suppose none of us does. Or where we're going. But we are here for a purpose, I believe.'

'What purpose?'

'That is your life's work. To discover.'

'And what's yours?'

'To serve God.'

'Is that all?'

He laughed. 'And to help others. I felt you touch me that day in the laundry and I knew that you wanted something from me.'

Jeanne looked down at the dry leaves. 'I . . . I don't know.'

When she looked up at his face again, she saw that it was framed with light, like the face of Christ on the cross in the orphanage church when the sun came through the glass.

He stood up and offered his hand. Jeanne allowed herself to be pulled to her feet. They walked together for a long time in silence, not touching, till they came to a narrow track with a farmhouse at the far end.

There was a feeling of peace that Jeanne had never known as they walked along the cart track between the poplars, towards the house, which had a commanding view of the countryside.

She felt that her life was about to take a decisive turn. Why should it be here of all places, she wondered – this old farm that had seen the generations come and go and would see her in the grave as well? But then again, why not? What are places for – but to keep watch silently?

'Shall we ask these people if they will give us some water?' said Bernard.

They crossed the yard, past a foul-smelling midden, and a chained dog began to bark as they approached the door. No one answered when Bernard knocked, so he cautiously opened it and called out a greeting. There was still no answer.

Jeanne hung back, but Bernard took her arm and led her into a gloomy passageway; they heard a horse shifting noisily in a side room. Eventually the passage opened into a parlour where the embers of a fire were smouldering, as though someone had recently been there and needed warming, even though the day was hot.

They stood opposite one another in the empty room with its cold stone floor and dark walls with unlit candles in wrought-iron sconces on the wall. Bernard held his arms wide and Jeanne fell to her knees in front of him.

'Dear Saviour,' she said.

There was a door that led into another part of the house. It swung open quietly. Bernard gestured towards it with his arm outstretched.

'Will you follow me?' said Bernard.

Jeanne stood up and looked into his eyes, deep brown and trusting under their black brows.

She felt the burden of her life shift inside her. She turned and went back quickly down the passage, the way they had come. Then she ran out into the dark, into the light.

PART V — YOU NEXT TIME

It was a hot evening in July, and I was sitting on the porch in a chair made from an old car seat. I had a six-string acoustic on my lap and was running my fingers up and down the fret board, gazing into the distance. There was a can of beer open on the deck. We didn't count alcohol as a drug and American lager almost wasn't beer. Lowri was inside the farmhouse, and through the closed insect door I could hear her singing. Janis and Grace, the dogs, were rooting around in the yard.

Times like this, I often used to just sit there and stare out towards the woods. And I liked the idea that Lowri would soon be cooking, and that Becky and Suzanne, the stray hitch-hikers, would be there too when it got dark.

There was the sound of a car coming up from the village. You could pick it out by the tower of dust as it snaked along the road, vanishing outside the clapboard post office with its tattered flag on a pole, coming into view again on the low-hedged straight beside the apple barns. It was an old Chevy pickup, painted green with a flower stencilled on the door, so I knew who it was before he even pulled over in front of the house — Rick Kohler with his kilo bag of white powder and the body panels of his automobile stuffed with grass.

'Hi there, my man.' Rick was a scrawny guy with glasses. His hair always needed washing and the trousers hung off his non-existent backside. He looked like the chemistry swot from school. He certainly knew a lot about drugs.

I offered him beer, but he waved me away. 'I got something special for you, man,' he said.

'Christ, what next?'

Rick looked towards the Chevy. 'Come on out, honey!'

The passenger door on the far side opened, and I saw a female head. Round the front of the car came a skinny girl of about twenty-two years old. She had a floral cotton skirt, sandals and a white peasant blouse. Her dark straight hair was half tied back, secured by shades she'd pushed up on top of her head. She had suspicious brown eyes and she carried a guitar by the neck. Her high cheekbones made me think of a Cheyenne. She paused, unsure, and at that moment the sinking sun came through her hair from behind, through the short sleeves of her blouse, lighting her up. This was my first sight of Anya King.

She climbed the steps to the porch and awkwardly shook hands. Normally at a moment like this, Rick would be talking, rattling on like a typewriter. This time, though, he was as close to quiet as he could be.

Lowri came outside and Rick introduced her to Anya, who stayed kind of reserved.

'I hope you don't mind,' said Rick, 'I asked a few other people to come up later on as well.'

'From the city?' I said.

'Yeah. Some.'

'Sure thing,' said Lowri. I knew she did mind, a little, but would think it wrong to say so.

'Guess they'll be here about nine,' said Rick.

I suggested we go to Maria's place to swim first, and Rick said that was cool. With the money from two platinum albums, Maria had bought the biggest house in the neighbourhood. A refugee from LA, she spent summers upstate with her husband John Vintello, who was a lawyer with MPR records in New York, kind of a straight arrow, not a shyster.

The pool was in the yard with apple trees round it. Maria put a Dave Brubeck record on the outdoor system. Rick came out through the French doors, naked, walked through the hissing sprinklers on the lawn and jumped in the water. Maria came out from the summer house at the far end of the pool, also naked, the skin of her breasts shining with suntan oil. I never much liked this communal naked thing, but it was OK once you were in. I looked back to the house, where Anya was sitting on a lounger, sipping a drink. She'd put on a straw hat and looked like she wanted to stay in the shade.

Rick leaned against the side of the pool, threw his arms back over the edge and talked to Maria. His hair hung over his shoulders and drops of water fell from his moustache. He was getting up to full speed now, yattering away, and I wondered if he'd had a quick snort indoors.

John, Maria's husband, came back from the city, driving his station wagon up from the railway halt. He was starting a month's vacation and was in a happy state of mind. His label had three acts in the *Billboard* top twenty and they had six people from A & R out on the road scouting for new talent. John was planning to sail a boat with Maria and a couple of friends from Key West down to the Caribbean. He'd asked a few weeks earlier if Lowri and I would like to come aboard, and we had both pictured storms blowing in from the Gulf of Mexico and Maria's pill habit in a cramped space. 'But you're a Brit,' said Lowri, 'you're meant to have the sea in your blood.' 'And you're a Yankee girl, you're meant to be a pioneer.' 'Horses, Jack. Covered wagons. We left the sea at Plymouth Rock and never got our feet wet again.' After the two of us had spent an entire evening calculating what might be the longest period between landfalls we knew it wasn't our scene.

There was no swimming for John. He brought out some beers and a jug of margaritas. The sun was going down and I called

Lowri from the phone in the hall. She said two of Rick's friends had already showed up from New York — Denny Roberts, whose band Blue Ridge Cowboys had had a top-ten album in the spring (a kind of country rock thing with interesting harmonies), and his folksinger girlfriend, Tommi Fontaine.

We took two cars back to the farm, and I finally got Anya to talk a little. Her voice was rich and low. She told me she'd been playing in a coffee bar in the Village when Rick came up and spoke to her after her set. 'I was, like, a little distrustful of this guy coming on to me. I've been handling my own material for three years. Making my own bookings.'

'You were still in a coffee bar?'

'Sure. But a New York coffee bar. To a girl from Devils Lake, North Dakota, a Village coffee bar's as good as Radio City.'

'How long have you been in New York?'

'Two years. I had a job in a kind of song-writing factory for a bit.'

'The Brill Building?'

'Yeah, like that, only worse. In Brooklyn. We were in a row of small cubicles. It was like a musical reform school. A state pen for tunesmiths. I sold two songs. Two B-sides.'

'And you left?'

'Yeah, I'd started hearing songs on albums that weren't crafted for commercial radio. Songs with real words. I saw you could write a song about . . . you know, anything.'

'Not just love songs.'

'Sure. And you could write for your own voice, to your own strengths.'

'Are we going to hear you play?'

She smiled — the first time I'd seen her smile. It was a little lopsided. 'It's a long way to bring a guitar and leave it in the trunk.'

'I look forward to it. Rick Kohler has great taste.'

She looked at the floor of the car, then back up at me. 'I liked your last record by the way,' she said. Her eyes were flaring with light, but guarded.

'Thank you. We've pretty much broken up. The band, I mean. I didn't like the production. I thought it was too West Coast.'

Anya focussed on rolling a small cigarette with tobacco from a tin in her Mexican shoulder bag, as though she felt she'd given enough of herself for now. She felt no awkwardness in just shutting down. There were no fade-outs, no goodbyes.

The farmhouse we lived in had once been little more than a barn and was still only half converted. In the music room at one end of the ground floor, there were a piano, three guitars, various harmonicas, maracas and tambourines, and a double-height window that gave onto the woods. At the other end of the ground floor, Lowri had made a living space with sofas and a kitchen and a brick fireplace, which we seldom used for fear of setting light to the whole building. There were red curtains at the window, cottage furniture and always jars of wild flowers. The two bedrooms were upstairs, in what had once been a hayloft.

Two more friends of Rick's showed up, plus Becky and Suzanne, and after we'd all eaten we went outside and sat on the grass. Rick and I took guitars and played a bit just to set the atmosphere, which was fairly mellow in any case, with red wine and some fat joints going round. It was still hot. We'd brought out a couple of hurricane lamps and some candles and you could see the moths zooming about crazily.

I remember so well how Rick laid down his guitar and stood up, smirking from ear to ear, like a kid who knows some stupendous news.

'Ladies and gentlemen,' he said, bowing, his red cigarette-end arcing back in the flourish of his hand, 'may I present to you something the like of which you have never heard before in your life, the unique . . . Anya King.'

Anya, cross-legged and unsmiling, took up her own guitar and began to finger a few notes, stopping to tune the strings. She had a delicate picking touch with the right hand, and the sound of the instrument was ethereal. It wasn't the metal six-string tone we were all used to. I wondered whether it was the guitar itself or the tuning.

'OK,' she said. 'I'll sing four songs. This first one's called "Genevieve".'

For a long half-minute, the fingers picked with a fussy precision, seeming to use the top three strings only. At last the thumb flushed an arpeggio, bringing the lower notes in for the first time, then it was back to the home chords, minor, frosty. And then came the voice. It was high and clear, much higher than her speaking voice. She went through the middle of each note like someone bursting soap bubbles with a pin. There was this terrible purity. The song was about a girl lost in the city, trying to make her way, and it was set in the dead of winter. And out there on the hot summer grass, all you could feel was the ice in your fingertips. You could feel the bone-freezing cold of the back alleys, hear the trash-can lids roll and the rattle of old fire escapes where the homeless sleep. In her song she built this fragile world, but hard, cold, made real by the force of her imaginative belief in it. She ended with a minor chord struck slowly down through all the strings, and lightly smacked down with her palm to stop the ring.

I had heard nothing like it in my life. Most of our group, sitting on the grass, were looking at their laps, fumbling, as though they didn't want to be the first to offer an opinion.

Anya coughed and plucked the A-string, twisting the tuning peg, perhaps for something to do. 'OK,' she said. 'The second song is called "You Next Time".'

Where 'Genevieve' had been sideways-on, like a short story about someone else, this song was so direct, so confessional it made you flinch. It was in the first person and it sounded as though it had been channelled that morning direct from her own experience. She'd loved a man she couldn't have, had given way to a cruel separation but vowed to meet him in another life. 'No mistake the second time around,/I will die and rise, the shadow on your wall,/My name will be the only one you call,/Oh, my darling, you next time.' The emotional openness, the lack of self-protection, was a little frightening.

In the break between songs, Anya smiled her thanks for the friendly clapping, but didn't really seem interested in our response. I didn't like the third song so much. It was called 'Reservation Town' and had a social edge. There was folk and protest music, a tinge of bluegrass, and it was less purely original. It had ancestry. What I did hear in this song, though, was the range of her voice. It wasn't just the three-octave span, it was the variety of tone when she went into the lower register. Here, the cold purity was touched by something warmer and more womanly. It was a beautiful sound. I'd always felt the best soul and pop singers, women more than men, had a few notes they needed to hit as often as possible. Anya had two or three of those notes where her midrange met her lower that you just wanted to hear again and again. The word she sang could have been 'toothpaste', it wouldn't have mattered; the sound was so exquisite it sent shivers through your skull.

The silence after the song was easier to live with this time. Anya looked round the circle, a smile twitching the corner of her lips, as though she was thinking, What is it with these people? She retuned again. She was a fussy, fussy musician. 'This song is really meant to be played on the piano, but I'll play it on the guitar. It's called "Julie in the Court of Dreams".'

There was another slow, finger-picking introduction. The song began as observational, a little like 'Genevieve', with an open compassion for the girl it was about. You felt how protective Anya was of this imagined Julie, and maybe of all women. Then the music opened out. The voice lowered and Anya brought herself into the song, with that sudden rushing confessional we'd had on 'You Next Time'. She somehow managed to fuse her true self with this invented girl and make it universal. It was a huge thing to do, but it seemed modest — and that was what was so moving. By the time she played the third verse, the melody had already become familiar. It sounded like a song that had always been there, yet like nothing you'd ever heard before.

When she finished, she laid the guitar down on the grass beside her and said, 'OK, I'm going to get a drink now. Someone else can play.'

But no one moved.

Anya liked staying with us. She seemed happy just to mess around in our farmhouse by day, go up to swim at Maria's in the afternoon, then join me playing music in the evening.

I wasn't a great pianist, but I could fill out what she was doing with some chords on the warmer songs. There was no point in trying to play guitar for Anya because her own sound was so distinctive. Right from the start she disliked any other voice on her songs, especially a man's, even though I could reach the notes in falsetto and could think up harmonies. When she saw my face, she started to laugh. 'All right, Freddy, you can play some chords.' I don't know why she called me Freddy. My name is Jack. She often did this, I discovered later, finding names she thought suited people better than their own.

Although for four years I'd recorded my own songs and several joint compositions with my band, and Anya King had recorded nothing, she only tolerated me as a session-man-cum-makeshift-producer. But I didn't mind; I knew I was at the start of something extraordinary.

Rick was always trying to shift Anya back to the city. He'd found her a gig in a bar in SoHo, still pretty unexplored country then. It didn't start till September, but he kept telling her she should get back to the city and rehearse, get a feel for the venue.

'Just another few days, Rick,' she'd say. 'I'm really getting my head together here.'

'You stay, honey,' Lowri said.

The summer slid by. Suzanne and Becky moved out of the second bedroom so Anya could have it. The girls took sleeping rolls out on to the porch or the grass, though they tended to get visited and licked by Grace and Janis.

Rick disappeared to an inn somewhere off the interstate, maybe to score coke, but after a few days came back and slept on the living-room couch. The general store in the village sold pretty much all you needed; we got vegetables from the local farms, and once a week one of us would go to the supermarket in town to get packs of beer.

The weather stayed hot by day and cool enough to sleep well at night. Every evening after dinner, Rick would say, 'We got to fix this chick a record deal, man.'

And I would say, 'Pass that joint over here, you mean bastard. There's always tomorrow.'

And Anya would say solemnly, 'Tomorrow is another day.'

Lowri would sit watching it all with her amused expression.

'Days like this don't come round that often,' I said one night.

'What about yesterday?' said Anya.

'Yeah,' said Rick. 'And the day before.'

'And tomorrow,' said Lowri.

This seemed the funniest thing that any of us had ever heard. For about twenty minutes we were in agony as the first one able to breathe would say, 'What about the Wednesday before . . . l-a-a-s-t!'

A telephone call did come, though, from MPR records. Some kid in A & R that John Vintello had put on to us wanted to come right on up – or send a train ticket for Anya to go down to the city.

'Screw that,' I said. 'You should play some more gigs. Let's get you in some places up here. Just till the end of August. There's plenty of small venues in town and a lot of tourists to play to.'

So next day Anya and Rick and I got in the Chevy and headed into town. We stood in daylight bars that smelled of last night's beer where the soles of your boots ripped up from the sticky floor when you tried to move. Rick did his spiel, Anya looked demure and icy, I kept an eye out for trouble. A guy with a white Afro and six rows of beads sat Anya on a tall bar stool to play while he slumped down at a low table so he could see up her skirt. An old woman in a pool hall said Anya could play for tips. A bar on the waterfront liked her enough to offer her a week, but not till September.

We went with the white Afro at five bucks an hour, beer and tips. He told Anya to sing some folk songs, which she had to do anyway because she didn't have enough material of her own to fill the time.

'I like that,' he said, when she'd played him one. 'Is that Appalachian or what?'

'Sure. See you Saturday.'

Back in the car, Rick said, 'Was that schmuck trying to get a look at your panties?'

'I think so.'

'What a pervert.'

'Don't worry, I wasn't wearing any.'

She was the only one who could shut Rick up.

Those few weeks, I was so happy I hardly dared inhale. I think it was the same for all of us. Households could break up as quickly as they formed and no one liked to talk about what made this one work where the last one crashed. I'd first met Lowri when I was in LA after my English band had broken up and she was living in Laurel Canyon in a house with six other people, three of them with giant egos. Lowri was the glue that held it together and no one seemed to notice how beautiful she was — with her brown eyes and straw hair and dusty freckles. She was always pushing herself into the background. I noticed her, though. She and I went to the Troubadour and the Whisky a Go Go and saw all those people who'd go on to be famous. That was way back, out West. But this summer, with Anya and Rick. What made our farmhouse run so well? It could have been the joker in the pack: maybe Rick gave people just enough to find annoying, so he was the lightning conductor. Maybe it was the bit-part characters, Becky and Suzanne, who went to work at the big neighbouring farm by day, saving up their wages to travel in the fall, and earned their keep by helping out and being cool (and in both cases, I suspected, visiting Rick on his couch in the night. The runty little guy had a way of getting girls to do things to him). Maybe it helped having Maria and John up the road for a change of scene. Also, there were no money hassles, thanks to the royalties still coming in from my last album.

We accommodated Anya. Softly spoken, young, unrecorded, mild-mannered . . . Was there anything that wasn't easy about it? The size of her talent, I suppose. The silent power of her self-belief. It left this kind of force field round her. She was in no hurry to get back to the city; it was like she knew her time would come and there was no need to rush. Perhaps she could foresee the limousines and the press officers and the chain hotels and all the other things that would threaten her ability to find the pure thoughts inside her.

The gig we'd set up in town turned out pretty well. The audience was folkies for the most part, but with plenty of vacationers passing through and a solid core of drinkers who took a lot of winning over. When she needed to retune or change guitars and they just wanted something to sing along to, there was kind of a big frost. She never played a note until she was one hundred per cent ready.

When did I begin to fall in love with Anya King? Before I met her. Before I knew her. The day her head bobbed up from the other side of Rick's car . . . I felt I'd known her all my life and here she was at last. But she was someone I was also dead afraid of, because she was too much in me, too much a part of me and, in some way I couldn't understand, stronger than me. She was more me than I was.

And I had to deal with the fact that I still loved Lowri. Yet the way I loved Lowri was full of respect. She was the opposite of me: she was fair, practical, considerate, wise. I was none of those things. We got on so well because we complemented one another. When I met her, it was like, I'll take this one, she's the deal, she's got all I need.

With Anya there was no weighing up and no decision. There were things about her I thought wrong, things I didn't understand and ways in which she was a lesser woman than Lowri. But none of them mattered at all. She was my destiny, and all I could do was ride it.

'Come on, Freddy,' she'd say each day in the evening light, banging on the bonnet of the Chevy. 'Time to go. I'm gonna try that new song tonight.'

She'd learned to drive an automobile when she was twelve – anything to get out of Devils Lake – but liked me to take charge of the expedition, like a roadie. In my bad moments I thought maybe she gave me roles in her life out of charity, but mostly I knew she needed someone to be between her and the world. She needed me to mediate for her. And I was thrilled, though I didn't let on.

'This time last year I was a guy with a top-twenty record. Now I'm an unpaid driver.'

'We make a left here, Freddy.'

The new song she was trying out was called 'Ready to Fly', and it made me excited and uncomfortable at the same time. It wasn't a fully personal-history thing like 'You Next Time', but it seemed to refer to her own life at that moment. The chorus had a see-sawing quality that had the people in the bar tapping their feet and humming along. The words went:

> There's a time you're unsteady
> This feeling is heady
> You know you could easily cry
> But you've spun there already
> This frightening eddy
> Now you know that you're ready to fly.

There were a few things that kept the song from being as simple as that chorus looked. The tune kept going from major to minor and back again, so you weren't sure how happy she was. The final word 'fly' was on that breaking verge between her middle and lower register, and she slid over two or three semitones. There was a 'he' or a 'him' in the song and if you were a woman listening then it could have referred to your man, but it could also have been someone in particular for Anya.

And was it just me or was there a rhyme-word that was obviously missing? And wasn't that word 'Freddy'?

I'd sit at the back with some of the rowdier guys and try to set an example by applauding like crazy at the end of a song. Sometimes they'd look up to see what I was on about, and sometimes they wouldn't bother. I'd first played at the age of fifteen with my brothers in pubs in south London, so I knew the score.

The middle of the set was given to folk songs and to covers of other people's material. It amused Anya to pass off one of her own as a song from the Appalachians. She liked to watch some of the older men nod their heads in approval, as though they'd had enough of this young woman's life and appreciated a real song now.

When Anya played, I was in the back-alley cold of 'Genevieve', in the wilderness of 'Julie in the Court of Dreams', in the vertigo of 'Ready to Fly'. And I was in her fingers on the strings, in her breathing, in her phrasing. I was pouring all my energy into her. I was part of something being born.

Late one morning, towards the end of August, I was sitting at the end of the house pushing a few chords up and down the piano, humming, and wondering if I would ever write my own songs again when I felt Anya standing behind me. This was a trick of hers, to materialise without a sound. She didn't make you jump; it was more like she'd been there all along. I pretended not to notice, and carried on playing.

She rested her head on my shoulder and watched my hands move on the keys. I could just feel the point of her breasts against my back. Then she leaned over, took my right hand away and replaced it with hers.

'You play with the left, Freddy, I'll play with the right.'

Her hair was tickling the side of my face and her left breast was pressed flat against me as she reached forwards. Her spare hand was on my shoulder. I played a simple rolling blues with the left hand and let her improvise with the right. I wasn't, as I've said, much of a pianist, and her body pressed against mine was making it difficult to concentrate. I felt myself hardening uncomfortably in tight jeans, but was determined to keep going. I didn't want her to think I was under her spell. As we played, Anya began to hum in my ear. The movement of her right hand seemed to be suggesting a melody to her.

'Hang on,' she said, detaching herself from me and coming round the other side. With her left hand she played a sequence of a few bars. 'Can you play that?'

'Sure. And just keep repeating?'

'Yup.'

She went back to the other side, squeezed back in tight against me and began to play the tune with the right hand. 'A little bit slower,' she said, 'more of a rocking rhythm. That's it, that's it.'

I watched her fingers going up and down, feeling out the melody while she hummed it in my ear.

'And what's it going to be about?' she whispered.

'Personally,' I said, 'I usually sing nonsense words with the right rhythm till I've figured it out. Any old words. "Sod this, it looks like turkey."'

'Nice try, Freddy.'

She kept humming for a bit, then sang, '"Susie, she's kind of lazy . . ."'

'Or, "Fuck me, you drive me crazy."'

'Ssh. "Hold me, I'm feeling lonely . . ."'

'Stay with that swoop you're getting when you slide between "hold" and "me". That's your killer. It goes through my teeth like a . . .'

'Like a what? Like a dentist's *drill*?'

'Yeah, but like it's drilling on a nerve of pure pleasure.'

'Shucks, mister. Really!'

'Find that note and stick it in as often as you can.'

'You saying I should construct a whole song just so it involves that note as many times as possible?'

'Why not?'

'Because my loyalty's to the song, not to people's pleasure.'

'Oh, Anya. Come to meet us. Come halfway.'

She pressed herself more tightly in and played the tune that was emerging. My left hand was still plodding away in the lower reaches.

'What do we call this special note, then?' she said.

'Search me, I just call it your "skull" note for where it hits me.'

'"'Hold me, you wondrous lady,' I heard him call,/When the lights from down the highway washed up the bedroom wall."'

'It sounds lovely, but maybe a bit comic.'

'Not by the time I've finished with it. Anyway, love is comic, isn't it? The fools we make of ourselves.'

'When you look back at it, maybe.'

She brushed her left hand across my groin and the fingertips lightly traced the straining outline.

'He must be awful cramped in there, Freddy.'

'He'll survive.'

It turned out Rick was playing a long game with MPR. He'd recorded Anya at the club and sent tapes also to Upright Records in San Francisco and to Antigone, a new label one of the big entertainment companies had spun off in LA. Anya liked the look of Asylum, but Rick told her they'd been gobbled up.

'In the end Warner Brothers swallows everyone, sweetheart,' he said.

'How are you going to tell John Vintello you've been going behind his back?' I said.

'We're allowed to look at different offers. But we need enough songs for the album.'

'I have maybe twenty songs,' said Anya. 'I just don't play them till they're good and ready.'

It was mid-morning and we were sitting on the verandah, drinking coffee.

'Oh, yeah?' said Rick, sceptically. '"Julie in the Court of Dreams"? How long you sit on that little baby?'

'I wrote "Julie" when I was nineteen.' Anya took a sip from her mug.

'Fuck me,' said Rick. He scratched his chin as he tried to regain his composure. 'You know what I think. Maybe split the album and do one side of, like, really personal things and the other of more story-like tracks.'

'Like a concept album, you mean?' said Anya.

'Yeah, kind of.'

She pushed the hair back from her face. 'That is a really, really terrible idea, man. Each song is a different world. You try and force them together, you diminish each one.'

'Yeah, maybe you're right.' Rick stood up. 'But one thing I can tell you for sure is you gotta get your ass back to New York City.'

'It's just so hard to leave,' said Anya.

She was gazing out over the farmland to the woods. I looked out there, too, and saw the first softening of autumn in the thick light on the meadow. My throat felt thick. 'Maybe we should clear up who's doing what in this little band,' I said.

Anya leapt up from the old car seat. 'I want you with me, Freddy. You gotta be my road man. I need you there. And Rick, you can suck the cocks of the record executives.'

We'd never heard her talk like this before and we exploded laughing, even Rick.

'Sorry,' Anya said. 'That just kinda slipped out.'

But we shook on a deal that we'd split the management fee, Rick and me, straight down the middle, and if one day he spent ten hours in meetings while I played a few piano chords and if another time I was on the road for a week and he was on vacation in Mexico, neither would complain.

'One thing I would say, though, Rick. Let's go with John Vintello. MPR is a good label. We need a bastard on our side and John's our kind of bastard.'

'Good title for a song,' said Rick. '"Our Kind of Bastard".'

'It's good in your Jersey accent,' I said.

'I already got a title from this conversation,' said Anya. '"So Hard to Leave".'

'Sounds kinda soppy,' said Rick.

'Oh, you big tough boy.' Anya put an arm round his shoulders, then her other arm round mine. We stood on the deck and looked over the fields towards the south, where, out of sight from us, behind the thick stockade of trees, the Hudson was winding down towards the city.

We had a place in the East Village, a cold-water flat that Rick had got hold of through a friend of a friend. It was a third-floor walk-up with three big rooms, which was enough for Anya to have a private bedroom and for all of us to be able to spread out and practise. I had a man come and fit a gas geyser and plumb in a bathtub. Rick said I should reclaim the money from our first record deal.

We did our best to make it comfortable, but Anya wasn't much of a homemaker. She sewed some curtains and liked to buy flowers from outside the late-night shop on Sixth Street, but that was about it. She had no interest in cooking. I was only meant to be there for a couple of weeks anyway while she got started with her thing in SoHo, then I'd be heading back upstate.

Lowri told me to stay in New York as long as I needed. She said it would give her a chance to get on with her own work, which was to write a play. She had been encouraged by some people she'd met to develop a one-act thing she'd done in her postgrad programme a few years earlier. She seemed set on doing it, and I never thought to find out how sincere her passion was, or even what the play was about. I just liked the idea that, like everyone else we knew, she had a talent.

Did Lowri suspect I was in love with Anya? It seems a crazy question now. Of course she did. Even Rick said, 'She's given you the rope to hang yourself, man.' What's even crazier is that I had no idea Lowri knew. It was so against the way we behaved to express jealousy or a sense of possession. We'd been together two happy years, but stayed out of each other's space. It was the way we all did things. And although it showed respect and granted a load of freedom, it also caused a lot of agony. She might have said something. She *should* have said something. And I should have used my imagination.

The place for Anya's residency was on Broome Street, near Thompson, in a cast-iron building that had been a garment factory. People could eat in the front, drab stuff, burgers and salads, though the place had about five hundred liquor bottles lined up behind the bar. The back of the building was mostly seats; you could get a lot of people in. Anya played two sets every night, one hour each, and all her own songs. There was an upright piano on which she allowed me to accompany her on a couple of guitar-based numbers, though if it was a real piano song, like 'Julie', she'd be at the keyboard herself. I don't think I contributed anything at all musically, but she liked to have me there. On one number I had to patter out a rhythm on the tom-toms, which was embarrassing for someone who, with his first band, had played electric guitar at the London Palladium.

The early-evening set tended to be a warm-up. There weren't that many people and they didn't listen. The later one, at eleven, was better. Word of mouth had begun to spread, but slowly. We needed to get her reviewed or advertised and it seemed to me the best way to do this was to sign the deal with MPR and let their publicity machine do the work for us.

Then one day we had a review in a music paper. It had clearly been written by some college boy who was using it as a platform to launch himself. It had some words like '*Weltschmerz*', but it seemed to do the trick. We stuck a line from it – 'Anya King is a sensation' – outside the door and took an ad in the *Village Voice* to push another line: 'Deeply moving songs of lost love and fractured identity.'

Without telling me, Rick sent the clipping to Upright Records in San Francisco, and their New York man finally came by and made an offer one evening after the show. Rick told him to stuff his offer, but he rang Vintello the next morning, used the Upright bid to crank up the MPR price and closed a two-record deal that afternoon.

Anya said she was appalled, but I think she was secretly pleased. She was to go into the studio in November for a springtime release.

And so it had happened that I found myself living with Anya. Like all things in those days, it was fluid. Sometimes a friend of hers would stay for a few nights, sometimes Rick would be there for a week, but he travelled a fair bit, and his folks had a place in Jersey where he kept his records and other stuff. The only ever-presents were Anya and me.

It was a sunny autumn with a cool edge to the air. We never got in before two, but we liked to get up early. I'd fetch the paper while Anya was in bed and sometimes I'd get rolls or pastries from the bakery. The early morning was her favourite time of day and many of her songs referred to mailmen, shop awnings being rolled up, birds singing. Once I knocked on her door and took in some coffee, but she obviously didn't like being disturbed in bed, where she slept naked. What she did like was to come out in her own time wearing a faded tee-shirt and brief cotton shorts. She'd pour a giant bowl of Sugar Frosted Flakes, which she'd work through without a word, sitting cross-legged on the couch. I could sometimes see she had nothing on beneath the shorts. I don't think she did this to taunt me. These clothes were a halfway stage to getting dressed and she only wore them because someone else was there. After the flakes she'd have some weird Turkish yoghurt as if to punish herself for eating processed cereal, then there'd be pancakes, or eggs with strips of maple-cure bacon and slices of wholewheat toast with redcurrant jelly. She was basically a vegetarian, except for bacon which 'doesn't count'. The square wooden table was a mess by the end. She'd slump back down on the couch with coffee and exhale loudly.

'Wow.'

'That looked good.'

'Did you want some, Freddy?'

'You always ask when it's too late.'

'I know you'll say no, that's why, skinny boy.'

In the course of these mornings I heard about her life. Devils Lake was old Sioux country that had been settled by some pioneer then filled with Lutheran immigrants. Her father's family were from Norway and she'd been christened Anja, but changed it to Anya because she thought it sounded more Russian and romantic. She said *Anna Karenina* was her favourite book and in the translation she'd read the lover guy called the heroine 'Anya' as a pet name. The grandfather had changed the surname from the Norwegian 'Konge' – a good move, I told her. She seemed vague about her mother's people. I wondered if there was some Sioux blood there.

Her mother ran off with a salesman in roofing materials when Anya was eight. They went up to Canada and never came back. Anya and her father had a card from Thunder Bay, where the mother had set up with this other man and was expecting his child. The parents didn't bother to divorce. The father never remarried and there were no brothers or sisters.

'So, said Anya, 'it was just me and Dad.'

She usually got dressed by mid-morning, so this far into a conversation she was in jeans and bare feet with some sort of peasant blouse.

'Were you lonely?'

'Not exactly. I went to school. It was a nice place and I had friends there. But when school ended there was not a hell of a lot to do. Dad didn't get back from work till late. The population of the town was only about six thousand. I used to go up to the train station and stare at the trains.'

'Just stare at them?'

'For hours. I liked it. Coming. Going. It made me feel there was always a future. Always another train. Nothing is for ever.'

'Nothing lasts?'

'Yeah, but also, nothing is lost. You just have to wait. The train was going to be my escape. Other days, I'd stand by the highway to Grand Forks and watch the cars and trucks.'

I pictured this kid standing by the side of the road watching the traffic go past.

'I liked clubs at school,' she said. 'Drama and painting. I learned to play the piano. I liked to stay after school as long as possible so I wouldn't be home alone. I wanted to go to drama school in Chicago. I used to write stories. Most evenings when we'd had dinner I'd go upstairs and write stuff.'

'Didn't you watch TV?'

'Dad did. He always fell asleep in front of it. I preferred making up people in stories.'

I must have looked unconvinced, because she said, 'It's what lonely kids do, Freddy.'

'But didn't you have boyfriends?'

'Sure. I kissed Dave Schneider when I was fourteen. I was always interested in boys.'

'I can tell from your songs.'

Anya frowned. 'They're not all me, you know. Some are, some aren't. Some of the ones that sound most like me – the "I" ones – are made up and some of the ones that sound most like they're about other people are really about me.'

'And that's how you keep your mystery.'

She put the coffee mug down on the table and looked back at me oddly. 'Am I mysterious to you?'

We were sitting very close to one another on the couch, but I felt all right about the way the conversation was going. One thing about us, even at this stage, was that we always *got on*. There was no awkwardness.

'Yes, you are mysterious to me,' I said. 'I don't know how someone who has that much talent can be so diffident. If I could do what you can, I'd be in the studio right now recording my third or fourth album.'

She laughed and flung her hands out wide, a favourite search-me gesture. 'The most exciting time is when everything is possible. As soon as I put "Genevieve" on vinyl it'll be like the death of the song. The arrangement, the exact notes and phrasing, whether we have a backing singer . . . I don't want there to be a definitive version. I want it to go on living. Every time I sing that song it feels different, like a performance in a theatre that's never quite the same.'

'And this "not committing," is that true with people too?'

'Yes.'

At this point there was, admittedly, a silence. But she didn't want anything to be unclear. She straightened up and made an effort, out of respect for me.

'Freddy, if I sleep with you, if we fell in love, I'd give myself to you completely. Do you really want that? Could you handle it? Could I? Is it what we both want?'

'I don't know. But I love you for telling me.'

'You're a beautiful man. Look at these hands. And this soft brown hair sweeping over your shoulders. You look like a troubadour, like a medieval knight. I know it would be wonderful. But like this, it's even better. Maybe. When everything is still just . . . possibility.'

In October, I went back to the farm. I think Lowri had been lonely. Becky and Suzanne had left to continue their travels. And as Lowri said, there's only so much time you can spend sitting at your typewriter with Grace and Janis for company. She'd got herself a job working in a bar in town three evenings a week. She liked having some money that didn't come from me, though mostly she did it for the company. This made me feel bad, but I wasn't sure what to do about it. When we went to bed my first night back, I looked at Lowri's beautiful face on the pillow next to mine and I kissed her and soon we were making love as we'd done so

many times before. But I came in a great blackout spasm thinking
of Anya, when she'd sit on the couch with her ankles crossed and
the soft hair I could see through the loose fit of her shorts. I let
out this roar of what must have sounded like pain, because Lowri
asked me if I was all right and I just made up some stuff about
it being a long time since I'd seen her and she said, 'Well, you've
certainly been storing it up,' and we laughed a bit. I rolled away
and she put her arm round me. I shut my eyes and pictured myself
pulling down Anya's shorts and bending her over the couch and
holding on to her breasts through the tee-shirt from behind, and
within moments I was hard again and twisted my hip so Lowri's
hand shouldn't accidentally discover. I couldn't keep my mind
from where it wanted to go. It was a sort of torment, but a torment
where I felt safe.

The fall was beautiful with the colours the eastern states are famous
for, and we could see it all without leaving the farm. Lowri and
I stood on the deck looking at the russet, gold, orange, red in a
great parade, lit by the thick, misty sun with breezes running
through the falling leaves and bringing the half-forgotten smell
of wood fires, and for Lowri, I suppose, memories of Hallowe'en
and trick-or-treat and freshman socials on the campus by Lake
Michigan and for me the clatter of football studs as you ran out
on the path that went down to the playing field, and for both of
us that quickening of the new term and shorter days and life
running on a little too fast. It was almost the first time we'd been
old enough to be aware of being grown up. Lowri was the first
person I'd shared this with, knowing these weren't random sensations, but they were wired in and would return.

I stayed until the last week in October, when I had to go back
to the city to help Anya and Rick finalise which songs she was
going to record and what session men we needed. After some
argument with the people at MPR, it had been agreed that I'd

produce the record. Anya had made it a condition. This was fine by me, except I didn't have that great a knowledge of the technical side of recording. John Vintello wanted us to work with this guy called Larry Brecker in Los Angeles, which seemed insane to me. I mean, to go all that way when there was so much expertise in New York. But I could be the sole producer and Anya could pick the songs, so long as we got them all down in three weeks at the studio in West Hollywood with Larry Brecker at the console. I guess MPR had some sort of deal with the studio, and it didn't seem too much to ask. It wasn't like they'd stuck in an arranger or an orchestra or something.

I called Lowri to tell her I'd be gone for a month.

'Where will you live?'

'In a hotel on Sunset. To begin with. But maybe we'll find something better.'

'Candy might have something in Laurel Canyon.'

'That'd be cool. Will you be OK?'

'Sure. I'll finish my play.'

'I'll call every day.'

'I'll be fine, Jack. Just don't forget to send the paycheck.'

Her voice had gone flat. She was trying to come over cheerful with the thing about the money, but she sounded like someone dying. And still, stupidly, I just put it out of my mind. Nothing had happened, there was nothing for Lowri to 'know'. I was going out to work, to pay the bills for our farmhouse. It's what people do.

In the last days in New York we went to a lot of art galleries during the day. After her giant breakfast Anya tended not to eat again until midnight, but she was happy to sit with me in a bar while I had a salad or a cheeseburger for lunch. I loved New York food and I loved the long wooden bars it was served at, with the signed photographs of boxers and baseball players on the walls. The city was a dream to me. I liked the way its history is all laid out. The names of the immigrant families faded on the brickwork in Lower Manhattan: Reuben, Kelly, Kasprowicz, Mancini. On parking lots, on warehouse walls, they'd left a printed mark on their journey between Ellis Island and the blank of midtown. It made me feel invigorated and so lucky that I'd never had to crawl off some stinking ship at the foot of the island and claw my way up the grid.

To be a part of this but not alone, not some London tourist, but in conversation all the time with this extraordinary woman — I was intoxicated, not on Michelob or grass, but on Anya's dark eyes, the way her teasing was becoming less defensive because she trusted me and was getting ready for what seemed inevitable. While I ate at lunchtime, she liked to drink a big glass of red wine and smoke a cigarette, then go back to the apartment and sleep for an hour to make up for the late night. It made a rhythm to the day. About four o'clock we'd have strong English tea with milk, to please me, and listen to records on the stereo. Anya liked to know what everyone else was doing, and we seemed to buy a new record every day. She'd slide the vinyl reverently from its waxy inner sleeve. She had a way of holding the disc up to the light, her fingers fanned out on the edge, peering at the grooves as though she could hear by sight. Then the turntable arm would drop, and the needle skated for a second with a hiss before it thunked into the groove. 'That's interesting,' she'd say. 'That middle eight.' Or 'That doesn't work at all. My God, that's not a pedal steel, is it?' She had a horror of pedal steel guitar, which she called 'the instant schmaltzer'. Then she'd practise for the evening and try out new ideas on me. We'd leave at six to walk to the venue, carrying her favourite six-string guitar, which she wouldn't risk leaving locked up at the club with the other instruments.

Audiences had been picking up steadily, and the last night at the club was packed. John Vintello and Maria came in for the late show. There were journalists from underground papers, the music press, and some guys from other record labels. There were also musicians, several I recognised, who'd come to hear what this girl was like.

The size of the audience gave her confidence. People who don't perform imagine that a big crowd is intimidating, but it's the half-full room that makes you feel like you've been rumbled, and makes the words stick in your throat.

Anya's last number was always a foot-tapper called 'Run Me Crazy, Run Me Wild', which was there to send them out happy, but before she did it she pulled the microphone a little closer.

'I want to thank you all for coming here tonight and the people at Blue Lounge for having me here these past few weeks. On Saturday I'm flying to LA to record my first album, which is kind of exciting, but kind of daunting too. Thank you, thank you! No, really, it's – wow, it's like a great opportunity for me.'

She looked about sixteen years old as she spoke, like a child showing off her artwork at a school open day. It was incredibly touching.

'Some of the songs you've heard tonight are going to be on the album,' she said. 'And maybe one or two you haven't. I'm not sure, yet. I'm going with my producer and my friend, Freddy here. Yeah, let's hear it for Freddy! And he's the person I want to thank most of all. He's been like an inspiration and a guide. So this one's for you, Fred. It's called "Hold Me".'

I had my hands poised for the barrelhouse piano of 'Run Me Crazy' and I didn't know what to do. But I recognised the chords she was ripping out on her jangly twelve-string. It was the song she'd written leaning over my shoulder in the farmhouse. I hadn't heard it from that day to this and thought she'd given up on it. She'd changed the words, though, and while it was still a lively song, it wasn't comic any more. 'Hold me, you brown-eyed stranger,/Don't let me go/There's a mighty road to travel/And some dangers I don't know.' It was the closest thing she'd written to a pop song, with a catchy falling melody and a shuffling beat and those little internal rhymes she liked.

But just then I wasn't thinking about rhymes. I was watching this absurdly talented young woman leaning forward to the microphone, striking rich chords and singing. I was picturing the weeks ahead.

We stayed drinking and talking till about two, then walked back through the cool night. Most of the old guys in the Bowery had stopped screaming at the dark and had slumped down in the doorways, but there were still a couple of hopeful hookers on 2nd Avenue. Anya was holding my arm as she always did on this walk back. We turned on to Seventh Street, and I had no sense of the big paving slabs beneath my feet, didn't see the fire hydrants or the iron braces on the kerb. I stuck the key in the lock and we reached the third floor slightly out of breath. We'd hardly spoken on the way back. She just held my arm. There wasn't much to say.

'You want a drink, Freddy? Scotch?'

'OK.'

She poured two tumblers and handed one to me. Neither of us liked Scotch. We clinked glasses and drank. I put mine down on the square table where she left the ruin of her breakfast things. I put my hands on her shoulders.

'You were good,' I said.

'I was OK. You were perfect.'

She reached up and kissed me on the mouth. I felt the shock go through my spine. We kissed again and she began to breathe quickly.

After a minute, she said, 'Wait. I'll call you in a moment.'

She went into her room, where I could hear her draw the curtains and light matches for candles. The bar of electric light under the door disappeared.

'You can come in now,' she said.

She'd taken off all her clothes and thrown them on the chair.

I was still fully dressed as she came into my arms and kissed me again. I let my hands feel the softness of her skin, on her back, down over her hips.

'Anya—'

She silenced me with her tongue. After a minute she said, 'You going to take your clothes off now, mister?'

'Sure.'

My hands were shaking as she shut the door behind us.

'I can't believe we—'

'I know, Freddy, I know. Just hold me. Hold me, you brown-eyed stranger.'

I laughed, but winced a little too.

Then she put her lips against my ear, pressed her body hard against mine and whispered, 'Now just fuck me, you beautiful, beautiful man.'

'Ask me nicely.'

'Please, Freddy. Please fuck me. I think you'll like it. Please, please, please.'

A few days later, we were on the plane. Anya was at the window, looking at the yellowish slabs of Missouri or maybe Kansas underneath. She was holding my hand in her lap while her other hand was swizzling the little plastic stick in her vodka and tonic.

'Hey,' I said, 'is that Devils Lake?'

'Looks a little too populated. Anyway, Devils Lake's way up north.'

'I know. I was just teasing.'

'Well, stop teasing.' She leaned over and kissed me chastely on the lips, but immediately there was a charge and I had to pull my head away.

'So,' I said, clearing my throat. 'Let's make that final list of songs.'

'How many we aiming for?'

'I think we should record twelve. They may want to bring it

down to ten. I guess we're aiming at not more than twenty minutes a side. Maybe less for a first record.'

'We get to choose which two we drop?'

'Sure. Unless there's some sure-fire hit they insist on keeping.'

'Well, I guess we're safe there.'

The definites at this stage were 'Genevieve', 'Julie in the Court of Dreams', 'You Next Time', 'Ready to Fly' and 'Hold Me'. That was one side of the record. There were about fifteen other contenders, and this was where the hard work would be. Anya wanted 'Reservation Town' and 'Run Me Crazy, Run Me Wild', though I thought her reasons were personal, not musical. The first one reminded her of travelling to Chicago for the first time at the age of eighteen and the second of the great evenings we'd just lived through in New York. I thought she had several stronger songs, but I decided to wait and see what emerged in the studio.

Then we were over the Rockies and Anya had fallen asleep with her head on my shoulder. As soon as she was unconscious, I thought of Lowri, back on the other side of the country. I pictured her mountains, the Catskills, and her weather, which would be getting cold. I'd call her from the hotel. The odd thing was that I only thought of Lowri when Anya was asleep. When Anya was awake I lived in her eyes and nowhere else existed. I nodded off, too, somewhere over the desert, and was awoken by the attendant telling me to fasten my seat belt for landing.

We took a cab from LAX and I felt what I always did arriving in this strange place and driving up Sepulveda. How Spanish, how low and spreadeagled it was compared to New York. It was a different continent. It must have been just as hard, in fact harder, to build a city here, where they didn't even have water. America always made you feel in awe of what previous generations had done. All these spaced-out people on the street, but someone strong had come before and done the work.

The Hotel Pasadena Star was on one of the dingier parts of Sunset. The reception desk was kicked and scuffed. It had a heavy dial telephone and there was a slow fan overhead that stirred the leaves of a potted palm.

The desk clerk looked like a sickly Sammy Davis, Jr. 'I have two rooms for you,' he said, holding out a pair of keys with heavy metal fobs. 'That's 274 at the front here. That's a premier room with a view over Hollywood, and 289 is in back overlooking our Japanese garden. You have a mini-bar in the room. The room charges are all taken care of, but not the extras.'

'Are the rooms near each other?' said Anya.

'Yes, ma'am. They're right across the hall.'

'Can we get something to eat?'

'We don't have a restaurant, ma'am, but there's a sandwich menu in your room. I can get something sent up. You also have a kitchenette in 274 if you'd care to make yourself a snack.'

'Is there a grocery store nearby?'

'I guess you'd need to take a cab. I'll get the bellhop to take your bags and I'll find out for you.'

The bellhop, a burly man who looked to me like Sam Cooke, tried to take Anya's guitar and found himself told not to touch it. Three other guitars had been shipped direct to the studio, but this one had had to fly with us as carry-on.

We took the elevator together. It was a squash and I could tell by the way she turned her face to the wall that Anya was trying not to laugh.

The rooms were drab, with 1950s furnishings. Number 274 at the front had that cracked grout in the bathroom that always made me think of cockroaches. There was no air conditioning, but when you opened the window you were hit by the traffic noise from Sunset. Number 289, overlooking the Japanese garden (a yard with pea-shingle in place of a lawn), was north-facing and dark, but much quieter.

I fumbled for a tip. I hadn't travelled for a while, and I'd forgotten the endless roll of ones you needed. Sam Cooke seemed happy enough as he left us.

Anya burst out laughing. 'Does everyone in LA look like a singer?'

'I know. And the other guy.'

'It's Sammy Davis. They should play together.'

'What do you think of the rooms?'

Anya pursed her lips. We were in 289, the back one. 'Let's sleep in here. We can use the other one for cooking and maybe rehearsing.'

'Good idea,' I said. 'At least this one's quiet.'

'We can make it comfortable' said Anya. 'I'll make it OK for us. My God, look at this mini-bar. My God.' She'd started laughing helplessly again. The 'mini-bar' was a wicker basket with a bottle of Four Roses and a pint of gin. There was a bag of potato chips, some Schweppes tonic and a Hershey bar.

'Where are we going to eat?' I said.

'I don't know. Where do you think Sammy Davis eats?'

'He probably does what you do — fills up in the morning then he doesn't have to eat till he gets home to Mom's cooking in Burbank.'

'Let's have some gin,' said Anya, trying out the bed. 'Did you see an ice machine down the hall?'

'No. D'you want to go and see?'

'I'm scared. There's a touch of "Psycho" about this place. You look, Freddy.'

I walked up and down the corridor, but there was nothing. Back in the room, I rang down to the front desk and ordered some sandwiches and ice.

Sammy Davis read it back to me: 'That's a Swiss cheese on rye with salad and a club on toasted white with extra pickle. Ice cubes. Potato chips. You want ice cream?'

'No thanks. But a lemon maybe?'

'You want a lemon? OK, we'll be with you in ten.'

I put the phone down. '"We'll be with you in ten," he said. Who's "we" I wonder?'

'Maybe the Temptations.'

'I'm half expecting the Four fucking Tops.'

'Is that your London voice? Do some more.'

'Blimey, love, 'oo d'ya think they'll bleedin' send up this time? Better tell the geezer when 'e gets 'ere you're the old trouble and strife.'

Anya was lying on the bed laughing. 'Give me gin, Fred.'

'You sure?'

'Yup.'

I poured some gin into a filmy tumbler. Anya sipped it and the tears stood in her eyes. 'This is gross.'

'I told you to wait.'

'I'm going to soldier on.'

I loved her at that minute, sitting cross-legged on the lumpy bed, still laughing through her gin grimaces.

The next day was a Sunday. We explored the neighbourhood, found a grocery store only half an hour's walk away, and went to Venice Beach to see the freaks. On Monday at ten o'clock we arrived at the studio.

Larry Brecker had long mousy hair, prescription glasses in an aviator shape and a moustache that covered both lips. His flared jeans were a little too short and flapped round the ankles of his boots. He'd listened to Anya's songs on a tape sent over by MPR and we began to discuss arrangements. He thought we should do 'Genevieve' first because it was a solo thing and would give her confidence. We had four session musicians lined up for later on – acoustic bass, percussion, sax and electric guitar. Brecker presumed Anya and I could cover any extra keyboards between us. There was an electric piano and a Hammond organ in the studio. They also had a girl singer on standby for backing vocals.

For our second track, after we'd finished 'Genevieve', he thought we should try a song he'd really liked called 'Boulevards of Snow', but maybe with some organ fills.

'Maybe,' I said.

'No chance,' said Anya.

'We can try it,' I said. 'We can always take the organ off again.'

'It's your call,' said Brecker, going back behind the glass.

I knew it would be a tough call to make because Anya would resist any additions to voice and one instrument. I could tell she was nervous, so we played a twelve-bar blues for a bit. Then she sang scales and a bit of Burt Bacharach to warm up while I got a feel of the piano, which was a much better instrument than I was used to. By three o'clock, after about fifty retunes and strings snapping, we'd got her guitar part on 'Genevieve' down in a way everyone was happy with. Brecker got his assistant, a kid called Russ, to order in some sandwiches and we sat around trying to relax. All this was new to Anya and I could see she was finding it a strain.

When Brecker was back behind the glass, I asked Anya if she'd maybe like her usual midday glass of wine. She put her arms round my shoulders and whispered, 'What I'd really like is my usual midday . . . this.' She ran her hand over my fly.

'Me too. I'll get Russ to send out for wine. Red or white?'

'Whichever. Red. I'm sorry, Fred. I'm doing my best.' Her face was an inch from mine and she smelled of throat sweets.

'You're doing fine. It gets easier.'

For the vocal, she had to go into a booth with cans on so she could hear her own accompaniment. She struggled for a long time. She even hit a wrong note, not something I'd ever heard her do before.

We took a break and drank some herbal tea. Anya was close

to tears. 'I feel as though once I've recorded it I'll have killed her off,' she said. 'She means so much to me. And this city. This heat. I can't see Genevieve here.'

I put my hands on her shoulders. 'You know the words by heart, don't you?'

'Sure.'

'So don't look at the paper. Shut your eyes. Think of winter. Make yourself shiver. Raise a hand when you're ready. Then get inside that girl's skin.'

'I'll try. For you.' She kissed me. I'd never seen her this fragile.

She stood with her hands on the headphones, clamping them to her head, while Brecker made 'What's going on?' gestures through the glass and I was signalling him to hold fire. Finally, Anya raised her hand and I nodded to him to start the guitar playback.

The middle eight, on which the song turned from loss to hope, went:

> She puts her nickel in the phone
> Been six weeks since she called home
> Frozen hands rake through her hair
> In the doorways of despair
> As she steps past sleeping men
> Scribbles numbers with her pen
> Says the city nights are hard and strange
> But she knows this life is hers to change . . .

Anya kept her eyes tight shut, breathing deep through her diaphragm; she seemed to let go and there it was at last – the voice like frost crystals forming on the glass between us.

Over his console Brecker made a 'Where did *that* come from?' face. I felt proud of Anya, and I felt intense relief. Something of her talent was going to make itself known to the world.

* * *

God, those Sunset days. We'd get the cab to stop at the grocery store near the UCLA campus on the way home but were so tired when we got to the Pasadena Star that we barely had the energy to cook. Having so hated gin at first, Anya was now obsessed by it. 'I'm gonna do this whole goddam album on gin and gin alone,' she said woozily one night, stark naked on the bed, waving her greasy tumbler at me. When we went past the front desk, usually at about nine, Sammy Davis, Jr. would say 'Good day in the studio, folks? You'd like a bucket of ice sent up with two fresh lemons, right?'

We developed a patter with him. He'd call us the Newlyweds and Anya would ask him how the other Ratpackers were doing.

'Seen much of Frank and Dino lately?' she said one night. I held my breath, but he laughed like a coyote, so I guess people had pointed out the resemblance before and he liked it.

We'd eat in the noisy front room and smoke some grass afterwards, then shift into 289 at the back, which we kept cool with the window open. I'd watch old cowboy films on the grainy black and white television while Anya lazed in the bathtub. By eleven we were fast asleep, naked, wrapped in one another's arms.

The album was coming together, and it wasn't just a run of songs, it had a shape. Some of this was down to Larry Brecker. He took me to one side early on and said, 'This chick sings like a fucking angel, man, but from where I'm sitting, you don't want two sharp instruments, her and that guitar, at the same time. We need bass notes, texture, some keyboards, whatever.'

I'd always known this. But there was that fragility of girl and guitar that was crucial, especially on a first record. There had to be that minstrel thing: here she is — one lonely woman travelling from town to town. The high point of the singer-songwriter fashion was over, but I didn't want Anya's tracks to sound over-produced. I had to find a middle way, or maybe both ways at once, the purity and the richness.

Another thing Brecker added was a conviction about certain

songs. What to include was Anya's and my choice, but Brecker made it clear that there were four songs we'd be insane to leave out. They were 'Julie', 'Genevieve' and two from the list of possibles – 'The Need to be You' and 'I'm Not Falling'. The first, addressed to a lover, showed striking insight into a man's weakness, and Brecker liked the second because it was an anti-love song, and as he put it, 'They're like hen's teeth in this business.'

The session men also helped. Anya had no problem with a string bass on some songs, and the bass player was a jazz veteran called Tommy Hawks. The sax she positively liked – an English guy called Stephen Lee, who was part of a prog-rock outfit who seemed to more or less live at the Hyatt House, renamed the Riot House by local wits. You had to remember to call him Stephen all the time because their bassist was called Steve. Apart from that, he was fine – one of those annoyingly talented people who could sight-read and play any instrument. Anya liked him because he didn't offer suggestions; he just played the parts. The electric guitarist, Elliot Klein, had a rough ride, though; she kept insisting on pushing him back in the mix. The drummer was a quiet guy called Joe Aprahamian. He'd also started out in jazz and had a light touch, but boy did Anya give him a hard time. One day I swear I heard her refer to him as 'Old Irongloves'. In the end, he was restricted to three tracks.

One of the ways I convinced Anya to have backing musicians at all was by letting her have tracks that were hers alone. In my mind I divided the songs into those that were personal to her and those in which she reached out to others. Then I had a headache about how to order them on the record. I tried it about thirty different ways. Part of the headache was 'sequencing' – making that transition between the last note of one song and the first of another. But I was also trying to make the album a coherent emotional journey for the listener – probably a young woman but maybe a man – listening to the album alone for the first time.

*   *   *

After we'd been in LA two weeks I felt I should be in touch with the guys in my band and take Anya to meet them, so I called Pete and told him where I was.

'Hey, Jack. Good to hear from you, man. Why not come up tonight? Jeff's here. Robbie's coming back later.'

'I thought Jeff lived in the desert.'

'He's through with that speedball shit. He's clean now.'

'You in the same house?'

'Yeah, but tonight we're going to Evie's. It's cool. Come when you like.'

Pete was a New Yorker and by a long way the most balanced of my band-mates. The others I wasn't so sure about. Cocaine had eaten into their brains.

It was a Sunday. I woke quite early, before Anya, and went into the front room, made tea and brought it back across the hallway. She was still asleep, lying on her side, naked, her hair falling on her shoulders and half hiding her face. When she was really tired she could sleep like a child and no noise seemed to trouble her. I put her tea on the table by the bed, then sat down carefully and looked at her.

There was her knee, the sweep of calf, and the bone of her ankle, all lying as still as if she were dead. I thought of the flesh packed in beneath her skin. And then I thought of the lyrical turn in 'Julie' where Anya changed from 'she' to 'I' in the dreamscape. I gently laid my hand on her hair so I could just feel the skull beneath. I pictured the sleeping brain where even then new microscopic pathways might be forming – connections that would body out ideas and melodies that would enter into other lives.

I guess all humans are the same, this miracle of thought in flesh, but with Anya it seemed more. I touched her right hand and thought how those fingers had gripped the fence at the Devils Lake Amtrak station, and how those same fingers had struck the chords of 'Hold Me'; how they'd pressed the nickel in the phone for Genevieve, brushed my fly and circled me and grasped me tight.

From the first day, making love to Anya was . . . Well, you can never tell in advance how it's going to be. In my bad younger days I'd often gone off the woman after just one encounter. Then there had been groupies. But with proper lovers, and I'd only had a few before Lowri, sex always played a different part. It could be a way of expressing need, of pulling me into their life; it could be just a recreation. With Anya it wasn't any of these things. In return for freedom to do what she wanted with me, I could take any liberty with her. I suppose the oddest thing was that it never felt finished – never, Well, we've done that three times today and there's no other variation left. More often, even as I was dropping off I'd think how nice it might be if she would just touch this bit, like that, while I looked on, or . . . And it would be something to remember for the following day.

That early morning as I watched her, Anya shifted onto her back, still breathing deeply. She unconsciously pushed a strand of hair from her face, and her lips opened slightly as though she was talking in her dream. Her breasts lay on her ribs, sliding a fraction under gravity to one side. Her legs were parted just enough for me to see the opening between. Giving in for the hundredth time to temptation, I softly kissed it, then dragged my tongue along the groove, up to the top. It was surprisingly damp, parting easily, so I could get the tip of my tongue to touch her there. Still with her eyes closed, she began to sigh and run her hands through my hair and the next thing I knew she was opening her legs wider and hauling me up by the shoulders.

Later on, I asked how long she'd been awake.

'A while. I could feel you staring at me. It got me hot, so I pretended to be asleep.'

'And that's why you were so—'

'Ready for anything, as the ice fishermen used to say in North Dakota.'

There were a few things going on when we made love. Sometimes I had that rare moment of balance, that control, when, without risking myself, I could make her come at will; then I had a sense of some long-kept secrets being told, some burden of memory being shrugged from her shoulders, as she tensed and shuddered. Eventually she'd beg me not to hold back any longer, as though she'd had enough pleasure for herself. But when I did what I was told, and as she felt me finally thickening inside her, it would set off her own most intense spasm and I'd have to carry on till she was through.

And afterwards. Well, Lowri used to lie on the bed for ages, tracing her fingertip over my back, softly singing me blues songs she'd heard in the clubs in the South Side of Chicago her uncle had taken her to when she was a kid. But Anya either fell deeply asleep or got up, got dressed and went to do something else.

I'm giving this detail about Anya and me because what was communicated through sex was more than a coupling; it was the powerhouse of everything between us. It roped us together. That and the music. It was as though we were becoming one creature. I did try to be careful, to check for signs that I might be letting myself into danger, but there still seemed so much that she needed from me.

For instance, she'd never been to Los Angeles before and was uneasy about the whole place. 'I don't really get it, Freddy,' she said later on that Sunday morning. 'Hollywood's a dump, isn't it? Nice weather, but the buildings are kind of tacky. Not even tacky, just ordinary. Square lumps with a few palms. And who's in charge?'

'How do you mean?'

We were driving up Melrose in a rented Ford convertible.

'I mean, like in New York,' she said, 'you're aware of Wall Street and the rich people on the Upper East Side and the immigrants moving up or heading out. You can kinda see under the hood. But here everyone's just hanging round. There're a few closed-up mansions on the hill there. What's going on?'

When we'd arrived at the Santa Monica Pier and were having lunch overlooking the ocean, I told her how I'd come to LA when my first band broke up in England. We'd been to the city on tour once and I'd liked it. I thought it would be a good place to go for a time, while I figured out what to do next. I called the promotions guy who'd done our tour and he told me he was going to a party that night off Wonderland Avenue in Laurel Canyon and it would be fine if I came along. It was fine. So fine that I didn't leave the Canyon for three years.

All the inhibitions and the grey rain I'd carried round from a childhood in south London . . . I dumped those at the foot of Laurel Canyon Boulevard. In their place, I took the vista from the top of Lookout Mountain over the steaming plain. I took half-naked girls, mellow grass and log cabins at the end of dirt tracks where everyone was happy to see you. It was exotic to a pale Englishman, the eucalyptus windbreaks, the heat, the Country Store, a jam each night at someone else's house, a party till dawn in the night scents of jasmine and acacia. This was how people were meant to live, sharing what they had, loving one another, patching together a better way of living than previous generations with their wars and wage enslavement. It was familiar and easy to me, as though I'd lived like this in some other life, in deep countryside enclosed within a giant city, a frontier adventure with owls hooting and coyotes calling in the night, yet only a fifteen-minute drive from the Whisky a Go Go and free passes at the Troubadour.

'I honestly felt I'd been there before. It was all new yet so familiar.'

'You make it sound like heaven, Fred.'

'I think it was.'

'And what was her name?'

'There were two in the Canyon before Lowri. Cathy and Roma. Not at the same time.'

'Good boy. And what did you do for money?'

'Odd jobs. House painting, joinery. Session work. I borrowed a lot. Then we formed the band and we began to get some gigs and then a record deal. At one point I owed Pete $35,000.'

'Shit! I've never seen that much money in my life.'

'Neither had I. That was the problem.'

'Didn't he mind?'

'He never batted an eyelid. That was what it was like. He'd had a big album with his previous band so he had money. He believed I'd pay him back.'

'And did you?'

'Eventually. He wouldn't accept interest, though.'

'I like the sound of Pete.'

'Well, let's go and meet him.'

That evening we drove up in the open Ford with the radio playing. For some reason I really wanted Anya to be impressed. I wanted her to like the Canyon and even to share in retrospect in the happiness I'd had there. I was talking hard, telling stories, and maybe this was why I overshot the turning. We did a loop past the Garden of Allah, which had been a place of assignation for old movie stars, and through the hairpins of Appian Way.

'The Country Store,' I said, 'another place of assignation.'

'Seems to have been a lot of sex going on up here.'

'Sure was.'

Weepah Way was a steep, precarious kind of trail with a drainage channel down the centre that someone high on acid thought it was a good idea to flood one summer, so you could surf down it on inner tubes.

'And how old were you, Freddy?'

'Maybe twenty-five?'

'Going on eleven.'

'Hey, look, this is it. Evie's house is down there.'

'And they don't know about you and me?'

'I guess not.'

There was a dirt-road dead end. Most of the houses in the Canyon were pretty ordinary, but Evie's place had a nice wooden palisade and a view over the Kirkwood Bowl. When we went through the gate, I felt anxious that people should like Anya. It was my old life and my new life in collision. Jeff was in a bad way, unshaven and suspicious; he didn't look that 'clean' to me. He disappeared midway through dinner and when he came back he talked non-stop for twenty minutes about the glories of the sandwiches at Canter's, a drab after-hours deli on Fairfax. He made you feel you were missing out on one of the great experiences of living and somehow doubting his word by not going there at once.

'And the pastrami,' he said. 'Wow.'

'Wow,' we said.

Pete and Robbie were suspicious of Anya when she refused to sing. It was like a tradition that anyone would perform if they were asked, but I didn't want to be seen to be hawking her round to build up some sort of reputation before the record came out. Also, I wanted her to reserve her voice for the studio.

Anya and I left before midnight, and although there had been all the usual talk of the band getting back together it didn't feel likely.

I put the disappointment out of my mind. My life had changed, it was as simple as that.

The recording was going fine until we came to 'I'm Not Falling'. I had this marked down as a possible final track because it would end the album on an upbeat. I wanted drums, organ and some tenor sax. Anya wanted just piano. Larry Brecker was with me, Tommy thought Anya had a point and Joe the drummer was keen to play on anything.

I went into the vocal booth so I could speak alone to Anya.

'I'm not trying to bury the emotion,' I said. 'We can mix it in a way that you and the piano are in the spotlight all along. But it's got such a good beat to it, I don't want to just throw it away.'

She earnestly grasped my wrists in her hands. 'Listen, honey, this is my life. It's not just my song, it's part of my experience of being alive.'

'Maybe you're too close,' I said. 'I guess we all need someone outside the creative moment, someone who's not so emotionally involved.'

'Do you really think you're not emotionally involved, Freddy?' Her voice had risen. 'With my life, my work, my body, my every living breath?'

Until this moment our intimacy had led only to exhilaration. Now I could see how such weird closeness, this connection of body and mind, could go the other way.

I saw how far we'd penetrated one another's lives. I didn't know what to say. We just kept staring. In her eyes there was anger, love, pride and desperation. God knows what she saw in mine.

She said, 'And if by any chance you *don't* feel that involved with me, my darling, don't sleep with me tonight.'

There were tears in her eyes as she spoke. Then the conflicting emotions seemed to resolve themselves. She reached up and kissed me on the mouth.

'You'd better be right, Freddy.'

'Do you trust me, then?'

'I trust you. But you'd better be right.'

Once Anya had committed herself to doing it with other musicians, she did let them play. Even Old Irongloves was allowed a look-in, though he was pretty far back in the mix. Stephen played a short tenor solo as well as some fills on the last verse, Anya was on piano and I thought it best for me to stay out of it altogether. It was a painful few hours, going over and over the arrangement, but Anya sang with conviction. Maybe she was thinking, If this is a fuck-up I can blame Freddy.

The last two days were spent on two Anya-only songs, and we were able to send the other musicians on their way. 'Thunder Bay' was about her mother leaving; 'Boxcar Days' was about watching the trains coming in and out of Devils Lake. It wasn't my favourite song, though it had some nice touches in the lyrics.

The final running order was this:

Side One	Side Two
Hold Me	Ready to Fly
Genevieve	You Next Time
Thunder Bay	Boxcar Days
The Need to be You	Boulevards of Snow
Julie in the Court of Dreams	I'm Not Falling

We felt the album had a balance to it. It kicked off and ended with the most obviously crowd-pleasing numbers. The slighter songs were hidden in the middle of either side. 'Julie', the album's masterpiece, had a good position. The second side opened strongly.

Delirious with pride, our quarrel buried beneath an avalanche of sex, Anya and I spent happy hours in room 289 roughing out album cover designs, drawing up the credits, making sure we left no one out, including 'Produced by Jack Wyatt at Sonic Broom Studios West Hollywood, Calif. Engineer: Larry Brecker. Assistant Engineer and sandwiches: Russ Gibson. Joe Aprahamian appears courtesy of A & M Records. Special thanks S. Davis, Jr., S. Cooke and all the staff of the Pasadena Star Hotel. This record is dedicated by Anya King to "Mom, wherever you are".'

As for the title of the album, there were plenty to choose from among the tracks. Anya liked *Boxcar Days*, I liked *Boulevards of Snow*, but when I called the people at MPR they'd already fixed on *Ready to Fly* and you could see their point. For a first record by a still-unknown artist it was hard to beat. Anya, uncharacteristically, gave way at once. She did want to sell records.

We said goodbye to Larry Brecker and sent a tape back to John Vintello in New York. We'd have to go back to listen to an acetate on lots of different speakers – plastic bathroom radio, automobile rear shelf – and fiddle around with sound quality on the master, but we could leave that for a bit.

It seemed like a good idea to get out of the Pasadena Star, though we'd come to love it in its crummy way. Your choices from LA are: south to Mexico, east into the desert or north to San Francisco. We flung two bags into the back of the Ford and started up the coast road with Anya singing 'Let's Go to San Francisco' in a high, mocking voice that made us both laugh so much I swerved into the wrong lane and was almost crushed by a giant trucker.

I grew up in a normal house in a normal street. My father was a sales rep and my mother was what most mothers were then, a housewife. There were five children. I was number four in a running order of boy, girl, boy, boy, girl – Ray, Susan, Simon, Jack, Gabrielle. As positions go, four out of five is as near invisible as you can get. My elder sister, Susan, used to mother me and dress me up in girl's clothes and my little sister, Gabrielle, looked up to me with open adoration. Ray and Simon shared a room, so I was put in with Susan. When she started having bras, I was switched to sharing with little Gabrielle, and this made girls familiar to me. For the first fourteen years of my life I roomed with one.

The sister thing was good, the brother thing was tough. Ray and Simon didn't want anything to do with me, and in an effort to get into their gang I started to stay late and practise music at school. We didn't have much money, but my parents were ambitious for us in their way. They pushed me through the eleven-plus so I got to a grammar school with a real music department.

I took up guitar as a way of impressing my brothers. The school provided an instrument and free instruction from the history teacher so long as I promised to study the piano as well. I sang in the choir, which I didn't like except when you did descants. At home, when Ray and Simon were strumming together in their room, I'd offer a harmony, but they wouldn't take me along to the pubs until my voice had broken. I think they were hoping it would go out of tune as well as dropping, but it didn't. By then, the revolution was coming from Liverpool. I never did my exams at school. I left at sixteen to be a musician.

These are the kind of drab life facts you tell on long journeys, with the Pacific slumped against the coastline to your left. The girl is on your right, the Santa Ana winds going through her hair, the radio struggling to make itself heard over the engine. Later, there are signs to wineries in San Luis Obispo. You wonder if you should stop and taste. You persuade your girl that it's her time to take the wheel and in return you'll find her a great salad and home-baked bread somewhere in Zinfandel Creek. She'll have to go easy on the wine, it's true, but she drinks only gin these days.

It doesn't matter, anyway. Nothing matters. You've just completed the most intense work of your life. Recordings that will be stamped on vinyl and reach a generation in their college rooms, in their cars, in their apartments, in their married houses. You're a king. You have a talent, not a great one, but by your determination and your work you're surfing on a twenty-foot wave of luck. You've done a great thing and enough credit will be yours, but most of it will go to the girl you love, who's sitting beside you.

The café at Chardonnay Gulch isn't quite what you'd hoped for, just an OK steak with field greens, and the waitress isn't a California girl but a heavy guy in overalls who generally services the machinery, but the wine stays good all the way down the bottle. You're burning the days, you're a millionaire of time, and the sun will never sink on the county of San Luis Obispo, where there are only two seasons, 4 January and summer.

You may as well head back to the car so you can hit San Francisco in time to find a good hotel. The girl sings 'Do You Know the Way to San José?' and you make the car hooter stand in for the Bacharach flugelhorn.

Up the coast road, with a stop, it's ten hours. You'll be in by eight o'clock. Maybe find a place on Russian Hill, where you stayed before with the band, or call that couple who said you should look them up. What do you think?

'I'd like a very clean hotel, Freddy. Sheets so white and starched they almost scrape your skin off.'

And by chance you find the very place on Powell and California, not far up from Union Square. A handsome building with shutters and tall windows. They have one room in the back with a balcony overlooking a yard of oleander and acanthus trees. The room price includes parking or breakfast.

Your girl, exhausted by her hours at the wheel, has barely time to phone down a hefty order to the front desk before disappearing to the bathroom.

You knock the hotel pen against your teeth. Parking or breakfast.

The man who rolls your food into the room looks like Henry Fonda. Salads, fresh rolls, grilled shrimp, butter discs on ice, vacuum flasks of almost-frozen juice and water, frosted white wine, fresh fruit with stiff cloths and napkins.

Henry Fonda is gone by the time your girl comes out, wet-haired, in a towel that falls to her ankles when she stretches up to open the window onto the balcony. She picnics naked on the bed, drains half a pint of wine and falls asleep at once on the starched, fresh sheets. You pull a light cover on top of her. How hard she's worked. God, she deserves to sleep. May her vast creative energies be knitted up, replenished. You think how much you love her. You can't wait for her to wake.

The next day, while Anya was at the drugstore, I called Lowri with a sick feeling in my gut. I told her the recording had gone as well as we could have hoped.

'You still on speaking terms?' she said.

'What? I . . . Why do you ask?'

Lowri laughed. 'I guess it's pretty intense. Someone's personal songs and someone else telling them what they're all about and how to sing them.'

'Well, we had our moments,' I said. 'But we're still talking. We've come to San Francisco for a couple of days. Then we'll fiddle around with the sound before they make the master.'

'What do they think in New York?'

'We're waiting to hear. How's the farm?'

'Lonely.'

'I'll be back in a week, ten days at the outside.'

Would I? Why had I said that? To make Lowri feel better? Was I going to leave Anya in LA? Or in New York, in the apartment on East Seventh Street that wasn't even ours? I wasn't going to risk losing Anya, but I didn't want Lowri to be unhappy or alone. I loved her and she'd done nothing wrong. So what was my problem?

I loved two women; that was all. It was hardly a sin. In the world of the Canyon it was considered pretty cool. Lowri and Anya were sophisticated modern women; they would understand. Oh God. Like hell they would.

'We had these awful rooms in LA I told you about,' I told Lowri, hitting the 's' on the end of 'rooms'. 'It's much better here in San Francisco. My room's got a balcony and a view.'

The 'my' wasn't quite a lie. It was mine as much as Anya's.

We talked on for a bit. Lowri had a beautiful manner on the telephone. Her voice was melodious, all concern for me and innocent good wishes. It made me feel terrible.

There was only one thing to be done. Go and find Anya. Re-engage with her.

We got back to New York in December, and there were still three months on the lease of the Seventh Street apartment. We eased out a couple of Rick's friends by giving them $200 towards a deposit on a new place, and I moved into what had been Anya's room with her.

John Vintello and the people at MPR were happy with the record. Based on the way the acetate had sounded, Brecker had done some tweaking at the mastering stage so the sound was neither shrill at the top nor muddy at the bottom, and would come through OK even on student record players. Anya didn't tell them we hoped for people in their thirties and even forties too.

Then I took the train up to the farm to see Lowri. I felt like an executioner as I watched the woods slide by the window. Like a hangman paid to travel up by train to some remote village and kill someone. I remembered a Methodist hymn my mother used to sing when we were kids, whose last line went: 'For this our task today we thank you, Lord.' Thanks a lot.

I hadn't planned what I was going to say. It seemed somehow deceitful to plan behind Lowri's back. We'd never held anything back from one another; in fact the success of our relationship had been that we developed our thoughts by sharing them from the start, so I wasn't going to go in with a speech or a statement.

I still hoped there might be a solution. If the Canyon years, if the 60s and all that, had meant anything, then surely it was that there was no 'right' way to live. Our parents had problems of fidelity, divorce and bitterness, because their rules were so rigid. One strike and you're out. It was so cruel.

Snow was beginning to fall on the woods. It was cold in the train compartment and I pulled my jacket tighter.

I was in the eye of a storm with Anya. It was inconceivable that I should not be with her and see how our story was to end. To leave her would have been to show a disregard for my own life, my own short time on earth and what it might be. But in going with this wonderful and inevitable thing, did I have to cut down the person I'd most loved and trusted before? Had all the philosophy and the Zen and the counter-culture so come to nothing that we had to make the same choices as married couples in Levittown?

To choose between Lowri and Anya was like being forced to pick between a guitar and a piano. Yet on the train I felt some drab nagging voice, like a parent or a priest, saying, You have to make hard choices. My hopes rested on Lowri. She might have some elegant plan. Perhaps she wouldn't feel bitter or rejected. She might be happy to be free of me. Or maybe in her company some answer would appear, and there'd be a shift of understanding that would bring ease to all three of us.

Anya's last words to me were, 'Be kind, Freddy. Be as kind as you can to all three of us.'

From the moment I saw Lowri, I could tell she knew. When she walked from the house to where the cab dropped me at the gate, her movement was as graceful as ever, but the bones in her body seemed to have gone soft. She threw herself into my arms, as she always did, but then seemed to hang there. Grace and Janis provided a distraction, snuffling and wagging round my legs.

We got into the house and I risked lighting a wood fire because it was cold. I wondered why Lowri hadn't thought of it herself. I noticed that the house was untidy and there didn't seem to be anything for dinner.

When the logs were flaming and we'd made tea, we settled

down on the couch together and I told her all about Los Angeles. There was plenty of innocent stuff to get through – the hotel, the session men and so on. Old Irongloves. It was easy to talk with enthusiasm.

'Shall we go into town for dinner?' I said eventually. 'We could go to the Fishermen's. Or Maxwell's?'

'Sure thing,' said Lowri. 'I'll call Maxwell's now.'

She went upstairs to change out of her jeans, and when she came down she was wearing a dress she knew I liked. It was black wool, quite short, and she wore it with knee-length brown cowboy boots and black woollen tights. She'd tied her hair back and put on some make-up, so her freckled face was revealed in all its lovely oval shape. I'd almost forgotten what a good-looking woman she was, and in what an original way. I told her how great she looked and ran my hand up her thighs, under the skirt. I put my hand between her legs and could feel the warmth of her body, those private folds, through her underwear. I turned her round so I could hold her breasts in my hands from behind while I nuzzled into her sweet-smelling neck. Her breasts were larger than Anya's and I thought about the way the freckles stopped there and the surprisingly white colour of the skin and the innocent pink of the nipple where the rest of her colouring was russet and straw. She sighed a little. I felt myself stir, and then I felt guilt. Would it be 'unfaithful' to sleep with my own girlfriend?

'I missed you, Jack.'

'I missed you too.'

She took my hands away. 'Come on. Let's go. I have a reservation in twenty minutes.'

I put a guard in front of the fire and followed her out to the car.

It was hopeless. We had dinner, drank wine, came back and stoked up the fire again. We'd both drunk way too much, three bottles, and I at once started kissing her and had my fingers inside her underpants, rubbing her gently until she couldn't take any more and knelt down in front of me and unzipped my fly while I lay back and closed my eyes in despair, my head on the back of the sofa, and almost at once I was on top of her on the white rug and her legs, still in their cowboy boots, were wrapped round me, and after some hard work, enough to make me sweat in the firelight, in the snowy night, I felt her beginning to gather herself, fighting it at first, then letting go and coming with a wounded cry that went through me like a spear.

Of course, I couldn't acknowledge the sound she'd made. I just stroked her hair and kissed her and carried her upstairs, and when we'd both wonkily cleaned our teeth, bumping into each other a couple of times and laughing, there seemed no other option but to hold her and kiss her and start to fuck her again in the kind of belief that if we stayed drunk and in each other's arms then things would work out, that reality was no more than an option, one of many.

I'm not sure Lowri and I ever did break up. Was there a word spoken? If so, I don't recall. I stayed at the farm for a week and then had a call from Rick Kohler saying I was needed in New York to discuss the spring tour to support the release. 'You're her manager, man. Get your ass down here.' I wondered if Anya had prompted him.

On the morning I left, Lowri and I talked about how long I'd be away this time and what Lowri would do while I was gone. She thought she might get her sister, who'd recently graduated from Northwestern, to come and stay. I encouraged her to stick with the bar job – not for the money, because I was making a regular transfer – but so she wouldn't be lonely. She said she'd try. We talked it round so it seemed quite natural that I should be disappearing for an unknown length of time, like a merchant seaman. It's what men do, work, is how we explained it to ourselves.

I packed my bag with a feeling of death in my hands. Lowri

stood in the doorway of the bedroom, watching me in silence. I turned and saw the path of silent tears on her skin. I said nothing because we'd fixed on a fiction to get us through and I didn't want to blow it.

The cab was waiting by the gate. Lowri was still in a dressing gown on the cold porch, by the old car seat. I held her close and said I'd call when I got to New York.

'Sure,' she said.

I forced a kind of gaiety. 'Shit, it's cold. Wrap up, honey. Take care. Bye. I'll call.'

'Goodbye, Jack.'

I crunched across to the waiting cab that was blowing poisonous exhaust clouds in the air. I didn't look back.

The driver put the car in gear and we began to move. Then I did look through the rear window. Lowri was still on the deck at the front of the house, but she'd fallen to her knees and her head was resting on the wooden rail.

There was a lot going on in New York. They'd taken some photographs of Anya in Laurel Canyon while I was tweaking the sound with Brecker. The art department wanted a kind of pioneer look and they'd faked a wood cabin for her to sit in front of. She was wearing a very short skirt and although her knees were together it was difficult to think of anything other than what underwear, if any, she had on beneath. She was unhappy with the picture and we had a big fight with the label. In the end, they used an out-of-focus close-up of her head and shoulders with a mocked-up rustic background. It was better than it sounds. Kind of folksy but dynamic. It worked with the title, *Ready to Fly*, and Anya King in big block letters. It had a real fuck-you, here-I-am look. We all liked it, but the label retained the right to use the short-skirt picture as a publicity still.

Anya designed the back of the cover, and the words to the

songs were printed on a single sheet inside. The first finished records came through in February. We all went into John Vintello's office on 6th Avenue to listen to it. Anya squeezed my hand when John's assistant slipped the shiny black vinyl from the inner sleeve. Static made it stick for a second as she eased it out. She held it carefully by the rim in both palms, lifting it like a priest at the altar, then placed it on the spindle and lowered the needle into the groove. The first chord of 'Hold Me' rang out with amazing fidelity on Vintello's thousand-dollar stereo system. I had a flashback to the front room in the Pasadena Star, the kitchenette, Sammy Davis, Jr. I could almost taste the gin.

Besides Rick, Anya and me, there were seven or eight people from MPR records. Vintello sat with his feet up on the desk, smoking a Chesterfield. Behind his head were framed gold and platinum discs. He nodded appreciatively at intervals and the other people took it in turn between tracks to say, 'That's my favourite,' or 'That was *so* beautiful.'

The whole thing was incredibly phoney. To defuse the tension, Rick and I talked only about sound production details. Eventually we got to the big close with 'I'm Not Falling' and broke open the champagne. Anya and I were glad to get out of there and back to Seventh Street.

When the album came out in March, Anya gave some interviews in the music and underground press. Journalists seemed interested by her story and didn't try to stitch her up, though one of them referred to me as her 'producer/manager/boyfriend'. I don't know if Lowri saw it, but I guessed other references might follow.

The reviews were positive. They even said nice things about the production — 'spare but warm' were one paper's words. None of the reviewers seemed able to grasp the size of what they'd heard. They weren't musically educated enough to analyse it. They also puzzled over which songs were personal to Anya and which weren't, and only one writer understood that what Anya had done at her best moments was to wipe out that distinction. But there was a good deal of air play on folk, rock and local radio stations. Sales were strong, and the album nosed its way into the top hundred, then the top forty. It was a slow burn, but people were responding to it and talking about it.

Then one day John Vintello called to say it had gone into the top twenty at number eighteen. By then we were on the road.

The tour was twenty-four dates in thirty days. It had been put together in a hurry. Some places we had local acts opening for us, usually singer-songwriters, occasionally a band. More often, it was just us at the student hall. Everyone knows what touring's like. There's the airport, flight, hotel, getting to the hall, sound-check, hotel, back to the hall, performing, party. But mostly it's being in a car. We'd asked Tommy Hawks to come and play some acoustic bass, but he had another gig with a jazz band. Then Stephen Lee called and said he could play bass if we wanted, as well as everything else, so he ended up on tour with us. I persuaded him to take over the tom-tom part on 'Reservation Town' while I sloped off for a cigarette.

Ann Arbor, about midway through, looked at first like a typical date. We got in from Detroit at about twelve o'clock and went straight to the soundcheck so we could have the afternoon off. After we'd dumped our stuff at the hotel, Anya came with me to a bar on campus that was famous for its cheeseburgers. She had the usual big glass of red wine and a cigarette.

'I like watching you eat,' she said. 'Just as well, considering how much time I've spent doing it.'

'What do you like about it?'

'Figuring out where it all goes.' She poked me in the ribs.

'Have a French fry.'

'No, thanks, but I'll have another glass of wine. I didn't sleep much last night. I want to make sure I get some sleep before the gig.' There was a slight tremor in her hand as she took the second beakerful of Merlot.

I tried to imagine what it must be like to see your inner life become common property. I'd sold a lot of records with my band and we'd been in the press a fair bit, but none of it was personal. With Anya, it was different. She'd laughed at most of the things in the papers, as though she didn't expect them to understand and was happy they were just polite. I think a part of her was disappointed, though. You didn't spend fourteen hours of your life recording 'Julie in the Court of Dreams' to have it called a 'mid-tempo closer to side one'.

Then there was the response of the audience. Anya wasn't a natural stage performer. She sometimes played as though she was in a conservatory or a recording studio. She was hypercritical, listening for the faintest flat or sharp, and the time she spent retuning between songs meant the set could lose momentum. When one of the songs had gone over really well – and it was often 'Genevieve' rather than one of the livelier numbers – she'd look puzzled. Occasionally she seemed to surprise herself by how much she'd enjoyed singing 'Hold Me', and she'd pause and smile broadly and wave at the end, but this wasn't exactly working the audience.

After lunch she slept in the hotel, for maybe an hour. She seemed very quiet when we packed up to go to the hall, and fell asleep again in the back of the car. I shook her awake.

'Are you OK?'

'Yeah, I took a pill. Rick gave me some in New York when you were away. I was having trouble sleeping.'

'Are you going to be all right for the gig?'

'Sure, let's just get some coffee.'

The dressing room was bare and squalid. There was no floor covering, just a slab, and the walls were only part-plastered, as though they'd run out of money. There was a broken hi-hat, some empty drum cases and two painted boards that might have been flats from a student play. We sent the roadie off to get coffee.

Anya sat on a moulded-plastic chair looking at herself in the mirror. The strip lights were harsh, the glare bouncing off the grey walls. She painted kohl beneath her eyes and put powder on her nose and forehead. She was crying.

There was a knock on the door and Stephen Lee put his head round it.

'I just wanted to check something,' he said. 'Are we still doing the new ending to "You Next Time"?'

'Yup. We take the cue from Anya, when she raises her hand.'

'OK. Is everything all right?'

'Sure. Is it a good house?'

'Looks full. The support's shit, though.'

Stephen looked at Anya, who was holding her head in her hands, and raised an eyebrow at me.

I looked at my watch. 'We still have ten minutes.'

Stephen nodded and left. I was wondering what the hell we would do if Anya didn't come round. We had no back-up plan.

I put my arm round her shoulder. She was shaking.

'Freddy, I don't think I can do it.'

'What's the matter, sweetheart?'

'I'm frightened. I don't want to do it.'

I pulled up a chair next to her and put my arms round her. I mumbled a lot of things – feeble stuff, I'm sure.

She pulled back and looked at me, black streaks all down her cheeks. 'It's one thing doing it for you, in the studio. Or on my own. But suddenly I feel – I don't know what. I'm afraid I've done the wrong thing.'

'I don't understand.'

'I feel guilty.' She was sobbing now. 'Perhaps I've used my own experiences and other people's too. To kind of boost myself. I think they're going to see through me.'

There was no point in telling her that she'd already performed a dozen times on tour without a hitch and people loved her music. Stage fright is not a rational thing.

I had to think quickly and the best I could do was, 'My darling, you're a messenger. The people you sing about, you're giving them a life. Remember when we did "Genevieve" in the studio? You climbed into her skin. Leave Anya King in this room when you go out there.'

It seemed to help a little bit. She washed her face, redid the kohl.

'I need a drink, Freddy.' She looked very pale.

'There's only beer. But any port in a storm.' I cracked a ring pull and handed her the can.

'Tomorrow I'll bring gin,' I said. 'We'll get through this. You'll be fine.'

She drank quickly, put the can down with a thump so it flooded the dressing table, then loudly burped out the gas. She smiled for a moment.

'Another thing,' I went on. 'All those people. They're mostly kids. Students. They're just thrilled to see you – a real live star. They're nothing to be frightened of.'

She looked up at me and tried to smile, but there was panic in her eyes.

When the stage manager came to tell us to get ready, I had to pretty much manhandle Anya down the dingy corridor and into the wings. The folkie who'd opened was coming the other way, guitar in hand, and squeezed past us without a word. I didn't see why we couldn't have a break between acts, but the venue insisted on pushing us straight in, something to do with local residents' bedtime.

The routine was that she did the first two numbers alone before introducing me. We watched the MC, who was a young guy, probably a college kid.

'. . . her hit album, *Ready to Fly*, ladies and gentlemen, you can tell your grandchildren you heard her on her first ever tour, the sensational Miss Anya *King*!'

I applied gentle pressure to the small of her back. OK, I pushed her on. A powerful spotlight picked her out. College or not, this was a big hall. She paused, as though dazed or lost, then made it to the stool and pulled the microphone a little closer. She was wearing jeans, as she almost always did after the row about the skirt picture. She licked her lips and cleared her throat. She looked about twelve years old.

She took her favourite guitar off the stand and ran her fingers through a chord. She fiddled with a tuning peg.

'Thank you for coming.' Her speaking voice was always low, but not this husky. She was supposed to kick off with 'You Next Time', the turntable hit of the album, but that was not the intro she began to play. Anya was a guitarist capable of improvising if she wanted to, and after a minute I still didn't recognise what she was playing. I was pleased that she hadn't thrown down the instrument or fluffed a note, but I felt my guts churning.

I took a deep breath and walked on stage early. I sat down at the piano and caught Anya's eye. She stopped playing. She looked at me lovingly, and with relief.

'This is my friend Jack,' she said. I don't think I'd ever heard her use my real name before. Even when introducing me to strangers, she called me Freddy.

'Good evening, everybody,' I said. One or two people called and whistled in a friendly way.

I looked back at Anya, but she was staring down at the fret board of her guitar. I took a chance. 'All right. Now we've tuned up, we're gonna start with a song called "You Next Time".'

Then I gave her the opening chord on the piano. Her left hand gripped the neck of the guitar and the fingers of her right began to pick. We needed only the voice. Come on, Anya, come on, little girl. Here it is, here it comes . . .

Two years gone, the passion's still unbound.
Another life, I'll know before we meet
This hill of pain cannot be mine to climb.
No mistake the second time around,
I will die and rise, the shadow on your wall,
My name will be the only one you call,
Oh, my darling, you next time.

There was a 'skull' note through the final word, 'time'. She nailed it with a kind of sob in her voice. The crowd went completely mad. I saw people in the front row with tears on their faces. They were on their feet and it was only the first song of the set.

Anya turned to me, her face a mixture of fear and amazement. For the second song, she came to the piano. I took a guitar and sat close by, but she seemed all right now. Her hands were steady on the keys and her voice grew in certainty. When she struck the opening chord of 'Julie in the Court of Dreams' there was a communal intake of breath. These kids knew their stuff. I caught Stephen's eye in the wings and we exchanged looks. Stage fright was not something either of us had been through before, and we weren't keen to go back there any time soon.

We got through the tour with the help of tranquillisers and bourbon. Their respective manufacturers sounded, Anya said, like a West Coast harmony band all their own: Hoffmann, Daniel and La Roche. We roughed out a record they might make called 'Slow Groove' with its double-sided hit single 'Past Caring' and 'Out On My Feet'.

We finished the tour in San Francisco, where we stayed in the same staid hotel as before on Powell and California and had people back to the room and partied till dawn with Henry Fonda ferrying in supplies. Then we went back to New York where we renewed the lease on Seventh Street, because Anya felt superstitious about moving.

In May, Lowri called me to say she was moving back to Los Angeles and what did I want her to do with the keys to the farm.

'I read the tour went well,' she said.

'Will you be OK?'

'Yes, I have a place with Candy on Beech Knoll Road and I've got work in town.'

'What kind of work?'

'Real estate.'

'Shit.'

'I know. But I have to do something.'

'I can send some money from my share of Anya's royalties.'

'I don't think I'd like that, Jack.'

The moment was hanging. I couldn't let her go.

'Can I see you again?'

'Sure thing. But give me a little time. Maybe a year.'

'I love you, Lowri. I'm so sorry. You know.'

'It's life, honey. It's a bummer from start to finish. A total fuck-up. Then you die.'

I could picture her face, unfortunately, as she spoke. She was beautiful. A complete original.

'Will we be friends?'

'We'll try, Jack. I can't promise, but I'll try. I guess it might go better in another life. The cab's here. I have to go.'

Another life, I thought: well, there's always that.

In June, Anya and I went up to the farm. Lowri had left everything tidy, the beds stripped, the sheets washed and put away. The pans were hanging on their hooks, the plates were clean and stacked. But her drawers were all empty. There was not a hairpin left behind.

Anya put her things in the second bedroom, where she'd been before. We went into town for dinner and Anya said, 'What we need is visitors.' Our life had been so secluded, so intense, that we barely knew anyone. My friends were in England or in LA. Anya had travelled light. There had been boyfriends, two or three big affairs, but she wasn't in touch with them, which was fine by me. We began to laugh when we recognised our plight – one moment, in the spotlight; the next, two friendless people in an empty farmhouse.

So we got Rick Kohler to come up. There was a girl called Sandy at MPR records Anya liked, so we asked her and her boyfriend to come that weekend. Down the road, there was a young high school teacher who was interesting to talk to and an ad-man who'd come up one summer from Madison Avenue and never gone home. He smoked about half a kilo of grass a day. A kind of scene began to develop, and during the long quiet days Anya wrote more songs.

We lived so close to one another I thought it might be bad for our health. Anya had tactfully stayed in the second bedroom and I gave her that space. I only went in there if she invited me and she never came into what had been Lowri's and my room. It sounds odd, looking back, but I think it helped. We made love downstairs, outdoors and in my lady's chamber when she asked me in – which was every night. But we kept to the fiction of separate lives.

While Anya wrote, I— Well, I kept house, I suppose. I went to the store, I got someone in to cut the grass and do some logging. I wrote a few things of my own and hoped Anya would ask me to help her with her songs. I dreamed of seeing 'King/Wyatt' in brackets after a track title on the next record. But she never asked.

She wrote two songs about the experience of touring. 'Out On My Feet', which had started as our joke but turned into a harrowing song about baring your soul for the delight of strangers, and 'Gate

Nineteen', a wistful number about airports and travelling on before
you've had time to breathe. She seemed to have material left from
older love affairs, from childhood and from the time she'd spent
in New York before I met her. And there were the songs about
other people, other lives.

The album *Ready to Fly* sold well in Europe, mostly in Britain,
but also in Germany and Holland, where to her irritation they
used the picture of her in the tiny skirt on the sleeve. John Vintello
talked of a world tour for the next record, but neither of us was
interested. We just wanted to make sure the second album was
stronger than the first. It was recorded in December, in New York
this time, though they flew over Larry Brecker to engineer again.
The Occasional Lover was released in February and there was
another tour. This time we had a support act – Blue Ridge
Cowboys, Denny Roberts's band. *The Occasional Lover* was well
received in the business, peaked at number seven in the album
chart – five places higher than *Ready to Fly* – and went on selling
steadily. The tour passed without bad incidents.

In May, we found ourselves back at the farm, rattling round
again. The weather was beautiful and I think it was good for both
of us to sleep off the rigours of the tour. But I guessed it wouldn't
last.

'Freddy,' Anya said one sunny day in the ruins of her giant
breakfast, 'we could go on doing this for another, like, decade.
Farm, write, city, record, city, tour, back to the farm. By that time
you'll be almost forty years old!'

I smiled. It was hard to picture, but it sounded all right to me.
At the same time, I saw what she meant.

'Shall we go somewhere?' I said.

'Where?'

'England. I could show you round. Paris. Rome. Greece. Africa.
Anywhere.' Anya had never been out of the United States,
except twice to Toronto. I'd seen her virgin passport with the

eighteen-year-old-college-girl picture. 'ANJA INGRID KING. May 24, 19—. Birthplace: N. Dakota, USA. Hair: Brown. Eyes: Brown. Height: Five feet, five inches.'

So the idea of what she called the Migration began. I had no doubt about why she wanted to travel. It wasn't for history, language, or art. It was in the hope of material for songs. We flew to Athens in June and found ourselves on a hot island soon afterwards. Greece was pretty unspoiled, though there were American backpackers on some beaches. They carried large books and, for all their naked hippy sun worship, were serious about politics, about Nixon and Vietnam.

We'd brought sleeping rolls and a two-man tent with a single change of clothes and, in Anya's case, one cotton dress. Touring had made her despise hotels and she was frightened of losing touch with the people she was singing for. The problem was that it was hard for her to sit round a beach fire at night and listen to someone strum a well-travelled guitar. She was not exactly famous, but she knew she might be recognised if she played.

There was a single taverna with a bathroom that was in constant use, you took in your own paper; and there was a shower outside. I don't remember what we did apart from lie in the sun, swim and talk with other people. We slept in the dunes above the beach. Books were passed round. Occasionally you'd make the long hike back to the port for dinner or you could get a boat round the coast for a few drachmas. The taverna didn't go in for the sort of breakfast Anya liked so she had to make do with yoghurt and fruit, then join me for a big Greek salad at lunch. I force-fed her chips, or Greek fries as she called them, as I thought she'd got too thin. After a couple of weeks like this, we went back to the port and put our tent up in a campsite. Every night we went down to a noisy taverna where there was a whole spitted lamb with pitta bread and salad, wine drawn from a barrel into jugs, and dancing. The locals seemed happy to dance with us and were fascinated when, high on retsina, Anya, for the only time on the island, gave in to the begging of a shy young man who was feeding her Karelia cigarettes and soulful looks.

She took the beaten-up guitar he offered and stood beneath a lantern hanging from the vines that made a makeshift roof outside. She had one foot up on a straw-seated chair to support the strapless guitar on her thigh. She didn't make a big deal of tuning it, just grimaced a bit and started singing. Her face was caught by the lamplight and her voice soared through the heat, the vines, the blundering moths. The locals looked on astounded. For Anya, there seemed no thoughts of stage fright, of how it would go across. She sang for the joy if it — 'Hold Me', 'Ready to Fly', some songs by other writers, one of her own I'd never heard called 'My Sister's Room' and finished with the whole taverna of people in a frenzied Zorba-the-Greek dance as she played 'Run Me Crazy, Run Me Wild'.

Her face, tanned by the Aegean sun, was radiant in the night as she threw back her head. Afterwards, I had to pretty much carry her home through the throng of sweating, laughing well-wishers. I had to hold her tight because she said the world was spinning.

I had arranged to go back to America in late summer to discuss a new record deal for Anya. She wanted to stay two more weeks, so I left her in Athens and flew to London, where I met up with my family for a few days before returning to New York. I spent a humid week arguing with lawyers about merchandising and marketing. I was pleased when I finally got back to the farm and happier still when Anya showed up a few days later.

Europe had changed her. She looked older, more mysterious in some way. It was as though she'd found a new horizon. The songs she played me had more rock and more jazz in them, they were less folky and in some odd way less American. I had to go back to New York again to finalise the contract, and while I was there she called me at the apartment to say she was going to meet her father in Chicago, but that she'd made a tape on the reel-to-reel in the farm of the ten songs she wanted to record for her third album. Would I please listen carefully and let her know what I thought when she got back.

It was about noon on a Saturday when the cab from the station dropped me off and I went into the farm. I showered, changed my clothes and drank a beer from the fridge before I went down to the music area.

Beside the reel-to-reel, which was rewound and ready to go, was a piece of paper torn from a notebook with Anya's scrawled pencil handwriting. Most tracks were familiar to me, but number eight was not. It was called 'Song for Freddy'.

I tried to listen to the seven songs before it, but I lost patience and fast-forwarded. I went to the fridge, got another beer, lit a cigarette, sat down and pressed Play.

It began with minor chords on the piano, yet quite a full sound. Her small hands could barely stretch an octave, and you could hear all the fingers at work. The introduction was repeated, unhurried, until I became desperate to hear the voice.

When it finally came, it wasn't what I expected at all. I thought of this magnificent woman, by a long way the most extraordinary person I had met. I thought of what we'd done in bed and out of it, the recording studio, the painful arguments, the grass, the gin, the Pasadena Star; yet she sang this song meekly, almost like a hymn.

> I'd loved you for so long before we met
> I trained my soul for you so it was ready.
> You purged those highways of neglect,
> For all of this and life to come, I love you, Freddy.

I lowered my head into my hands. There was a cascade of falling notes that bottomed out as she slipped into her lower range in the last line. There was a 'skull' note through 'love' and another through the first syllable of my name, which she stretched into two notes so you could hear a smile in her voice, as though she was chiding me.

I believed Anya's work would last for ever, and to find myself the subject of such a song was more than I could take in. The refrain was so melodic that it was on the verge of being a pop song until she switched suddenly into a minor key, making it more difficult, a little bleak, as though she had decided she didn't want her private song too widely liked, or played to death on the radio.

There were two verses, a middle eight, the chorus twice, and then the third verse, with the same meek, respectful quality as the first, like a girl talking to her father. And then it just stopped. There was no third chorus, no fade, nothing.

It was perhaps the most beautiful tune she had ever written, it was sung by a heart with nothing but love in it. Why then did it sound so unbelievably sad?

The third album was called *No Turning Back*. Anya allowed me much more freedom in the production and even suggested parts for brass and strings. Her idea of harmony remained to double-track herself, and I was happy with this because it gave a certain depth while keeping the focus on her. But for the first time, on three tracks, she also had female backing singers. The girl-and-guitar thing was over, though even with this new sound she remained clearly a 'solo artist'. The words of the songs had become a bit harder to follow; not many were as simple as those lines from 'Freddy'. There was no US tour this time, but she appeared on national television and in festivals in San Francisco, Britain and France.

It was impossible for me to tell Anya that I didn't think *No Turning Back* really worked. It was all very well to have writers in the national newspapers saying how great you were, and there were sublime moments on the album. But it was a bit of a mish-mash. She could hear jazz rhythms, but she wasn't a jazz player;

her roots were in folk – and, to some extent, pop, from her years in her Brooklyn equivalent of the Brill Building. It was great that she was ambitious, but I didn't want to hear a kind of anthology of influences, I wanted concentrated Anya King.

I didn't tell her any of this. We talked about which of the tracks might make a single. MPR had belatedly put out 'You Next Time' and it was a sleeper hit, though most people we knew tended to look down on the idea of singles. Anya had felt it cheapened a song to be taken out of context when we'd spent so much time sequencing the tracks and making the album work as a whole.

With time, though, people change. One day at the farm we listened to *No Turning Back* and tried to figure out if any of the songs would stand up to repeated play on car radios and in clubs and bars.

Anya came and sat on my lap, as she sometimes liked to do, curling up against me like a cat.

'Do you think you really want a single?' I said. 'Do you want to go on television chart shows for kids?'

She made a face. 'Well, I wouldn't *mind* a hit, Freddy . . .'

We were getting on fine, thanks to my holding back my musical opinions, and in other respects we were honest; she had recently told me much more about her life before we met.

At the age of seven, when her mother was still at home, Anya had caught rheumatic fever and missed a term of school. She had a high temperature, which they put down to a throat infection. It was only when she had pain in her joints that she was taken to hospital so they could look at her heart. Her mother was ashamed because she thought rheumatic fever was a slum disease, and although their home was poor it was respectable. A visiting doctor from Duluth said it was nothing to do with living conditions but was caused by being allergic to certain bacteria. Two years later, she had a second attack, which put her back in hospital. After that, as she put it, 'the bastard fever cleared out of town', though it left her underweight and frail in her teenage years.

When she was fourteen, her father lost his job at the fibreglass factory and this dumped him into some kind of depression. Anya was expected to keep house for him when she got back from school. He'd be asleep in front of the TV, ankle deep in beer cans. She took to driving his automobile to escape, but could never get far enough in the time available. Eventually she had to find part-time work, serving in a hardware store in school vacations and babysitting for neighbours some weekday evenings. Most of the money she earned went into the housekeeping, but she saved enough to buy herself a ticket on the train for Seattle. She travelled only a few stations until she got to Wolf Point, which was the main town on the Fort Peck Indian Reservation.

'I just got out there because I liked the name,' she said.

'And what did you do?'

'Wandered around. You have to understand, Freddy, things were real different. It's only a few years ago but it could have been the 50s. Low rectangular buildings on Main Street. Most of the men in cowboy hats. The badlands stretching out far as you could see. Wheat farms, cattle ranches. In town the pawn shops, thrift shops, the gas station with guys in overalls who'd pump the gas, check the tyres, wash the windshield all for thirty cents. Fifty cents was money. There was no rock 'n' roll, no modern world.'

She'd met a man there, some drifter. He took her off in his car to a place called Jordan, down the side of a huge lake. They went to a bar called Hell Creek, which had a neon sign in the shape of flames. They drank a lot and left. She wouldn't say exactly what happened. I think maybe he raped her. But she didn't want to tell anyone and she stayed with this man for a week or so, although she was only fourteen. I think she felt she had to grow up very suddenly, she was tired of being a child and her father needed her to be a woman now. I think she figured this brutal transition was what it took.

She didn't cry when she told me about it. 'I'm not gonna tell you all the things that happened. But I'll tell you this. I knew what I was doing. I thought I should get my pain over and done with.'

We were sitting on the deck of the farm, looking down towards the trees that hid the Hudson.

'Why? Why would you look for pain?'

'I already knew I wanted to be an artist of some kind. I'd seen paintings in books at school and in magazines. On another vacation I hitch-hiked through Grand Forks to the big gallery in Minneapolis. I saw this Austrian guy called Egon Schiele. I couldn't believe my eyes. You didn't have to take the world at face value, you could see it how you wanted. I wanted to be a painter after I saw Schiele. But I wasn't good enough, so I decided to put all my energy into music.'

'What does that have to do with this guy in Wolf Point?'

Anya sighed. 'If you're going to draw on your own life, you need to be authentic.'

'So you wanted pain to write about it?'

'No, I wanted pain to get it out of the way. So I could see more clearly what I was and what path I should take.'

'And what did that mean?'

'It meant I took decisions for my life on the basis of what they meant for the music.'

I'd feared she meant something like this, and she must have seen the alarm in my eyes.

'Don't worry, Freddy, I'm not a masochist. I'm not insane.'

Although she was laughing, I felt hollowed out. I hated the thought of Anya suffering at such a young age because her mother had run off. But there was more to it than that. The weird strength of her character would have emerged in any event, and in a cowardly way I was wondering what this kind of ruthlessness might one day mean for me.

She left high school at sixteen to go to music school in Chicago, paying her way with evening jobs. She didn't see it through, and by nineteen she was in New York City with nowhere to live. She slept rough for some time in parks and doorways until someone took pity on her. It struck me with a sudden lurch that 'Genevieve' was her own story. No wonder it had been so hard for her to record in the studio with Larry Brecker. How stupid I'd been to take the songs at face value, assuming the third-person ones were about others and the first-person about herself. As she'd told me, it was almost the opposite.

I volunteered not to produce Anya's next record. I felt she needed a new sensibility and that I'd given all I had to offer. Rick Kohler and I were still managing her, the album sales were strong and all of us were comfortable – on the surface.

But the more she became respected by the music press and the mainstream newspapers, the more her music seemed to me to lose direction. I blamed her ambition and her modesty about equally. The ambition meant she was always listening to new things, hoping to stretch herself. Every night when we were in New York we'd go to a club or a gig of some kind – African music, folk or classical as often as rock. She'd take in different time signatures and so on, then set to work on them. This was fine, but her modesty meant she always assumed that anything new she heard, especially if it came from some other culture, was superior to her own music.

I went with her to Los Angeles to record her fourth album, *Atlantic Palisades*, because she asked me to, and because we were inseparable. The title was a play on Pacific Palisades in LA, of course, but also a reference to America's East Coast and what lay beyond – Europe. Yet for all the new melodic influences, the words of the songs looked backwards: it was as though her present life was no longer providing inspiration. There was a catchy song called 'Don't Talk Spanish', which drew on her feelings about Lowri and me. '*Kalimera*, California' was a political song about Americans abroad with a re-creation of that night in the Greek taverna. 'City on a Hill' was an affectionate account of our hotel in San Francisco, with humorous words: 'Tramcars shake the window frame/Travelers see no lovers' shame,/Tongues on frosted glasses sing/My darling, is this now *la vie bohème*?' In other songs, the lyrics were vague and hard to understand, and I had a bad feeling that sometimes this was not because they were saying something difficult but because she was trying to disguise the fact that they weren't saying much at all.

We did a few dates to support the new album, all of them in places Anya liked. Her stage fright had made major tours impossible, but with careful preparation and a good rest between dates, we were able to agree to two nights in each of seven venues. Hoffmann, Daniel and La Roche were lined up and off we went.

On 2 May we were in Austin, Texas. Anya looked out from the wings ten minutes before we were due to start. She saw the audience gathering, turned and ran back to the dressing room, where she began dry-retching.

Back on stage, it was humid and hard to breathe. Halfway through her set, she began to choke. The band played an instrumental while I took her off stage to get water, washed down with plenty of Jack Daniel's. We stood under the bright lights of the dressing room, face to face. Her pupils were dilated from diazepam and marijuana. She leaned over the basin (our dressing rooms were better equipped now), splashed cold water in her face and turned round to me with black runs of kohl and mascara down her cheeks.

'What the fuck am I doing, Freddy?'

I held her trembling hands in mine. I remembered as a kid being given a rabbit to hold and feeling the captive flutter of its heart.

'I don't know, sweetheart. You don't have to do all this. I mean, we have to finish the set. But next time . . . Just do a TV thing. Playing live is only worth doing if you're trying to make a name. Or if you enjoy it.'

She scrubbed her face dry with a towel, which she then threw down on a chair.

'Can I go home now?' she said. 'I want to be back at the farm. It's my favourite time of year.'

'It's almost hay-fever time too.' I was trying to keep it light. 'We'll be back in two weeks. We can't pull out now.'

I knew MPR had insurance against no-shows because we'd had discussions with their money men after Anya's previous difficulties. But I felt we had to complete the tour, especially the two dates in Los Angeles, which had sold out within minutes.

Anya looked at me hard. 'Who are these fucking rednecks out there anyway?'

They were in fact a good audience, they knew their music, it was just a bad evening. The sound mix was not that great, she was exhausted.

'Do you want me to go out and say you're unable to finish? I will if you want.'

She looked at the floor. When she turned her face up to mine again, my heart filled with love. She looked so mournful, so proud, so wrecked.

She said, 'I don't know why I have to do this thing. I have to kill myself to do this fucking thing. I literally shat blood last night. Did you know that? It's like I've scoured my heart with steel wool and I'm bleeding out of my ass.'

I kissed her and held her for a moment. Then, without a word, she turned and began to walk back along the corridor towards the stage. My heart was aching as I followed. On some level, I must have sensed what was coming, any day now.

Anya sat at the piano. 'Sorry about that,' she said into the microphone. 'Unforeseen . . . Stuff. I hope the band kept you entertained. This is a song from the new album. It's called "*Kalimera*, California".'

There was no tremor in her voice. You would have thought she'd merely gone to the bathroom.

The next day we flew the short hop to Denver. I always like arriving there. It's at altitude and the air is fresh and cool, especially if you've come from the South. You feel better at once. We were staying in a nineteenth-century hotel in the middle of town, a triangular brownstone with a pointed nose like the Flatiron. I was so pleased to be there I just peeled off some dollar bills for the bellhop and flopped down on the bed. Anya went to tidy up in the bathroom.

It was an off day. There was time for lunch and a sleep before we'd even need to think about the soundcheck. We decided to go downstairs to eat. It was kind of an interesting place. You could look up from the lobby straight to the sky through a big glass dome eight floors above. There was a fancy restaurant and an upmarket pub with a baseball game on television, so we sat on stools at the bar and drank wine and I ate grilled shrimp with salad and Anya had a cigarette.

She looked shaken and pale, but I put this down to the strain of performing. I tried to talk to her about the set lists for the next day and the day after. I thought if she played more early songs she'd feel less like she was trying to thrust this new album down the public's throat.

She just nodded and kept saying, 'Maybe you're right, Freddy. Maybe you're right.'

At one point she put her hand on my thigh and looked lovingly at me, but in her eyes there was something else as well.

'Listen, sweetheart,' I said. 'We have a whole day of doing nothing. Let's go and sleep. Tonight we'll go out and I'll find you the best dinner in Denver and a club to go to afterwards and we'll get back not too late and have one little joint of that grass Rick gave me and sleep till nine in the morning.'

She nodded, but seemed unable to speak. We went upstairs, pulled the blinds, kicked off our outer clothes and curled up together under the cover. I must have fallen asleep at once.

I awoke bewildered in a late-afternoon light. I couldn't work out where I was. The farm? The Seventh Street apartment? Austin? I kept pressing buttons in my mind and they kept coming up blank.

Then I went to the window and raised the blind. Denver. Of course. Anya King. My love. I remembered now. My pulse quickened at the thought of the gig tomorrow and dinner out tonight.

The bathroom door was open, but Anya was not inside. I looked round the room and there was no sign of her anywhere. I went back to the bathroom and saw that her toothbrush, which I'd seen her use before lunch, had gone.

I walked round the room about five times, wondering if I was losing my mind. She had been there, surely? We'd had lunch together. I wasn't hallucinating or anything. Then I saw it. An envelope with the hotel's printed name and mine written in pencil in Anya's hand: Jack Wyatt.

Well, I didn't want to open it, but I didn't let myself admit that. It was a short note, and the writing was shaky. 'My Darling, You are the most wonderful man I ever met. I don't want to, but I have to travel on. One day I can maybe explain, but don't try to reach me now, let me do this awful thing I have to do. Don't grieve for your little girl. For all of this and life to come, I love you, Freddy. A x'.

The fallout from the cancellations was horrific. Some of the venues threatened to sue. I had Vintello's people in my ear for weeks, though I must say Rick Kohler was fantastic. He had our lawyer

in New York go in and read the riot act to MPR. He was a litiga-
tion partner from a London-based firm. His name was Cheeseman
and when he could be torn away from reading the cricket scores
on the Reuters tape, he was afraid of no one. 'I thought he'd be
a typical old-style Brit,' Rick said on the phone, 'but he knows
Anya's songs by heart, man!' This Cheeseman guy threatened a
million-dollar counter-suit for mistreatment of the artist, for all
Anya's medical expenses and for knowing underpayment of royalties – or words to that effect. Apparently his last words to their
lawyer were, 'You fight me on this and I guarantee you'll never
hire a female artist again.' He then had an accountant go in and
do an audit and discovered an underpayment of $140,000 over
four albums. We made a one-off 'goodwill' gesture of $20,000 to
MPR to cover the incidental expenses of Anya's disappearance
and they settled with the venues from the insurance payout, so
no one lost – financially.

When the business side was sorted out, I took the train upstate
to be alone. The person I most wanted to talk to was Lowri, but I
felt it would be a cruel thing to call her. It was only when I'd got
up to the farm that I allowed myself to think about what I'd lost.

Then I guess I went a little insane. I remember one afternoon
lying naked under a tree, a tall tree with thin branches and leaves
a grey-green colour like olive or birch. The wind made a restless,
metallic sound in them. I thought I could hear Anya's voice in
the rustle, then if the wind veered even a tiny bit, the human
words were lost, only to come again a few seconds later. It was
driving me frantic with despair that I couldn't hold on to that
voice. I could sense her presence so strongly it was as though I
could see her. I don't think actual vision would have added
anything to the power of her presence there, in the leaves.

Sometimes by chance I'd hear her voice on the radio and have
to run across the room to switch it off. In the farm I put all my
copies of her albums in a deep, dark drawer so no visitor should

chance to put them on the stereo. Once in New York I turned the corner of 41st Street to see a sixty-foot Anya smiling down from a billboard. *Atlantic Palisades* said the lettering above. She had that look in her eye she'd have when she was about to suggest some new love game. I couldn't quite believe that she still existed – for other people, somewhere.

I had no idea where she'd gone and I didn't look for her. I knew that for all sorts of reasons I had to let her do what she wanted to do. It was only a pity she had left me with this mountain of a puzzle. How to get through a day, then how to put the days together into something that might be a life worth having.

Then I wondered what it was like for her. If it was as great a torture, minute by minute, for her as it was for me, why on earth had she done it? And if it wasn't so bad for her, did that mean that she'd never felt as deeply as I had?

Press speculation was hot for a time. Anya was 'temperamental', a 'prima donna' and other newspaper words. It was strange, but till I read them it had never occurred to me that Anya was difficult. All the dramas in her life had sprung naturally, I thought, from the scale of what she was trying to do. Maybe the papers had a point. I don't know – but luckily they seemed to tire of it quickly.

Anya's friend Sandy at MPR had a telegram from Anya in Paris in August saying she was fine and not to worry. Paris. I wondered why. It wasn't like she spoke French or anything.

Oh, Anya, Anya, sometimes I used to hold the pillow like a child. At the farm, I moved into 'her' bedroom, and at night I tried to conjure her, body and soul, from the darkness. All I could see were the timber beams above my head and I envied them their painless existence. I actually envied a piece of wood.

I don't want to admit how much I missed her being there, her body. The culture I was raised in – London, respectable but poor – and the one I'd moved to – LA, not so respectable, less poor – had one thing in common when it came to men and women. They both thought 'sex' was the delinquent brother of 'love'. To my parents and their friends I suppose 'love' meant 'marriage' and to the people in Laurel Canyon love meant Zen and Buddhist wisdom and transcendental this and that.

They were both wrong, to my mind. We seem to be alive just once – in a random skin and bone that starts to move towards disintegration as soon as it's old enough that you can kiss it. What Anya and I did with one another wasn't the poor relation of anything. Once when we were making love, and she was propped up on her elbows, she looked down hard at where our bodies met and whispered, 'Freddy, this is who we are.'

I knew what she meant, and I knew she was right and that was why I loved her.

More than a year passed before I had a letter from her. In that time I'd taken up an invitation from Pete in Los Angeles to put together a new band from the ashes of the old. I didn't want to go back. I'd done LA. But I was dangerously unhappy. I thought about Anya every minute of the day. I used to go and help with the logging on the farm, work till it was dark and I could barely stand. Then I'd drink bourbon and beer, watch a movie on the television turned up loud, maybe with my stoned ex-ad-man friend, and fall into bed. This way I could force Anya to the edge of my mind, keep her out beyond the stockade. But then when I was asleep, when all my defences were down, she'd creep into my dreams – as real a presence as if she'd been in the room, but always with some hard twist in our situation. I'd awake with tears on my face, cursing her. Leave me alone, woman, leave me alone.

Music might yet save me. At least it would be another way of keeping me occupied, of shutting my ears to her calling voice. I went to the local store, which acted as a post office, and left a forwarding address care of Larry Brecker at Sonic Broom Studios. To begin with I'd stay at Pete's, but I didn't expect to be there long.

Anya's letter came – fifteen months after Denver – from an

address in Paris. 'My Dearest Freddy, I hope you're OK. I think about you all the time. I don't expect you'll ever forgive me for walking out like that and I don't think you should. Just so you know, I've been in Paris for a lot of the time. Also, I went back to Athens, then spent some time in Italy. It's been difficult. I think I've lost my ability to write. But people have been kind. I have enough money forwarded from the bank. Thank you and Rick for looking after that. I keep trying to write songs but nothing seems to come. Be well. I will come back to the US one day. I wish you every happiness, day and night. A x'.

It didn't make me feel any better, but I guess it wasn't meant to. I sent a very short reply: 'You must do what you have to do. I'm not bitter. I just miss you, night and day, day and night. Back in LA. Looked in at the Pasadena Star last night. S. Davis, Jr sends his love. Always here, F x'.

The re-formed band did fine. Ted Fox, the new guitarist from Seattle, turned out to be good — loud and bluesy, with a flair for catchy tunes though a voice too deep to sing them in. It was a kind of baritone and you need a hard tenor against electric guitars. This meant I had to do a lot of the singing, which made a change after being banned from the microphone for four years with Anya. We got gigs round LA, we got a record contract, we made a little money.

When I'd been in LA six months I finally called Lowri. She sounded pleased to hear from me and wanted to meet up. She named a café-restaurant in Santa Monica with an outside terrace and a view of the sea. I thought a hell of a lot about what I should say to her and how I should come across. I even spent time thinking about what to wear, which would have amused her — and Anya, come to that. 'Well, look at you, mister, pair of black jeans and a white tee-shirt. My oh my!' she used to say when she'd got dressed for some big occasion in a vintage dress with beads and coloured eyeliner, and underwear I'd find out about later.

I got to the café early. It was the best kind of place, with green awnings and bright white tablecloths and an air of freshness in everything – the iced water, the clean menus, even in the waitress's laundered shirt and LA teeth. There was a basket of different home-made breads and chilled butter pats of different flavours, anchovy, parsley, and a dish of fresh sliced radishes and carrots. I also had a large bourbon and a cigarette.

Lowri came into view, swinging down the street from where the cab had dropped her in a knee-length navy linen dress and shades, the dark of these colours against the fair-russet of her swept-back hair and freckled skin, bare legs and sandals. She looked amazing. I sucked deep on the last of the Camel, stubbed it out and stood up to kiss her. I felt we'd never been apart. She threw herself into my arms, as she always did, but this time she had the firmness back.

We ordered grilled fish – grouper, snapper, I'm not much good at American fish, but they all taste good. Lowri ordered Coke, I had beer. After a bit, we began to laugh. She told me about her household on Beech Knoll Road, with Candy and a couple of weirdo performance artists. She'd quit the real-estate thing and now had a job with a music publisher also based in Laurel Canyon. A couple of times she referred to someone called Nick – Nick said this, or Nick and I were going there anyway – rather as though I ought to know who this Nick guy was. I guess I did, really.

As I watched her talking in that even California sunlight I could sense she'd re-found her inner balance. It pained my heart to think what I'd lost, but I didn't go with the feeling. Sometimes with these powerful emotions, you're crushed. You just flail around and hope for the pain to stop, for some bastard to stop stabbing you in the guts. Other times if you're very lucky, you can kind of skate along the rim, look into the precipice and it's almost like you have a choice – to plunge in or turn your head away.

A small flush of excitement was under the skin of Lowri's throat as she described her new life. I thought of all the happiness she'd brought me and of how very lucky I'd been to find her in that oddball household all those years ago.

I could let her go now. Did that mean I'd never really loved her, as I loved Anya? Was friendship greater than love, did good-will outlive passion? Hardly, because given half a chance I would have taken her to a hotel straight after lunch. But it seemed enough that Lowri was happy and that I could send her on her way laughing.

She turned at the end of the street and waved. She blew a kiss. Then I did feel a little desolate.

It was almost three years after Anya left me in Denver that I had a call from Rick Kohler in New York.

'Hey, man. Have I got news! Anya's been in the studio again. She finished recording an album last week with Adam Esterson and Larry Brecker and half the session men in New York City! We can hear a tape next week.'

'Why the fuck weren't we told?' I was dumbfounded. 'We're still her managers.'

'Not been much to manage. Anyway, Vintello's people are beside themselves. Get your ass over here, Jack.'

'But we don't have a contract with MPR.'

'Well, they sure as hell want to buy it.'

I flew to New York and checked into the Gramercy Park Hotel. It turned out Rick had known Anya was back in America and had been in negotiation with Vintello for a while, but 'hadn't wanted to bother' me with it.

'Why not?' I asked by phone from the hotel.

'Well, I didn't want some kind of fucking psychodrama with you and Anya and all that crazy shit. I just wanted MPR to pay for the studio. We haven't signed the deal yet. You can see all the papers.'

'How is she?' I said.

'I haven't seen her. Just spoken to her a few times on the phone.'

'How did she sound?'

'Take it easy, man. She was fine.'

Rick had arranged for the two of us to listen in a studio in SoHo on the Tuesday afternoon. Brecker would be there to play the tape, otherwise it would be just the two of us.

It was a large bare room with a piano, drum kit, music stands and a booth for the singer, the usual things. Rick and I sat opposite one another on a couple of hard chairs while Larry Brecker cued up the tape on the other side of the glass.

My heart was pounding when Brecker came through with a piece of paper.

'Sorry, guys, this is the best I got.'

It was a list of tracks, written in ballpoint in his handwriting. He went back into the control room, then his voice came through the intercom. 'OK, I'll give you a pause of a couple of minutes between tracks, but if you want more time just hold your hand up.'

My eyes raced down the list of songs. It went: 'Side One: Wolf Point, Esmé Sings, Hollybush Lane, Frida. Side Two: The Doctor From Duluth, Forget Me, Boulevard Haussmann, Another Life.'

Only four songs on each side, so they must be pretty long, I thought. There was the balance we'd got on the first album in which each track reflected its opposite number on the other side. You might think 'Esmé Sings' would be about someone else, and 'Forget Me' would be personal, but I knew otherwise. 'Wolf Point' and 'The Doctor From Duluth' obviously balanced. 'Frida' and 'Another Life' would be about other people – superficially. The other two were about places, real or imagined.

I tried to clear my mind, to keep calm so I could listen properly. It wasn't easy. And then it began.

How can I describe it? When you're with a child, you can't picture how they'll look at forty. But when you know someone as a grown-up and you look back at photographs of them as a kid, you can see that all the adult features were there already, at age two, six, fourteen — it's just that no one knew which ones would come to dominate. All the best aspects of Anya's early songs had grown and flourished, all that was unsure had gone.

The word for the record would, I think, be 'liberation'. She wasn't dabbling in different kinds of music any more, she'd taken the whole lot under her wing — she'd absorbed them into her own bloodstream. There was confidence, power, soaring melody. There was the exhilaration of a talent that was not ashamed of itself.

'Wolf Point' began like a mournful piano recital, like something a student might play in a Conservatory, very proper. Then there came a hint of strings, of picked guitar and then, of all things, a gospel choir. A piano bridge led to a string quartet, the whole thing still anchored by the left hand at the piano. There was a plucked mandolin, a bassoon and flute and as that began to fade, a little cry from what sounded like an oboe before it touched the opening verse again, ending with assertive piano chords. It had the range of a symphony in four minutes and five seconds. It was a song of strength and desolation. Anya's voice had deepened, but only a fraction. It was still a young woman's, but it now belonged to someone thrillingly in control.

'Shit,' said Rick.

'Yeah.'

There was no longer any fear of sounding too popular. It was as though her mastery had given Anya the right to sound as tuneful as she wanted. 'Esmé Sings' rocked slow, like sex in a sleeping car. 'Hollybush Lane' had the soprano charm of early songs like 'Ready to Fly', but with sly words that switched from 'she' to 'you' to 'me'. 'Frida' was the longest track, placed in the 'Julie in the Court of Dreams' position, at the end of side one. It was about the painter, Frida Kahlo, whose physical

struggles following a streetcar accident had been an agony, an
obstacle, but also a subject of her art. 'The Doctor From Duluth'
had jazz-style muted trumpets and clear enunciation in the words.
It was very intimate, as though she was talking to someone, and
the 'you' of the song didn't sound like a lover, it sounded like
you the listener. 'Forget Me' was a breathy pop song, dangerously candid, with brass, sizzling hi-hat, jangly guitar and – for
a few bars only – the hated 'instant schmaltzer', the pedal steel.
She was half laughing as she sang and the slight barrelhouse
feel of the organ and brass saved it from sounding overproduced.
'Boulevard Haussmann' was a song of agonised regret, and I
guessed she'd written it soon after leaving America. But while
it told of her misery, it seemed to have a love of men, or a belief
in them. There was even a saving touch of humour, as well as
a downbeat ending with two or three of her best 'skull' notes.
For such a sad song it was oddly uplifting. Just as on the day
we met, when she played sitting on the grass at the farm, I had
the sensation of listening at a double level – thrilled senseless
both by the song and the fact that there was someone alive with
the talent to write and sing it.

The record ended with its title track, 'Another Life'. Everything
Anya had worked at in her musical career seemed to be contained
in it. She had squared the circle by suggesting that there was no
real difference between her own life and that of the women 'characters' she sang about because they were essentially part of the
same consciousness – 'Another life would be the same/My heart
existing by a different name . . .' There was an unexpected key
change that introduced the melodic heart of the song, which then
returned to a sort of recitative before the crux, a heart-stopping
major to minor chord change that confessed her powerless identification with a woman she glimpses in a station waiting room.

Then the record ended. I'd been avoiding Rick Kohler's eye
until this point, but now I looked across at him. He was holding

his face in his hands, but I could see two tears squeeze out over the webbing between his fingers.

I stood up, went out into the corridor and lit a cigarette. I didn't trust myself to speak.

What had she done? What had it cost her — what had it cost me — to produce this thing? There seemed no point in doing an audit of what we'd paid for these songs. I might have felt differently if the result had been less glorious, but one hearing had made it clear that this music would be listened to with joy as long as people had ears and a brain.

I inhaled the last of my cigarette and went back into the studio, where Larry Brecker had come in from the control room.

Rick was still sitting on the same chair. He shook his head as he peered up at me. 'Yeah, well . . .' he began, then trailed off.

'What d'ya think?' said Larry Brecker.

'What do I think?' said Rick. 'I think I've done one good thing in my life.' He sniffed loudly. 'Now people can't say, Oh yeah, Rick Kohler. He was that putz from Passaic, New Jersey, never had a real job in his life. Now they'll say, Rick Kohler, yeah, he was the guy who discovered Anya King. And they'll bow down in front of my fucking grave.'

Brecker and I laughed.

'What do you think, Larry?' I said.

'I guess she's pulled off what other people dream of.'

'Congratulations,' I said.

'I just sat at the mixing desk,' said Larry. 'Esterson did a great job. But she knew what she wanted all along, she ran the show.'

'I can imagine,' I said.

There was a silence.

We sat around for a time, reflecting on what we'd heard. Brecker played a few bits back — the ice-cold muted trumpet on 'Wolf Point', the shimmering lead guitar break (by Elliot Klein) on 'Boulevard Haussmann', that chord change on 'Another Life'. But

I really just wanted a copy of the record and to listen to it a thousand times alone. I think we all did.

Eventually, we fell silent again, kind of exhausted, so I said goodbye to Rick and Larry and went out on to the street. I so much wanted to see Anya, to tell her the size and wonder of what she'd created – funny little girl from Devils Lake with her fevered heart and her deep brown eyes. But I knew I would never see her again unless by chance. My contribution to her life was over, and only in retrospect could I see that it was a supporting role, not the lead part I'd imagined it to be all those times I held her in my arms.

I walked up Thompson Street towards the great divide of Houston Street, where the dumpster trucks rumble as they go over the potholes, where the big lorries push across the city, loaded down from the waterfront. I stood among the throng of people waiting patiently to cross and tried to mingle with them, to disappear into a greater mass of human life, hoping I might lose my pain, my sense of self, in that tireless commotion.

I did see Anya again once, though I was in the auditorium and she was on the stage. It was at the London Palladium during her farewell tour at the age of almost fifty, in one of the closing years of the twentieth century. I'd read an interview with her in which she explained that this was definitely her last performance. She'd suffered from a recurrence of rheumatic fever and had had two heart valve replacement operations. She had arthritic pain in her joints. 'Also,' she told the journalist, 'touring is such a king-size pain in the ass.'

She'd carried on making records after *Another Life*, but none of them had been anything as good. She reopened her box of influences and went into folk and jazz and world music, and while almost every record had one or two moments of magic it was hard not to feel she was on a lonesome journey. Public appreciation trailed away. She became known as the singer who had made that one perfect thing. There was a five-year gap before a *Greatest Hits*, though no single of hers had ever actually charted. She'd lived with various men, mostly musicians, been married once, but was now living happily, said the interviewer, 'alone in San Francisco, in a large, airy apartment on top of Nob Hill, near the junction of Powell and California'. She had had no children.

I carried on working in the music business. When my second American band folded I moved into production, and when that work dried up I released a solo album. After *Another Life*, I stopped managing Anya and left her in the care of Rick Kohler, who rose to the challenge, while taking himself pretty seriously as the keeper of the flame. With song-writing royalties from my original British band as well as the two American outfits, I had enough to live on. One night in 1986 I bumped into our old lodgers Becky and Suzanne at a gig in New York. They were insanely excited to see me again, I don't know why, but I asked them up to the farm for old times' sake and invited Rick to come along too. We had a hilarious weekend, and a few months later I found myself married to Becky. It could easily have been Suzanne, as Rick never tired of pointing out. Those sisters made my soul sing, after all the years. They made me laugh.

I was so glad I hadn't sold the farm in an attempt to purge the memories of Lowri and Anya. I had come very close to getting rid of it in the lowest of my low days, but it was still a wonderful place to live. Becky, who was by now in her thirties, became pregnant almost straight away. We had two little girls, Loretta and Pearl, and Becky indulged me by giving Pearl the second name of Anya.

I'd been over for my mother's funeral in south London when I saw the large newspaper ads: 'Anya King. Last Ever Performances.'

I didn't tell Ray or Simon or my sisters that I'd be going to see Anya, but I had to leave the house while there were still people there with the sausage rolls and tea and beer. An old person's funeral is not such a terrible thing, and some of my mother's younger friends and neighbours were enjoying themselves.

I bought flowers from a barrow in Soho and took them to the stage door on Great Marlborough Street. I put in a card that said: 'Good luck. Hoffmann, Daniel and La Roche on standby? Love F x'. Then I went to a pub, because I felt nervous for her. It was full of smoke and tourists and it smelled sweet, of old booze and sweat. I drank a pint of bitter, then switched to bourbon on ice and raised a glass to Anya. There was a man with a grey ponytail who kept staring at me and I had a bad feeling he recognised me from an old album cover. He was probably going to the concert himself and I didn't want to have to talk to him about what had happened to Pete or Jeff and what Anya had been like in the old days or what had really happened in her 'missing years'.

One thing I had discovered, from Rick Kohler, was that when I'd flown back ahead of her that summer in Greece, she'd met a man in Athens. He was an Egyptian, or maybe Tunisian, wealthy, and he'd made a big play for her. He'd told her he had a flat in Paris and it was there that she'd fled when she left me in Denver. I guess that explained why she went to live, as she did, on the Boulevard Haussmann, which, I discovered, is a wide street with chain stores and offices on the Right Bank – not at all her idea of the '*vie bohème*'. The man had a large apartment where she could be alone and write. I tried not to think of when he visited or how he took his rent.

I didn't feel much about my mother as I walked towards the Palladium. Perhaps the full force of her death would hit me later, but for the time being I was so intensely anxious about Anya I could think of nothing else. I found my seat in the theatre. The house was full and the atmosphere was charged. Many of the audience were my age, with bald heads shining under the house lights, but there were younger people who must have sampled Anya's work from her back catalogue and come to like it.

The stage was set up for a full band with keyboards, drums, microphones for backing singers, as well as guitar stands. This was encouraging. Although I was high from the bourbon and nicotine and half a spliff I'd had on the street, I was consumed with anxiety, not only for Anya but for myself. This woman, the love of my life — after twenty years. Would she be old and unattractive? Would I still love her at a distance? Would it rip me apart? Or would I feel nothing? I saw that my hands were shaking.

The lights went down and the MC strode on. He was superbly brief. 'Ladies and gentlemen, for the very last time — MPR recording artist Anya King.' The audience rose to their feet as the spotlight picked up a slight figure coming on stage left. She wore a knee-length green gypsy dress with boots and big gold earrings. She carried an acoustic six-string guitar, held at arm's length by the neck. As she made it to the middle of the stage, I noticed that she limped. On a stool, beneath the spotlight, she sat and pushed back her dark hair, cut back to just above the shoulder, thickly streaked with grey. There was no kohl beneath her eyes, but there was powder and lipstick on her face as she turned it up into the light. Without speaking, she ran her thumb down a single arpeggio, leaned forward and at once began to sing:

> Platform lights are furred with cold
> In December's freezing hold,
> Genevieve, you've made your plan,
> Now you must stay . . .

Tears erupted from my eyes. Her voice had changed. This was much more than the slight deepening I'd noticed on *Another Life*, this was a new register. At the end of the song, the members of the backing group came on stage. They included tenor sax, trumpet and two female singers. The next song was the popular 'The Need to be You', where the backing vocalists provided the top notes, then came 'Boulevard Haussmann', with a clumsy guitar solo that tried to replicate the record note for note.

At this point, Anya left the stool, went over to the piano and addressed the audience. This was the first time I had heard her speak since lunch at the hotel in Denver more than twenty years before.

'Thank you all for coming tonight. My name is Anya King and this is the last public performance of my life. I guess you can tell from my voice why I think it's time to call it a day.' There was some good-natured whistling. 'Later on I'm going to introduce you to the band, but for the time being just sit back, stand up, whatever you want to do, and enjoy the show. We're going into a little melancholy mode here. This one's called "The Doctor From Duluth".'

The audience responded enthusiastically, calling out suggestions or 'We love you, Anya.' How much I'd missed that voice – that pure diction, the North Dakota accent with a resigned self-awareness that always seemed to put her one step ahead of you. It was the voice that had phrased intimate words to me so many times, the self-same voice that had whispered and sung 'I love you, Freddy.' At this point I wasn't sure I'd make it through the set and had started to look around to see how quickly I could escape.

The lights dimmed, except for one spot on the piano. 'This is called "I'm Not Falling",' she said. After all this time she had the arrangement she wanted – voice and piano alone. She'd also changed the tempo, slowed it down, so it was no longer a kind of novelty anti-love song that Larry Brecker had liked: it was a self-critical account of her inability to give herself to another person. She blamed what the song called 'a greater need', which I suppose referred to her music. She'd written the first draft of the song when she was nineteen, but it was as though it had taken her thirty years to understand it.

She stood up and walked stiffly back to the middle of the stage, where she strapped on her guitar. 'All right. Here we go. One, two, three, four.' Off they went into 'Forget Me' and for the first time the band seemed to gel, to pull its weight. Also for the first time, Anya began to look as though she might be enjoying herself. She stayed up-tempo with a light-hearted 'Ready to Fly', her voice see-sawing all over it. When she came to the final verse, with its key change, she thrust her hips forward and pointed up to the sky in a very literal reminder to the other musicians. And up they went.

Then there were introductions to the band, at the end of which she said, 'OK, for the last little bit of fun, we're going to do a song which has a special memory for me. And Freddy, I don't know if you're out there. I kinda think you must be. So, thank you for the flowers. And this one's for you.' I was fearing 'Song for Freddy', but the bubbling bass line and the ringing guitars led into 'Hold Me'. She sang it just as she had in the SoHo club that first night. Her voice was gruffer, but she still managed to convey a sense of excitement when she sang 'There's a mighty road to travel/And some dangers I don't know.'

Back at the piano, she gave a mesmerising 'Julie in the Court of Dreams' and 'Wolf Point' with its chilling trumpet solo. She then played 'Another Life', and that was too much for me. I put my hands over my ears and waited for it to stop.

There was another upbeat section with Anya back on guitar for 'Don't Talk Spanish', which featured a fantastic tongue-in-cheek flamenco solo from the guitarist, then 'City on a Hill' and 'Gate Nineteen' before she thanked everyone for coming and prepared to leave. There was a lot of calling out and pleading from the audience for more.

'Sure, you can have more,' she said. 'This is "more". This is my last song.'

She seemed to flinch as she straightened up in front of the microphone, and I wondered where the pain was – hips or knees or heart. There came a slow dreamy tenor sax, fizzing cymbals, exploring bass. For a moment, I didn't recognise the song, then I heard the diminished seventh chord ringing out from Anya's guitar and the words beginning, 'Frida, don't you let them have their way.'

The song was eight minutes long on the record and I looked down at my watch as she began. It was almost unbearable to think that there were only seven, then six minutes of this magnificent voice left for the world to hear. The audience was motionless as the song unfolded heat-soaked plains, dust clouds, the smell of oil paint, the roar of Mexico City – and in amongst it all the hard-edged voice of a lonely girl from Devils Lake.

I'd done nothing, I'd played a few things for fun and money, but I felt as she sang then the enormous stretch of what Anya had tried to do – that outreach of imagination, to feel your heart beat in someone else's life – and I saw how much it had cost her.

I looked at my watch. There was about a minute left as she entered the final verse with its doubtful ending, 'Maybe it was more than you could take, my darling,/Were these choices really ours to make . . .'

And when the final note faded, she did what she had done the first day I met her at the farm and she thought she'd said enough for the time being. She just shut down. There were no fade-outs, no goodbyes. She took the guitar off and propped it on the stand, bowed briefly to the audience, turned on her heel and walked off the stage – trying hard, I could tell because I knew every pore of her skin so well, to limp as little as possible as she left the spotlight – went into the blackness of the wings and disappeared.

Becky wanted me to buy a flat in London because she was keen to visit more often, and the next day I went to see a new development near Hoxton, an old Victorian building with its name chiselled above the lintel: St Joseph-in-the-West, once a workhouse or something, now full of saunas and fitness rooms.

I didn't really go for it. I didn't want to be swallowed up by so much history, by the failed existences of others. At my age I'd begun to pity the struggles of the young and I was resigned to all the lives I wouldn't now have time to lead. It was no longer a matter of envy when I saw beautiful women sharing plans with laughing men.

So I told the estate agent I'd call the next day, then went and sat outdoors at a pub. Beside me were guys in suits, shouting over lager to female colleagues in their shiny work clothes. I didn't know their world. They looked fired up and engaged, but I'd never even had what they would call a proper job.

I was almost sixty years old, but I didn't understand anything. It all in the end seemed to have been a matter of the purest chance. But for a succession of tiny pieces of good fortune, I might never have had a glimpse of Weepah Way, the farm or Anya King. Yet I also knew that if any of those bits of luck had fallen out a different way and I had had another life, it would in some odd way have been the same — my heart existing, as Anya put it, by a different name.

I don't feel I'm the same person as the kid who walked across the park to school each day. I saw an article in the paper the other day that said that at my age I'd have no cells or whatever in common with that small boy. Maybe someone else has his cells now. I look ahead and I can see the years spooling out of me like tape from an unhinged reel-to-reel, spinning out of control, tangling, never to be rewound. And the past seems like something I imagined. The guitarist I was in my first band in England, at the poll-winners' concert . . . I remember the grain of the wood beneath my tapping foot; but in what sense was that me?

Sometimes my whole life seems like a dream; occasionally I think that someone else has lived it for me. The events and the sensations, the stories and the things that make me what I am in the eyes of other people, the list of facts that make my life . . . They could be mine, they might be yours.

I'm an actor playing a part I've never mastered. I've stood here – back to the bar window, beer in glass, slight jet lag, old leather jacket – maybe a thousand times before. And it never adds up.

So when eventually my hour comes and I go down in that darkness, into the blackness of the black-painted wings, there'll be no need to mourn me or repine. Because I think we're all in this thing, like it or not, for ever.

www.vintage-books.co.uk